A Last Dance in Liverpool

Elizabeth Morton was born and raised in Liverpool, spending much of her formative years either at convent school, or playing her piano accordion in Northern working men's clubs. When she was 18 she trained as an actress at the Guildhall School of Music and Drama and went on to work in TV, film, and theatre. She is known for the Liverpool sitcom, *Watching*, playing Madeleine Bassett in the ITV series, *Jeeves and Wooster*, and performing in Willy Russell's plays, including the role of Linda in the original cast of *Blood Brothers* in the West End.

She began writing after winning The London Writers Competition and has written plays as well as episodes of *Doctors*, the Radio 4 drama series *Brief Lives*, and CBeebies.

She was shortlisted for the Bath Short Story award in 2014, also shortlisted for the Dragon's Pen competition, Fish Short Story Award, and in 2015 won prizes in the Exeter Short Story competition, and the Trisha Ashley Most Humorous Short Story. In 2016, she was one of six shortlisted in the CWA Marjorie Allingham award.

She is married to *All Creatures Great and Small* and *Doctor Who* actor, Peter Davison.

Elizabeth
MORTON

A Last Dance in Liverpool

First published by Ebury Press in 2020

1 3 5 7 9 10 8 6 4 2

Ebury Press, an imprint of Ebury Publishing
20 Vauxhall Bridge Road,
London SW1V 2SA

Ebury Press is part of the Penguin Random House group of companies
whose addresses can be found at global.penguinrandomhouse.com

www.penguin.co.uk

A CIP catalogue record for this book is available from the British Library

ISBN 9781529103533

Typeset in 12.5/16 pt Times LT Std
by Integra Software Services Pvt. Ltd, Pondicherry

Printed and bound in Great Britain by Clays Ltd, Elcograf S.p.A.

For my mother

Acknowledgements

Thank you to the people whose lives I based this book on. My husband's father, Claude, who joined the British Army from the colonies, and whose wartime diaries when he arrived in England from Guyana were a treasure trove of stories. Thank you also to my talented grandparents, Renie, a dancer, and Ernest, a pianist, who ran a dancing school together. This book is written in memory of them and of the many ordinary people who led extraordinary lives in World War Two.

Special thanks to my agent, Judith Murdoch, and my editor, Gillian Green. Thank you also to Peter, my best friend, for his humour and patience when I drift off for many hours of the day. Thank you also to my sons Louis and Joel for continuing to be the distraction that keeps me grounded. Finally, thanks to my mum, who spent happy times dancing with my dad at the Grafton in Liverpool before they were married, is still dancing and shows no signs of hanging up her tap shoes just yet.

Prologue

January 1940

Lily Lafferty followed Father Donnelly into the parlour of St Jude's. It had just begun to snow, and she brought in with her a blast of cold air from outside. Blowing on her fingers and rubbing her hands together vigorously, her distinctive, lively brown eyes, darted up to the framed print of Jesus hanging from the picture rail, then over to the wooden crucifix on a plinth on the cluttered desk, and back across to the mirror blotted with cauliflower-shaped rust. She noted the pale, discoloured plastic daffodils stuck in a vase and shivered.

'And who's this?' asked Sister Assumpta.

Father Donnelly smiled. 'Lily Lafferty. She's here to help me collect the sheets.'

Sister Assumpta gave a brisk nod.

'Ah, one of the famous Laffertys?' said the nun.

Lily, standing tall and beautiful, but awkward, as if she didn't quite know what to do with her arms, took off her beret embroidered with the words Women's Voluntary Service Civil Defence in red letters. Her long brown hair with undertones of red tumbled over her shoulders.

'Here we are. They're boiled and sterilised,' Sister Assumpta said, hauling a wicker basket filled with bundles of laundry tied together with old stockings out from behind her desk.

'Thank you, Sister,' said Lily. She was grateful to the nuns. She would be able to make a mountain of bandages out of these old sheets, but she was also glad they weren't staying here long. This place unnerved her with its draughty corridors and ill-fitting, ornately carved wooden doors and ugly ecclesiastical furniture.

'She's doing a grand job for the WVS. The centre will be delighted, isn't that right, Lily?' said the priest.

'Yes, Father,' she said, nodding.

'Take them out to my car. I'll see you there in a minute.'

But just as she was about to leave, the door was flung open, pushed heftily from the other side by a foot.

'I have cake!' said an excited Sister David, bustling into the room, carrying a tea tray with mismatching cups and saucers, a pot of tea, and a sunken Victoria sponge oozing with jam and cream sitting on a glass stand with an elaborate gold handle. Her smooth white skin pillowed out from the stiff white coif that framed her smiling face. 'You're not going? Stay and have cake. Will you have a bit of cake, dear?' she said to Lily. 'Perhaps you would like to lead us in grace, Father?'

Sister Assumpta, now seated behind her desk, rearranged the skirts of her black habit and twitched an impatient frown.

'I don't know . . .' said Father Donnelly.

'Oh, have a bit of cake, Father. Go on. It'll not harm you.'

'Very well, Sister David. Just a small piece.'

Sister David beamed.

'Are you the WVS girl?'

'Aye. I'm Lily. Just here to collect the sheets.'

'Grand. Have a seat, dear. You have *lovely* hair. You'll have a bit of cake?' said Sister David as she pulled up a chair.

Embarrassed, Lily nodded a smile and sat down.

Father Donnelly settled himself on the sagging chintz sofa and interlocked his fingers. 'Bless us, O Lord, and these thy gifts which we are about to receive, may the Lord make us truly grateful, Amen.'

Lily lowered her eyes and mumbled along.

'So, Father,' said Sister David, and after a hurried sign of the cross, poured the tea that was stewing in the pot into a china cup and handed it to him on a saucer. 'Isn't it exciting? We're all on a knife-edge. Waiting to see what Hitler is going to do next. On *pins*, we are.'

'*Exciting*?' he said.

'Exciting, Sister?' said Sister Assumpta, wincing.

'Sorry, *sorry*, wrong choice of words. I mean, overwhelming. Terrifying, this war,' she stuttered.

Lily pressed her lips together and cast her eyes down as she fought a smile.

'Yes. Well, that's what I need to speak to Sister Assumpta about. The evacuees. Lily, do you mind?'

He gestured to Lily that she should leave, with a small nod towards the door.

'So you're not just here for the sheets, Father,' said Sister Assumpta, flatly. 'You're here to talk about the evacuation programme? Whatever you've got to say, you can say it in front of the girl. Because there's not much to talk about, I'm afraid.'

Lily, standing now, hovered, uncertain what to do next.

'Stop shuffling and sit down and finish your tea, Lily,' said Sister Assumpta. She continued to speak, directing the full force of her words at the priest. 'Father, if it comes to it, we'll all be pulling our weight. But there's a limit. We can only accommodate twenty evacuees here at St Jude's.'

'Is that all?' He hooked his finger under the edge of his dog collar, as if doing so allowed himself to breathe in an extra gulp of much-needed air.

Sister Assumpta's fierce dark eyebrows knitted together. 'We have fifteen fallen girls here. Four of them are due to give birth in a month's time, so we will be left with eleven. The classrooms are large, but there's only a certain number of beds in the dormitories. There's a limit, Father.'

Lily could feel herself blushing. She saw the nun glance across the room at her and felt sure she was enjoying her discomfort.

'Come now, Sister. Surely you can manage another dozen?' said Father Donnelly.

'We have discussed it. But we are a Mother and Baby home. We wouldn't want the evacuees to see the girls – it might—'

'Upset them,' interjected Sister David.

Lily made a show of looking out of the windows with the snow now drifting against the glass panes. She fixed her gaze on the expansive lawns, at the overgrown rock garden with grass clumping up between the granite stones, and the lopsided statue of Our Lady, now wearing a white cap, set back in a small ivy-covered grotto. She felt she ought not to be interested in the discussion going on around her, though of course she was. *Fallen girls* . . . how shocking! And there had been so much talk at home as to whether her younger brother and sister should be evacuated since war had been declared six months earlier, and the decision to keep them in Liverpool had been a constant source of argument between her parents.

'Sister, we have a duty to our children in Liverpool to educate and accommodate them when the bombing gets underway, as they say it will. Soon enough, most likely. St Joseph's in Hertfordshire have drawn up plans; in Wales the nuns have already sent out letters; St Mary the Virgin in Derbyshire have got the decorators in.'

'And what do you propose to do about the fallen girls? They don't stop getting pregnant just because there's a war on,' said Assumpta. She turned to Lily. 'D'you know any fallen girls? I'm sure you do. There's always one who mysteriously leaves school without explanation or apology, isn't there?'

'I-I couldn't rightly say,' stuttered Lily.

She sipped the weak tea and prayed the nun would stop asking her questions, looked outside again and hoped it would seem as though she had a sudden fascination with the red squirrel zig-zagging up the trunk of a pine tree. There was a knock on the door and a girl with pale skin freckling about her lips and long curtains of limp red hair came in to collect the tray. She held it in front of her bump, but there was no hiding the fact that she was at least seven months pregnant. Lily, shocked, looked at her and met her gaze momentarily, but the girl's eyes darted away. Sister Assumpta flinched as the girl picked up the tray unsteadily, making the crockery rattle.

'Take this. That will be all, Doreen,' she snapped.

'Lily, get the door for Doreen and wait outside,' said Father Donnelly, firmly.

Lily did as she was told and sat on a rickety chair in the corridor. Looking through a diamond-patterned window, she saw the girl's hunched figure scurrying across the lawn, creating footprints in the snow.

In the parlour, meanwhile, Sister David was trying to swing the talk back to the matter of the war. 'If anything, it's worse. When they think their men might die at any minute, common sense and chastity goes out of the window. It's a hotbed of sex out there. We had more girls coming through our doors in the last war than in peacetime. They seem to go at it like rabbits when the bombs are falling,' she said, dabbing at the corners of her mouth, collecting cake crumbs.

'*Sister*!' said the older nun, admonishing her with a look.

Sister David blushed pink.

'This building is huge. You can easily keep the fallen girls out of the way in the annex where the nursery and the labour wards are. The children will be in the main building. Shall we say thirty?' pressed Father Donnelly, clearing his throat. 'Besides, our evacuees from St Columba's school on the Dock Road and other parishes in Liverpool are in greater need than the unmarried mothers for now. When war starts to take its toll on—'

'*If* war starts to take its toll,' said Sister Assumpta. 'Nothing's really happened yet in Liverpool. And it looks like it might never happen. This phoney war has gone on for months. The bore war. Isn't that what they call it?'

'That's right, Sister. Plenty have brought their little ones back from Wales and the like, because so far it's been just one long yawn – but like Father Donnelly has said, it'll liven up soon enough and they'll be looking for places to keep their kiddies safe again.'

Once again, Sister Assumpta threw the nun a look. Sister David knew all that it contained, nervously took a biscuit and crunched it between her white teeth.

'You're walking blind, Sister Assumpta. It's only a matter of weeks before the bombings start, they say. So please think about it. That's all I ask,' said the priest. He needed to move the conversation on. 'Now, how about I leave you to have another slice of cake? I best get Lily back with her sheets. I'll be in touch, Sister,' he said, taking Assumpta's hand in his, pausing for a moment before he committed himself to the gesture, then patted it lightly. 'May God bless you and guide you in his infinite wisdom.'

'Infinite wisdom, indeed!' she said after he had left, absentmindedly twisting the band of gold on her ring finger whilst beadily looking out through the window at Father Donnelly hurrying Lily towards his Austin Seven car as the snow fell harder.

Chapter 1

Seven months later

Lily went downstairs to the large, airy high-ceilinged front room of their ramshackle home in Caryl Street, just off Liverpool's Dock Road. The Laffertys had lived here for as long as anyone could remember. Lily's mother had grown up here, and her mother before that, but with each passing year a few more roof tiles slid off, a few more floorboards turned as soft as marzipan, and the chimney stack had begun to crumble. But it suited them. The rent was cheap because nobody else in their right mind would have stayed there. The front room was the beating heart of the Lafferty household and when the chaise longue was pushed back and the battered armchair shoved against the wall, this was where Lily's mother, Stella, gave dancing lessons. They called it the ballroom and every Saturday and Sunday it would be full of the sounds of her mother yelling 'Eyes and teeth!' at the gaggle of children who came to learn how to shimmy and polka and step in time whilst her father bashed out 'You Are My Sunshine' on the piano with a Woodbine cigarette permanently dropping from his lips.

There was a residue of dust on the surfaces from all the preparations for the bombing that they had been waiting for since the previous autumn. When Lily had put her hands on the wooden rail screwed into the wall that they called the barré, her fingers left long slender imprints so she had brought a bucket of water in from the kitchen, placed it on the floor, and wrung out the cloth to wipe it down. Lily slid the cloth across the piece of wood, then dropped it, with a splash, into the bucket, pushed the sleeves of her pale blue blouse further up her arms and wandered over to the piano where she played a couple of notes. The keys were brown with muck – you could barely tell the black ones apart from the white ones – but it didn't matter. Her father might not be sitting there with cigarette smoke curling from the side of his mouth, now that he was working at the docks – that was the war's fault as much as her mother's – but the sound of him thumping out a tune still rang in her head. She paused and looked at the poster that sloped to one side, one corner hanging off the wall It was a picture of her and her younger brother, Matt, in Pierrot costumes. 'Liverpool Empire: Puss in Boots,' it said in bold letters, and underneath, in tiny script, below the names

Arthur Askey and Gracie Thompson, you could just about make out 'The Laffertys Limber Dancing Babes'. On the piano top there was a framed photograph caked in dust of her nine-year-old brother, little Bobby, in his sailor suit and tap shoes. Then one of Deirdre, aged seven now, the youngest of all the Laffertys, with a blob of shoe polish on her nose, and her head, a mass of quivering ringlets, tipped coquettishly to one side.

She ran her finger over the sideboard, regarded the black smudge on the tip of it and was about to wipe it down when she heard the slam of the front door.

Oh no, she thought, not Luigi from Bertorelli's, asking her to go and do a few extra hours at the mobile cafe, or the woman from the WVS centre seeing if she was free to do practice with the firewatch girls or cut up a few more sheets to make into bandages? But, to her delight, it was Vincent Wharton who stuck his head around the door. She beamed and thought how much he had grown. She hadn't seen him in three months since his job with the civil service had taken him to St Anne's just outside of Blackpool. He looked so strikingly handsome, with his steel grey eyes and his light brown hair swept back off his face, his broad shoulders perfectly in proportion to his long legs. He grinned, stepped inside, and undid the top button of his collar. When he walked in, she noticed that he almost had to duck to avoid hitting his head on the door frame.

He was wearing brogue shoes, a suit with baggy knees, and a shirt that was fraying at the collar, but he had finished it off with a white silk scarf tied loosely around his neck and, with his hair slicked back, he looked as though he was trying to be someone from the movies – she couldn't quite put her finger on who, maybe Leslie Howard?

'Vincent!' she cried.

'All right, lovely? Mam and Da out?'

Lily nodded a yes.

'You look grand,' he said.

She pushed a piece of hair behind her ear. He had made her blush. Had he noticed, she wondered, that she was different from when he had last seen her, that her clothes, tighter now, showed off her newly developed curves? Everyone had been saying it lately.

'Thanks,' she replied.

'Though this place looks a bit sad since I was last here …'

'We're broke. Things have slid. Like painting the Forth Bridge, it is, keeping this house clean. And us being so near the docks, it's worse every day. All the army vehicles coming and going and tearing the place up under our flaming feet.'

He grinned.

Lily continued, 'Mam doesn't really care. Impossible to keep on top of it, she says, what with all the bulldozing and digging, so why bother? Though that's just her excuse for choosing a natter over cups of tea and glasses of cheap brandy over chores.'

'That's unless she can get someone else to do it,' he joked.

'Of course. She's just the same.' She smiled.

'And the school?'

'No one comes any more for dancing lessons. In fact, no one's here much at all. What with me working at Bertorelli's and then in the evenings I'm doing my WVS work, and Mam's at the parachute factory and Dad's at the docks.'

He jangled coins in his pocket. 'Shame. I miss it here.'

He picked up the photo of them both when they were fourteen, dancing. He blew off the dust and rubbed at the glass with the heel of his hand. 'I remember this day. The Grafton, wasn't it?' he said.

Lily smiled again and her brown eyes shone.

'Look at you, dressed up to the nines in that suit and dickie bow. Smart little fella, you were,' she said, standing beside him, squinting at the picture.

'Your mam hired the hall and we made a grand pair, Lily. First prize, wasn't it? The tango? Right couple of bobby-dazzlers we were.'

She laughed her tinkling laugh. 'Lindy Hop,' she said. She peered at the photo. The shimmering drapes hung at each side of the raised dais, gathered in folds, looked like waterfalls, the men looked dapper in their white dinner jackets, their instruments held casually at their sides. It was another world – one of Palm Court orchestras, sweet sherries, whisky sours, patent leather shoes and high heels. She was wearing her mother's frock; it bagged around the waist, but she was holding the frilled skirts out to her sides – there were small loops that she'd slipped her fingers through – and it fanned into a shell shape. She remembered how beautiful she'd felt wearing it. Vincent looked pretty good too, in his smart suit that had belonged to her father. The cream jacket sloped off his shoulders and he'd turned up the white trousers to shorten them, but he looked just the ticket. She remembered her mother saying those words. Just the ticket.

Now he took a packet of sandwiches from his pocket and sat on the dusty, faded piano stool after he had brushed it down with his cap. He unwrapped the greaseproof paper and offered her one. 'Want a jam buttie?'

She nodded, took one, and ate it greedily.

'You working later, Lil?'

'No. I did the early shift. Shame, that's changed an' all. Supposed to be an ice-cream bar but there's no ice cream at the moment. There's not much food either. Except spuds. It's potato pie, potato mash, potato cakes,' she said, smiling. 'So I'm mostly peeling potatoes.' She laughed. 'Still, it pays. People – mostly Italians and Irish – come to chat and drink tea and there's plenty of beer. Sometimes Dad turns up and plays the piano with a couple of the accordionists – my cousin's new husband is a wizard on the squeeze-box – and they sing songs. "O Sole Mio" and "Danny Boy". The old stuff. Mam hates it, of course. Says it's common.'

He grinned, then got up from the stool, flicked breadcrumbs from his trousers, tilted his head and smiled at her.

'What's the matter?' she asked. He didn't answer the question, just shrugged.

Looking at him leaning against the piano, one foot crossed over the other, just staring at her and grinning, she repeated the question.

'*What*?' she asked.

'You,' he said. He moved a step forward to her. 'You've changed.'

What was this? This strange look on his face? His loitering gaze and smile? She felt a pang of something, unsure what it was exactly, a mixture of excitement and nervousness. This wasn't the Vincent she knew.

Feeling herself blushing, she looked away from him, down at the piano that had sat there in the corner for ten years now. The one that had plinked and plonked as she and Vincent had sashayed around the room together, had grown up dancing to the sounds of. Other memories came of her and Vincent, all mixed up with cascading hairpins, slipping her feet into tiny salmon-pink shoes, and her mother wielding a can of hair lacquer saying 'Shut your eyes, this will sting!'. There were the concerts at the Rialto and the pantos when they would swell the dance teams at the Empire. Memories of standing on this battered old piano stool, with Vincent laughing at her until he cried, wearing wilting ears made out of corners torn out of the *Liverpool Echo*, an old stocking stuffed with newspaper pinned to her bottom, supposed to be a cat's tail, the sharp sound of her mother's hand slapping her thighs as she sewed a white bib onto her leotard and told her to stop being so bloody daft, playing up to Vincent.

'So how'd you fancy a quick belt around the Rialto before the crowds arrive, if Betty will let us?' he asked.

'That'd be grand,' she said.

He plucked at the Senior Service cigarette pack poking out of his jacket pocket.

'Be like old times.' Until now, when they hadn't been dancing, she and Vincent had mostly spent time together when he would visit her at Bertorelli's after Luigi had nipped out to put a bet on a horse, giggling and flicking tea towels at each other, racing around tables, until a customer walked in and she would have to shoo him out. This was different.

She cast her eyes down to his brogue shoes. They were in a right state. She could see the shape of his feet moulded into the leather, those lovely feet that she had stepped in time with since she had been six years old.

Shoving her hands into the sleeves of her jacket, she said, 'Give us a ciggie,' turned off the light and, with Vincent pulling on her hand which was gripped tightly in his, they set off to Upper Parly Street.

After dodging a tram with the covers on its headlights that shot out into the street from nowhere and swerved to avoid running them over – the inky blackness in Liverpool had already taken more lives than Hitler – they arrived at the dance hall. There was a blast of music, noisy and brash, a cacophony of trumpets and horns, the sounds of a piano, heady and giddy. It was one of those clubs that craftily manoeuvred itself around the law by saying it was a dancing school as well as a club, but everyone knew the only lessons that had been taught here were how to slip an arm around a girl's waist and whisper come-ons in her ear whilst doing the tango without getting a slap in the face.

A fog of cigarette smoke rose from the basement door, wove itself up the steps and into the street and hung in the air. Lily inhaled the smells, felt herself intoxicated, excited by the sounds as Vincent led her downstairs. Someone at the piano started up with 'In the Mood'. There was a fellow on a trumpet and a saxophone who took up the tune, one of the Walker boys. It felt warm, familiar. At seventeen, she was a little too young to be here, but in the dim lighting, she hoped no one would notice. The small red lamps at each tabled glowed like beacons, throwing pools of light onto the tables. Half an hour and her mother would be only just leaving the parachute factory in Bootle to head home. And as Vincent slipped his hand around her waist, cigarette drooping from his lips, and steered her on to the floor to dance, the dark undertones of the music, sweet and rhythmic, made her forget herself. It was true what they said. You could lose yourself and find yourself in dancing, she thought. His hand sliding down the curve of her hip as they moved together, she wondered again, was she imagining it? Vincent? Her best friend? Her partner in crime? Surely not. And yet . . .

This early, they had the floor almost to themselves. They could call out to the piano player for the songs that they wanted – 'South of the Border', 'Sunrise Serenade'. The men in the band in their white jackets and dickie bows, imagining they were Victor Silvester or Glen Miller, nodded and smiled back at them.

Vincent spun her around, twisted and turned her about the floor, lifted her off the ground, his chest pressed against her breasts, so that when she locked eyes with his, her head felt dizzy and her nerves tingled with excitement. People couldn't help but stop and stare at them as they began to dance a tango to the music of D'Arienzo – 'King of the Beat,' whispered Vincent. With their fingers interlocking, her slender legs winding around Vince's muscular ones, coming together, moving apart, leaning in to one another, it looked almost as though they were about to kiss at times.

Finally, Betty appeared with a broom. 'Off you go now. Paying punters about to arrive.'

'Thanks,' said Vincent. 'That hit the spot, eh Lil?' They went outside into the street, breathless, sweat glistening on their brows, and stood leaning with their backs against the wall. He lit another cigarette and, without warning, turned in to her.

'What, Vincent?' asked Lily, smiling, wiping her forehead. But she knew exactly what. Dancing with him had left her in no doubt about that. She could feel it. She had felt it from the moment he had arrived at Caryl Street that evening. Felt it for years, all her life maybe, just never really noticed. The little puffs of hot breath on her cheek, the rise and fall of his ribs, the searching look in his eyes, the way he pushed a tendril of her chestnut hair off her face and behind her ear, was familiar, but different.

And that was the first time – after so many years of friendship, and both of them wondering why they had never done it before, because it was so natural and right and good – that suddenly they kissed: passionately, ferociously, fiercely.

'You took your time,' she said, when she broke the kiss and they paused for breath. Is this what it felt like to begin to fall in love? She felt a little sick at the thought of what her father would make of this. 'Our children are pieces of the heart,' he would often say to her mother. And Lily knew then, as Vincent's hands tugged at her blouse, what he wanted to do with her, and how it would break her father's heart in two. She wondered also what her mother would have to say about this if she could see her bare legs, skirts pushed up her thighs, top three buttons undone on her blouse, as Vince breathed hard into her face.

'Some things are worth waiting for,' he said, and as he leaned in for more, he added, 'Feel that …'

'What?'

'You know what,' he said, as he pressed his body against her. She was used to this body, she knew it so well, but not that – that was something new and dangerous – and it made her sick with excitement and a little terrified as to what all this might lead to. Is this what the nuns at her convent school had been trying to warn her about when they had talked about *men's ways?*

Suddenly, he moved away from her.

'Come on,' he said. 'I'll walk you home. Have to be up early tomorrow.'

'To go back to St Anne's?'

He paused. 'No, love. I've left. Pushing papers is not for me, no matter how much me ma and da say civil service is a good job.'

'Heard they are busier than ever at the dockyards, converting their liners to warships. Why don't you try that? There's jobs for everyone.'

'That's right, love. But I don't need another job. I'm joining the merchant navy. I've already started my training.'

'The merchant navy?' she said in a panicked voice.

'There's a war on out there, despite what everyone says about it being a phoney war. This country is going to need supplies of every kind if it's to survive – and I, for one, want to be part of it,' he replied.

Chapter 2

They decided to take the tram back as it was getting late and Lily began to worry about arriving home after her mother.

'The thing is, Lily, I'm eighteen now,' he said, speaking loudly to be heard above the lightbulbs rattling in their sockets and the hiss and squealing and clanking of metal as the tram moved along the rails.

'I know, but …' she said. But what? It felt so sad that the possibilities stretching out in front of her when he had kissed her might be about to slip through her fingers like grains of sand, but she couldn't say it. It seemed such a shame that he was about to go away again, such a waste that she had only just realised now what he meant to her.

'I can't stand these fellas who say they want to do something for this war and do nothing. Couple of them last night at the George, sitting around giving it all the big "I am" talk, and then finding excuses as to why they had to stay with the horses at the stables in St

Domingo's or keep up dock work. I could never be like that.'

She looked at him sitting next to her on the tram seat. Headstrong and adventurous, of course the war was going to be irresistible to him – he would be the first to post back his papers, front of the line if need be, racing up the steps at St George's Hall two at a time to sign up, no doubt, but it still felt like the ground moving under her feet to hear the words being said out loud. And why the merchant navy, for goodness' sake? It was dangerous. Everyone knew that the very first British ship to be sunk was the SS *Athenia*, torpedoed by a U-boat on the evening war with Germany was declared. Britons, Canadians and Americans had lost their lives. Vincent's father had been in the merchant navy, and his father before him, so he knew the risks, all right – why put himself in harm's way like that?

'As soon as I finish my five weeks' training, I'm off.'

Her face fell, her large soulful eyes became worried and sad.

'When's that then?' she asked, straightening her skirts.

He paused. 'Well, here's the thing. I'm over halfway through it already. I went straight from St Anne's to a camp in Sharpness. Now I'm on a ship here moored at the docks. You must have seen it – the one with the sloping funnel. You have to learn knots, splicing, steering, boxing the compass. And the gunner training, of course.'

She could see his eyes shine with excitement as he spoke and once again she felt a little sick. Just the words 'gunner training' made her worried.

He chattered on. 'You have to buy all your clothes and gear for sea – can't carry on spending every penny of my wages in the pub until I get the next pay packet like I'm the flaming Aga Khan.'

'No.'

'You'll miss me when I go to sea?' he asked.

'I will. St Anne's was bad enough but at least I knew you were safe. And I'd forgotten what it feels like to waltz with you until you reminded me tonight. Who'll waltz with me while you're away? Our dance. Nobody knows it but us two. All those whizzy twists and turns we made up. Mind you, I won't miss you treading on my toes with your great big size elevens.'

'When I have ever done that?' he laughed, and she smiled.

But then the smile slid. 'Is that why you wanted to see me tonight? To tell me you were going away?'

'Just wanted to put you in the picture, like.'

She wanted to say, don't go, why d'you have to go? What if something happens to you? Don't leave me with my mad-as-a-March-hare mother, unreliable father, and unruly brothers and sister, but she didn't dare. She didn't want to stray into unchartered territories, a place she knew she would find it difficult to come back from.

'Didn't want you to think I'd just taken off.'

'That's nice, Vincent.' She enjoyed saying his name out loud. Turned it around in her mouth. Vincent. Her friend who she worshipped and adored. Vincent, her dance partner since he first took lessons from Stella as a boy. Vincent, who looked out for her, slipped three-penny bits down her back, and made her laugh, who had the power to make her feel that the two of them together could even take on Hitler and win. Vincent, who had just *kissed* her.

'Grand that you'll be worrying about me,' he said, moving up closer to her on the tram seat, nudging her in the ribs. She could feel the sweetness of his breath on her face as he leaned in to her.

'Exactly. You can't go, please don't . . .'

There, I've said it, she thought, hoping the smile she said it with would mean he might think she was joking. She blushed, felt her cheeks reddening.

He smiled. 'I'll be back on leave after each voyage. They even pay you whilst you're waiting for another ship. Three pounds a week.'

She picked at a thread on his jacket, let it swirl in the sickly yellow glow of the lamplight.

'And how long before you'd be off again?'

'They send you a telegram. Five days, probably. Maybe the next day. Who knows? Everyone has to put themselves in a bit of danger if we want this war to be won.'

'Why not sign on as a reservist? Like me da.'

'I'd like to see him working on the docks, you know.'

Lily exchanged a smile with Vincent. The thought of her father, hauling sacks and cargo at the docks, was hard for either of them to imagine.

'No, reservist isn't for me,' he continued.

'Mam has been canny. She wanted him to get the job at Huskisson dock so that he wouldn't have to be called up and she could keep him close to home. But hard graft doesn't really suit my da,' she said.

Vincent nodded. Cliff Lafferty, sitting at the piano wreathed in a blueish fog of cigarette smoke, with his long delicate fingers and graceful ways, wasn't made for hauling sacks of coal about.

'Mam said he would just have to put up with it, but he doesn't like it. And can you believe it, she went along with him to the interview for the job? The man interviewing saw through that ruse straight away, saw her poking him in the ribs, whispering in his ear, telling him what to say. Sent her out of the room, the fella did.'

'Can't picture him at the docks. Your da would look right out of place with his cravat and patent leather shoes,' he said, laughing, and Lily smiled. 'You Lafferty lot are different. You're not like other people. Can't imagine your da getting up at seven o'clock, sitting behind a desk for eight hours, either.'

'My father didn't used to get out of his dressing gown five o'clock, some days, and some days not at all. And Mam needs freedom. "*I need to breathe*!"' she said, mimicking her mother with elaborate fanning gestures, and making Vincent laugh. 'He's doing his bit. But he's still mad at Mam. They won't tell me exactly why. I just hear snippets of conversation, or rather arguments, through cracks in the door.'

'Bet your Matt wishes he could get stuck in. Only sixteen, isn't he? Not quite ready to go off to the army yet.'

'Mam would find that hard to watch an' all. So would I. Let's hope this war is over before he's eighteen.'

'Well, no one knows what Hitler will do next.'

The tram stopped at the end of Caryl Street and they got off together, Vincent clasping her hand tightly as they jumped off the board onto the pavement. Lily paused and looked at him. She straightened his jacket, placed her hand on his lapel, and let it rest there for a moment.

'And what if you d-don't come back?' she asked.

'Of course I will,' he said.

'You might not. What if one day there's the telegram boy's bike at your mam's door?'

'Stop fretting. You can't think like that, Lily. Go down that road and you're done, love. I've never been one to sit at home in my slippers and vest waiting for the world to come knocking at my front door.'

She moved an inch towards him. She could smell him this close. But it wasn't one she was used to. Instead of the smell of battered old dance shoes, Brylcreem and chalk dust, it was another smell – an intoxicating, strong male musky scent that made a wash of goose pimples rise under her flesh.

'Lily, are you all right?' he asked.

'I had a lovely time tonight,' she murmured. 'With you, I mean. The best.' It was difficult to put into words what she was feeling. But she had tried. And as she walked up the steps to her house and waved goodbye to him, while he struck a match and lit a cigarette, she was glad that she had.

When she got in the house, she pulled her coat around her, trying to rearrange her dishevelled clothes, and set off up the stairs, avoiding the loose bottom step that always creaked loudly whenever anyone trod on it.

'Is that you?' called her mother, her disembodied voice floating through into the hall from the parlour.

'Yes,' she replied, wincing, raising her eyes, and mouthing 'damn, damn' silently to herself.

'Come in here, love.'

Lily turned and went downstairs again and into the parlour. Her mother was sitting on the battered armchair, wearing a pair of stained fluffy pink mules and a long, flowing chiffon dress with holes in the flounces around the hem where her heels had caught in it when she had been dancing. 'Turn around.' She struck a match to light the cigarette in her mouth, and the flare from it as she held it to her red lips lit up her face to reveal a cold, expressionless stare.

Lily's heart beat faster. 'What, Mam?' she asked.

'Turn around and lift up your skirts.'

'Why?'

'Lift up your skirts,' she said firmly, taking a long drag on her cigarette as if to prolong Lily's discomfort, as if she was enjoying the look of panic on her daughter's face. Her mother gestured with the cigarette. Lily shuffled around so she stood with her back to her mother.

'Go on.'

Lily clutched the material of her tea dress and lifted up her skirts tentatively.

'Higher.'

'Oh, Mam!' she said, twisting her head around and speaking over her shoulder to her mother.

'I said higher, Lily.'

Lily sighed. She was used to doing as she was told – anything for a quiet life with her mother – but she was finding this excruciating. Nevertheless, she clutched her skirt again, and hiked it up another inch, revealing the backs of her thighs.

'The pencil line. The pencil line you've drawn on the back of your legs to fake stockings.'

'What, Mam?' She had been begging her mother for months now to get her some silk from the parachute factory to take to her best friend Rosie, the seamstress next door, to make into stockings.

'It's all smudged. Like you've been rubbing up against something.'

Vincent's leg, coiling around hers as they had kissed, flashed into her head. She pinked to the tip of her ears and stammered a reply. 'I-I . . .'

'Have you been with Vincent Wharton? I've heard he's jacked in his civil service job and he's back in Liverpool. I've heard he's joined the merchant navy, doing gunnery training, so his mother told me.'

Lily twisted the belt of the dress around her finger. 'No . . .' she mumbled, realising that she was going to have to come up with something better than that.

'Speak up!'

'No.'

'Where to? The Rialto?'

'I went down to the Rialto on me own. Betty gave me half an hour,' she lied. 'Me and her were trying the tango. You know that. It's tricky.'

'You are not to go there again!' her mother said, slamming her hand down on the arm of the chair, making her glass of sherry rattle about on the surface of the small battered side table.

'Mam, I'm sorry. It's this place. I can't stand it any longer. I just needed to get out.'

'I'm not saying you can't go out. Just not to the dance halls.'

'Why? Plenty of people head there when the sirens go off. Some stay there all night until the all-clear. They say they're safe.'

'Safe? When they're swarming with men looking for a woman, any woman, as long as she's got a heart-beat and a smile?' Her mother rested the cigarette on the glass ashtray. 'I don't want to be worrying about you and Vincent. I've enough on my plate.'

'What do you mean?'

Her mother stood, walked over to Lil and grabbed her by the chin. She didn't answer. 'Have you been plucking your eyebrows again?' she said, squinting into Lily's face, twisting her face to the ceiling light. 'Are you sure you haven't been with Vincent?'

'No,' she lied.

'He's soft on you, love. Look at you. You're beau-tiful. But you're too young. And what about when he goes off to war?'

Lily's heart kicked at her ribs. She didn't want to be reminded of that. She sighed deeply and looked vaguely into the distance.

'This war has changed other things, not just the dancing school and leaving us with hardly a bean. It's changed the way men think about women. When you know you might walk out that door and never come back, it changes things.'

'What are you saying, Mam?'

'Well, there are some round here who think that artistic types have loose morals. People like us.'

People like you and Dad, you mean, thought Lily.

'I've seen the way that Vincent looks at you. Seen it for years. You've just never noticed. This isn't easy for me to say. But you know this running off, it's not doing any of us any good. I know things are difficult at the minute, but I don't want you spending time with Vincent if he comes knocking. This doing up your face in war paint and rubbing gravy all over your legs when you go dancing? It's only going to lead to disaster. Getting carried away in the heat of the moment, letting your passions get the better of you.'

'Gravy? Mam! I don't do that! You know I don't. That gravy trick makes your legs smell to high heaven. It's disgusting,' she said.

'Well, you might have chosen the less pungent alternative tonight, but I'm telling you, all these amorous shenanigans will only take you to hell in a handcart. There's a lot of it around at the minute and I don't want you getting into trouble. Can you imagine what it would do to your father if the same happened to you as Nellie's girl?'

'Nellie's girl?' What was she going on about?

'The one who went off to have her baby and never came back. The one who drowned herself in the Scaldies. Remember?'

'I don't know Nellie's girl. Anyway, getting pregnant doesn't always mean the sky has to fall in on you. What about that girl we know from Kenty who I'm working with at the WVS? She had a bun in the oven at seventeen. That turned out all right. She got married.'

'Yes, to someone who works in a *pub*! All I'm saying is: you need to be good. I was never going to be a good example to you, but at least I can be a horrible warning—'

Lily frowned. 'What does that mean?' she asked.

'We'll save that for another time,' Stella answered, mysteriously.

Chapter 3

'Damn! Damn!' said Lily. Those bloody sirens again. It had been a week of running back and forth to the shelter. News of a bomb killing a poor unfortunate housemaid in Birkenhead, and Wallasey feeling the full force of Hitler's Luftwaffe, had left everyone fearful it was only a matter of time before something dreadful was going to happen in Liverpool. She had seen Vincent a couple of times when he got off training at six, but it had been snatched hours where she had mostly sat at the side of the boating lake in Stanley Park with her head on his shoulder, or walked up to the Pier Head holding his hand so tightly it gave her pins and needles. The wailing sound meant Lily was supposed to follow the instructions on the bit of paper that was pinned to the back of the larder door, and start making her way to St Barnabas School at the end of their road, to wait safely inside the shelter – a heavily fortified brick bunker, reinforced by corrugated iron and bucketloads of cement, situated between the gym and the girls' lavatories. She certainly wasn't meant to be here at home in Caryl Street. She should have been at the shelter twenty minutes ago, but she had lost all sense of time. Besides, she hated the place. Who would want to spend the night there? It was impossible to sleep with the coughing and sneezing and whimpering of everyone around you. Rows of bunk beds, kids sniffling – and the previous week, after another false alarm, a couple had lain together in the bed next to her, doing heaven knows what under the sheets, grunting and moaning like animals. It was horrible. And the smell! The smell was awful, worse than a pigsty. She would put her handkerchief over her nose and mouth but it did little to stop making her gag when she went down the stairs to enter the shelter. The wardens tried their best, but the bleach and tins of Vim they used every day, never quite got rid of the pungent musky human stench that she hated so much.

'What the hell are you doing here?' Matt's face was purpling with exasperation. She could see circles of sweat darkening his twill shirt at his armpits. 'Have you not heard the sirens? What if this isn't just a practice run! What if this is actually happening? You heard what happened over the water a week ago? Someone was killed!' he said, raking his hand through his reddish brown hair.

'I heard. But then I could ask the same of you. What the hell are you doing here?'

'Mam sent me to get you. You're sending us all daft. What do you think you're playing at?'

'And who d'you think you are? Pushing me around, just because you're a fella. You're my kid brother and I'm not going to put up with that. Anyway, I can always go in the cupboard or under the table.'

'Don't be so flaming idiotic.'

She humphed and her eyes flashed blue-black. He might be her brother, but he was still younger than her, though you wouldn't think it at times. He had certainly inherited their mother's domineering nature.

'Were you born stupid? Or did it take years of practice?' he asked. He grabbed her roughly by the arm. 'Get down to the shelter. Just because a bomb hasn't killed anyone in Liverpool yet, doesn't mean tonight won't be the real thing. This is serious, Lily!'

'Hold your flaming horses! Stop prodding me!' she said.

'Get a flipping move on!' he barked.

'My shoes. I'm not going without my good shoes. I'll see you down there—'

'Forget your bloody shoes! Can't you hear the sirens? What the hell do you need them for? At this rate you won't need shoes where you're going. What's the good of shoes if you're in a bloody box?'

'Why do you always have to look on the grim side?' she said.

'Look, run all the way to the shelter, OK? I'm going to check on Gram. Make sure she's safe with Auntie Annie.'

She nodded and tutted. When she heard the sound of the front door slam, she went over to the window, pulled the blackout curtain aside and checked to make sure he had left. As she watched him racing down the street, she called, 'You can come out now, Vince.'

Vincent stepped out from the cupboard.

'He's right, love. You need to get down to the shelter toot sweet. Too dangerous here,' he said, buttoning up his jacket.

She moved towards him, pulled him to her by the lapels, stood on her toes and kissed him full on the lips. 'You as well? Go home to your ma and I'll be round as soon as the all-clear goes. I'll be fine, I know I will. I feel lucky tonight.'

'Lucky?'

'Of course. Because, well … This. Us. You know what I mean, Vince?'

'Aye, love. I do,' he replied.

It was the deafening sound of an aircraft's engines that she heard first. She had just waved goodbye to Vince when they went their separate ways at Caryl Street Gardens. When she looked into the sky, just above the roofs of the row of houses up the hill, she saw the square tip of the wing, then the black cross. Good God! Matt was right! This *was* the real thing, she realised, panic gripping her. Suddenly she heard a terrific whizzing sound, followed by an explosion. The warning sirens began blaring louder now. She felt every muscle tightening and flexing, pressed her hands over her ears and winced. Bit late for the sirens, she thought as the plane swooped over her head and looped back the other way. She was sure it was crashing; it looked as though it was nose-diving right behind the Liver buildings, but it curved up into the sky and went away back across the river towards New Brighton.

Her thoughts turned to Vincent. She was worried for him, wished he was here with her, but, with her heart pounding, hurried on to find the shelter.

'Stand back!' cried the ARP man as she raced down Stanhope Street, clutching her thin cardigan around her body. Those tin hats gave these fellows a jumped-up air that some of them didn't deserve, she decided.

'What are you doing out here?' a second fellow cried. A right jobsworth, blowing his whistle, waving his arms about like a proper fool, Lily thought. She shoved past him and sprinted down the hill. She could hear more clanging and the ringing of the police car warning bells. Maybe her brother had been right. She had become too complacent, too tired of nothing happening. She used to go racing down to the air raid shelter at the first warning sounds, then she got bored when time after time it turned out to be a false alarm. More often than not she would just crawl under the bed or slip into the broom cupboard. Her mother never seemed that bothered. But this time it was real, all right.

'Where are you going love?' shouted the ARP man at the top of Crow Street.

Phump. Phump. Then again, phump. The sound of bombs falling. Vincent had told her that before they flew back home they would open their flaps and drop everything they had left as a goodbye present. The air thickened and parts of the city were lit up with a greenish glow. Must be the sulphur from the bombs. Ash was beginning to fall. She could feel it sitting on her eyelashes and her cheeks. And then another explosion. Closer. Too close. Around the corner, maybe. That one must have been a whopper. Worry descended on her like a cloud. And the voluminous dust that made it hard to breathe was ominous. Please God, the debris in the air and the black particles that were making her nose itch and eyes stream wasn't a result of the shelter where her mother and brother and sisters had headed off to being hit. Please God, Vincent had got home safely. A sharp pain stabbed her throat as she gulped more air. Her stomach somersaulted. She pushed her hand into the side of her waist, trying to abate the painful stitch in her side.

Someone called out to her to turn back. 'You don't want to go down there!' said a man with a mucky face and a bag stuffed full of *Liverpool Echo*s slung around his neck. But something, a fear gripping her again, tightening again around her chest like an iron band, was compelling her to drive herself on. 'St Barnabas School's been hit!' he called after her. And in an instant her fear turned to a hurtling, blind panic.

How could I have been so stupid? she said to herself. The elementary school at the bottom of the hill? But that's where her mother had taken shelter with the little ones! What if her brother and sister, her mother …? What if …? What if …?

An ambulance came screeching around the corner, but instead of heading towards the school where the bomb had fallen, it raced off the other way, up the hill, in the opposite direction. Had there been another, worse, bombing down the road, more casualties? Surely not? Or was the driver lost? And then a thought occurred to her. St Barnabas. St Barnabas School was where the bomb had fallen, the man had said. But St Barnabas *church* was up at the top of the hill. Everyone round here knew that the school, now being used as makeshift air-raid shelter, was half a mile away from the church, but maybe this was their mistake. She ran into the road, waving a handkerchief she pulled out from up her sleeve, shouting after them, 'Hey! Come back!' But her voice was hoarse and hollow.

It was the smell that reached her nostrils first, then a choking, dry feeling hit the back of her throat as she tried to breathe. More clouds of dust, small fires breaking out everywhere, a car with its tyres flattened and deflated, looking as if it had almost melted onto the pavement. Oh God, oh God, were her sister and brother in the school? Her mother? What would she do if they had been hurt? What would she do if they were dead? The thought was unimaginable, but it remained stuck in her brain, terrifying her as she charged on, tears gathering in her stinging eyes.

The first thing she saw was that the front wall of the building had completely collapsed. The windows had all been blown out of their frames and glass crunched under her feet. A man was shouting unintelligibly into a loudhailer. A few people were clambering over the mounds of debris, desperately pulling away rubble to clear their path. There was a burst pipe with water splashing all over the pavement and she could feel her shoes letting in water. For a moment she stood there like a statue, rooted to the unyielding ground, just watching the scene being played out in front of her, people carrying out children in their arms, some barely alive, some ... No, she didn't dare think about it. Then suddenly, as if waking from a dream, her body jolted into action and she ran over and pulled away at some of the stone and the brickwork that had fallen in piles all around her. She tore at the broken bricks, dirt pushing up beneath her fingernails, scrambled up the pieces of wall to get a look inside one of the windows. As the smoke cleared, she could hear shouting. People started to appear from inside the building, clothes ripped and torn, faces covered in dust, some tearful, some dazed, some sobbing and calling out for help, indicating that there were others inside. A man said to Lily that she had to leave immediately. He had a handkerchief over his mouth and was waving a flag and yelling.

'Get away from here!' he cried. 'This is no place for a child!'

'I'm not a bloody child!' she shouted. 'I'm seventeen!' She didn't want to leave. And he shook his head and muttered something, stomping off. He had no time for this silly girl and her arguing.

'Who are you looking for?' asked a kind-looking woman, touching her gently on her arm.

'My sister. My brother. And my mam – they're here. *I* was supposed to be here,' she said in a tremulous voice.

The ARP man, relenting, joined them; he could see what state she was in. 'This is my job, love, this is no place for you.'

'I need to – I need …' she said, gasping. She felt herself choking, felt more ash on her eyelids tasted sulphur in her mouth.

Another man in a tin hat came out. She had seen him go in – he had been carrying a shovel and had pushed her aside. This time, though, he wasn't carrying a shovel, he was carrying a child bundled up in a sheet and she saw a mass of red curls poking out from under it. Thankfully, not her brother or sister, and instantly felt guilty for the thought.

'Whilst there's life, there is still hope,' she heard a woman muttering to a young man sobbing beside her as he uncovered a still figure from the rubble.

The woman turned away. 'Oh God, poor wretch. To have been buried alive! And look at the kiddie in her arms. Perfect. Perfect face. Not a mark on her. That's the gas that does that. Your lungs just explode!'

'Don't look, love. Please don't look,' said a voice beside her. 'Cover your eyes ...'

Then suddenly, clambering through a large hole in the wall, came Lily's mother, face covered in soot, her hair in sponge curlers poking out like pink sausages from under a headscarf, her favourite red dress, now filthy and hanging off one shoulder. She was trying to avoid the shards of broken glass, with Bobby, his straight shiny brown hair that usually looked as though a bowl of melted chocolate had been poured over his head all matted and ruffled up, and little Deirdre, her soulful eyes wide with fright, clutching each hand.

'Mam!' cried Lily. 'Over here!'

'I'll bloody crown you! Where have you been, Lily? We thought you were still in there!'

'Cleaning the house. I lost track of the time. I'm sorry, Mam.'

'*Cleaning the house*! We've been going out of our minds! Is our Matt with you?' she said, grasping both Lily's arms and shaking her.

'Gone to check on Gram and Annie at Gladys Street. They've got an Anderson shelter there. Matt said Dad's there.'

When Stella let go of her, Lily looked at the red mark her fingers had made.

'I've been worried sick about you, Lily. We were in the back room. The cloakroom. It was the front of the building that got hit. Thank God.'

Then relief was overtaken by anger as she suddenly hit Lily about the head.

Lily cowered and protected herself with her forearms. She didn't know what to do; she just shouted, 'Mammy, *Mam*!'

A dog, a cocker spaniel, came up behind them barking. Deirdre stooped to stroke it, but the man holding it on the leash, shouted 'Get back! Are you out of your mind?'

Startled, she jumped back. The man bent down, unclipped the leash and let the dog off; it started sniffing about.

'Why's he sniffing, Mam? He's sniffing all over the place,' said Deirdre.

'Sniffing for dead bodies,' replied Bobby, flatly.

'You had no need to tell her that!' said her mother. 'Look what you've done!'

Deirdre's little face crumpled and she wailed so loudly someone came over and offered them tea and asked them who they had lost.

'We're all here. All alive, thank you,' said Stella. He nodded and walked briskly away; he had other people to worry about.

Lily opened her mouth, about to speak, but was stopped abruptly by her mother, a flat palm held up in front of her face.

'No, don't say anything. I don't want to hear. I'm sick of your excuses, day in, day out. We can never find you when we need to and you lie about where you've been. I know when you're lying because your mouth twitches. Do you know it does that? I had to send your brother down back to the house with the sirens wailing above us and you're wandering around, waltzing the length and breadth of Lime Street, for all I know, without a bloody care in the world. Just selfish! Lily, do you realise that you're just selfish!? I'm sick to death of it.'

Lily frowned, chewed at the skin around the base of her thumbnail.

'I don't know what the fuss is about,' she said. 'I'm OK, aren't I?'

The man was shouting, 'Where are the bloody ambulances?'

'Three of them went down Brownlow Hill,' said Lily. 'I saw them on the way here.'

'Oh no, oh no, they gone to the church! I knew they had,' muttered the man. 'Didn't they get the message to say it was the school that had been hit?'

Four men left to find out if it was true, meanwhile others were bringing out more people, carrying some in blankets and asking for sheets.

'To cover the dead bodies,' whispered Bobby, which only stared Deirdre off again.

'Take a photograph!' someone was shouting. Another yelled, 'Please return to the shelters ... please return to the shelters ...' But it didn't do any good. More people arrived, some come to help, some just to gawp in horror, and then, as the chimney leaned dangerously to one side, it wobbled and fell in on the school house, crashing down in a heap of bricks, cement and clouds of dust, accompanied by a collective gasp of shock and a cry of disbelief.

Meanwhile, they were using the doors that had been blown off as makeshift stretchers. A young man lay on one of them. He was perfect – apart from the pool of blood under his head ...

'Go to your nearest shelter, please go ... This isn't a circus. Please go as quickly as you can and wait for the all-clear,' someone said into a megaphone.

They set off, a bedraggled group, clutching each other's hands, frightened, worried and, with the sound of the clanging bells of engines and ambulances, seeing the sky light up blood red because of fires all over the city, finally coming to the realisation that the phoney war was over. If, indeed, it hadn't just been lying in wait and had never been phoney at all.

Chapter 4

Two of the windows in the front bay of Caryl Street had completely shattered. The black crosses taped to the panes, 'kisses for Hitler' as Deirdre called them, had held the upstairs ones together after a fashion, but the top of the chimney had completely collapsed in on itself. The blackout curtains were torn in places and hung off the rails. The house hadn't been hit directly, but there was enough damage from flying shrapnel to have caused 'a right old mess of the place', as her mother had said. That morning was the start of a sweltering hot day; there was the sound of birdsong and an incongruous sweet smell of roses in the air, but it belied the devastating consequences of the previous two night's bombing. Lily shaded her eyes with her hand at the window. Bobby was popping tar bubbles in the melting tarmac with a stick in the street outside. He blinked against the sunshine. Lily mouthed his name and knocked on the glass, beckoning him to come into the house.

'London is bracing itself for casualties,' said the voice on the wireless.

'What about here in Liverpool?' asked Lily, turning her head. 'We've already been hit pretty badly.'

A breathless Rosie, from next door, came rushing into the front room, strands of her dark brown hair escaping from a paisley-patterned turban, her clothing slightly dishevelled as though she had just been interrupted while dressing. 'Have you heard? Hitler is about to take another step. You know what he said to the Germans? That if we drop thirty thousand bombs, he'll drop a million on us! I didn't believe it at the time.'

'A step too flaming far!' said her father, and he sat there with his mouth agape.

'Now, Rosie, you've always been prone to exaggeration. Are you sure you've got that right?' said Stella.

'In retaliation for Berlin,' she answered.

It felt like one minute they were all joyously practising Stella's favourite tap step – 'Shuffle off to Buffalo' she would rhythmically chant to keep them in time as they linked arms and danced together – and the next minute, shuffling off to Buffalo was a thing of the past and dancing at Caryl Street was over for the time being at least – and they were crowded around the wireless, listening to a disembodied voice talking about poison gas attacks, and bombings and gas masks, and telling them that they all might die at any moment.

'Thirty-three killed in Guernsey, sixty-seven injured, nine killed in Jersey ...' said the voice on the wireless.

'Good God!' said Cliff, a Woodbine drooping from his lips, raking a hand through his thick, blue-black hair.

'For those families who still have children in the cities, the time has come for a second wave of evacuations ...' continued the voice. 'Those of you who have children who returned home after the first wave should make arrangements to leave again immediately.'

Amidst the commotion, Lily slipped out, went into the larder, busied herself behind the stippled glass window amongst tins of condensed milk and sardines and then, when she was sure no one had noticed, headed outside through the back door. She found Deirdre sitting on the step with a jam jar full of rose petals turning into mush in water.

'I'm making rose perfume,' she said. 'Want a sniff?'

'I haven't time. Tell Mam I've nipped off to get a bit of Spam from the grocer's. I won't be long,' she said, leaning over her sister. 'Where am I going?'

'Gone to get a bit of Spam.'

'Good,' she replied. 'Gone to get a bit of Spam.'

Lily ran all the way to Vincent's house, past Caryl Gardens Estate and Gallagher's stables, towards Stanhope Street and then to the small row of terrace houses in Fisher Street where Mrs Wharton opened the door to her.

'Are you all right, Lily? I heard you were at the school the other night. Terrible. Terrible. Unbelievable,' she said. 'Never thought it would actually happen to us. Don't know why. Foolishness, I suppose.'

'Is Vince here?' asked Lily.

'Didn't he tell you?' she replied. 'He's just left. His boat sailed from the Pier Head at ten. Everything on red alert now.'

A wave of sadness rippled through Lily. It made her hands sweat and her eyes fill with glassy tears.

Mr Wharton appeared at the door. 'Come and sit down. We had a long night. Everyone did. We were holed up in our cellar, cups of tea, wireless ... we've been waiting months for this, held up pretty nicely, I might add,' he said with his chest puffed out, rocking back on his heels, toes curling upwards to the ceiling with pride, hands jangling coins deep in his pockets. 'Quite cosy, all things considered. Mind, this war is cruel all right, taking against innocent folks. Kiddies as well. I know the newspapers are going on and on about how we have to keep our chins up and morale is good. But I don't know. I haven't seen much morale around here. Hard to find morale when you hear stories about what lies ahead. Have a banana. Vincent brought them. One of the perks of being in the merchant navy.'

Why was he talking so much? thought Lily. She took it, peeled it and sat eating it numbly, thinking merchant seamen like Vincent were risking their lives to bring bananas and oranges to Liverpool so that people could stuff their faces with barely a thought for their sacrifice.

'I heard you were at the elementary school in the shelter? What happened?' he said.

'Whole place collapsed. It was grim. A little girl died, I think ...'

'Vince left this letter for you.'

She took it, apologised when she almost snatched it out of his hands, she was so desperate to tear it open and read it. Her eyes scanned the page, when she did.

18 *August 1940*
Fisher Street

Dear Lily,

They knocked for me at eight this morning. Pandemonium at the docks and all hands on deck, which is why I had to leave so suddenly. I'll probably be heading off to Scotland, there's talk of escorting our boys to the Panama Canal, picking up survivors from ships the Italians have torpedoed in the waters around the West Indies, but that's a longer voyage than this one. I'm sure what they say is true. Distance makes the heart grow fonder. I will call and see you the minute

I'm back so keep practising those turns and spins for when I take you dancing again to the Rialto. If you've upped sticks and left the Pool, leave a note with Ma and Pa saying where I should find you. I should be back home in a few weeks or so. Stay lucky, Lil.

Vincent.

P.S. I know it sounds sentimental, but wherever I go, you'll be my compass. I'll find you. Don't worry. Everything comes back to you. You're my star of the sea. You'll always be the place where I'm heading. I love you, Lil.

Her heart thumped. Pressing it to her chest, and then to her face, hoping to breathe in the smell of him, she murmured, 'I love you.' It was there in black and white in his sloping handwriting. She absentmindedly touched the necklace she wore that had a small locket that sat in the hollow of her throat. Then she folded the letter in half and then into quarters and slipped it into her pocket. 'I *love* you,' she murmured.

'Where's the Spam?' asked Stella, when Lily returned half an hour later. 'Deirdre said you'd gone to get Spam.'

'Oh!' replied Lily. 'I forgot it.'

'You forgot it? You stupid girl. How could you have forgotten it?'

'I left it on the tram,' she stuttered.

'Oh, you silly girl,' sighed Stella. 'You'd forget your head if it wasn't screwed on. Wouldn't you? I said, wouldn't you, Lily?'

But Lily wasn't listening. She was thinking about Vincent. Vincent. He loves me. Those were the words that were turning around in her head, not Spam left on a tram seat, or the scarcity of bananas, or tragic stories of war and death.

Chapter 5

Lily woke to a beautiful warm September day. She pulled back the blackout curtains and the sun streamed into the large front bedroom. Through the window smeared with dust particles and flecked with black, she saw a glittering River Mersey ruffling up as if someone had sharpened a silver pencil over its surface. You would hardly know there was a war on, she thought. And yet over the past two weeks there had been more air raids with Mill Road hospital damaged and houses in Mossley hill and Everton hit badly. No doubt today would bring more awful stories.

She came downstairs to find her grandmother Ivy, known to all as 'Gram', sitting at the kitchen table, trying to thread a needle.

'Shame,' said Gram, putting it down in frustration. 'My eyesight's not what it used to be.'

Lily leaned across the wine-coloured, balding chenille tablecloth. 'Give it me.'

'What you cooking, Gram?' asked Matt, coming into the kitchen. He was just about to leave for work at Cunard's. He strode over, lifted the lid of the pan, and peered into it.

The Laffertys had a meal routine they rarely strayed from: Sunday, roast; Monday, cold meat; Tuesday, sausage; Wednesday, stew; Thursday, fry-up; Friday, fish; Saturday, egg and chips. And even with the war and rationing, today was no different. The stony soil in the makeshift vegetable garden on the patch of land behind their house had, miraculously, seen a few carrots sprout that week, so peeled and scrubbed, they sat in pans of water on the stove. In a large tureen was a stew that had puddles of dumplings in it and a skein of white lard on its surface.

'Scouse.'

'Blind Scouse?'

'*Scouse* Scouse. Got a bit of mince from Harts'.'

'Smashing,' he said.

'Any news?' asked Gram.

'Custom House hit last night. And Cleveland Square shelter. Doesn't sound good.'

'Oh no,' she said.

'Aye. They say folks have died. And talk of even more bombing is on everyone's lips,' said Matt, stirring two heaped spoons of sugar into the cup of tea Gram placed before him.

Cliff, Lily's father, came in noisily from the front room, braces looped around his thighs. He sat at the kitchen table and began drinking a glass of milk. When he had drained it, he burped loudly and unselfconsciously and began tearing into the heel of a loaf, glowering at it.

'I heard more rumours today, Da. That now Hitler has got his sights set on Liverpool, he won't stop until he's completely destroyed the docks. No one knows what's going to happen. Should we be doing something? Like evacuating the kids?' said Lily.

'Ask your mother. She's the one who makes the decisions around here,' growled Cliff. 'You can count me out of any discussions for now.'

'Dad!' said Lily, as he barged past her to go into the hall, grabbed his jacket off the bannisters and stormed off as her mother appeared puffing on a cigarette.

'Leave him,' whispered Stella, resting a hand on Lily's arm to stay her. 'He's in a mood. '

Lily eyed her mother suspiciously.

'What?' asked Stella.

Lily noticed the crumpled piece of paper in her mother's hand.

'He'll get over it,' said Stella. 'He wants to go down to Drury Lane in London and audition for the entertainment corps – ENSA. I ask you! They refused him before. Said that they'd got enough piano players. I told him that's a blessing in disguise – everyone knows ENSA stands for Every Night Something Awful – but it didn't help.'

'*Will* he get over it, though?' asked Lily.

'He's fine at the docks. I don't want him going off, touring army bases with some dreadful variety act – second-rate crooners, acrobatic dancers and rubbishy illusionists. Or worse, off to flipping Burma, like he's been going on about. Apparently, for some unknown reason, they're in desperate need of a piano player out there. Can you imagine? My God, the heat! He hates the docks, and it's dangerous, I know that, but I want him here.'

'Lily, I've a splinter. It hurts,' said Deirdre, having just come down from upstairs in a threadbare nightdress full of holes that Lily recognised as an old one of her own. She was clutching her hand, her rosebud lips pursed into a small 'o' shape.

'Come on,' said Lily, pulling her towards her, lifting her up under her arms, and plonking her on the edge of the table. This war, she thought. Dust everywhere, splinters, grit in your eyes. 'Let's get this over with … Show me.'

Deirdre upturned her grubby palm and showed her the fleshy part at the base of her thumb, with the splinter embedded into it. Lily squeezed the skin either side, and said 'Whatever you do, don't move.' As usual, it was a performance and a half and ended with

Deirdre yelping, squirming away and running around the table before Lily was finally able to catch her by hooking a finger under her cardigan and twisting her to her. She grabbed her sister's hand and removed the splinter with one sharp tug between her thumb and fingernail, finally announcing, 'Got it!' Smiling, she showed it to Deirdre on the white handkerchief that she took from her pocket. 'That was brave,' she said.

After she had washed the handkerchief under the sink, her grandmother pestered, 'Lily, can you make me up a cup of Ovaltine?'

'Gram, I'm trying to get the kids ready for school.'

'Lily, can we knock for Fred on the way? We can walk to St Columba's together!' shouted Bobby as he tore through the hallway and into the kitchen, brumming a red matchbox car along the walls.

'Not today, love,' Stella said, snatching the car from him. 'Stop that! My nerves. Have you forgotten? Fred has gone to Rhyl.'

'Oh, yes,' said Bobby. His face clouded over. 'Do we have to evacuate like the man on the wireless said?'

'I think you might,' said Stella, wafting around the room, flapping her hands to disperse the veil of cigarette smoke wreathed about her head. 'Mr Churchill, the Corporation, the Welfare Officers, Father Donnelly – they are all telling us it's safer. Bad enough I'm being a terrible mother for keeping you in Liverpool, but now I'm helping Hitler as well! Apparently, he would be delighted if you stayed here and he could blow you all to pieces. Well, this war is about to destroy the country, but it's not about to destroy our family.'

'I don't want to go,' said Bobby.

'You'll like it at St Jude's. It's near the beach. In fact, you'll love it.'

Lily looked shocked and her horrified expression told her mother what she thought about the idea. Please God, she didn't mean the grim Gothic monstrosity that she had collected the sheets from with Father Donnelly? The Mother and Baby Home? Why would she pack them off them there?

'You don't actually mean St Jude's?' she gasped.

'Yes. Why not? The nuns have finally agreed to open their doors to those in need. And that's us. We're desperate.'

'You shouldn't let them anywhere near that place,' Lily said. 'It's horrible. They'll hate it!'

'And I don't want to leave Mr Binks,' said Deirdre.

Bobby chewed his lips worriedly. The cat appeared as if on cue.

'You don't want us to go, do you, Mr Binks?' said Deirdre, stroking his tail. She drew him up onto her knee, buried her face in his fur, and gave a small sneeze.

'Lily, where's that Ovaltine!' cried Gram.

'I'm getting the kids ready, Gram. I'll see to you in a minute!'

'If I had a penny for every time you said a minute, and an hour passed, I'd be a rich woman,' retorted Gram, with a sigh.

Lily turned back to her mother.

'I mean it, Mam. There has to be better places for them to go than that awful Mother and Baby Home. What about Wales?'

'Too far,' said Stella, flatly. 'St Jude's will be grand. Perfect. Just perfect.'

When Lily set off to take the children to school the first day back after the summer holidays, she saw Rosie scrubbing her front doorstep. Rosie was a few years older than she was and beautiful, with hazel eyes and creamy skin; hard work had still to take its toll. They were good friends, had grown up together and had become even closer through their WVS work. It was amazing what you found out about another person whilst you relieved the tedium of darning socks and cutting up sheets. Lily had recently discovered Rosie had once served Arthur Askey a cup of tea at the Kardomah in Church Street, that she was allergic to tomatoes, and that her dad wasn't her real dad. Today, she was wearing an old pair of pink bloomers on her head, tied in a topknot, and an old ragged pinny. A necklace of sweat circled her neck – she looked like she was scrubbing the doorstep half to death, so much so that the sandstone underneath had begun to show through. Lily thought she looked as if she was taking out whatever she felt about Hitler and this dreadful war on that step.

'All right, Rosie?' asked Lily. Rosie put the pail down, wiped her forehead. 'Mam says do you want to swap your bacon ration for our sugar?'

It was something they did every week. Stella had a passion for bacon and Rosie had a sweet tooth, but she seemed in no hurry today. She dropped the scrubbing brush into the pail. Water splashed over the top of it and Rosie smoothed her hands over her apron.

'Have you heard there's more bombing on the way?' she said.

'Aye,' said Lily.

Through the open door, Lily caught a glimpse of the room beyond and noticed there was something different. The furniture had gone; a packing case sat in the middle of the floor and, next to it, a rolled-up rug.

'Oh no. You're not leaving?'

'Not right now. But soon ...'

'Rosie ...' she said sadly. 'Don't go. You're my best friend. And what will Mam do without you? You know how close you two are.'

'I know. And I'll miss her something dreadful. Your mam ... well, since my mam died she's been a mother to me – and more than a mother. Which ... well, considering ...'

The sentence tailed off into a piercing, troubled thought that flashed across her face.

'Considering what?'

'Nothing. Nothing. But like I say, I have no choice. You must have heard people died last night at Cleveland Square. Da wants us to go. Being as old as he is, I've got to think of him. Look around,' she said. 'We're choking on all this dust, all this worry of the bombs. We're too near to the docks, here. Can't hardly bear to see the little 'uns playing outside in case a plane comes flying over and this time it's our houses in Caryl Street they hit.'

She grabbed the pail up and water slopped onto the floor. 'Come inside,' said Rosie. She got up, rubbed her sore knees, and led Lily into the hall. 'Hear that?' said Rosie, gesturing to the ceiling.

Lily cocked her head. There was the sound of scraping and thumping above them. At first she thought it was coming from upstairs, but then she frowned.

'Yes, that's right. Great big clodhopping footsteps on the roof. That's kiddies nicking the lead. Bluey hunters, that's what they call the little blighters. Because of the blue colour of the lead. Scavengers, the lot of them!'

'It never is,' said Lily.

'Aye. Like vermin. Sometimes they climb in through them houses at the end of the street that are empty. They come in through the holes in the roof and you can hear them running from attic to attic. They hack away at the walls in between each house and I hear them scuttling about like cockroaches, sneaking into the empty houses and seeing what they can burgle. Last week I found one of the little devils standing on my landing. He'd come through the back window.'

Suddenly Rosie grabbed a broom, ran upstairs and thumped it on the landing ceiling. Plaster and dust showered down on both of them. 'See what I mean?' she said, as the sound of scurrying followed her banging. 'Like vermin.'

Lily wiped her tongue with her fingers, spitting out the dust. She fiddled with the ties of her pretty wrap-around skirt. All this talk of evacuating only made the threat of St Jude's all the more real.

'It's dangerous here,' said Rosie, 'and the kids don't see it. Can you believe it, one bloke came in the other day when me and Da were having our tea – he's been up on the roof, he's climbed over from next door, bold as brass. And then a great big pair of feet comes in above our heads as we're sitting there listening to Lord Haw-Haw. And it's not just him, he's brought his little lad wi' him. The bloody nerve of it. There we are supping us tea and the very roof is being stripped off under our noses. I don't know how long I can stand it, Lily. They say everyone's pulling together with this war, but there's plenty around here who are taking advantage of it! You heard about Father Donnelly and the little lad come to him for confession? "Bless me, Father, for I have sinned. It's Robin, Father." "Ah, Robin," says the priest. "No, Father, *robbin'*. Robbin' me mam's purse, robbin' the offertory plate, robbin' the blueys off the roofs . . ." '

Lily smiled, and Rosie laughed her tinkling laugh. Rosie could always cheer Lily up with her stories, but when she started to speak again, she grew serious, and the sound of her voice nervously skittering up the octave made Lily worry.

'I've heard that we've seen nothing yet. It's going to hit us hard. It's real now, this war. And we're right in the line of fire,' Rosie said.

They nodded in agreement, and sighed, and Rosie gently placed her flat hand on Lily's cheek. 'Look after yourself, Lil,' she said.

'Please stay, Rosie. You're not just my best friend, you're my *only* friend. Who'll chat to me when we're darning the socks at the cabin? And you know it will break Mam's heart. Who'll she swap her sugar with now?' Lily said plaintively, as she stood on the door-step, about to leave.

'I can't stay here, love. I've got to think of Da. But it's not forever. You can come and see me whenever you want.'

'*Please*?'

'Why is it so important?'

'Because … because Mam's talking about sending the kids off. And that means I'll probably be packed off to Morecambe to her Aunt Mary's. I don't want things to change around here, just when …' She stopped, not wanting to say more.

'Your mam's right to be thinking about making plans. It's dangerous here. I've spoken to her about me leaving Caryl Street and she thinks it's a good idea. She wants me to be safe, just like she wants you lot to be safe.'

'We don't know how bad it will be yet.'

But Rosie hadn't the time to continue the conversation. China needed to be wrapped in newspaper, cases needed to be packed.

Banks of white cloud gathered on the horizon. Walking through the streets with Bobby and Deirdre, Lily pressed a handkerchief to her mouth. All the digging and the tons of cement being poured into basements to reinforce the houses, the concrete to build shelters, corrugated iron, gardens being unearthed, was taking its toll on the city. There was now a constant stream of lorries trundling up and down the hill outside Caryl Street and the children's eyes were full of grit from the rubble. The preparations for this war had been going on for months – the boarding up of buildings, the uprooting of back gardens for the Anderson shelters, the work at the munitions factories – and the barrage balloons bobbing on wires were a sinister and eerie sight along the river and the edges of the parks. Bobby trailed a stick across the railings and enjoyed the clattering sound. He was old enough to run on ahead. Lily planned to drop them off at school on her way to do the early shift at Bertorelli's. As she approached the bend in the road, she listened out for the handbell clanging and the usual chants from the playground: 'We are St Columba's gang, we know our manners and how to spend our tanners, we are the Columba gang.' But this morning she heard neither. It was so much quieter than usual and sandbags were stacked up against the walls, up to the height of the windows.

Looking around she noticed, apart from two mothers fussing over their children, it was almost empty – the Mulrooneys, the O'Neills, the McVerrys, the Leddys – no sign of them yet. But then it dawned on her. The reason they weren't there was because they were probably all gone now, all evacuated. Especially now the bombing had started in earnest. Hitler had set his eyes on Liverpool, all right. Father Donnelly had been knocking on people's doors with his stick for days, searching out and admonishing, with disapproving head-shaking and sighs, those with children. After Winston Churchill's announcement saying that the assault was most likely to increase in severity, it was no surprise that more had left. There were another dozen children fewer than last week, whole streets had emptied.

The city, she now realised, was becoming full of old people; either they had no reason to leave, or they were too stubborn. Or stupid. Standing and looking around her she thought it was as if the youngsters had disappeared into thin air without her even noticing. In churches, the christening fonts were bone dry, pregnant women had left for the suburbs and had their babies in country hospitals, and now you could arrange a wedding at the drop of the hat. Most of the young women at the altar, it had to be said, were pregnant. Up the duff. In the club. She tried to think of the good things the war had brought to Liverpool in the past few months – the war spirit, the comradeship, the morale – but all she could think of was that there were fewer queues to hear Mr Sunshine playing the harmonium outside Rushworth's music shop; no more pushing and shoving to get a good look and pet the monkey dressed in its bright red waistcoat. Bobby and Deirdre could sit on Mr Sunshine's knee all day if they wanted.

Miss Postle came out into the playground, clanging the handbell. She wasn't much older than Lily, and she was friendly, and when Lily had met her at the wash house once when she had gone there to do the laundry, she had no airs and graces. Some were snooty about using the wash house, they saw it as something poor folks did, but Miss Postle didn't seem to care.

However, she seemed older suddenly, with her solid perm and sturdy practical shoes.

'Miss!' cried Bobby, beaming.

Bobby and Deirdre both adored her; she would encourage them to sing and perform their tap dances to the class, and she even said they were clever enough to pass the eleven plus.

'Watch me!' Deirdre skittered across the playground, hands on hips, head cocked to one side. 'Shuffle off to Buffalo,' she sang in a breathless voice as she danced. 'Shuffle off to Buffalo, shuffle off to Buffaloooo.'

'Good, Deirdre, marvellous. Now go inside and put your coat on the peg. And Bobby, you can take that crate of milk from in the sun – it's going sour ...'

Bobby left, struggling with the crate, milk bottles clinking.

'Terrible night with the air raids, wasn't it?' said Miss Postle. 'Was Father Donnelly telling you should leave again? I saw him talking to your mother the other day.'

Lily shrugged. 'Yes. He says Mam should let the kids go to St Jude's if she doesn't want to send them to Wales.'

Miss Postle's face grew serious and a worried frown appeared. 'He's right, Lily – we're too near the docks here. And they're closing down the school. I'm surprised you're even here today.'

'Closing it down? Why?' she answered, shocked.

'Not enough kiddies left because they're all being evacuated again.'

'But what'll happen to those that stay?'

'Provisions will be made – Dame schools and suchlike. Tutors.'

Not the awful Dame schools. There was one in posh Rodney Street, a miserable place from what she'd heard, with only a handful of children trooping in, just sitting at a spinster's kitchen table doing algebra and reciting the catechism, no playground, or classrooms.

'Oh God!'

'Indeed. Your mother's only being sensible and I've heard St Jude's is not so bad. The kids who went from here to St Asaph's convent in Wales are having a riot so St Jude's would be a lark as well – and a lot closer to Liverpool than Wales. Only a half-hour train ride away up the coast and the beach is on the doorstep, so the sand dunes and pinewoods would be their playground. Besides, they might learn something because the nuns will teach them well. They really are clever enough to pass the eleven plus but not if they don't go to school. You've got to think about their education, Lily. Someone has to.'

Miss Postle was right about that. Stella had used her brother and sister in pantomimes, variety acts, clubs, dance competitions – she would take them out of school at the drop of the hat.

'Can you talk to your mother? Tell her she needs to move quickly.'

'Yes,' replied Lily.

'And what about you?'

'What?'

'Will you be leaving Liverpool?'

'Me? I'm not going anywhere.'

The very idea of it horrified her, now that there was something else to consider. Vince. She would never see him when he came home if she were stuck miles away in the country. What a ridiculous suggestion. No, she would be staying in Liverpool for Vince, so she could see him on his leaves. She couldn't even contemplate an alternative. But Miss Postle wouldn't drop the matter. How long could she stand dodging the shells? Wouldn't she love fresh air in her lungs and to sleep peacefully at night?

Lily shrugged. I'm not leaving my Vince. Not for anything, she thought. What an absurd notion.

Miss Postle suddenly clapped her hands and blew on a whistle. The noise made Lily start and she made a small inward gasp.

'Air-raid practice!'

A small group of children came running out of the classroom.

'Stand up over there!' she said. 'Fingers on lips! Hands on heads! Now what do we do if we hear the sirens?'

'Take cover in the shelter, miss!' someone shouted.

On the other side of the playground, at a bottom of a grassy slope, there was a large shelter that had been hastily been built with a door that was designed to shut so tightly it would prevent those who were inside being harmed from any poison gas attack. However, it wasn't without its faults, and though there was an escape tunnel that led out into the church graveyard, the teachers complained the tunnel was too small for their adult bottoms; they kept getting stuck and the gas-mask boxes kept jamming up against the walls, so that it was pretty useless.

Suddenly, the children started to gallop across the playground towards the grass beyond the square of tarmac, and when they reached it, they began to scramble down the sharp incline to the ditch at the bottom where the air-raid shelter sat on the piece of waste ground. It was a sight, all flailing limbs, and shrieks and gales of laughter, some of the children sliding on their bottoms, others tripping over their heels, and yelling.

'Stop! Stop!' Miss Postle cried, blowing on the whistle and clapping her hands. 'You *wait* until I give you the signal! Come back, Maureen! And you, Kevin! Come back here now!'

The children scrambled back up the slope, grinning. Lily watched through the railings, smiling, as on the count of three and a sharp piercing blast of the whistle, they all ran down the slope again, apparently not having listened to a word Miss Postle had just said. She saw them rise to their feet when they had stumbled and landed in the ditch, twist around and looking amazed that they had vivid smudges of green on their skirts and shorts. Lily wondered what their mothers would say when they went home later. The children didn't seem the least bit worried. It was their spirit she admired. The Liverpool spirit.

And it was that same spirit that made her toss her head back with resolve as she walked on down the hill. No, she was staying in Liverpool to be with Vince. Whatever happened. Damn Hitler. Damn his bloody bombs.

Chapter 6

Lily said goodbye to her last customer at Bert's cafe, a thin man in a shabby suit, who looked like he hadn't bothered to shave for days. Shooing out the poor soul she shut the door and put the CLOSED sign up. She began to complete her chores, just as she had done the day before and the day before that. On the instructions of the landlord, they were closing at three because of the trouble at Gino's a few doors down the previous night. She wondered if it would ever open again now that Italy had declared war on Britain. Bertorelli had hinted as much. The week before a brick had been thrown through the window, and there had been shards of shattered glass all over the black-and-white tiled floor. She twisted the key in the lock then she went over to the window to pull the heavy blackout curtains. Light flooded her face.

'Vince?' she cried. 'Is that you?'

It *was* him! Standing on the doorstep. 'Vince! What the flaming heck are you doing here!? I thought you wouldn't be back for weeks!'

'Got as far as Barcelona. Had to rescue some poor fellas whose boat had been split in two like a kipper. Brought them back to Liverpool and I'm off again tomorrow. Couldn't stay away from you, though, Lil.'

He grinned, stepped inside, bringing in muggy summer city air. He was wearing a navy jumper and trousers, the no-nonsense uniform of the merchant navy. Taking her face in his hands, he kissed her. Her skin was warm and he put a hand on her cheek. When she took it away and kissed his fingers, she noticed the lines and creases in his palm beautifully mapped out in oil.

'Am I glad to see you, love,' he said, one hand squirrelling up the front of her blouse, searching out her breast. 'I've missed you something rotten these past two weeks.'

She clung on to his fingers kissed them. And then, in a volley of words, she said, 'It's been awful. I've missed you so much too.'

He put his hand around her waist and his cheek against hers, breathed in the smell of her newly washed hair.

'This bloody war . . .' He faltered. 'I wish I could do something.'

'You're here,' she said. 'I can't believe it! Tell me more. What's it been like at sea? Did you steer the boat?'

'Not yet. I'm pretty low in the food chain. Though I can fire a gun now,' he added, a sense of pride creeping into the tone of his voice. 'There was an opera singer when we arrived in Spain, with pineapples on her head, singing from *Tosca* on the quayside, can you believe it? And a band and everything. And, if I'm being truthful, it was exciting. Most of the fellas are looking for some kind of action, that's why they're there. Delivering tins of goose fat is not quite the same when you might lose your life doing it – takes on a different edge,' he said, his breathing low and shallow against her ear.

She looked at him. His newly cut hair flopped in a front lick over his eyes as he bent his neck forward. With a finger he tilted her chin up so that her eyes met his.

'Been awful without you.'

'I don't know how to make it better, love. But I do know if you let me kiss you, we might forget about this war keeping us apart, just for a moment.'

'Oh, Vince. I keep hearing these stories. About ships being blown up.'

'You're my lucky charm,' he said when they separated. 'I just want you. Every bit of you. I'm sorry. I can't help it. Come here …'

What harm will it do? she thought, twisting in to him to kiss him. But she knew then, as he led her over to the corner of the room and laid her on the floor, the feel of the tiles hard against her flesh as they searched each other out with tongues twisting and turning around teeth, it was only a matter of time before kisses would not be enough.

It had been Luigi Bertorelli, banging on the door after returning earlier than expected, that had interrupted them from 'getting carried away in the heat of the moment', as her mother would say. Half an hour later, they walked along the quay in the shadow of the Liver Building beside the harbourmaster's office, holding hands, him striding out beside her in his navy blue trousers and serge jacket, her feeling her heart beat faster knowing how close they had just come to something so terrifying and so wonderful in equal measure. They stopped and she clung on to him when he took her into his arms. Pushing the lick of hair from his eyes and kissing his forehead, she didn't care about the people who were staring at them. They walked towards the Pier Head from Water Street and, after a while, they sat on a wall and watched the boats slip in and out of the estuary. It was a beautiful day and, looking across the Mersey, they had to shield their eyes from the sun. If it wasn't for the sinister barrage balloons moving back and forth surreally and gently, tethered by their ropes to the harbour wall, she thought, you would never have believed that there was a war on and that people had died in Liverpool, or that Hitler had invaded Poland and France, or how many had lost their lives at Dunkirk. Her paisley frock fluttered in the breeze, and she squashed the skirts of it down between her thighs. But then, suddenly, her face crinkled up with worry.

'Every week I read how dangerous it is, the U-boats, I mean. If anything is going to be hit first it's you fellas in the ships; you're sitting ducks out there.'

'Yes, well, we're not going to think on that any more. We're going to think about beating Hitler. And me coming back on leave before you know it, and by God we'll make up for the time we're apart.'

'Why didn't you join the army? Or air force?' she said breathlessly. 'What if . . .?'

'What if I don't come back?'

'I heard about the ships torpedoed off Dunkirk. And they said on the wireless that there was one hit last month in the Indian Ocean with twenty men left in lifeboats for days and nights, as if they were being swirled around in a washtub, and they'd gone half crazy when they were rescued. One was eaten by a shark when he fell overboard and the rest died on the journey home.'

'Don't believe everything you read in the *News of the World*. Churchill knows what he's doing. Besides, it might be German propaganda. Someone told *me* the fella was eaten by a whale.'

'But what if that happens to you?'

'I won't be around to worry about it, will I? And I'm not going to meet a shark in the North Atlantic, am I?'

'Don't make a joke of it, Vincent.'

Vincent breathed straight into her face, pushed her heavy fringe off her forehead.

'Thing is, they're desperate. Dunkirk wasn't the victory they said it was. All coming out now. Tens of thousands of British troops safely home, unbeatable, victorious, all that rot, was what they crowed about. It's only now that the steamers and barges are coming back that we're getting the truth from ordinary folk. They need more men. Lots more men. So wait for me, Lil,' he said as he took her in his arms. 'It will fly by. Just as long as you won't get bored and run off with some fella? Don't know how anyone wouldn't fall in love with you the minute they set eyes on you. Lil? What's the matter?'

She could feel her anxiety, her shoulders shrinking inwards and a worried frown knitting her eyebrows together.

'Just don't flamin' die on me. I mean it, Vincent.'

He smiled, placed the palm of his hand lightly on the crown of her head, pulled her into his chest. She felt the brass button of his jacket, pressing cool against her cheek. 'I won't,' he replied. 'They won't put me on the guns permanently yet and I'm not going to die learning how to tie knots.' He lifted her face to his, then kissed her again.

'Take this,' he said. He put his hand deep in his pocket, drew it out and uncurled his fingers. 'I bought it for you. You'll wear it?'

She gasped. 'It's beautiful,' she said, turning the necklace over in her hands. Hanging on the end of it was a small silver ballerina. He showed her how, when she put her thumb under the ballerina's legs, they moved back and forth on a tiny hinge under a billowing skirt.

He took each end of the chain, fastened the clasp about her graceful neck, and touched the silver ballerina lightly with his fingers, positioning it in the hollow part of her throat. He stood back and looked at her, pulled up once more by her rare, wild beauty. 'You look a picture, Lil,' he said.

A plane flew overhead, swooped towards the mouth of the Mersey and then looped back towards New Brighton, followed by two more in close formation. Lily and Vincent followed it with their gaze. It was a reminder of what lay ahead.

'Lily, I have something else to tell you.'

'What is it?' she asked. His expression worried her. He looked serious all of a sudden.

'You shouldn't stay here.' He frowned. 'Word is, it's going to be bad for Liverpool. Especially where you live. Being in the shadow of the docks.'

'What d'you mean?'

'This war is suddenly moving faster than anyone thought. Just make sure you have plans.'

'Mam might be sending the kiddies away. To St Jude's. But it's a home for unmarried mothers and I don't care that they've opened their doors for evacuees – it'll still have that horrible air of gloom about it. I've been there, I know what it's like. And they still have some girls there who are in the club, I bet. Poor wretches.'

'If they'll be safe, though, why wouldn't she do that?'

'You wouldn't say that if you had seen it,' she replied. 'It's like something out of one of those Dracula movies.'

Kisses triumphed over words in the short time they had left. Finally, he announced he had to leave, but at the last minute he paused.

'Fancy a quick belt around the Rialto later? As a final goodbye? One last dance?' he asked.

She thought of her mother.

'I'm not allowed,' she said.

'What about we go somewhere else? The Grafton? They call it Liverpool's Bombproof ballroom now. Mrs Hamer conducts the dance band wearing a tin hat when the sirens go off. Remember we used to always go there when we were nippers? Anyway, if we go to the Grafton, you're not strictly breaking her rule, are you? As long as it's not the Rialto.'

'You're a devil, Vincent Wharton,' she said, as a smile tugged at the corners of her mouth. 'But what the heck! I'll think of something to tell me mam.' She paused and grinned more. Her heart had been breaking with the thought that this might be one of the last times she was to see him, at least for a while, but now this feeling was overtaken by excitement, knowing that she would be able to spend a few more hours with him. 'I'll meet you there at seven ...'

She watched him leave, walking towards the overhead railway where he would take a train two stops to his home as a ship sailed around the headland, guns on board firing in practice, sparks and flashes flaring and the smell of sulphur and smoke filling the air. It blared its foghorn as a cloud scooted across the sun, and Lily set off in the direction of home.

St Columba's was empty and Lily's footsteps echoed as she made her way down the aisle. She shuffled along the pew, joining her hands together as she knelt down on the cracked kneeler. Someone was singing, a priest and an altar boy in a white lace cassock were laying out hymn books in the pews. The sounds lisped through the church. She started to mumble a Hail Mary but couldn't see the point of it and lost heart halfway through.

She went over to the side chapel and lit a few candles. She didn't have a single coin to put in the slot of the tin box, but hoped God would forgive her just this once, and promised she would bring some coppers next time. IOU. One for her mother and father to stop arguing about 'flamin ENSA' one for her sister and brother to be happy at St Jude's – and one for Vincent to stay safe. As the flames bent and flickered, she screwed her eyes tight shut and pressed her hands together. She heard the soft chimes of the church bell. People would start arriving soon and Father Donnelly would pad out from the presbytery in his white lace chasuble and vestments and make his way on to the altar – and as long as he had seen she was there, she would have the excuse she needed. And then she was off.

'Ah, Lily. God Bless you,' said a voice behind her. She turned around sharply.

'Father …' she said in a low voice, crossing herself.

'You're here for Benediction?'

'Yes, Father.'

'Good girl.'

He nodded and walked off to the sacristy.

That had gone better than she'd expected, she thought; that would get back to her mother, all right, and as the church started filling up, the small assembly of people allowed her to mingle with the congregation. She slipped out through the ornate double doors, leaving the sounds of Tantum Ergo behind her, and skipped down the steps and towards the bus that would take her across the city.

As Lily approached the Grafton, she took off her lightweight coat and carried it over one arm. Underneath she was wearing a pretty sleeveless white cotton blouse with a sweetheart collar. The blouse revealed her smooth, tanned shapely arms. The skirt she had chosen to go with it, showed off its stripes that were the colours of sugared almonds when she spun around. She knew that because she had practised it looking at herself in the ballroom mirror before she had left. It was sweltering. Fifty pans of spuds, she'd peeled earlier and her hands were so sore that her knuckles had reddened. Embarrassed by them, she thrust them deep into her pockets. She reached West Derby Road. The crane was swinging above her, screeching and clanking, the wrecking ball smashing against the side of a building. A man in work overalls and a tin hat called out to her.

'Mind, love. This is dangerous around here. War preparations.'

There were a dozen or so men, playing cards sitting at upturned packing cases. One of them turned his head and wolf-whistled. She felt her cheeks sting with embarrassment and lowered her eyes to the pavement. Not that she minded, much. She would rather be noticed than not.

When she arrived outside she heard the music coming from one of the buildings. It seeped into the street as she passed the doorway of the Olympic dance hall next door, made her stop for a moment and listen to the sounds. The music, the blaring trumpets, the sound of the brushes sliding over snare drums, always gave her a warm feeling. From inside she could hear someone at the piano playing the same few notes over and over again. She could have stood and listened to this for hours. It was seven o'clock. Someone flung open the window from the first floor. She swore she could smell stale smell of beer, as if the dance hall itself was belching the leftovers from the night before.

The Grafton felt reassuringly familiar. Immediately it hit her when she went in through the door into the huge airy ballroom with the tiered stalls and huge crystal glass chandeliers – the smell of beeswax polish, cigarettes, and cheap cologne. It was here, as a girl, she had watched her father and mother dancing every Saturday night in tulle ballgowns and dress suits, it was here where she first danced as a child. It's what made her feel alive and helped her to forget the humdrum existence of chores and school and work. Of course, despite that – or maybe because of it – her mother would be furious at the thought of her coming here on her own to meet Vincent after she had forbidden her to.

She was surprised to see that Vera, the woman who used to run the place, was still here behind the bar, though she looked much older now, and the veins on her hands looked like worms under the skin which was chapped and inflamed from years and years of bottle washing. Please God, thought Lily, my own hands aren't going to end up the same. Vera paused from pushing a tea towel around the inside of a glass and smiled. 'Oh God, it's good to see you here, Lily. Been a while. You look a picture.'

'Thanks,' she answered with a grin.

'How can I help you love? Fancy a beer?'

'No thanks. I'm here to meet someone.'

'Vincent?'

'Yes,' she replied, blushing.

'I remember you two coming in here with your mam, aged fourteen. You know you'll always be welcome here, love …'

'Thanks, Vera,' said Lily. 'How's business?'

Vera smiled. 'There's always someone who'll step up and offer to tinkle the ivories. But to be honest, we're losing people. Business is not what it was. I heard Stella has closed down the school.'

'Who told you that?'

'Gossip.'

'Aye. School has shut up shop for now.'

'Shame. How are you?'

'I'm all right.'

She wanted to tell her that she was happier than she had ever been, that she and Vincent were courting, but of course she wasn't going to tell Vera that. It would only get back to her mother.

'And the children?'

'Fine. They're enjoying the chance to miss another day off school now it's closed, to go and play on the reccy, or try and steal apples from Croxteth Park estate. Dad says it will be dangerous to stay here. Especially after this last week. This war is ramping up in Europe, he says. And with us so near to the docks, we're sitting ducks. The kids might be going to St Jude's.'

'The Mother and Baby Home?'

'They've opened it up for evacuees.'

'Bit grim, is that,' said Vera.

The floor was nearly empty. The spotlight carefully angled to hit the mirror ball made coloured ovals glide across the few couples as they danced. It was hypnotic and slow-moving and watching these points of light drift gently about the room, she felt her muscles relax and a calmness come over her. Usually these rooms were full of chatter, and dancing, best dresses, best suits, polished brogues and high heels. The promise that you might get a kiss from a game girl at the end of the night after a dance had brought men flocking, but tonight, the place felt quiet.

'Lily,' said a voice behind her. It was Vince. She had felt his warm breath on the back of her neck when he spoke her name and she beamed a smile at him as she turned around. 'You look a picture.' He led her to a red banquette with split plastic seats, and scooted her along to the corner with him, snaked his arm around her waist and kissed her on the lips.

'All right, love?' he said. He undid the top two buttons of his shirt, and she glanced at his chest hairs, springing in tufts from inside his collar.

'Mam doesn't know I'm here,' she said.

'I better not tell her then,' he said, grinning, chucking the end of her nose. He knew what to say to make her feel better about things.

'Fancy a dance?' he said.

She smiled and nodded; sometimes dancing was so much easier than talking. And she let him take her hand, clasp it tightly and interlock his firm, warm fingers with hers. He led her to the edge of the sprung wooden floor and they swirled on to it as the conductor raised his baton. The music, chords piled upon chords, a slow, lazy rhythm, sighed through trumpets and the smell of the chalk in the slip trays, the smoke in her lungs, the whiff of alcohol, was intoxicating. Joyfully, they took advantage of being one of the few couples to have arrived early, with fast and slow turns, forward and backward glissades, measured swings and graceful waltzing.

When the medley finished, the band members took a bow and put away their instruments so they could take a short break. He walked her back to the banquette, and she could feel him sliding his hand under her blouse after he pulled it out from her waistband, feel his hot, sweating hand on the hollow of her back.

'Come with me,' he said suddenly. He moved past the banquette and, leading her by the hand, took her straight out through the swing doors.

'Where are we going?' she asked, as he led her down the corridor.

He didn't reply, just looked furtively across each shoulder and opened another door that led to a room where there were stacked-up chairs and upside-down tables. It was musty and dimly lit and there was an alcove, well, more of a cupboard, behind a wooden beaded curtain with brooms in it, and a bucket with a mop in it.

'What the heck are you doing?' asked Lily. 'What is it about you and dark cupboards?'

But she knew all right.

The alcove was airless and unventilated; it smelled of damp socks, Vim and mothballs.

He kissed her and she kissed him back. He struggled to undo the button on her blouse as his tongue pushed between her teeth.

'Vincent …'

He placed a finger over her lips. 'Don't say it,' he said. And he kissed her again with breath that smelled of whisky and cigarettes. But as he pulled and tugged at her clothes, deftly popping buttons and unhooking clasps, she didn't care. She didn't care at all. This is what she wanted from him, for him to kiss her and touch her and taste her, and get so carried away in the 'heat of the moment' that she felt that she might burst into flames. And so she decided that this time she was going to let him do whatever he liked. Because she was a Lafferty, and maybe her mother was right: the Laffertys had loose morals. And he might be dead in a month.

She felt waves of pleasure shudder through her body from the tips of her toes all the way up to the top of the head; perhaps because death was on everyone's lips in this city, she felt more alive than she had ever felt before, as if every single part of her, when he touched her with his fingertips, was about to set her on fire, and she found it impossible not to be overwhelmed by the feel of his hands moving down over her body as they began to make love, he pushing his way inside her, she urging him to do so, in a way that shocked and surprised Vincent.

And then, when it was all over and they lay in a tangle of damp clothes and sweating bodies, there was the sound of sirens starting up again. She sat up and began buttoning up her blouse. He wriggled back into his trousers, stood and fastened his belt. But then he stooped and took her face in her hands. 'I'm sorry. I couldn't stop meself, Lil. Were we stupid?' he said, suddenly.

'Stupid?' she replied.

For a moment he didn't know what to say, just pushed a tendril of hair behind her ear and pulled her closer to him.

'How can something as lovely as that be called stupid?' she said, lifting her head, and raising her wide blue eyes to his with a look that was searching, innocent and hopeful.

Chapter 7

At the same time as Vince and Lily were making their way home, Stella had invited Rosie in for a drink. Suddenly there was a knock at the door. It was old Peg Leg from the house opposite who always turned up when he got a sniff of a free tipple. The Laffertys' doors were always flung open to anyone who wished to drop in for a whisky and a gossip, and tonight was no different.

'Room for a little 'un?' he asked, squashing his wide bottom onto the threadbare chaise longue between Deirdre and Bobby, and told his famous story that they had all heard a hundred times before, of how he had lost the bottom half of his leg in the Great War, and everyone rolled their eyes at each other because they all knew it had happened when he had fallen off a tram, drunk on Guinness, outside St George's Hall. 'Still, mustn't grumble,' he added at the end of his speech.

A minute later Cliff came barrelling in with a pal who he had collected along the way from the pub. And then, just as they were about to start on the sherry, Matt appeared.

'Read this,' he said shoving the *Liverpool Echo* into his father's hand. His face was pale and worried.

Stella paused. She could see from his expression that whatever it said was serious.

'What's the matter?' she asked.

'Just read it!'

She scanned the headline. Its ominous, bold black letters made up the sentence that would change their lives forever: HITLER PLANS BLITZKRIEG FOR LIVERPOOL.

'This Hitler is a monster,' she said, her hands trembling and the newspaper quivering.

'They say there'll be an announcement this evening. On the wireless ... About what we should all do.'

'Oh no,' said her mother, steadying herself with a hand on the mantelpiece, trying to think through what the consequences of all this might be. Stella paled. The realisation hit her.

It had been a blistering hot summer's day and it was still a warm evening now, at nine o' clock. The room was stuffy and hot and they all sat huddled around the wireless, wiping their brows, the men loosening their collars, the women wafting themselves with their hands.

'You've heard what Hitler is doing in France? You've heard about the blitzkriegs in Europe? Terrible business,' said Peg Leg.

Cliff Lafferty usually had to demand quiet at this time. He followed the news and enjoyed his favourite radio programmes, Henry Hall and his dance band, and Arthur Askey in *ITMA – It's That Man Again*! they would all chorus – but he didn't have to tell anyone to shush, or pipe down, or throw his shoe at them to stop them talking.

'Let us remind ourselves of *Hitler's inflammatory statement* on the tenth of July,' said the voice coming out of the radio.

'The Fascist dictator in his speech to the Reichstag said, "*Mr Churchill may well belittle my declaration again, crying that it was nothing other than a symptom of my fear, or my doubts of final victory. Still I have an easy conscience in view of things to come.*"

'I ask you!' said Stella.

She reached out a hand, placed it gently on her husband's shoulder, and squeezed.

'It's baking hot in here,' she said, fanning herself down with her hand. Her copper hair was tied back in a loose ponytail with a brightly coloured floral scarf. Beads of sweat appeared on her brow like fresh dew.

Peg Leg took the rolled up *Liverpool Echo* out of his pocket, opened it, but after a second, put it away again. He paused and shook his head. 'I don't know. I can't look at these pictures. It's too grim. What's the world coming to?'

Stella could read her husband's expression. He looked worried.

'Are you all right, love?' she asked.

He turned to her, shrugged, and raked his hands through his hair. He stared ahead blankly, and absent-mindedly rubbed at a speck of black on Bobby's cheek with his thumb.

'This is happening finally. We live so close to the docks. We're right in the line of fire, Stel. We've got to take it seriously.'

Stella nodded and turned to Rosie suddenly.

'You as well, Rosie. Lily's told me you've started packing. Well, you should go as soon as you can. No more sitting under your stairs or a table or holding a tea tray over your head or, like I caught your da the other day, wearing a stupid saucepan on his head. As if that would do any good. Far too dangerous for that nonsense. I mean it. You should leave as soon as you can,' she said urgently, clasping one of Rosie's hands tightly as she spoke.

'M-Mam . . .' stuttered Matt suddenly, as he looked out of the window. They all saw the panic in his wide eyes, heard it in his voice.

'What is it?' she said, alarmed. She repeated the question urgently, her bottom lip quivering. 'What is it, son?'

'D'you think they've dropped another bomb? You can smell the smoke. What should we do?'

Stella clutched her cardigan to her in a panic. They all raced over to the window, shoving and pushing each other out of the way to get a better look, though at nine at night there wasn't much to see. Just the stench of acrid smoke hanging over the Mersey.

'Looks like they're on their way here,' Matt said.

The sounds of the sirens began to wail.

'Where's Lily?' she cried. 'Anyone know where Lily is?'

That must have been close, Lily thought, as the sound of a whistle followed by a wump wump accompanied a tremor beneath her feet. Vincent grabbed her around the waist and pulled her into a pub doorway, threw his arms around her and hugged her tightly. She could feel his heart beating beneath his shirt and coat.

'All clear,' he said, poking his head out.

They set off again down the road towards Caryl Street.

'Off you go, Lil. Run. I've got to go home and then straight back to my ship by seven tomorrow morning. I don't know for sure where we'll be going but gossip is it could be North Africa.'

'North Africa!'

'Keep that to yourself. Now go. And be careful.' He brushed a strand of hair off her face and kissed her one more time.

'And you,' she said. 'Your ma will be out of her mind.'

'Pa is delighted that this is finally the real thing. He's enjoying testing out his precious cellar that he's spent so long doing up. And Ma too. She's so proud of how she's chintzed it up with cushions and the like and whitewashed the walls!'

'She got the tins of condensed milk stacked up?'

'Aye. Stacked to the ceiling. I said to her, Ma, you've enough conny-onny to take us into the next century.'

'That's good,' said Lily, smiling.

'Even got electricity down there.'

There was another sound of an aeroplane in the distance and this time the ground shook slightly.

'Did you feel that?' asked Lily.

'Aye,' he said.

Pulling her towards him for a final kiss on the doorstep of her house, he could sense the waves of fear that shuddered through her body.

'Go. Now,' she said. Then, checking that the coast was clear, she leaned in to him and pecked him on the cheek. 'And be careful.' She watched him from the window and saw him running down the road, then glance back up and wave at her before he turned the corner. Please God, be lucky and stay safe, she murmured.

*

When Lily arrived, shattered and exhausted at the shelter at St Columba's church three streets away, and met Stella and the children, they were all told to wait in the kitchen downstairs in the crypt. It felt that a new fear was everywhere and nowhere more than in the faces of the people that came through the doors that night. A room full of camp beds was being prepared, and the wardens, they announced, would lead them through when they were ready. Matt appeared at the door.

'Jesu Cristo! So much for your phoney war, Mam!' he cried. 'Where's Gram?'

'Gone to Aunt Mary's in Morecambe with Annie for a few days, thank God. They left this morning.'

'Get down!' yelled Matt suddenly, as another bomb made the ground shake and the china, stacked up on a shelf, rattle.

'That must have been close!' shouted someone from across the room.

They all crouched, eyes stricken with panic, and the woman who was trying to organise things raced around the kitchen in the crypt looking for tea trays to hold above the heads of those who hadn't found a space under a table.

'I don't like it, Mam!' sobbed Deirdre. The familiar waves of panic and fear rippling through the cramped damp smelling room grew in intensity.

'Come here, chicken,' said Lily, her voice trembling. Her heart beat in thuds and she felt that her chest was about to rip right open.

'I don't like it either,' said Bobby, competing in volume with Deirdre's wailing.

Matt began to sing a song. 'Oh, me name is Ernest, Chimney Sweep I am, love me Chimbley Chimbley . . .' And in a desperate effort to cheer them up, said, 'What do you call a man with no body and no nose?' he said, grinning. It was the kiddies' favourite joke, but this time, when he gave them the answer, 'Nobody knows!' they didn't laugh. They just looked at him worriedly, round-eyed with fear.

Half an hour later they were led into the room where the camp beds, about fifty of them, were all lined up in rows with threadbare blankets draped across them and a small pillow each.

'Vera!' exclaimed Stella. 'What are you doing here? Awful night we've had.'

Vera, red-faced, turned. 'Stella!' she cried. She told Stella in a volley of words that she had run all the way from Laxey Street and thought she was going to die. 'I felt the iron claw clutching my heart, Stel! I did!'

Lily moved away quickly. She was praying that Vera wouldn't tell her mother she had seen her with Vincent at the Grafton. All hell would be let loose if that happened. But seeing them in deep conversation, seeing the look pass between them, she became worried. When she saw her mother's expression darkening, her eyebrows knitting together, then glancing back towards her, she knew immediately that whatever they were talking about had something to do with her.

The women stood huddled together. Heads bent, nodding, they were both looking over now.

'I can't sleep. Them planes. Is it the Jerries? Are they bombing Caryl Street?' Bobby pestered Lily, pulling the thin linen sheet over his hunched shoulders.

'No,' lied Lily, distracted, still worried about her mother. 'Just practice runs ... Try and get a bit of shut eye, sweetie.'

Bobby sighed. Matt came over, knelt beside him, pushed a cigarette in his ear, produced it from his other ear with a flourish. 'Tah dah!'

'How d'you do that?' Bobby asked, amazed.

'Magic,' he replied.

Lily put each child into a bed and sat on a third bed between each them. Matt pulled up a stool beside her. 'This really is enough now,' he said. 'This is just too dangerous. It's the docks they're targeting – and that's us.' He turned to Lily. 'The kids can't stay in Liverpool. They have to go to St Jude's.'

Lily looked shocked. Did Matt also think this was a good idea? How could he even suggest it? The grim Gothic monstrosity that she had collected the sheets from? The Mother and Baby Home? Why would they pack them off there?

'You shouldn't let them anywhere near that place,' Lily said.

Suddenly, she felt her mother at her side.

'Why not?' asked Stella.

'It's pitiful. And what about the girls?'

'What d'you mean?'

'The fallen girls? What's going to happen to them?'

'Let's not worry about the details,' said Stella, crossly. 'You'll find out when you get there.'

Lily's eyes widened with the shock of what she had just said.

'Who, *me*?'

'Yes, you. Don't look so appalled. There's a place for you as well. The nuns need more girls to help with the domestics. I want you to go there to look after the kids. St Jude's are taking whoever's still left here from St Columba's parish next week. Father Donnelly has arranged it. The bombings will start getting worse because this is a proper blitzkrieg, all right, just like the ones in Belgium and Poland – and this time Deirdre and Bobby should go. The nuns are doing it to be kind. Helping with the war effort.'

Lily's jaw dropped open. 'No! I'm not going! I've told you, it's an awful place!'

'Of course you're going, Lily. Don't be ridiculous. I'm not having these children go on their own,' said Stella.

'I can't!'

'What do you mean, you can't?'

'I mean I won't!'

'You will do as I say, young lady! I'm sick of you defying me. Don't think I don't know about you running around town with boys when I told you not to! You're going. And that's the end of it.'

'You're sending me away because of *Vincent*?'

'No. Yes … no,' she answered.

Bobby, with his thumb stuck in his mouth, clutched Lily's hand.

'Is everything going to be all right? I'm scared,' he said. He dropped his head fiddled with his fraying cuffs.

'Fine. Everything is fine,' answered Lily, as another plane roared overhead and her nerve endings tingled with the vibrations.

'Go to sleep, Bobby. Everything will feel better in the morning,' snapped Stella.

And then she turned on Lily again.

'You'd really abandon your brother? Look at him, poor lamb,' she said. That was unfair, thought Lily, as he stared at her worried round eyes. 'You're going to St Jude's, Lily.'

'But—'

'No buts. You're going and that's final.'

'But—'

Stella held the palm of her hand flat up to her face in a gesture that Lily understood was telling her that there was no point in arguing. Lily, sensing this was a hopeless situation, humphed, and lay down. She turned her back and lay on her side, drawing her knees to her chest on the sagging camp bed whilst the ground shook again suddenly and a terrific whizzing sound came from overhead. Everyone shrieked, and ducked, and prayed for it to stop. Everyone except Lily, who at that moment was so upset, and so furious with her mother, that she wouldn't have cared if a bomb had dropped right there and killed the whole flaming lot of them.

Chapter 8

The following week after work, Lily headed off to the makeshift cabin at the top of Canning Street where the WVS supervisor was waiting for her to start her shift. Rosie's small chair was pushed up against the sewing machine and another girl was sitting at it.

'Start on this,' said the supervisor, dumping a pile of socks in a wicker basket.

Lily hesitated.

'What's the matter, love?' said the woman.

'Where's Rosie?'

'I have no idea. But I do know these socks won't darn themselves.'

Lily frowned. Had Rosie left? Had she left without saying goodbye? Surely not! She couldn't bear it if she had. It was Rosie's lively chatter, accompanied by the comforting whirr of the machine, the spools whizzing around and the pedals clacking, that made her work here tolerable.

She looked around. The two girls sitting at the end of the bench – one with a painted gash for a mouth, her legs winding around each other, the other with her hands placed flat underneath her thighs and her hair in pink sponge curlers under a yellow chiffon headscarf – were gossiping about some fella being as useless as a soggy candlestick. That's all those two ever spoke about – men, and how hopeless they were – and she ended up doing more than her fair share of sewing whilst the pair idled the time away nattering and drinking tea.

One of them looked up. 'Rosie popped by earlier. Left that for you.'

She pointed at an envelope that was propped up against the sewing machine.

Lily opened it. She frowned when she saw the cheap tarnished locket on a nickel chain tucked inside. It was shaped as a small heart and Lily recognised it as the one Rosie wore around her neck, the one she said brought her good luck.

Dear Lily, said the note. *Sorry I missed you at Caryl Street earlier but you were out when I knocked. You always said you liked this. I want you to have it. For luck. Stay safe. We're closer than the closest sisters and always will be. See you when this damned war is over. Rosie.*

The girl threw her a pile of serge and a cotton reel and Lily reached out her hand. The needle scraped the inside of her wrist and she winced. She began to turn the socks inside out, then she took a pair of scissors and cut a hole in the heel.

'What are you doing? You're supposed to be darning the heel, not cutting holes in them.'

Lily pushed her hand through, stuck her thumb through the hole. Wiggled her fingers. 'See, fingerless gloves.'

The second girl smiled. 'Neat trick. Rosie teach you that? I saw her do it once.'

'No,' she answered. 'My mam.'

'Funny. That's what Rosie used to do an' all. Never seen it before.'

Lily nodded, thought no more of it, thought nothing about why Rosie hadn't left the envelope with Stella instead of coming all the way here to drop it off, and returned to cross-stitching the sock.

She left after a couple of hours, fingers sore from pushing a needle and thread through thick linen material and without a thimble to help her. She made her way down Caryl Street. The night had drawn in and the sky was studded with pale stars. When she arrived home, she started on the grate, but there was a knock at the door. Father Donnelly came in, swirling his black cape over one shoulder, and Stella showed him to the kitchen where he took his place at the table and called Lily to join them. He had brought with him a bottle of holy water, and a ginger cake. Baked by the nuns, he announced. He placed the tin on the table and when he took the lid off, he made the sign of the cross.

The clock ticked softly. Annie brought a pot of tea and the priest took the best and only delicate china cup and saucer that the Laffertys owned, trying not to look directly at Deirdre and Bobby hopping from one foot to another, mouths salivating and eyes widening – hardly surprising as they hadn't had anything as delicious as cake for months, they both wriggled with excitement.

'All right, have some cake. You look like you've swallowed jumping beans, you two,' said Stella.

Little Deirdre took a piece and nibbled at it fussily, whilst Bobby stuffed it down in almost one go. The sound of Father Donnelly's slurping punctuated the silence whilst they all concentrated on the sweet taste in their mouths. A lady's face gradually appeared in the bottom of the treasured china cup the priest was drinking out of and when they finished their cake, Deirdre and Bobby watched, anticipating the priest's smile when the lady's face became visible. They didn't want to tell him that Matt had nicked it from the Chu Chin Chow restaurant in Liverpool – they knew that wouldn't go down well – but they could hardly contain themselves, and fidgeted feverishly in their seats.

Father Donnelly placed the cup on the table.

'Did you drink it all?' asked Bobby.

'Shush,' said Stella.

'I did,' he replied.

'Did you see the lady?'

'I told you shush!' said Stella.

'On the bottom of the cup?' said Deirdre.

The priest took the cup, peered into it. 'Ah yes,' he said 'I see now. Very good. Very good indeed.'

Deirdre, thumb stuck in her mouth, padded over in her frayed cotton hand-me-down shift dress, dragging her rag doll, and clambered onto her mother's knee.

'Will you not have another piece of cake, Deirdre?' asked Father Donnelly. He bit into his piece, wiped crumbs from around his mouth.

'She's had enough,' said Stella. 'We'll save some for Matt.'

'Very well,' he said. 'Now. The nuns at St Jude's are making preparations for the children. God works in mysterious ways.'

'Yes, he certainly bloody does,' Stella said, looking at the pile of plaster on the floor that had fallen from the ceiling rose. Must get Lily to sweep that up, she thought.

She felt a quick kick under the table from her sister Annie.

'What?' she said, defiant. 'Stop kicking me under the table.'

'Father, we're very grateful,' said Annie.

And so it was decided. Soon satchels and bags would be packed and Lily would be dispatched to Freshdale with the three children to settle them in. No more pinching themselves to see if they were dreaming, war had come to Caryl Street; it was finally happening.

'Make sure you give these to your mother,' said the man from the Corporation who knocked on the door ten minutes later, delivering pamphlets. 'There's everything you need to know in there,' he continued, as he handed over labels to Lily and told her what they must do next.

She unfolded the paper, read the list: two vests, two pairs of knickers, two pairs of socks, mackintosh, nightclothes, plimsolls or house shoes, warm coat.

'Get the children ready as quickly as you can, the trains are leaving tomorrow. You should plan to be at Lime Street Station by twelve at the latest. Please God more bombing won't start before then.'

The next morning after another night without incident, thankfully, September sunlight sliced through the window. There was the sound of church bells clanging in the distance. Matt had arranged all the travel details and Deirdre and Bobby were going to St Jude's with Lily. There was to be no argument and no turning back. Faced with her mother's determination – *no one* crossed Stella! – Lily had no choice but to accept it for now. She followed her mother into the tiny kitchen. The table was laid. Each mismatched chipped plate had a fried egg, fried bread, and black pudding on it.

'Where on earth did this come from?' exclaimed Stella.

Cliff stood with his back to her, facing the hearth, reading the *Liverpool Echo*, a cup of tea held against his cheek and a lit cigarette dangling from his mouth. He replied, 'Peg Leg provided the eggs from his hen, meat is from Kerryson's butchers. Thought I'd give Lil and the kids a bit of a send-off.'

'Oh, you are a darling,' said Stella, in a rare moment of tenderness.

Deirdre came downstairs. Lily scooped her up, took a moment to look at her sweet face with her snub nose and pretty eyes and ruffled the top of her head. Annie, who had left her home in Gladys Street and had arrived at the house earlier, was Stella's sensible sister. She wore thick horn-rimmed glasses, and she was fond of saying to Stella and Cliff when she occasionally joined in the dancing, 'Don't look at me like that. These two left feet have kept me out of trouble. And isn't about time you two got proper jobs?' She was proud of her job as a clerical secretary for Liverpool Assurance, proud she didn't have a man to complicate her life and drink her earnings down the pub. Stacking plates left over from breakfast and running them under the tap, she turned to Stella. 'I've spoken to the sisters. It's all in hand and they will be well looked after,' she whispered.

'Rosie's finally left,' announced Cliff, suddenly. 'I must say, you can't blame her. Hooligans nicking the lead off the roof. Her da looked up and saw a pair of bloody feet coming in through the roof. Paddy went mad.'

Gram's face crinkled up into a smile.

'It's not funny, Mam,' said Stella.

'Paddy Doocey has always been a miserable sod. I wish I'd been there to see it!'

The children sat down at the table and gulped down the glasses of milk that Annie was putting under their noses.

'I don't want to go. I want to stay in Liverpool and shoot the Jerrys!' said Bobby. 'Pow! Pow! Why do I have to go to the flipping country now there's going to be a real war?'

For a moment Stella wavered, until he started racing around the kitchen, arms outstretched, pretending he was an aeroplane, crashing into furniture, pushing chairs out of the way, knocking a small vase of sweet peas from Peg Leg's allotment off the table.

'Bobby! You daft 'apeth! Stop running around like that and shouting like a lunatic. You're getting all over-excited again, you big chump! Look what you've done! Water all over the place. Help me clear this up. Remember what happened when the King came on the wireless to tell us about Mrs Simpson? We don't want a repeat of that, do we?' said Annie.

Bobby humphed. Lily, mopping up the water with a dish rag, raised her eyes as an image of him of him marching around the kitchen, saluting, and hollering LMS! LMS! *Lousy Mrs Simpson!* and walking straight into a door and breaking his toe came into her head.

'You felt a right fool for a month, didn't you? Have you forgotten already?' she said.

'I want to stay here and see the bombers. Niaow, niaow, pow, pow, pow! Mam, I don't want to go.'

'OK, Bobby. I've had enough. Listen. This is serious. You're going away to be safe,' said Stella, getting cross with him, grasping his arms and bending down so that her eyes met his.

'I'm staying.'

Stella shrugged. 'All right, you stay if you want,' she said, standing and walking away with a casual wave of her arm, trying to make him think she didn't care.

'Can I stay, Mam?' asked Lily, one last try to get her to change her mind.

'No, you flaming can't,' she replied. 'You should be setting an example to Bobby and Deirdre.'

'I'm staying, I'm staying,' chanted Bobby.

'I give up,' Stella said, her voice rising in frustration. She placed her hands on her hips and shrugged. 'Right then, go and get your pulley on. Here's your hymn book.'

'What?' said Bobby, faltering.

'Go and get ready for church if you're staying here. School might be shut but Father Donnelly is saying morning Masses all this week,' she said. She shoved a chair under the table, took a piece of her hair, deftly wound it around her hand, and piled it up on her head in a neat chignon, secured it with a grip, and pretended to ignore him.

'I don't want to go to church.'

'Well, if you don't want to go to church, stop mithering and moaning about getting evacuated then. It's not as if you're going far.'

Deirdre, who had been sitting on the edge of the table, watching this exchange, her feet on the seat of a chair, looked adoringly at her brother. With her face lit up and her eyes open wide, she cried, 'Does it mean if we get evaccied we don't have to go to church *ever*?'

'Don't be stupid, love.'

'No more church! No more church!' cried Bobby. He grabbed his hymn book from the table and chucked it into the air. It rose like a flapping pigeon, flew up to the ceiling, then landed back down with a thump on the floor. Little Deirdre, clutching her precious doll, covered her pert lips and burst into a fit of giggles.

'Is it like going on holiday?' asked Deirdre. 'My friend says we'll get the mange if we stay here with all the bombing and that—'

'Eugh!' said Bobby. 'I don't want the mange. Shirley Hooley's got the mange ...'

Lily took in the scene. Bobby was now trying on his gas mask, shouting, 'It smells like wellie boots!', which made the glass steam up inside. And then Deirdre started to mock cry, sticking a grubby thumb in her mouth when she saw him, saying he looked like a sea monster.

Lily went upstairs for one last look at the house. The musty smell of stale air and mothballs hit the back of her throat. She rubbed the toe of her boot at the silver trail a snail had squiggled across the floorboards and then her gaze shifted to the bare walls stained with spreading damp, sooty marks reminding her of vanished paintings; only one picture left now, hanging crookedly, a cheap print of Degas' ballet dancers.

'Have you looked under the beds?' she asked Bobby, who had just come up the stairs.

He brought out an old stained porcelain potty.

'Won't be needing that at St Jude's,' she said.

The two poky rooms, one with peeling purple wallpaper and chunks of plaster falling off the ceiling, the other, a small dark bedroom in which the children slept, had certainly seen better days. Leading Deirdre by the hand, she pushed open the door of the box room with her foot. Ivy twisted in under the gaps between the window frames and the sills, its tentacled fronds creeping up the walls. Ragged striped curtains hung limply from a sagging nylon wire at each small window. She put her head around the bathroom door, took a last look at its chipped tiles and stained bath, and checked nothing had been left.

They were finally leaving Caryl Street.

'Is this the right thing to do?' Cliff asked Stella, later. 'To be sending the kids away to that place? As if they're parcels, or pieces of luggage, with those dreadful brown labels around their necks?'

'We'll soon find out if it's not,' replied Stella, and she shrugged and sipped more tea, and decided that it didn't do to make problems where there were none. At least, none to speak of yet . . .

Lily, Stella, Deirdre, and Bobby, shut the door behind them and came out blinking into the sunshine. The letter from the nuns had said they should send the children to the meeting point at St Columba's school and from there Miss Postle would escort them to the station to begin the evacuation with the other children. But Stella, never one to do as she was told, had insisted she should go to Lime Street to wave her children off.

They took the tram into town. It rattled all the way, and as it finally pulled up outside the station, Lily noticed a number of kids coming towards them from the Adelphi. It was a line of older schoolchildren in their uniforms, led by a teacher. They were walking under a banner with the name of their school on it:

St Matthew's. As they approached the entrance to the station, seeing the sheer numbers of children spilling down the steps, fanning out onto the concourse, and crowding onto the platforms, she gasped.

'Good God, Mam. Who knew there were this many kiddies in Liverpool? What's going to happen to us all?' said Lily. She had always been such an optimist, the person who believed that this world was the best of all possible worlds, but even she was beginning to worry.

A woman wearing a beret and holding a clipboard turned down the sides of her mouth into hospital corners and pulled in the belt of her mackintosh another inch. 'Line up over here,' she shouted. 'LINE UP OVER HERE!' Then she grabbed a megaphone from a man in a ARP tin hat, and repeated it. 'Listen to me, everyone. You need to pay attention and line up in an orderly manner!'

Lily bustled little Deirdre and Bobby over to the magnificent clock. She thought there was something noble about this clock, with its huge white face and Roman numerals.

'Listen!' the woman said. Then she stopped. She turned to the man beside her. 'That's Stella Lafferty – the woman who owns the dancing school, married to the fella with the cigarette permanently hanging from his lip who's after every bit of skirt in Liverpool,' she said in a low voice. She walked over to Stella. 'What are you doing here? Parents were told to leave their children with their school teachers. Or priests.'

'I wanted to wave them off,' she replied.

The woman raised her head and tutted. 'Did you not read the pamphlets? You should have stayed at home.'

Stella bridled. 'Is there a law against waving good-bye to your kiddies?'

The woman rolled her eyes.

Lily couldn't help noticing that amongst the gaggle of rowdy and excited boys, a good number of them were crying; a few were even carrying a pathetic plastic bucket and spade. Did they think they were going for a short holiday at the seaside? Is that what Bobby and Deirdre thought as well? It was the sound of a few of them singing and smiling, faces raised to the vast Liverpool sky, arms linked as they marched towards the platforms, that made her stomach somersault. One of the teachers was waving her arms, mock conducting, urging the kids to sing along.

'Glory, Glory Hallelujah!'

'Teacher hit me with a ruler!' a few chorused together and laughed.

'Hitler has only got one ball!' sang a lone voice.

'The other is in St George's Hall!' shouted another.

'Less of that!' said the teacher with an umbrella that looked suspiciously as though she had brought it to use to prod any unruly pupils. She marched over and cuffed a few kiddies over the head. The woman with the clipboard threw a stern look in the teacher's direction and a group nearby chortled.

'Does everyone know where they're going? Or just us?' Lily asked Stella.

'The letter said the billeting officer decides which homes they go to. Most of this lot are going to Wales. You'll just head off to Freshdale. Think about it, it's lovely. It's the countryside, it has the beach and fields and it's on the way to Blackpool. Much closer to here than Wales – *and* they speak the same language, thank the Lord. Only an hour or so away, and the nuns will be waiting for you.'

Surely not everyone speaks Welsh in Wales, thought Lily. Her mother's tendency to exaggerate never failed to surprise her.

'Wish I was going to Wales,' said Bobby.

'No you don't,' replied Stella. 'St Jude's will be lovely.'

Bobby wriggled out from Lily's arm. 'I want to go where Frankie is. Not St Jude's. Frankie said he's going back to Mrs Pilkington's posh house in St Asaph where they bang a gong at dinner time, like in the movies, They have to do that because the garden is so big and there's a river at the end of it! He says it's got hot running water and maids and servants. Frankie says you can click on one switch and the whole place lights up like a flipping Christmas tree. And there's *no damp or mould. It's clean.* And white. So white it makes your eyes hurt. White like in heaven.'

'Don't listen to Frankie,' said Lily. 'How would he know what heaven is like? Listen, just because his dad works at Pilkington's doesn't mean he'll end up going back to Mrs Pilkington. The Pilkingtons are millionaires and Frankie is dirt poor like we are. That's about the only thing he's got right. He'll be lucky he doesn't end up in a barn this time.'

A lorry arrived, a removal van it looked like, trundling into the holding space, dust rising from its tyres in great clouds as people moved out of the way for it. The sun appeared and flashed its rays through the glass of the vaulted station roof. The fingers of bright light cut through the clouds of steam as the lorry stopped and a group of children were instructed to climb into the back.

Stella turned to Lily. 'That woman with the clipboard. So rude,' she said. 'No need for it, the way she's yelling at everyone to stay back, miserable old shrew. She'll end up with the face she deserves, mark my words.'

Lily looked around. More families were beginning to arrive. A man, with cymbals held by elastic bands strapped to the inside of his knees and a trumpet, walked up and down the lines, trying to entertain everyone. People laughed as he crashed the cymbals together. He looked like a demented chicken and his face, full of boils, finished off the picture.

'What's the point of him?' asked Stella. 'And his flaming trumpet playing! So out of tune. What a horrible caterwauling. Besides, letting the kiddies believe that being evacuated is going to be as much fun as going to the circus seems cruel.'

Lily murmured in agreement. But then she asked, 'So why are *you* sending us away? Why are you sending *me* away? I'm not a kid.'

'It's for the best,' Stella replied, brusquely.

Finally, the children were instructed to get onto the train. Stella made a great show of ruffling hair, planting of kisses and hugging Bobby and Deirdre so tightly that they could hardly breathe. Then she kissed her fingers, reached out and placed the tops of them gently on Lily's lips. Bobby ran towards the platform and barely gave her a backward glance.

They took their places on the train. Deirdre nervously nibbled on the cardboard label slung around her neck with her gas mask and cardboard box, her face staring out of the window. She looks frightened, thought Lily. Suddenly, Stella ran through the barrier and raced alongside the train as it slowly hissed and chuffed away. She banged on the window and waved goodbye as the train pulled out of the station.

'You be careful!' Stella shouted. 'Be careful of those bloody nuns! And look after the little ones, Lily!'

Chapter 9

After the ten-mile train journey that headed north through the docks, then Bootle, and then skirted up the coast all the way to the open countryside and the beach and pinewoods, they arrived in Freshdale. They got off the train, planted their feet on the ground and filled their lungs. The fresh air lifted their gloomy spirits and Deirdre and Bobby dashed around in excited circles, playing tag. Lily yelled that they were going to fall on the track and screamed, '*Stop*! You're putting the fear of God in me, you silly children!' as Bobby nearly slipped onto the railway sleepers. Lily yanked him back to safety and there was a commotion from two women further down the platform when they saw what had just nearly happened, and the ticket collector came running out of his office. One of the women, a kind-looking pink-cheeked lady with a wicker basket full of cabbages, asked Lily if she was all right, and they all stood round and chatted, and before they knew it, the kiddies were gone, in a flurry of waves and a hauling of the bags and more stamping of feet, delighted to have darted past the ticket collector and off down the road. Old habits die hard, thought Lily, handing over the travel vouchers. There had been no need to try and dodge the fares today. 'Ta ra and thank you,' she said politely, and set off dragging a suitcase to catch up with the children who, carrying their small bags and gas masks, were racing on ahead.

The road to St Jude's – one of the houses furthest down the street and nearest the shore – was wide. This place was quiet, but not the kind of quiet the city could be, especially at night between air-raid sirens, with the awful feeling of dreadful anticipation as you looked up at the sky, waiting for the planes that might appear at any minute. Nor was it eerily quiet as in the morning after the all-clear had sounded and people were afraid to come into the streets for fear of what they might find, or mournfully quiet in the way the playgrounds had felt so empty after the first wave of evacuations; or worse, the awful, deathly quiet when news reached folk about casualties and death and bombing. No, this place was a calm, peaceful quiet. A comforting quiet. It gave Lily hope that the houses being demolished in the city, leaving great gaping holes in the ground like open wounds in the earth, might rebuild, and one day be like Freshdale. It felt safe here, as though life was flourishing and that time was moving forward.

'Nice here, isn't it, kids?' said Lily.

They passed a parade of shops. A woman, sitting out on the steps in the sunshine, sleeves rolled up, sorting out stems of roses outside a florist's, smiled at them, and as they passed a baker's shop with the aroma of freshly baked bread in the air, a man in floury overalls, standing on the step and smoking a pipe, nodded a friendly hello.

'What now?' asked Bobby, when the road took a sharp bend. The hedges were tall and the cow parsley growing in the verges was waist height. 'Are we at the seaside, Lil? Is there going to be ice cream?'

'Rationed, love. But if we're lucky maybe the nuns will have some strawberries.'

Bobby's eyes widened.

They could smell the sea now. Up ahead they could just make out the sand dunes rising in peaks. As they got closer, Lily saw the fuzzy Gothic towers of St Jude's beginning to take shape. Soon the road disappeared into a mass of potholes. With each footstep, they grew closer. The sand underfoot on the pavements had been blown inland from the beach and softened their tread and pine needles were heaped in the gutters. The children grew more excited. Even frightened Deirdre began to smile. Lily began to think that the countryside could change you into a different kind of person. How different your life would be if you lived here.

'Hold your nose,' said Deirdre, laughing. 'I can smell a fishy smell!'

'That's the sea,' said Bobby, breaking into a run. 'How much further to St Jude's?'

'Just around the corner.'

They made their way further down the road. A blue sky was bulking up with white clouds but finally, they stood outside the wrought-iron gates of St Jude's. Lily noticed Deirdre lingering, bending to tie a shoelace that didn't need tying. As she did so, she squinted up at the huge house with its turrets and dozens of windows.

'What's the matter?' Lily asked.

'Scared,' replied Deirdre.

It was true the building looked foreboding and unwelcoming. Lily paused for a second.

'Who's that lady?' Deirdre asked. Lily followed her gaze, up towards a high window set back under a gable fashioned with wooden curlicues. A girl with loose dark hair, wearing a black dress with a light-coloured collar, was peering out at them, but she moved away quickly and disappeared behind the black curtain. Lily felt a rash of goose pimples rising up over every inch of her flesh as a wave of panic washed over her.

'Lily, who is she?'

'Nobody,' she replied. 'Now, come on, that's a good girl. They'll be waiting for us. May as well start by trying to make the best of it. Let's go and ring the bell. Lickety-split, now.'

A smiling nun came out of the building, keys jangling on a chain around her waist, ready to greet them. She undid the padlock on the iron gates, pulled one side open, and welcomed them in.

'Ah, 'tis the famous Laffertys!' She looked kind and spoke with a soft Irish lilt. 'Sure, you must be Lily. And these are the little ones. Lovely! You are *most* welcome. I'm Sister David,' she said, sticking out her hand.

'Look at that statue,' whispered Bobby to Deirdre. 'She's got a stump for a hand.'

'Yes. That's St Theresa,' replied Sister David, 'our patron saint. We all love St Theresa with a *passion*. She's a beauty, isn't she?'

Bobby nodded, not quite knowing what to make of it all.

A second nun bustled out of the side door. 'I'll take over, Sister David. Welcome,' she said. 'Welcome, welcome. I'm Sister Bernadette.'

Lily looked at the washing line strung over part of the gravel forecourt and attached to two posts at the side of the house. There were bloomers and shirts hung across it, sheets bucking and tossing and flapping in the sunshine.

Bobby, meanwhile, had stopped and was balancing on one leg, pouring stones out of his shoes.

'Come this way,' said Sister Bernadette.

When Bobby had finished, they followed the nuns up the wide gravelled drive. 'The boys and girls are just coming out of morning Mass,' she said.

A line of about twelve children appeared from the back of the house, all walking with their hands behind their backs as instructed by a laughing nun with her hands deep in the pockets of her habit and a set of keys and rosary beads hanging from her waist.

'That's the University Walk that Sister Assumpta is so fond of,' Sister David said, with a smile. It seemed difficult for most of the children who were wobbling unsteadily, as if they were trying to walk along a tightrope.

'I said hands behind your backs!' said the laughing nun.

'Saints preserve us! What a hoot!' Sister David said to Lily.

'There's Alice!' cried Deirdre suddenly, excited to see her friend. 'Alice! She was in my class at St Columba's! Hey, Alice!'

The girl she was pointing at looked over to them, squinted and frowned, then when she realised it was Deirdre, stood on her toes and waved back excitedly.

'We teach them in the schoolroom in the wing at the end of the building. But when it's sunny, like today, the children bring their desks outside. They enjoy that,' said Sister David.

Lily nodded. One of them, a small boy, feverishly concentrating, lost his footing.

'Would you ever have thought walking with your hands behind your back would be so difficult?' said the nun to Lily, smiling.

Lily smiled back, for a moment reassured.

They followed her up the steps and inside, the nun swishing down a parquet floor corridor, past the alcoves with statues of the Virgin Mary, and beautiful flowers in glass vases, whilst branches of fuchsia were pushed into the holes in the lids of silver vases. They came into a cheerful refectory with yellow curtains and a picture of a serene Sacred Heart of Jesus hanging on a cord from the picture rail, his punctured palms upturned and dripping blood, but smiling, as though he didn't seem to mind at all, a golden halo hovering above his head. They drank tea and orange squash sitting at a long trestle table in the large airy room that smelled of steamed cabbage, and ate biscuits that the children sniffed, licked, and nibbled at, savouring the taste. Lily wondered where the nuns got such treats from. The Laffertys had had nothing like this for months now because of rationing. It was all prune roly-poly and Spam hash back in Caryl Street.

'I'll take you on a quick tour,' said Sister David when they'd finished and they walked down more corridors with more smells of polish and pungent flowers and wax candles and, through windows, glimpsed children at desks in the garden, chattering and colouring, and they looked happy, and there were even more crystal vases full of cut flowers and everywhere looked clean and smelled like freshly laundered linen.

'Lovely to see, isn't it?' said the nun.

But then Lily stopped suddenly. 'How does it work?' she asked.

'I'm sorry?' said the nun.

'With the girls. The unmarried mothers?'

The nun hesitated, then glanced at Bobby and Deirdre. 'They're in the annex. You won't see much of them. We keep them quite separate,' she said quietly to Lily.

Lily nodded, unsure whether this was good thing. Or a very bad thing indeed …

They finished by going on a short walk around the nuns' garden, and talked about Father Donnelly, and Sister David said what a grand time everyone would have, that the war had done ghastly things, but opening their doors had been a positive step, and a bright light in a dark tunnel for the children of Liverpool. She added that the nuns were enjoying helping with the war effort, that it was the least they could do, and they were grateful to have Lily as an extra pair of hands. Sister David made the sign of the cross, and when they stopped at the kitchen, she wrapped cake in greaseproof paper for Lily, and slipped home-made biscuits with lumps of glistening ginger into Bobby and Deirdre's palms.

But as they left, on the way to the building at the back of the main house, Lily saw the girl again, or rather just the shape of a girl this time, moving about at an upstairs window. Lily paused and stared up at her. But this time the girl just stood there, she didn't move quickly away, and it was as if, when she finally tugged the curtain back across the window, for some reason she had wanted to be seen.

'You one of the new lot?' said a voice. Lily looked up to see where it was coming from and saw, at the top of the staircase, a blonde-haired girl leaning over the bannister, chewing gum. 'Come up here,' said the girl.

As Lily climbed the stairs, she saw the girl had yellow dusters tied around her feet. Must be her idea of a convenient way of doing the job of polishing the parquet floor on the landing, Lily thought. Quite ingenious.

'I'm Janet,' the girl said, sliding and skating across the floor, thrusting out her hand, and then, after shaking Lily's, in an impressive show of bubblegum skills, stuck out her tongue, blew, and then popped an enormous quivering pink bubble. She was smiling and seemed pleased with herself and happy to see Lily. She was about the same age and her fair hair was cut into a short bob. She had sturdy legs and lively blue eyes, and was wearing a loose smock dress with the sleeves rolled up to reveal shapely, freckled arms.

'You the new girl to help with the evacuees? Sisters have told me to take you to your dormitory. Want some chewy?' she asked, offering her a stick of bubblegum.

Lily took a piece to be polite. Janet untied the dusters and, as they set off, shoved them in her pockets and told her a little more about the place. Through the small gabled window she pointed out the large, old, rambling stone building at the back with ivy creeping over every inch of its walls and choking the guttering in the roof, so that even the windows were barely visible. This was called Ambrose Hall, she said. Built before the First World War, it had been used for the laundry where the girls washed the shirts and sheets. It had fallen into disrepair, but it had reopened, and although it was totally unsuitable to be used as a school, it was available, and large enough, to teach a class of thirty children. Everything had been transported from Liverpool – chairs, tables, desks, crockery, blackboards, piano, boxes of chalk, dusters, old Janet and John, Arthur Ransome and Enid Blyton books, all delivered safely, just like the children who had arrived in various stages over the last six months.

'The first lot came walking in a crocodile down Virgin's Lane, with their gas masks and cardboard boxes around their necks. Then there were more dribs and drabs. So three more nuns arrived from Manchester.

They're a lot nicer than the awful cow, Assumpta, who runs the place. She's an old witch. Sister David's all right, though, and Sister Bernadette.'

'And what about the fallen girls?' asked Lily.

Janet laughed. She talked over her shoulder as she spoke. 'The few unmarried mothers still here who do the laundry are given strict instructions to remain out of sight, so as not to corrupt the sweet, innocent children. Though Sister David got a shock one day when one of the sweet, innocent children asked, "Sister, where are all them fallen girls who like riding the flagpole?" Well, you should have seen the other sweet innocents giggling behind their hands, trying to stuff the laughter back into their mouths, they were.' She grinned.

They walked further down the parquet-floored corridor with its high, leaded windows. With the sun streaming in, Lily thought how nice it was not to have the dreadful blackout curtains as in Caryl Street, bringing an air of gloom and worry to the place. At the far end of the corridor there was an impressive alabaster statue of a worried St Francis holding a curly lamb, a staff, a Bible and a bunch of flowers, looking as though he was going to drop one of his precious objects at any minute.

'In here's the bathroom. We all share it. There's always a fight over the two baths. Once every month if you're lucky.'

Janet opened the door. 'And look at them, with the bloody lids on them. That's so the nuns don't see their boobs. Their own boobs! They're scared of them. Or their hairy things when they wash. They think all that kind of thing is a sin.'

'Do they?'

'They do, love. But don't worry. We nick off and go to the local swimming pool, the Lido, you know, in Southport? If you can sneak out and don't mind swimming in your pants and vest it's a smashing day out. Or the beach, even. Though it's dangerous with the tides. Remember that.'

She told her how they were divided up into boys and girls and by their different ages, and all allocated a dormitory, though she and her pal had a room at the end of the nuns' corridor upstairs to themselves as they had been there longer than most. The dormitories were all named after saints and some were in a better condition than others – Southwell had a smashed window that let in rain.

'Ambrose has a squirrel infestation, and even though the squirrels happen to be red with bushy tails and look awfully pretty and sweet, the droppings aren't that sweet and stink to high heaven. Swear to God, squirrels will eat anything. Gnaw through the wood and paper, they do. Gnawed through the Bibles in Ambrose Hall. Squirrels don't care, though. Why should they? They're squirrels. They don't give tuppence. Unlike the nuns. Who had a hissy fit when they saw the destroyed Bibles and made us all say novenas that it wouldn't happen again,' she said laughing.

'And what about the girls? The ones who are pregnant?' Lily asked again. 'Where do they sleep?'

'Ambrose. They have a dorm in there and you don't see them much. Except the other day, one of the lasses, her fella tried to climb over the wall, and Sister David ran after him with a broom. Everyone laughed and the kids cheered to see him scramble over the gates, but then they all got walloped on their backsides for laughing, which didn't seem fair as the real culprit should have been the fella who climbed over the wall. Bloody hilarious.'

Lily smiled. 'I would have liked to have seen that,' she said.

'You got a fella?' asked the girl. She took a piece of gum from her mouth again, wound it around her finger as if it were a long piece of elastic, then popped it back in again and began chewing ferociously.

'I do. But he won't be scrambling over any wall. He's at sea.'

'Where?'

'Can't exactly say at the moment.'

'I don't think I'd like that.'

'It's not so bad. He says he'll take care of himself.'

'And what if the Jerrys blast his ship out of the water? You hear terrible stories about them U-boats and their torpedoes.'

'He's brave.'

'Some call it brave, I call it being flaming stupid when he could have signed up for something safer.'

They shared a smile, but Lily had rather Janet hadn't reminded her. Leaving the dormitory, they walked down the corridor to the wooden staircase, which took them to the floor below. Janet rested the side of her bottom on the polished rail and slid down in one go. Lily's eyes widened in shock. She spluttered with laughter and thought how nice it would be to have a friend like Janet. She had always been close to Rosie, but she didn't really know anyone her own age, apart from the WVS girls who she did mobile teas with and helped cut up the sheets to make them into bandages. She spent so much time looking after her brothers and sister she hadn't met anyone who she could share secrets with. The girls at her school had always thought of her as an outsider. The one from the dancing family, she would hear them say. The funny family, without much money. The one that eats potato pasties outside on the wall at lunchtime because she couldn't afford school dinners. It was Stella's fault. She had spent so much time at dancing competitions and teaching and practising, there hadn't been much room for friendship.

'The refectory down there . . . you do the washing up on a daily rota and you have to take the supper trays to the nuns upstairs. You'll be given a Saturday job, like sweeping the front steps and cleaning the front hall or washing the nuns' undies.'

Janet stopped, dipped her fingers into the holy water font screwed into the wall at the bottom of the staircase, and made a sign of the cross. And then, just as Lily thought this was some kind of sign for her deep love of Jesus, she dipped her fingers in the font again, but this time she flicked the water at Lily's face and laughed.

'Got you!' she giggled and then they headed towards the end door. 'You'll be in here with a few of the twelve-year-olds; the little ones sleep in another dormitory at the end of the corridor,' she said, opening it.

Lily put her head around the door and looked around at the large bare room with its eight bunk beds. It was undecorated, shabby and some of the plaster in the eaves had come off, leaving the bare wooden slats exposed. There were another couple of the obligatory framed pictures of the Virgin Mary hanging off a picture rail and when she noticed an old stained potty poking out from under one of the beds, she couldn't help but wrinkle up her nose in distaste.

'That's yours,' said the girl, pointing to the top bunk in a corner.

Lily was glad; partly, because she would be able to see what was going on from up there, and partly because she didn't want to bump her head every time she sat up, which looked likely if she had been assigned a lower bunk.

Each bed had a small locker beside it for clothes, and, at one end of the room, there was a large table with tin bowls on it and tin jugs of cold water.

'They're for washing in,' said Janet. 'You have to tip the dirty water into a bucket. The other night, one of the girls kicked over the bucket and the water dribbled through the gaps between the floorboards, onto the room below where the nuns were saying evening prayers. So bloody funny when Sister David came running out saying there had been miracle, praise be to God! It had only gone and dripped onto the statue of the Virgin Mary and when it dribbled all down her face, she thought Our Lady was crying real tears. Assumpta put her right on that one and came raging along the corridor, convinced one of us had done it deliberately to make David look stupid. Fifty Hail Marys a day and on our knees scrubbing the cracks in the paving stones with toothbrushes for a week.'

'Sounds awful.'

'It wasn't so bad. They've made us do worse,' Janet said. 'You should hear the fuss when we have to wash in cold water.'

'What's that curtained-off cubicle?' asked Lily. On a sagging wire, there was a frayed calico curtain.

'Oh, that's where one of the nuns sleep sometimes. They take it in turns, making sure we're not up to mischief. That must be a penance and a half for them because the bed is tiny and uncomfortable.'

'I can't imagine a nun without her black habit,' said Lily, picturing a nun padding about the place in a diaphanous nightie such as Stella sometimes wore.

Janet giggled. 'My friend, Aggie, dared me to pull Sister Assumpta's habit off. She said their heads are shaved after they take their vows. But I told her that their hair grows back.'

'Did you?' asked Lily, wide-eyed.

'Not yet,' Janet replied with a grin.

She sat on the windowsill, took a packet of Embassy cigarettes from her pocket and offered one to Lily who politely said no. Janet lit hers and started blowing the smoke outside the window, waving it away with her hand.

'I actually saw one naked once. Getting out of the bath. All hairless and shiny.'

'You didn't!'

'I did.' She paused as she sucked on the cigarette. 'I peeped in through the crack in the door. That was a sight,' she said, making a face. 'Scarred me for life. I'll never get that moment back,' she paused. 'So, do you think you'll get used to living with a whole lot of people, instead of with just your own family?' she asked.

'There's plenty of us. Six. Seven with my gram and my Auntie Annie's always coming and going. So I'm used to it.' She thought of her father but she didn't want to talk about him, of how unhappy he still was at the docks, how he felt Stella was making a fool of him when he could be fighting the real war, but she knew it would change the tone of the conversation and she was enjoying this girl and her mischievous chattering.

'I've made friends here, especially Aggie, a lovely Irish Catholic girl, who's just as mad as I am. We're older than all these kids, like you, and we call ourselves the Terrible Twins. But we can be the Terrible Triplets, if you want. Would you like that?'

Lily smiled. It sounded a laugh.

'We pick flowers and make them into chains to thread through our hair for dancing in the evening, tuck our skirts into our knickers and the nuns go mad to see us throwing ourselves around like lunatics, but the kids love it. If you're good at dancing, you'd enjoy the craic, as Aggie would say. Aggie's speciality is the sand dance. You should see her. I'm not much good.'

She jumped off the windowsill and made an attempt at sliding across the floor and pushing her neck back and forth like a strange pecking bird.

Lily grinned.

'One thing we cannot *stand* is that they send us to bed at seven thirty each evening. Silent, lights out and sleep. So we have to keep our voices down, with the girl nearest the door primed to cough loudly when she hears footsteps. In the mornings, because it's still a convent, all the Catholic girls – that's you, I suppose, and Aggie, not me, thank God. All those brothers and sisters you lot have! Unbelievable! – anyway, you left-footers have to get up and be ready for prayers at six. So are you Catholic? I'm assuming you are?'

'Yes,' she replied. 'But sometimes I think my mam is only in it for the hymns. She loves a good hymn, always likes to sing her heart out on high days and holy days, but she's not organised enough to go to church every week.'

'I'm glad I'm not. I have the luxury of staying in bed for another half an hour before I have to get up for breakfast,' she said, smiling. 'Unlike you. You have to go to Mass every morning.'

'The nun who showed us in seemed kind.'

'She is. Sister David's heart's in the right place. But they can't control all these children twenty-four hours a day. They're used to an ordered life, rules and such-like, and that's is why they have the bed rule – to get rid of us, I suppose.'

Lily nodded, stared at the sagging bunk beds, the faded sheets folded over green woollen blankets that made her feel itchy just to look at them.

'What about the unmarried mothers? With their babies?'

'Oh, that's a different thing altogether. Like I said, there's not many. And you hardly see them. Not since they've cleared the lot of them out to make room for the evacuees. Though sometimes you hear crying through the walls. And I don't mean their kiddies, I mean *them*. It's a rotten thing, so it is.'

She went on, rattling through sentences, barely pausing for breath.

But Lily wasn't listening. What went on behind those walls? That's what she was turning around in her head.

Chapter 10

17 September 1940
St Jude's
Freshdale

Dear Vincent,

I have been here just over a week now and the children seem to enjoy the new surroundings, they are full of life, but I'm not so sure about this place. They appear happy enough and were delighted to meet up with their friend, Alice, again. They are a different kind of breed to normal people, these nuns. Some are kind. There's one called Sister David, who's always smiling. But the ones who have been here longer are quite frightening. I suspect, beyond that door, in the annex where some of the unmarried mothers are, it's quite a different story.

I met a girl called Janet, who is great fun and larks about – she told me she has a friend called Aggie who does the Wilson, Keppel and Betty sand dance. Janet had a go at the dance to show me. You should have seen her! Had us both in fits. But I don't think she's telling me the whole truth about this place. I had an idea something was badly wrong when I was sure I heard crying through the walls last night. At first, I thought it was a cat mewing, or a fox, but I think it could have been a baby.

I am counting the days until your ship arrives back in Liverpool again. It feels so long since we last saw each other. And it's so hard when the only news is from the wireless, and of course that's mostly about the British walloping the Germans; when it's the other way round, no one wants to hear that, so we don't get to know much.

When can I see you? I'm worried I've had no word from you. Did your parents tell you where I am? Please reply as soon as you get this, which I hope will be left sitting on your pillow or propped up against the wireless. I'm praying you will see it first thing when you walk into your house on leave as I'm posting it to your address. Try and get a message to me and I'll come straight back to Liverpool. I must go. The only complaint I have is that the food doesn't agree with me here – there's stewed cabbage and tapioca that feels like eating frog spawn when it slips down your throat and overcooked liver that's like chewing rubber and hearts that we have to cut into pieces to boil and you can see actual ventricles and aortas!

Yours, lovesick,

Lily.

The pen wobbled. She felt queasy and laid it down, rubbing her stomach to ease the churning sensation. This food, especially the disgusting tripe and mash they had had that evening, really was making her feel ill.

Chapter 11

Four days later, lying in bed, she heard strange sounds that travelled across the lawn – an animal, maybe a fox, and though she couldn't be quite sure where they were coming from, she was convinced she wasn't supposed to have heard them at all. But the next day at breakfast, when she asked Janet about it, she just answered, 'What noises?' and casually licked her spoon, then regarded her reflection as if the question didn't really warrant a response.

Lily never liked sweet porridge and it was making her feel sick, but to her dismay, once again a dollop of sickly sweet honey had been already liberally slopped on top.

'Sister Assumpta, can I could have a bowl without honey? It's a little sweet,' she said.

'Young lady, you will eat what is put in front of you! What makes you think you're so special that we are going to indulge Lily Lafferty's likes and dislikes?' she replied. 'Be quiet. Empty vessels make most sound.

Now eat up and clean the plates after you. I want this place spick and span when I get back. That's why you're here. To help with the domestics, not complain about the porridge.'

'Considering honey is rationed, I thought I would be doing them a favour,' she whispered to Janet as the nun walked away.

'What was that?' said the nun, turning on her heel, suddenly. She placed the wire-rimmed spectacles that hung on a chain from her waist on the bridge of her nose.

'Nothing, Sister,' said a frightened Lily.

'Nothing, indeed.'

The nun left, sweeping up her black skirts, spectacles glinting, the keys on her belt swaying back and forth against her thigh.

'Usual rules don't apply in here,' whispered Janet, leaning in to her. 'Everything's topsy-turvy. You'll see.'

After breakfast, it was back to the dormitory for bed-making and tidying up, then off to sewing classes to learn how to make string vests for the troops and darn their socks. Those who couldn't sew helped the children with arithmetic and spelling. All exercise was taken out of doors, even on chilly autumn mornings like today, and as she went out she saw Bobby and Deirdre in their pants and vests, already skipping across the lawn.

She wondered what Vince would make of this place. Everything she did, thought, saw, or felt, she wondered what Vince would have to say about it. Would he also laugh at the sight of the skinny beetle-like kids, leaping about like whirling dervishes? Would he have found the taste of the curdling sour milk as revolting as she did? Would he have decided Sister David was really rather lovely, whilst Sister Assumpta was not to be trusted?

'Hello. I'm Aggie,' said a voice behind her. Lily turned to see Aggie, small, perfectly proportioned, and with cascades of dyed bright-blonde curls escaping from under a blue turban. She stood with her hands thrust deep into her pockets. She was wearing a baggy trouser suit that looked like some kind of WAAF overalls with badges and buttons and on it.

'Heard you're here with your brother and sister.'

Lily nodded. 'Aye.'

Aggie squinted, tilted her head to one side. 'This place what you expected?'

'I came here a while ago. To collect sheets for the WVS.'

'You still in the WVS? You one of them stitch-and-bitch lassies? Sewing for Victory?'

'I do what I can to help. Medical supplies and stuff. Do the mobile teas as well.'

Aggie looked her up and down, took in her curves, and paisley skirt, the shirt with the frayed Peter Pan collar. 'They're outside doing PE. Just finished writing their weekly letter to send home.'

Aggie grinned. She wandered over to the window, looked over to the manicured lawn where the children had gathered in a small group. They were wearing plimsolls and culottes or shorts and pale blue aertex T-shirts, and sat cross-legged, fidgeting, with their arms crossed over their chests.

'God help them. At least they're with David. Assumpta has a thing about vests. She doesn't like you wearing them, even in the freezing cold. You have to lift your shirt up to show her you've not sneaked one on. Apparently to toughen you up. Vests are for sissies, she says.' She paused for effect, raised an eyebrow, and then gave an explosive laugh. 'Nice that, isn't it? Jesus, will you look at her!' she said pointing to Sister David, doing star jumps in front of the children. 'She's the only one in this place whose legs and arms I've actually ever seen moving like a human being's. These bloody nuns never run – doesn't even seem like they walk, just glide along as if they're on wheels. Sometimes it's as though they hover above the ground. The one thing we have over them is that they never break out into a sweat. Scarper and they just stand there blowing on their flaming whistles in a fury and shouting, getting red in the face whilst we race off. They don't even bother to try and catch us. It's dead easy to escape from his place.'

'Do you do that a lot?'

'Every so often. Me and Janet are planning to go into Southport later if we can skive off the Saturday walk. Fancy it?'

'What for?' asked Lily.

'You'll see,' Aggie answered, smiling impishly.

Lily came into Deirdre's dormitory and found her examining the regulation navy blue knickers that had been left on the bed for her.

'What's this pocket for in the knickers, Lil?' Deirdre asked.

'To keep your hankie in, instead of wiping your nose on your sleeve,' she said, with a smile.

'Ugh,' said Deirdre.

Bobby ran in and jumped on the bed. He grasped the end of the metal bedstead, bouncing up and down, kicking his bare feet up behind him.

'Bobby!' she cried, as he bounced higher and higher until, no surprise, his feet hit the ceiling. 'You're making footprints!'

He jumped down, landing with huge thump on the floor which made the statue of the Virgin Mary on a high shelf wobble.

'You'll catch it if you smash Our Lady,' she said. 'You shouldn't even be in the girls' dormitory. And that's a great game, kicking your legs up like that until your foot goes right through the plaster and you have a gaping hole above the bed! Like to see you explain that away to Sister Assumpta,' she said.

'I've got bites on my arms,' complained Deirdre.

'That's because we're in the countryside and you're wearing short sleeves,' she replied. 'There's all sorts of creepy crawlies here. Try not to scratch them. It'll only make them worse. Now, off you go to lessons.'

She left her brother and sister and set off to collect the socks that needed darning from Sister David's office. Or was it the kindling she was supposed to be doing today? She had been told to do both but didn't know which was the more urgent. Coming down the corridor, she saw Sister Margaret ahead of her, entering the doors of the chapel. She should just ask her what chores she had been assigned that morning. Moving quickly, she followed her in to the chapel but, as she entered, she took a sharp intake of breath, hit by a strong smell of incense and burning candles. There was a priest kneeling on one leg in front of the altar, head bowed, arms outstretched from one end of the altar table to the other, with his back to the pews. A girl, with a man standing beside her, stood in the middle of the altar rails, and she could see that the girl was holding a baby. A second girl, also with a baby in her arms, stood in the front pew. She, unlike the first girl, was alone, there was no man, but she had a nun at her side. She couldn't be sure, but it also seemed as though she too, had a baby in her arms. And then it was confirmed by the sound of a mewl, the sound of an infant crying.

Sliding into the back pew, she wondered if she had stumbled in on some kind of service. Something was happening, that was for sure. Lily stood for a moment watching the ceremony continue, listening to the priest murmuring through hushed prayers. The candles bent and flickered, throwing soft light onto the statue of the Sacred Heart suspended on wires on a crucifix. He looked serene and accepting of his fate, despite his ghastly predicament. She wondered if the girls at the altar were supposed to take some kind of comfort from this. She decided she wasn't about to stay around and find out and turned around to leave but knocked her foot against one of the threadbare kneelers hanging from the end of a pew. Suddenly, the nun twisted her head sharply and looked to the back of the church, then swept down the side aisle towards her, her feet clicking over the marble tiled floor, forehead puckering into a troubled frown as she marched past the gory paintings of the Stations of the Cross.

'Out!' she hissed, grabbing Lily roughly by the arm. '*Get out*!'

The girl at the altar shuffled around to turn and look at what was happening. She seemed bewildered and sad, even shocked, thought Lily, meeting her gaze. She was wearing a flimsy battered bluebell-shaped hat, a scarf patterned with roses, and a loose-fitting pale blue shift dress. It was as though she had tried to dress for the occasion. The young man, in a threadbare suit and flapping shoes, looked embarrassed, as though he had been caught in the act of doing something he was ashamed of. Perhaps the nuns were hoping for conversions, or repentance, but the whole thing seemed odd.

Lily bit her lip.

'But Sister, I just wanted to ask you—'

'I said out! Are you deaf?' she cried, and pushed and shoved Lily back through the door.

Head down, cheeks burning and concentrating on her feet as she walked down the corridor, Lily hurried off towards the stairs. She shivered. Whatever she had witnessed, she had an instinct it was something she should keep to herself. For now.

An hour later, after a quick belt through 'Guide Me O Thou Great Redeemer' in the refectory, after cups of milk were drunk and heels of buttered bread were demolished, Sister David announced they would all go on the Saturday Walk.

'Can we go to the beach, Sister?' said a small voice.

There was a rustle of excitement. Deirdre and Bobby's eyes were round and hopeful.

'No, most definitely not.'

There was a collective groan.

Whilst there was a commotion over stacking chairs and collecting tea trays, Aggie signalled with a wink, for Lily to come and join her and Janet. Outside she whispered instructions to Lily.

'OK, keep to the back of the line, stick with the stragglers, and then shoot off when we tell you. The nuns never notice. They'll think we're on an errand or something. So flaming boring this walk, everyone wants it over with.'

Half an hour later, the crocodile of children with Lily, Aggie and Janet lagging behind, reached the end of Virgin's Lane, Sister David, pointing out highlights on the way, blackberry bushes still with fruit on them, tracks made by a fox, a red squirrel leaping mid-air from one pine tree to another in a dizzying display of aeronautics. Just as they were about to turn and walk along the railway track down the path with the hawthorn bushes on either side, Janet poked Lily in the side and they peeled off from the group and took cover behind a gorse bush with its explosion of vivid yellow flowers, thorns pricking their shins as they crouched down, giggling.

Ten minutes later, they were on a train rocking on its tracks to Southport. They talked for the whole journey, Aggie and Janet taking it in turns to powder their noses and put on bright red lipstick, admiring their work in Janet's silver compact mirror.

'Go on, Lil,' said Janet, offering her a small pot of rouge from her beaded bag. When Lily hesitated, Janet said, 'Give it to me,' and took her chin. 'Use the tri-dot system. Three dots. One here, on your cheekbone, and one just below the tip of your nose, one under your eye. Smooth in the triangle like this,' she said, dotting blobs of the rouge on her face and vigorously rubbing at it with her thumb. 'Secret to perfect make-up is to use a good vanishing cream. You could look like a movie star because you're gorgeous, Lil, with all that lovely hair. You're just not making the best of what God gave you. You could have any fella you want.'

'I don't want any fella. I want my Vince.'

'Yes, but we all know Hitler's trying to blow our ships up with U-boat torpedoes. It's risky, all right, so I'd say keep your options open.'

It turned out that Janet was quite rich. 'Proper posh – they say "barth" instead of "bath",' said Aggie, which explained why she was happy to pay for the tickets, and she was the one who suggested they head off to Lord Street, with its elegant Victorian arcades and genteel department stores. The sea air was invigorating and the sun was bursting through the clouds, bleaching the paving stones. The three girls were an arresting sight. Janet and Aggie didn't seem concerned about the stares they received as they walked along, linking arms. It was Saturday; and Saturday, announced Janet, was not the time for church and endless Hail Marys and Rosaries, or darning socks for soldiers; it was the time when they should be having a laugh.

They arrived at the Copper Kettle and Janet took them straight to a table in the alcove with an arched bay window that looked onto the street. The ruched net curtains, the plastic daffodils gathering dust, the paper napkins seemed the height of sophistication to Lily.

'So tell us about your fella. What's he like?' Aggie asked Lily as she licked her teaspoon after unwrapping two sugar cubes and stirring them into the cup.

'What do you mean?' said Lily.

'I know you have a fella. Janet told me. You got a photo of him? Bet he's lovely in his navy uniform. Gorgeous.'

Lily flushed red with embarrassment.

'Bet he's the bees' knees,' persisted Aggie.

'Merchant navy don't get to wear the smart stuff. Just blue trousers and pullovers. Don't half make you itch and scratch, Vince says.'

'Merchant navy? Bad luck,' said Aggie.

Shifting about in the chair, Lily blushed as they fired questions at her about what he looked like: was he handsome? How long had they been courting?

'How did you meet him?'

'My parents run a dancing school. I used to dance with him. Competitions and the like.'

'So did you manage to get in a bit of how's your father while you hot diggety dogged around the dance floor?' Aggie said, and smiled.

Lily blushed deeper. It was always her blushing that let her down but this was her big love and she didn't like it that the girls were reducing it to a cheap joke.

'Come on, you can tell us. What's the matter? You don't need to be shy.'

'There's nothing much to tell.'

'Ciggie?' asked Aggie.

'When does he come home?' pressed Janet.

'I'm not sure.'

'Just as long as he comes back, I suppose. Can't ask more than that. That he's not coming back in a coffin or drowned at sea.'

Her heart lurched as she thought about Vince. Still no news. It had been almost three weeks now.

'Chin up,' Janet said. 'Now *this* is why we're here, Lily. Not the bloody scones and jam.' She nodded over to the small group of men in uniform who had just come in, the tinkling of the bell signalling their arrival.

'Jesus, would you look at the coloured fella! Not like he was born, more like he was dropped from heaven right here into the Copper Kettle,' Aggie giggled. She was talking about the tall, handsome soldier with tight black wiry curls and lively brown eyes. He had taken sheet music out of his bag and was propping it up on the piano.

The others, a skinny fellow and a chap with mousy hair, also in uniform, and a short, rotund fellow in civvies, began taking out instruments from cases

– a trumpet appeared and a banjo. 'Are they going to play?' whispered Lily.

'You wait,' said Janet.

The handsome fellow sat at the piano.

'Feast for the eyes, isn't he?' said Aggie, grinning and winking, as she lit up yet a cigarette. 'I would, in a heartbeat.'

'Would what?' asked Lily.

Aggie giggled. 'You really are a bit of a dozy mare, Lil.'

She suddenly realised what her new friend was talking about and blushed.

'Just a bit green, aren't you love?' said Janet, placing her hand on hers and giving it a reassuring squeeze.

He certainly looked a grand sight, even Lily had to admit, in his khaki uniform as he sat on the red velvet stool, finding the piano pedals with his feet. But it was only when he began to sing 'By The Sleepy Lagoon', after playing a few bars of introduction, that the tinkling of teaspoons against china and the low murmur of conversation reduced as people turned their heads in his direction, which explained why Aggie and Janet were behaving so giddily. The natural musicality of his beautiful voice, mellow, sweet, lazy, and smooth as treacle, was hypnotising, with the lilting West Indian cadence adding to the charm of the song. This was the kind of music she was more used to hearing in the dance hall than in a cafe full of old ladies. And even then, the jazz men she knew, friends of her father's in dance bands, or fellows she had met through her mother? None of them could have hoped to capture even a tenth of how this chap sounded.

Finally, after a few choruses, and a polite round of applause, Janet stood up and beckoned him over. What on earth is she doing? thought Lily. But he smiled back. And he *was* coming over to their table.

'Well, hello, Janet. You make a nice threesome, ladies. Who's this?' he asked, taking a cigarette from a silver case, tapping the end of it on the case, and lighting it with a Zippo lighter he produced from his trouser pocket.

He was smiling at Lily.

'I'm Clarence,' he said. 'Pleased to make your acquaintance ...' The first thing she noticed was the flash of gold in his smile. A gold tooth! How wonderful. It looked strange and unfamiliar in this refined Victorian seaside setting with old ladies with stiff hairdos sipping tea from delicate china cups, pouring in milk from silver jugs and stirring in sugar from bowls with lids and tongs.

The banjo player, one foot on a chair, continued to strum. A man at a table suddenly got up, produced a tissue and comb from his pocket, and started playing along and tapping his feet to 'Blame It On My Youth'. Music, conversation and laughter filled the smoke-laced cafe.

And then, without warning, Janet suddenly stood, snaked her arm around Clarence's waist, and began to sway in time, clicking her fingers.

'Hey, Lil. Watch this,' she said, leaning in to whisper to her.

Janet put her hands around Clarence's neck and there was a ripple of consternation around the tea room. Not that she cared. She was laughing now, twirling into him. He looked uncomfortable, as though he knew exactly what Janet was doing, and it made Lily feel uncomfortable too.

People began to stare, but Janet seemed to be enjoying it. She held her head up and swivelled around to face the ladies sitting behind her.

'What are you looking at?' she asked. And when they didn't answer, she repeated, 'Hey, can't a girl dance with a fella? What are you gawping at?'

She grinned as they shook their heads, tutted, and returned to their tea.

'Go back to your mates, Clarence ...'

She pecked him on the cheek, then leaned down to whisper to Lily, 'They love it when he sings, but they don't like it so much when he doesn't know his place. The old cows. Come on, Lily, let's get out of here. The nuns will have a hissy fit of they think we've lied about where we are, and if this gets back to them, we'll all be sent to hell.'

Clarence, on his way to walking back to the piano, stopped and turned. 'I didn't get your name,' he said to Lily, sucking a match, and smiling at her.

'I'm Lily.'

'Clarence Aimé. Pleased to meet you,' he said, sticking out his hand.

'Aimé. Means loved. Isn't that romantic, Lil?' said Aggie.

'Pleased to meet you too,' said Lily, ignoring her new friend and feeling her cheeks reddening slightly.

'You enjoy the music?'

'Yes. Grand. I liked the way you played "Sleepy Lagoon",' she stuttered. 'Real twist on it. Never heard it like that before. Syncopated rhythm on the chorus.'

He smiled. 'That's jazz,' he said. 'If you can make a song your own, that's the trick. Musical trick of the light.' And he grinned, revealing the match stuck between his teeth. 'I'm impressed. Bet you two featherbrains don't even know what she's on about,' he said, to Aggie and Janet. 'Syncopation, if you do it right, gets to your soul, isn't that so, Lily?'

'We need to go,' said Janet.

'Bye, fellas.' Aggie waved to the two other men, wiggling her bottom, shouting over the heads of the people in the cafe, as they left, giggling and happy, glad to have escaped the nuns for a few precious hours.

'Hey, fancy hiring a boat? We've got time,' said Janet on the way back as they walked through Floral Gardens. She pointed to the line of small rowing boats bobbing about on the lake. 'Love boats, they're called,' she said, with a grin. 'You and Clarence should take one out, eh, Lily? Mr Aimé and the lovely Lily in a love boat!'

Aggie, seeing Lily blush again, seemed to find this hilarious and giggled all the way to the edge of the boating pool.

They went over and Janet hooked one with a stick, pulled it to the jetty, stepped inside it and held out her hands to Aggie and Lily. Gingerly, Lily followed Aggie and they all shrieked as the boat wobbled. Janet shoved her fingers into her mouth and whistled, and Aggie creased over with more giggles, pushing a fist into her side as she was laughing so much. The boy manning the booth squinted out across the lake. He came over, handed over oars to them and, strangely, didn't ask for money.

'I saw the way Clarence looked you up and down. Like he wanted to eat you up,' Aggie said, pulling on the oars. 'You think he's good at the piano? You should see him dance. Every Friday he's at Sullivan's Dance Hall. Send shivers down your spine. Does this thing with his hips ...'

She stood up, mimed thrusting her hips, curled her lip, and the boat wobbled dangerously and nearly tipped over as she did so, causing them all to shriek as she lost her balance and roared with laughter as she thumped down, gripping the sides to steady herself, which only made it rock more and everyone shriek louder.

They set off again, Lily rowing now. After a little while she faltered, and let go of the oars, allowing them to rest in the rowlocks. 'I've told you, it's Vince I love. And besides I could never go with another man.'

'Don't be such an idiot. You only live once. I've had loads of fellas. I've had two on the go at the same time, three actually,' Janet said, and winked, and Aggie smirked. 'You never know what's going to happen with this bloody war so it's good to have someone on the back burner. Now start rowing again, we're drifting.'

She heard Aggie laugh. The wind was picking up and the water ruffled up across the surface as they floated to the centre of the lake..

'You're right, Lily, I know. But war changes the usual rules,' said Janet more gently.

'So what d'you say? That chap. Did you see the way he looked at you? Did you fancy him or what?' said Aggie.

Lily frowned. 'No!'

'All's I'm saying, it's good to keep your options open. Your Vinnie could be dead in a month, could be dead now. When did you last hear from him?'

Lily's face fell.

'Don't be such a cow, Ag. You've made her cry.'

'No, you haven't. It's just the wind,' replied Lily, with a toss of her hair, and thrusting out her chin. 'Here, take the oars.'

After half an hour rowing, Aggie and Janet singing snatches of the songs Clarence had been singing earlier and urging Lily to join in whilst trailing their hands in the water, they set off back to St Jude's on a train that swayed on the tracks, with the countryside rushing past them in streaks of autumnal oranges and yellow.

'What about the girls?' Lily said suddenly, still troubled by what she had seen that morning in the chapel. 'The fallen girls at St Jude's? We never see them. But I've heard crying through the walls. No one talks about the girls.'

There was a pause.

'The girls? Well, here's the thing, love. We *are* the girls,' replied Aggie, sharing a look with Janet. 'What do you want to know?'

Chapter 12

The way Aggie had said it, so straightforwardly, so simply, had probably been the most shocking thing of all. When they got back, they told Lily to wait in the rectory for half an hour and then meet them in the dormitory. When she arrived there, still reeling, there was a girl sitting on a sunken camp bed, pale and wan with hollowed-out cheeks and pockmarked skin, limp hair with one plait undone that looked like it hadn't been touched by a brush for weeks. Lily recognised her straight away. It was the girl at the window, she was sure of it. She was fiddling with a rubber band on her lap as though she didn't want to be here, as though she had things to do. Janet was sitting on the window ledge, a pillow wedged under her bottom, one leg crossed over the other. She fixed Lily with a look and then nodded to the girl.

'This is Bridget. Go on, Bridge,' she said. The girl stared into her lap, then lifted her head tiredly and raised her eyes. 'Tell her,' repeated Janet.

The girl just sat there silently, picking at the frayed skin around nails, her socks sagging around her ankles.

'Why d'you think we're here, Lily? For the craic?' Aggie said.

The girl shifted and the bedsprings squeaked as she exchanged a look with Janet. Then, with her head drooping again, winding the rubber band around a purpling finger, she sighed.

'Tell her about your baby, Bridget,' said Janet. 'Don't be frightened of Lily, she's all right.'

'Oh,' said the girl. She sighed again and opened her mouth to speak, then blinked away a tear and gazed out of the window.

'They took her babe away last week,' Janet said. 'They gave her to a woman, didn't they, Bridget?'

The girl nodded and Lily could see that the skin on her hands was cracked and sore.

'Looked like a bloody movie star, this woman,' said Janet. 'All done up in a posh Rothmoor coat and her husband drove a Jag and wore a trilby hat. Kept talking about his flipping car. "Corners like it's on rails," he said to Sister Assumpta. I heard him saying that when he walked up the path with her. They made me meet them at the gate and bring her to Assumpta's office. What did Assumpta care about the Jag? Apart from it meaning she could get a sack load of money out of him for Bridget's baby!'

'Sure, she smelled like a movie star,' said Bridget in a small voice. It was the first thing she had said. And after a long silence: 'You know, the lady's perfume? You could choke on it, it was that strong …'

'Vol de nuit? Guerlain?' asked Janet.

Bridget turned to her and frowned.

'What you on about?' said Aggie.

'Never mind, go on, love,' said Janet.

'She held me baby, only for ten minutes or so, but when me bairn was crying for me, hungry, and I had to feed her … well …'

She winced at the memory of taking her back, of how her baby had smelled of the woman. That milky creamy smell of her little girl was contaminated by the woman's perfume. 'She whiffed like Mrs Hardbottom – that was her name, that'll be me baby's name I suppose, poor lamb …' She frowned, as though this had just occurred to her, and that was another stab to her heart along with all the other piercing wounds, in this sorry business of her stupid Ivor getting her up the duff, again. She continued, 'Ah, the smell was beautiful. Expensive. Like Parma Violets. But it wasn't the smell of me little mite, Dolly.'

'And your bosoms. Still full of milk, aren't they? Show her,' said Aggie, who was listening, leaning against the doorjamb, chewing gum.

Bridget lifted her shirt and showed Lily two wet patches on her greying brassiere.

Aggie handed her a handkerchief. 'It always starts at the same time, doesn't it?'

'Aye,' she replied, stuffing the handkerchief down a bra cup, and wincing.

Lily saw more tears gathering in Bridget's eyes. Instinctively she touched her stomach.

Bridget continued, 'I live in the annex. That's where the wards are. The nursery wards and the labour wards. My last baby, well, he . . .' Tears filled her eyes.

'*Last* baby?' said Lily, shocked.

'Her last baby died. Bridget nearly did an' all. Terrible shame. A day old, wasn't he, my love? At least this little nipper, Dolly, she came out kicking and screaming and went to a good home, didn't she?'

Bridget nodded.

'Her mother, your mam, Nellie, she won't have anything to do with you, will she? Disowned you, hasn't she, love?'

Bridget winced, and Lily was reminded of something her own mother had said once. 'You don't want to end up drowned, like Nellie's girl.' Was this *Bridget*? Was her mother telling everyone she was dead?

'And you, Janet? Why are you here?' asked Lily, nervously.

Janet took a cigarette out, puffed on it, and waved the smoke away.

'Six weeks ago I had my daughter. It still hurts me down there, you know. It's knackered my privates up, that's for sure. I had sixteen bloody stitches. They didn't tell me that. Had to sit on a rubber ring for a week until Assumpta said she was taking it away as she didn't want the little ones, the evacuees, asking questions. God forbid the children would think a person might actually have sex! Or that they might find out the real truth about bloody storks and whatnot.'

Lily was shocked as much by their low throaty laughter, as anything else. They almost seemed to be enjoying themselves, as if their predicament had brought some darkly comic humour into their lives.

'I was supposed to go to the hospital because there were complications, so too risky to have my baby here and I had my Woollies' wedding ring and vanity case all laid out on the bed. But the baby decided to come before I got to the end of the path. Oh, that was a sight. The nuns screaming and howling like bloody banshees. They took me into the scullery – that was as far as they got me – and pulled the little lass right out of me. Used a pair of flaming salad tongs to finish the job. There was such a commotion. And the St Columba's kids, who were having a PE lesson outside, were all peering in the window to get a look, standing on buckets and each other's shoulders. Some of them were crying when they saw the blood because it was *everywhere* – on the floor, all over the table. One of the sisters ran out but she'd forgotten to wash her hands and there was blood all over them, up to her wrists, and the kiddies started screaming their heads off when they saw her. And God, Sister Assumpta was *furious*. That was the best part.'

She laughed. How can she *laugh*? thought Lily. Doesn't she care about her child?

'If you had your baby, why are you still here?' she said.

'Why are any of us still here?' she said, mysteriously. 'Why are *you* here?'

'I've told you. I'm here as a sister's help,' Lily explained. And then she began to wonder. Why *was* she here? She was the only one who slept in the same dormitories as the children. Aggie and Janet were on another floor, Bridget was hidden away in Ambrose Hall. Also, no one had asked her to do anything much, apart from clear dishes away and chop up wood, which was not much more than the other girls seemed to do.

'Janet's here because her parents will pay the nuns when she leaves. Up until then, though, they want her to stay here and work. Sort of penance, isn't it, Janet? They want her to go home pure and reformed. They think after making all those Rosary Beads for the nuns, she'll have grown angel wings and her only love will be Jesus and she'll never want to have sex again. Crazy.'

Lily frowned.

'Crazy, for sure,' murmured Janet in agreement.

'Bridget will tell you *that*,' said Aggie. 'Ivor was pulling down your drawers the minute you got out of here, and Jesus went right out of the window, didn't he, love? Jesus didn't even get a look in. You just wanted your Ivor and you were going to let him do whatever he wanted to you, because to hell with it, that's what you wanted as well.'

'Couldn't have put it better, meself,' said Bridget, regretfully.

'Anyway,' said Janet. 'Where else can I go? My mother and the nuns have decided I can stay for a few months as long as I help with the sewing. I'm good with a needle, can stitch something out of thin air any day of the week. So I'm working the debt of shame off – and at least I don't have to sleep in Ambrose any more now that I've had my baby and I can mix with the evacuees. My mother at least made sure I was moved out of Ambrose, though Sister Assumpta would much rather I was still hidden away there. "Jesus is love, you little whore", she whispers in my ear when she stands over me, watching me do blanket stitch when I'm buttonholing their shirts. Anyway, I'm off soon. Not sure where. My father doesn't want me back. Just chucking money at the nuns buys me some extra time, though, and my own room which I share with Aggie.'

Lily shivered.

'I expect you're wondering about me?' said Aggie. 'My baby isn't due until March.'

Lily's eyes widened.

'Didn't have a clue, did you?'

She smoothed down her dress. And, of course, now Lily could see it. The rise of her stomach? Well, it wasn't too many scones and jam after all – she had a baby in there!

'Oh God!' said Lily. 'I had no idea.'

'Why would you?' asked Aggie. 'I'm about four months pregnant. I can still hide it pretty well. Except for these bloody things, they're already enormous.'

She cupped her breasts in her hands, jiggling them up and down as if she was weighing two bags of flour, deciding which one was the heavier of the two. 'Can't bear this bloody brassiere! Over Shoulder Boulder Holder, I call it! Anyway. It's my dirty little secret that I'm supposed to be ashamed of. I'm supposed to tell no one. That's the pact between my parents and the nuns. They pay handsomely, like Janet's parents. As long as I say nothing, they even pay so I don't have to do the laundry, like poor Bridget here. I just have to help with evacuees until I can't hide it any more. Then I'll be shoved in the annex with the other poor wretches. In the meantime, Sister Assumpta gets rich on the back of it.'

Bridget, with her long lifeless curtains of hair hiding her face, twisted the band around her very purpled finger. There were no concessions for her. It was obvious she was as poor as a church mouse. Lily turned to Janet.

'Your baby. Where is he now?'

'Who bloody knows?' she replied with a shrug. 'Probably on his way to Canada.'

Lily gasped. 'Canada!' She sat in frozen silence.

'Or Australia. I'd rather Canada. Because of my freckles. What if my baby has my freckles? Imagine him burning up in that hot sun? My parents have said I have to stay here until all that is settled as well. They don't want me running around Liverpool, trying to find my baby. Though there's no chance of that. What do they think, that I'm going to jump on a ship or something? Hammer on folks' doors asking if they've got my child? If I'm truthful, I'm not so sure I'd want him anyway. I just want my life back. What can I give a baby? Nowt!'

One thing Janet has to be admired for is her honesty, thought Lily. She was unflinching. She looked again at Bridget, now straightening, and re-straightening the hem of her dress. It was a disturbing sight.

'And Bridget?'

'Bridget's going round the bend, aren't you, love? Third time she's been in here, poor mite. Bridget's never leaving this bloody place.'

There was a silence.

'Chin up, love,' said Janet to Lily. And she tossed back her head, full of spirit, and smiled. 'We had a grand day out, didn't we?'

Chapter 13

Back in Liverpool, life had continued more or less as usual for Stella, and for all the dark cloud of worry, the Laffertys managed to put aside the thoughts of what new horror each day might bring with this blessed blitz and did what they were good at: carried on carrying on. And Stella had enough to be preoccupied with. Food had become so short, she was getting sick of Woolton Pie and she couldn't face another swede, cauliflower or turnip so she was permanently hungry. Thank God for the coupons. She stuck them in her ration book and enjoyed waving it at John at the fishmonger's, not having to beg for what he had leftover under the counter, but demanding that she got her fair share. Even though it was a paltry offering, it was better than nothing. Everyone was doing their bit. Then, one morning, Stella came bustling into the kitchen after a trip to the grocer's and found Cliff sitting in front of the range, taking a swig of the tea then nursing it against his cheek.

'What are you doing here?' she asked. 'You should be at work.'

'Aye. I should. But the foreman has laid me off. The truth is, I'm not suited to this dock work. It's not for me.'

'Not for you? What d'you mean?' said Stella.

His sinewy body shifted in his seat.

'Hauling stuff around. In the end it does for you. You know I'm not brawny, like the other lads. There's more to me than Cliff the docker.'

Stella looked at him. 'Of course, I know that, but if you've got something to say to me, just say it. I don't need you dancing around the blackberry bush like this, and I've got other things to worry about.'

'I do need to say something, actually.'

Stella stood up, tried to ignore him, and began opening and closing cupboards as if she was looking for something.

'Did you hear what I said?'

She banged a drawer shut, which gave him his answer.

'There are other options to help the war effort. There are things a man can do where he can be respected,' he said, raking his hand back through his hair.

Stella sighed. 'What's wrong with the docks? There is nothing wrong with a fellow who works hard with his hands. There's dignity in work. Anyway, what *things*? You *are* respected. You've always been respected at the dance school.'

'I've made a decision. You tried to put me off it once, but this time I'm putting my foot down. The army needs pianists. I have to go to London, the Palladium, for an interview, but it's just a formality.'

Stella's mouth gaped open. 'A job! I don't understand, Cliff. You're not talking about Every Night Something Awful again?' she snapped, tossing her head back for emphasis. 'I thought they had turned you down?'

His brow creased into a frown. 'Give over, Stella.'

'So you're determined to sign up! What now then?'

'Not really sure, love. I've only really talked about it to the fella at the pub. Came in wearing a suit. Bought me a drink.'

'What is it about fellows in bloody suits?' snapped Stella.

'He said Egypt could be on the cards. Camp in the Western Desert. They've lost their pianist.'

'Egypt! What? Are you mad? No!' she said, slamming her fist on the table, the strength of it making the crockery rattle on the Welsh dresser.

'Oh, Stella, what are you talking about? How d'you think it makes me feel? Everyone doing their bit, seeing my friend desperate to get out there and pull his weight, and me, just sitting here pretending I'm a docker so as to skive out of my duty. They need as many pianists as they can get to play for the troops out there. As a morale booster. Besides, I hate the docks,' he said, bitterly. 'Look where it gets them all? They're shells of fellas, dead at forty-five, half of them. I'm the *man* around here, Stella. It's time for me to make some decisions.'

'What about if we took the act on the road again?' she asked, plaintively. She clutched the collar of her dress, winsomely, tilted her head to one side.

'What do you mean?'

'I could sing again. We could dance. Tour. People here need cheering up. I could sing for money – you know I'm good at it. Everywhere in this city there are people making money from music and dancing. They can't get enough of it.'

He paled. 'Is *this* why you wanted to send the kids off? So we could be free to do the act again?'

'Don't be stupid!' She wavered. 'But now you mention it, have you not seen the fella driving around in his Rolls Royce, hanging around the pubs, looking for people to make a fortune out of? Look at Vera Lynn. We knew Vera when she was playing those awful dives and gin joints. Perhaps we could—'

'No, that's an idiotic idea.'

Her tone modulated to a sweeter sound. It was as if the idea was beginning to take shape in her head. 'We could do competition dancing again,' she cooed.

She reached out to him and, in a desperately sentimental gesture, grabbed his lapels, pulled herself to him and placed the palms of her hands flat on each of his cheeks, then swayed back and forth. 'We were good, Cliff. Still got the magic, I bet. Remember how many medals and cups we won? No one could touch us, Cliff.'

He pushed her away in a sharp, angry shove.

'Woman, you're insane! Why would you want to stop me feeling like a man? Look at you, mincing and preening like a tired old has-been. It's not good for people to see me like this. They know I'm only shifting sacks and hauling stuff to get out of the war. All the other dockers laugh at me, Stella. They know it was you who organised me to get the job at Huskisson Dock and I cringe every time I hear some fella muttering under his breath, "That's the piano fella who thinks he's too good for the war. He's not a real docker. He's just a war dodger." I want to wear a uniform, Stella. Simple as that.'

'Since when have we cared about what people think?' she said.

'You talk a load of bloody nonsense, Stella. I'm going to London to see what's what. Everyone is saying I'm stupid not to just tell you how things are. You're my wife, damn it.'

'Don't listen to them! Seriously, when did we ever care about what people think of us?'

'No, Stella. Bring Lily back from Freshdale and she can keep you company. I don't know what she's doing at St Jude's in the first place.'

Stella pursed her lips, lit a match then turned on the gas. The noxious smell hit the back of her throat.

'You know I'll never bring Lily back – or the kids. As long as this war is going on, she's staying out of harm's way.'

'There you are, at it again. You always want to be in the saddle or pulling the strings, Stella. You might do it with your children, but you're not doing it with me. I love you, but this time I'm deciding what's what.'

'You'll regret this, Cliff,' she said bitterly. 'And to think I thought it was Hitler who was splitting up this family, and now it turns out to be you!'

'Don't talk rot.'

Suddenly the sound of the sirens went off again.

'Not again . . .' she said flatly. She put her hands over her ears. The long moan was low and flat, the horrible sound that they all loathed so much. 'Can't stand it!'

There was a silence for a minute or two, followed by another unbroken wail that crescendoed to an ear-splitting pitch. It was a howl, like that of an ancient creature being awoken from the depths of the Mersey.

He stood, opened the cupboard door, and the handle came away in his hand. 'This place is falling down around us. There was no water this morning.'

'I'm fine with the wash house.'

'They say that'll be gone soon. I don't know. I think, if I go away, you should go with your mam to

Morecambe, and when this war is over we can all have a fresh start somewhere else.'

'Look, Cliff, I know everything is going to be different soon, when the bombing gets even worse, I know that. I've heard what's happening in Europe. But when I look around at these walls, I think they'll outlive me now. So why bother? As long as we survive.'

He sighed. 'The fact is, I don't want to be organising the kids' funeral, or yours, or your mam's, because this place has been bombed and you're the fools who all stayed put.'

'My funeral?' said Gram, who had wandered in, puzzled. 'What about my funeral? I'm not dead yet.'

'Shurrup, Mam,' said Stella.

'Wouldn't you like to go somewhere safer? Maybe think about a fresh start, Gram?' asked Cliff, twisting around to face her.

'Fresh start? I'm fat as a sow and the wrong side of sixty. No fresh starts for me,' came the reply as she picked at a piece of carrot roll congealing on a dish and popped it into her mouth.

'I don't know that you are, Mam,' said Cliff.

'Give over, Cliff. Don't drag Mam into it,' snapped Stella.

Ivy sucked her teeth. 'The Corporation have stopped doing repairs. That's why everything has gone to pot. It's a disgrace.'

Stella, sitting in the armchair now, stared ahead resolutely. One of her legs crossed the other, an old sling-back sandal dangling off the end of one foot.

'You're trying my patience, woman. You really are,' Cliff said, exasperated. 'Do you realise how little money we have left now since we've closed the school? I can't make a bean at the docks. Standing in the pen each morning, hoping to get chosen by the foreman for a pathetic day's work, is no way to make a living. The rivet work is paid per flaming screw and I'm not trained for it! But I have a *skill*, Stella. I can play the piano. And I'm going to bloody use it.'

Stella shrugged.

'What?' she said, glaring at him as he opened his mouth then shut it.

'Nothing,' he replied. And with that, he drew himself up, grabbed his cap, and marched off in a whirl of disgruntled huffs and sighs, and shut the door so hard the reverberation caused the poker to fall and clatter onto the floor.

Chapter 14

It was the house being so quiet that Stella found the most difficult. Matt had his job at Cunard's and, when she wasn't bickering with Cliff about him leaving the docks and signing up for ENSA, every night whilst he was at the pub she would sit alone at the kitchen table with a glass of cheap gin cradled in her hands. She talked to no one, apart from Matt and Annie and her mother, if she could help it. The constant bombing, the running back and forth to the shelters, meant she went to bed exhausted, and woke up exhausted. Some days she just wandered about in a negligee that gaped at the neck all day, and Annie had to tell her to stop making a dreadful show of herself, especially in front of visitors.

Then one morning, Annie came in and announced, 'I've decided, Stella. You're going to Freshdale to see the children. It will do you good. You can take the kids out for the day. You promised you'd go and visit them, they must be missing you,' she said. 'Besides, you need to get out of this city. Seaside will put a bit of colour in your cheeks. No more moping around the place. It'll do you good. Do you hear me, Stella?'

'I don't know. The seaside?' asked Stella. 'It's not exactly the seaside, is it? And it's hardly the weather for buckets and spades. It's October!'

'Why not?' Annie said with a sigh.

'Well, for a start, the beach is so bleak. The tide never comes in and you have to walk miles just to dip your toe in the water. Either that or there's a good chance you'll drown when you get stranded on those shifting sandbanks. Not what you'd call a day out, is it?'

'It's not about a *day out*. You just need to see those kiddies. Nothing's stopping you from going to see them. They'll be missing you. Little Deirdre especially. You'll have a lovely time. Small children don't notice the weather. They'll just love running about in the dunes and having a paddle. They don't feel the cold. It's all been arranged,' she said as she fussed around the kitchen. 'I'll go and find the kiddies' costumes.' And then, without waiting for a reply, she went upstairs to look for them.

'Swimming costumes!' cried Stella, shaking her head as she thought back to Ivy spending hours unravelling old jumpers and knitting Bobby a pair of trunks from a pattern until her fingers were sore. Stella suspected this was more about Annie getting her out of the door, than worrying about how the kids were coping, otherwise she wouldn't be talking such nonsense.

'You're going to give those kiddies a smashing treat. Perfect weather for it. Bracing. But not too cold,' Annie said determinedly as she came back into the room.

Stella nodded vaguely, turned back to pumping the bellows of the range, and shrugged a non-committal shrug. 'I'll go. But I'm not taking woolly swimming costumes. Useless at the best of times,' she muttered.

An hour later, the train Stella was on pulled into Freshdale Station. Ten minutes after that she was standing outside the huge iron gates of St Jude's, wearing a serge puppytooth coat that looked like it could have been Matt's and a woollen hat. She could already feel her bones aching in the damp autumn sea air. The Gothic turrets and the bars on some of the windows made her shiver. Pushing open a smaller side gate with a padlock hanging loosely on a chain that she looped over the swirling iron work, she went in. Taking a deep breath, she made her way past the flower bed and across the manicured front lawn.

She went up the steps and pushed the bell. It was Sister David who opened the door.

'Mam!' cried Deirdre and Bobby, appearing from behind the nun, hurtling past her and flinging themselves at their mother. Kisses and hugs exchanged, they wrapped themselves up in their mother's skirts and clung to her legs, breathing in the scent of her. Deirdre suddenly started stamping her feet in delight, running up and down on the spot, making small thudding sounds on the wooden floor. 'Will there be donkey rides, Mam?' she cried.

'It's not that kind of seaside,' replied Sister David, thinking of the windswept beach, the dunes with the marram grass that whipped your shins, the tide that never came in.

'Give us a kiss, Lil,' said Stella when Lily came along the corridor. Lily offered her cheek to her. Stella planted a warm kiss on it and Lily backed away quickly, shifting from foot to foot, a little embarrassed. She was sure she had smelled the whiff of alcohol on her mother's breath.

'How are you, love?'

Lily wanted to tell her about Aggie and Janet and the tragic Bridget, but now wasn't the time or place. 'I'm fine,' she said.

'Let's give these children a smashing day out and go and make some memories,' said Stella, squeezing her hand.

She was trying her best, Lily could see that. But she looked tense. Like she wanted to get out of the place as quickly as she could. And who could blame her?

'Let's go and see the sea!' said Bobby.

'Let's go and see the sea,' echoed Deirdre. And they giggled and chorused their new song, feeling very pleased with themselves.

'Give over with that racket!' cried Stella. 'You're already giving me a splitting headache. Now, let's go and see what's what, shall we?'

'Are you sure this is a good idea?' asked Lily.

'According to Annie, it is!' said Stella, leading them out of the door.

When they got to the track that led to the beach, there was a car parked in the clearing, sheltered under a circle of pine trees. It was a rusting blue Morris Oxford and, as they approached, Stella shooed them on, hoping they would ignore the steamed-up windows and the blurred shapes of the couple inside.

'What are they doing, Mam?' asked Deirdre, turning back to look with a curious stare.

'Never mind,' she said. 'Let's go and see if the tide's in.'

'Courting, necking, snogging,' whispered Bobby to Deirdre, who giggled.

'The tide never is in, but we could go and have a look,' said Lily, diverting their attention.

When they reached the bank of dunes with the sea just beyond, Stella's feet were getting tired. The damp air filled her lungs. Her hair, blown by the wind, went sticky, and at the back it became glued together in a clump. They climbed over the sand hills, using their hands and feet to pull themselves up, the marram grass pricking and scratching the skin of Bobby's calves through his trousers, and making him shriek and cry out that he was being stabbed in the leg.

When they got to the top of the dunes, Lily gasped. Along the beach were the rolls of barbed wire that everyone had talked of. Even though she was expecting it, it was startling to see it.

The children's faces fell.

'Does that mean we have to go back, Mam?'

Stella gathered herself. 'It does not,' she answered and, shading her eyes with her hand, scoured the shore. 'There's a gap!' she said excitedly. Her mood was lifting. Stella had always loved a challenge. 'Follow me!' she cried, and marched on ahead.

'Wait!' Deirdre shouted as her brother, without stopping for thought, bounded on ahead.

'Come on! The tide's in! Come and see! The tide's in! Isn't it brilliant?' he cried.

'I've never seen it like that before,' said Stella, shoving away the stray pieces of hair that were blowing in her face. Bobby jumped off the top of the sand dune and, tripping and leaping, stumbling and rolling, landed in a heap at the bottom. Stella and the others followed more slowly and then, pulling the bottom of her sleeves over her hands, Stella carefully moved the barbed wire away so that they could run onto the shore.

They raced towards the crashing waves that foamed brown surf instead of white and the sea tossed up broken bricks and pop bottles. A ship in the distance belched as it sounded its foghorn.

'Watch this!' Deirdre shouted and did a running handspring, falling on her bottom with a thump. Then she lay down flat and opened her legs into a V-shape and moved her arms away from the sides of her body, up above her head.

'An angel!' she called, standing up and pointing at the sand. 'Come on!' she cried, beckoning wildly to Lily. And she looked so happy. If only I could freeze this moment in time, thought Lily. 'Come on, Mam! What are you waiting for? We've come all this way!' cried Deirdre, trying to make herself heard above the roar of the waves.

Stella danced up to Bobby, hoiking her skirts up. The sea seemed to stretch away from them for miles and miles.

'Isn't this smashing?' she cried. 'Just what we all need!' as they all took off their wellington boots and shoes and socks.

Shielding her eyes from the stinging particles of sand, Lily shrieked as the cold water dribbled between her toes and over her feet. She took Bobby's hand and together they paddled up to their ankles. Deirdre, meanwhile had tucked her skirts into her knickers, and raced along the beach. With a stick she drew a large heart in the sand, and wrote her name in the middle of it.

Lily shivered. The corners of her mouth were caked in a salty white residue and the sand beneath her feet felt ice cold.

'Your face is wet, Mam!' cried Bobby.

'It's the spray,' answered Stella. 'I can't hear you!'

Their clothes flapping against their bodies sounded like drum rolls.

'The spray from the sea!'

Stella stood next to Lily to catch her breath, watching the children race back to the sea and shriek as they jumped over the breaking waves.

'I've got some news, love. Your dad's joining up. Been offered a job as a pianist with ENSA.'

'That's good,' said Lily. She placed her toe in a pool of water and rearranged her wavering reflection. But when she saw her mother's eyes fill with tears she said, 'Isn't it?'

'He could be gone for months, years, even. The job is in some godforsaken place in Egypt, can you believe it?'

Lily frowned. She thought of Vince.

'Let him go, Mam,' she said.

Stella shrugged her shoulders. 'I don't think I can stop him, even if I wanted to.'

'Then let him go, Mam.'

She felt a tug on her sleeve suddenly. It was a shivering Bobby, panting, exhilarated and exhausted, pulling her towards the foot of the dunes. 'Let's sit here,' he said, collapsing and catching his breath, when they reached a place where the sand had piled up on one side creating a kind of windbreak. 'It's quiet here.' He cupped his hands around his mouth and called over to Deirdre who was cantering along the beach pretending to be a horse, shouting, 'Giddyup!'

She joined them in a jumble of limbs and shivering curls and giggles, and here, out of the wind, the foot of the dunes felt like a gentle place, a secretive, quiet place. They all stared out to the horizon, knees drawn up to their chests and shoved up their jumpers, happy, tired, and contemplative. 'There's an old shipwreck out there, half sunken into a mudflat, and sometimes you can see its mast poking out. And that's Blackpool Tower, round that corner bit. Look at the horizon, now look there … follow my arm … Can you see …? Put your head behind my shoulder and look down my arm …' said Stella.

Both younger children close now, Stella turned and, smiling, looked over her shoulder at Lily. 'It's lovely here, isn't it?' She picked up a handful of sand and let the grains trickle through her fingers.

'Mam, are you crying?' asked Bobby. He touched his mother's cheek.

'Must be the sea,' she answered, wiping away the moisture. 'All this fresh air.'

The disused tramlines, the blinking lights of the docks, the container ships and cranes, swung away into the distance. They could just about make out the barrage balloons bobbing about like strange, alien creatures. Lily looked up into the sky and Bobby pulled his sleeves over his fingers and stuffed his hands into his armpits.

Meanwhile, Lily unwrapped the jam sandwiches Annie had made and they all felt granules of sand as they bit into the butties and the sandwiches crunched, and they wondered how that had happened as they had all wiped their hands thoroughly, just like Stella had told them to.

Stella stood, brushed the sand off her skirts, then stood back and looked at Lily. 'You look bonny,' she said. 'The fresh air has brought some colour into your cheeks. And those nuns are certainly feeding you well,' she said, pushing a strand of hair off Lily's face. It was about to rain, and it was time to go home. 'Let's go. Kiddies are dead on their feet.'

'Just one more paddle,' Lily said. And this time she tucked her skirts up into her knickers. 'Here, take my cardigan, I don't want to get it wet,' she said, peeling it off and flinging it at her.

Stella couldn't help looking her daughter up and down, marvelling at her dark hair cascading over her shoulders, her graceful limbs and plump lips, taking some pride in Lily as she did so. But when a sudden gust of wind whipped Lily's skirts causing them to cling to every contour of her body, Stella frowned.

'Your bosoms!' she said. 'Mind you, I'm not surprised you're putting on a bit of weight. You wolfed down those sarnies!'

Lily cast her eyes down at her body, and shrugged. She didn't know what she was talking about. 'I'm a little fatter. It's all the bread-and-butter pudding, Mam, and the nuns feeding me their horrible sweet porridge.' It was the first time she had thought about her thickening waist, her brassiere that was pinching under her arms, tighter now, but ...? No! What on earth was her mother suggesting?

Stella rattled on. 'Well, thank God for that, Lil. For a moment – for a moment, I thought ... oh, dear me, thank goodness ...'

Lily didn't say anything but worry took hold of her. Stella's words had planted a seed of anxiety in her head and as she looked out to the sea, she mentally counted on her fingers the days and weeks since she had had the curse, only for the thoughts to become a muddle inside her head.

But, ever optimistic, she pushed it aside with a shiver, shrugging away the idea, reassuring herself that this war had meant everything was behaving differently to how it usually did. Nothing arrived on time – trains, trams, buses, food deliveries, even cinema and theatre shows, couldn't be relied on any more, stopping halfway through, starting again only when the bombing finished or the sirens stopped. Maybe, just maybe, the upheaval of war was what was causing chaos inside her body as well as inside her head. Yes, that was it. Of course, that was it. The other would be just too terrible to contemplate.

Chapter 15

'Rosie? Dead?'

Lily stood in Sister David's office with the Bakelite receiver pressed so hard to her ear it was making it burn. She felt her legs buckle beneath her. Her face, expressionless at first, crumpled into sadness moments later.

'Looks like it. I'm sorry I'm telling you on the phone. Are you all right, love?' said her Aunt Annie. 'We don't know anything much yet, apart from the house was badly hit from the air.'

Lily looked at the ceiling in order to blink away the tears. 'Oh, Auntie,' she said. 'She should have stayed in Liverpool.'

'I know. To think she left Caryl Street to be safe and then got hit in Belle Vale.'

'Is Mam there?'

'She's too upset to speak, I'm afraid.'

That made sense. Lily knew that, for Stella, losing Rosie would be almost as painful as one of her own children dying. Feeling numb, an hour later Lily stood at the door of St Jude's refectory where she had just finished clearing away the plates of bread and milk. Janet and Aggie were the first people she told.

'I'm sorry. Were you close?' said Janet, when she saw Lily beginning to cry.

'She was a neighbour, but yes. She was my best friend – she was like a sister to me. We grew up together. The house was hit by the Germans in broad daylight.'

Janet handed her a handkerchief. They started to ask her about funerals, and going home, and what she thought was the best thing to do next.

'How have the children taken the news?' asked Aggie.

'I haven't told them yet. What would you say?' Lily replied, sniffing.

Janet faltered. 'I should tell them the truth, perhaps …'

'But how do you tell a child such a shocking thing, especially as we don't even know ourselves exactly what happened?'

'Perhaps nothing for now,' said Aggie. 'But …'

She glanced at Janet. It was as if something unspoken had just passed between them.

Lily had an instinct Aggie was wrong and Janet was right, that she should say something to Bobby and Deirdre, at least tell them part of what had happened. But how could she find the words? She stood and walked over to the window. Outside there was a line of children in hats and scarves and coats, crossing the lawn to the chapel, doing that strange, unsteady walk with their hands behind their backs. They were being led in song, an 'Ave Maria', by Sister Assumpta. What exactly should she say to them?

For lack of something to hold on to, she gripped the countertop.

'God prevail over us in everlasting sorrow. I heard you've had bad news, Lily,' said Sister David, bustling in. 'Let's say a quick Hail Mary for the repose of her soul. Come on, girls.'

Janet and Aggie rolled their eyes behind Sister David's back and Lily, letting the words wash over her, joined her hands and mumbled through the prayer. She suddenly felt a tug at her sleeve. It was Bobby, with Deirdre at his side.

'Why are you praying? What's wrong? Is it Dad?' asked Bobby.

'No, it's nothing, sweet pea,' she replied. 'Dad's fine. Apart from getting a dickie tum. Still finding his sea legs. He sent another letter home to Mam last week. Now go to your dormitory. I'll follow you up. Wait, Deirdre!'

She untied her sister's plaits, brushed her hair out with her fingers and replaited it.

Bobby and Deirdre must not see her cry. She was going to keep this show on the road, get on for the sake of the family. It was up to her now, especially as Stella would be in such a state about Rosie.

Janet made them all a pot of tea. They had been told they had to eat their carrot pasties in the scullery whilst the sisters ate their corned beef fritters in the parlour, but they didn't mind about that. Lily cupped the mug around her hands and, sitting with one knee drawn up to her chest, her foot on the seat of the wooden rickety chair, listened to the radio for news about the raid that had killed Rosie, but there was none.

'This war has only just got started and it's destroyed so many people,' said Lily.

Aggie nodded. 'It's destroyed so many things. It's not only all the people who have died. I know teachers whose schools are shut because children have been evacuated, who now work in the wash house or down at the docks. Aye, and it's made ill people out of healthy people, you should hear the sounds of hacking coughs from the cement and dust.'

'The girl who used to help my mother with our laundry now works in the munitions factory and she's turning yellow because of the sulphur. Toxic it is. Swear to God,' said Janet. 'Her hair and skin are as yellow as a banana. She's one of those they call canary girls.'

'Me aunt,' said Aggie. 'She lost her two little boys when their shelter collapsed in on them all and now she's lost her marbles ...'

They sat in silence, Lily resting her chin on her knee. Suddenly a voice from the wireless crackled. Another ship had been bombed. Lily froze. The news was brief, perfunctory, but the short announcement was enough for Lily to imagine it in her head: the bodies in the ice cold water, the limbs floating in the dark, Vince calling out for help. The officers in the rescue boats watching him slip under the water, thrashing his arms about for someone to save him. Might it be better to be dead than this? How could a person recover from such horror? But then she stopped herself. It didn't do to start imagining tragedies when there were none. It was enough to cope with the dramas that they already knew about.

'Oh, love,' said Janet, swishing her hair up into pony tail. 'What's the matter?'

'Nothing. Except ... It's bad enough hearing about Rosie. Can we switch it off?'

Worry consumed Lily. She thought of Vincent again as she stared stupidly at the wireless knobs, and then snapped it off as the announcer began talking of another air raid on the city. Twenty-two bombs dumped on Bootle. How awful.

Janet knelt and sat on her heels, stoking the fire in the grate with a poker.

Suddenly, Sister Bernadette bustled in. She was carrying a wooden box with a lid on it, the words Maguire's Bakery stamped on the side. She slammed it on the table and opened the lid. There were a dozen or so loaves inside.

'Girls! Can you slice some of these loaves into pieces? And remember, they have to go around thirty children *and* the sisters.'

She tipped the loaves onto the table out of the box.

Lily, still in a daze, started laying them out one by one. When she had finished, she took the empty box and made off towards the back door out of habit.

'Where d'you think you're going with that?' asked the nun.

Aggie and Janet glanced at each other.

'Bring the breadbox to my office when you're done,' said the sister.

'Don't we chop it up for kindling?' said Lily.

'And why would you do that?'

Because that's what we always do with the wooden grocery boxes and crates at home, she wanted to say, but instead she frowned. A cold chill had filled the room and she felt the hairs stand up stiffly on the back of her neck.

Aggie picked at her nails, looking up at Lily from under her heavy fringe. She widened her eyes, tried to signal something to her. Lily compliantly placed the box back on the table.

'What was that about?' she asked after the nun left.

'I hope you never find out,' murmured Aggie. And before Lily had time to ask her what she meant, as she turned, there was Bobby, standing in the doorway.

'Bobby, why aren't you upstairs?' she asked, weaving the silver chain around her neck through her fingers.

Great pendant-sized tears spilled from his eyes and dropped silently onto the floor.

'Is Rosie dead?' he asked. 'Sister Assumpta said she's gone to be with Jesus, that she's in God's waiting room, but she'll be on her way soon, something about a pear in a tree, and I shouldn't snivel about it because heaven is a far better place than being here on earth.'

Lily felt rage course through her veins. Purgatory, Bobby must have meant. How did Assumpta know? How does anyone know? Purgatory's not even in the Bible, she wanted to yell. Just a made-up load of nonsense. She felt like finding Sister Assumpta and hitting her over the head with one of the frying pans hanging from a hook on the iron bar over the range. How dare that nun tell Bobby about Rosie before she had had the chance to do it? And so casually, it sounded like.

'Come here,' said Lily, hugging him to her, enfolding his little body, a mess of quivering bones and heaving sobs.

He looked at her with swollen red-rimmed eyes.

'Rosie's gone straight to Heaven. She's with Jesus already. Now try not to worry,' she said, pulling him onto her lap and wiping his tears with the hem of her dress, wishing she had something else to say to make him feel better. She placed her hand on Bobby's sleek hair, bent and kissed the top of his head.

What kind of a person was Sister Assumpta, that she would tell a child this in such a heartless manner?

Then, half an hour later, after Bobby dried his tears, she went upstairs, to write a letter of her own. She read it back out loud to herself. Her throat ached when she spoke.

17 November 1940
St Jude's
Freshdale

Dear Vincent,

Did you get my last letter? I have some sad news. Rosie has died in an air raid. It's upset me terribly. I'll miss her so much. I can hardly bear to even put it down on paper, it makes it feel so much more real. And I hear another ship has been sunk at the docks in Liverpool. Forty-three of them lost at sea. I wonder if you've heard already.

This war is taking its toll, all right. They say we have to be strong, Father Donnelly might organise a blessing for the parish, as folks in Liverpool are getting desperate. Night after night this bombing, Mam says. Netherfield hit real bad.

The other day a ship was hit as it sailed out of the docks, I expect you heard. Someone suggested a parade down Scottie Road, someone even suggested they carry the Virgin Mary statue, Star of The Sea, that she is, but someone else said that would confuse things so I think it will be just Father Donnelly swinging incense and everyone else just saying prayers and singing mournful hymns, 'The Old Rugged Cross' and 'Ave Maria', most likely. It's an awful thing. A body washed up on shore in Blackpool last week, but it was bloated and disfigured, and everyone is arguing over who it belongs to. A foot washed up on the beach at Seaforth and it turns out you can have a funeral with a coffin, even if you just have someone's finger, so I've heard there were some folks, who lost their loved ones in the sinking, fighting over this flipping foot, insisting it's their loved one, just so they can have a burial and a bit of a send-off and a knees-up. Matt says Mam listens to all this talk, then raises her eyes and still says she'll never get over Rosie. It has sent her into a spiral of despair, and now she's worried about Dad, wanting him to come home, so you can guess where that's got us. Anyway, for now, I'm staying here with the little ones at St Jude's. Mam wants me to stay out of the city as it's so bad now, but I don't know. Maybe I can get a job in Southport and take lodgings. Or I'm hoping

Mam will change her mind and I can come back to Caryl Street, but that seems pretty optimistic.

It's hard getting anything much out of anyone how it is. Probably for morale, they don't want to say. Government wants to pretend half these tragedies didn't happen and the numbers of the dead are hard to come by, but one thing's for sure, the bombs are raining down in Liverpool now. I hope your ma and pa are all right. Thirteen were killed last week in the raids. You'd think people would be safe and sound in their shelters, but a friend of Mam's was in theirs and there was a gas leak and when he lit a cigarette the whole place blew up. Anyway, I'll stop with the bad news. Being so far away from you is so hard but in a way it means nothing, because it means everything and when I see you, I will fall in love with you all over again. Vincent, I do love you, and I miss you something dreadful.

I am counting the days until your next leave. I am praying that you get this. I love you,

Lily

PS I have some other news. I really don't know how to say this, which is why I've saved it until the end of this letter. It's been so long now that I can't deny it even to myself. The fact is, I'm pregnant.

Chapter 16

The next morning, Lily woke, got out of bed, turned down the bedclothes, took off the sheets and the greying quilted coverlets, shook them out to air, and draped them across the metal bar of the bed frame. She swept back the frayed cubicle curtains and began to tuck the bottom sheet under the mattress.

Aggie was sitting on her messy half-made bed, watching Lily fold and pleat the sheet into hospital corners. Janet stood in the doorway of the dormitory, arms across her chest, her head lolling against the door jamb. When Lily finished and wiped her glistening brow, Aggie suddenly said, 'We found your letter.'

Lily paled. 'What?'

Aggie readjusted the crocheted collar of her knitted blouse and paused for effect. 'Your letter. To Vincent. At least, the one you wrote first with all the scribbling and crossing out. Did you send another?'

Lily stood there, shocked. Aggie took the letter from her overall pocket, opened it, casually waved it in the air, and then began smoothing out the creases on her knee.

'What on earth are you going to do about it?' she asked – the same question Lily had asked herself over and over again over the past few weeks since the realisation had hit her. Apart from waiting to see what Vincent would say about the situation, she hadn't come up with an answer yet.

'How far gone are you?' said Janet.

Lily gazed at her, bewildered.

'I don't know,' she sighed, fighting tears. She slumped onto the bed, dropped her head in her hands and curved into herself. 'You shouldn't have read my letter.'

'You left it on the bedside table under the Bible, you chump!' said Janet more kindly. 'What if Assumpta had found it?'

Lily clutched the pillow. 'I didn't want to believe it. Mam suspected first. At least how . . . I'd changed,' she blurted out, sadly.

'Did she go crazy?'

'I think she accepted it when I said I was just getting fatter because of all the porridge, but that's probably because she can't get a grip on anything at the moment either. That's also because I didn't really know myself what was happening to me.'

'Oh God, Lily. You're so innocent. Did you really have no idea?'

Lily dropped her eyes and shook her head.

'Didn't you realise when you didn't get the curse?'

'I did get it. Well, I thought, I did. But it wasn't like I usually do . . .'

'That happens sometimes,' said Aggie. 'It's not your proper Auntie Mary. Confuses the issue though, that's for sure.'

Lily shrugged and sniffed and snivelled and Janet handed her a handkerchief. Then, when they asked her how far gone she was again, she said the last time she had seen Vincent was nearly three months ago but still, everything was topsy-turvy. She climbed up the ladder and onto the top bunk, lay on her front, and cried and cried into the crook of her arm, and then cried some more. Aggie climbed up, rubbed her back and gave her another handkerchief as the first was sopping wet, then lay down next to her, and propped herself up one elbow.

'All I'm saying is, dearie, you don't want to stay here. Trips to the arcades, skiving off, Saturday morning picture house. The Lido. The Copper Kettle. That won't happen. Unless your mam is real rich, like Janet's. She makes sure I'm looked after as well, doesn't she, Janet? That's why I've not been shoved into the annex yet. But unless you have special dispensation, you'll be left here washing sheets and scrubbing shitty nappies, could be for years, like Bridget.'

Lily rolled over and sat up with her knees shoved up under her skirts, chin resting on her kneecaps. 'It's not fair that there's one rule for some and another for others,' she said, her cheeks streaked with tears.

Janet paused from chewing the skin around her thumbnail.

'No one's arguing with that,' she said. 'But it's complicated. The one thing we can agree on is that they see girls like us as stains on God's grand plan. They can't understand why we would want to have sex before we are married. Though I reckon, given the chance, Assumpta would do it even with any one of us girls! I swear, I've seen her looking at me the same way as a fella would.'

Lily winced and felt her cheeks flushing red.

'What's wrong? Don't you believe me?' asked Janet. 'Swear on the Holy Virgin's life, it's true. Sister Assumpta, when she's off on one with the love of Jesus, she goes all hot and bothered, a mass of quivers and sweats, and it's like she's imagining what she's missing out on, right there on the altar when she's praying for all the sin in the world. You can see it in her face. It's *hilarious*.'

'Please don't be sad, Lily,' said Aggie, stroking her hair.

Lily wavered. She really couldn't trust anyone. Especially after they had been the ones who had taken her letter and read it in the first place. She lay down again, put her hands behind her head and stared up at the ceiling. Janet was right about the hole in the skylight. Looking through it, she could see the sun. Was that same sun also shining on Vincent? Or would it be the moon? How many miles across the sea? She couldn't imagine where he might be, but felt that she wanted him, *needed* him, with her now, this minute, more than ever.

Aggie spoke again. 'You can't stay here, Lily. The nuns, even the kind ones like Sister David, are awful when they see us pregnant girls; it's like they become a different sort of person.'

Janet agreed. 'I think it's because they've given up their whole lives to God and it makes some of them go all bitter and twisted about it when they see anyone who's up the duff; all that life on show – big milky boobs and huge bellies, you can't escape it – we're a constant reminder of all they've given up when they married Jesus. All that sex we're having with our fellas, sex in strange places, or with married men, sex in cars, dirty, filthy, filthy sex that has nothing to do with making babies.'

Janet had enjoyed her speech, but Lily just felt sad. She remembered seeing Sister David earlier, laughing and holding hands with two small boys as she scythed across the grass in her swishing habit then twirled a hoop around her waist, gyrating her hips. She seemed to be one of the good ones. Surely Janet was exaggerating.

'Nappy sluicing is the worst. The smell is awful.'

'You really can't have your baby here. It's like torture to hear the crying on the birth ward. I'm telling you, you'll have no gas and air. Just pethidine, and that's only if it goes wrong. And if all goes well, they announce in the ward, "Lily's had a baby boy. Seven pounds!" All happy, like. As if we should be celebrating. "Three cheers for Lily and her wee one! Hip hip hooray!" And they make everyone clap, and it's awful, because what's it to you? Who cares if your baby is bonny and healthy if they're taking him away?'

Lily listened to the speech. It was as if Janet had started off talking to her but finished talking about herself.

Then she thought of Vincent again. She squeezed her eyes tight. Only God could help her now. You *stupid*, dizzy, dozy, girl, she could hear her despairing mother saying. Just like she had once said to her when she had taken the jug to the corner shop for a tuppence worth of black treacle to fill it from the urn with a tap, and when the shopkeeper had asked her for the money, she had realised she had left the coins inside the jug. 'You *stupid*, dizzy, dozy, girl,' her mother had cried, when she had told her. Only this time it was a baby, not a couple of coppers, she had made fool of herself with.

'What are you going to do?' Janet asked her again, wrenching her back to the present.

She wanted to say, she would just simply have the baby and marry Vincent when he came home. Of course, he would want the same. Why wouldn't he? He loved her. In her mind, the only scenario where that might not be possible was if Vincent were to die in this terrible war, and it would still mean he would be hers and she would be his, and the child would be a symbol of their love and would bind them together forever.

But she didn't answer. She was afraid that they might laugh at her.

Chapter 17

Stella was lingering on the stairs, coughing. It had started after the visit to the beach. Ludicrous, paddling in the sea in October, she had muttered to herself. No wonder I'm ill. She was beginning to cough harder these days, everyone had noticed. It was getting to her chest. Hearing the hacking sound, seeing her go purple and her eyes bulging, Matt was thankful when she caught her breath as Gram bustled in and offered stockings, no questions asked about where the money had come from to buy them. Rosie's funeral was at twelve. It had taken weeks to organise. Death in this city had become a complicated affair. There were so many to bury, and identifying bodies was often a gruesome and long drawn-out task. More than 150 people had died three weeks after Rosie, in Durning Road in Edge Hill. The most cruel and horrific act of destruction that was hard to see how anyone would recover from.

The funeral procession coming up the hill was a tragic affair. The carriage, from Spall's yard, that normally carried old rags, was done up with black drapes and a single balloon on a stick, as a gesture to Rosie's father who was a rag-and-bone man in Everton. There were flashes of white handkerchiefs as the well-wishers came out of their houses to wave and wipe their eyes.

It turned into Caryl Street. When Stella came out onto the front step to pay her respects and follow the procession, walking behind it as they made their way to the church, it made her heart break just to look at it. *Rosie*, it said in flowers on the side of the coffin. It acted as a sombre reminder of how fleeting a life could be in this monstrous war and it was hard not to get swept up with the drama of the four top-hatted pallbearers walking behind, and the men's voices singing, and the majestic Gallagher's horses. Stella, staggering, grief-stricken, held up by the arm on one side by Matt and the other by Peg Leg, wearing black from head to toe, striking in ink black velvet and a hat with a black plume of feathers, only added to the drama.

'Buck up, Mam,' whispered Matt. 'Funerals have always raised your spirits.'

She looked at him with tears swelling in her eyes and frowned. 'What are you saying? This is *Rosie*.'

'I mean, you've always loved a good send-off, that's all,' he said.

She turned away from him and shook her head sadly.

The crowd slowed to a halt outside the church. One of the big funeral horses, with its oversized fringed hooves, stopped, bucked its head, whinnied and snorted. When they went in, it was already packed full. There was a heady smell of incense and Rosie's father, a small, hunched shell of a man, twisting his cap in his hands, looked alone and sad, as though the only thing in this life that he could wish for now was death. Prayers were said for Rosie over a coffin, prayers not only for her but all the others whose loved ones had died in this miserable war, and afterwards the group of people who stood outside on the steps whispered to each other about how Rosie would be talked of in years to come, even though there had still been hardly a mention of how the bad the bombing had actually been on the wireless. So many more bombs dropped each day and sometimes you'd read the papers and it was if as it hadn't happened. Morale, someone said, got to keep morale up.

'Rosie was one of the good ones,' said Peg Leg to Stella.

'You're right. She was one in a million,' said Vera, touching Stella lightly on her shoulder with a lace-gloved finger.

'Don't cry, don't you dare cry,' Peg Leg whispered to Aunt Annie. 'It'll set Stella off again. She's in a shocking state.'

Stella fought back more tears. Sobs rose up through her body but she swallowed them down, shook her head, took a forefinger and wiped it under the line of her eyes, rubbing away the tears as she crossed herself.

And then a few Hail Marys, and the woman from the WVS saying this was drawing the wrong kind of attention when people came out of shops to gawp, and back to Caryl Street for corned beef sandwiches and toasts to Rosie, and it was all over.

Stella, exhausted, sat with her calves aching, and slipped off her high-heeled shoes. She stared into the burning embers of the fire. Annie had brought a pan of Scouse and parsnip pie, and when that was gone, another miraculously appeared on the stove. Then Peg Leg Wally came around to finish the Scouse, and there was more talk of the reports of the bombing and about what had happened. 'Would've been quick, Stella, if that's any consolation,' he said, as Matt came in with hot cups of tea. Stella stirred in heaps of sugar, then asked, 'Haven't we got anything stronger?'

Peg Leg offered Stella a biscuit but she shook her head. He offered it to her again and, out of politeness, Stella nibbled at the end of it.

'Mustn't grumble,' said Peg Leg, munching away, savouring the custard cream, and Stella wondered how some people could do things as ordinary as eating a biscuit in the midst of all this tragedy. But maybe they didn't see it like that. People just carried on. Just got on with their lives. That was what the government wanted everyone to do. Make the best of it. But she never would be able to do that if anything happened to her Cliff or the children.

Annie sighed. 'Rosie has always been such a presence. So larger-than-life. And such a good neighbour to you, Stella, always swapped the bacon and the sugar, little things like that. All she wanted to do was make everyone's lives better.'

'We should have spent more time together,' Stella said. 'All the things we had said we would do. Trips to see the Blackpool illuminations. Days out to see New Brighton gardens. She was going to teach me how to bake her plum pie and how to cross-stitch embroidery properly. And now she's gone,' she said regretfully, sniffing away tears, before tailing off into silence.

'Stella, are you all right, ducky?' asked Annie.

Stella looked at her vaguely. She was a little drunk now.

'Are you all right?' Annie repeated.

'No,' she answered. 'I'm afraid I'm not. I don't know how I'll recover from this. And I also have a bad feeling.'

'What about?'

'About Lily not coming today,' she said. 'I sent a letter and asked her and she wouldn't have missed it for the world. I thought she'd leap at the chance to come home to Liverpool for a couple of nights. Doesn't seem right. I can feel something's not quite as it should be.'

'Feel it in your waters, you mean?'

'Aye. Feel it in my waters. That's about it, Annie.'

Chapter 18

January 1941

More dire news came from Liverpool to Freshdale. The Christmas blitz brought sad and chilling stories of personal tragedy and the collective mourning of a city that had been under siege for days, and as much as the nuns wanted to pretend it wasn't happening – too much distraction, they said – word reached Freshdale soon enough. And yet, despite the devastation, Stella still refused to budge. She sent Christmas cards covered in kisses and said how much she missed them all, but said she was too exhausted to get on a train to see them. The truth was Rosie's death had hit her hard, and she had barely stepped out of the house for weeks, not even down to the shelter.

It was probably a good job they had stayed in Freshdale for Christmas, Lily had decided. Her body was beginning to really change now, and even though she had managed to hide it from the nuns by wrapping herself up in old jumpers and borrowing one of Aggie's baggy dresses, there would be no hiding it from her mother. The sickness had stopped but at over four months pregnant, it had been replaced with other horrors – she felt tired all the time and her back seemed to constantly ache.

They all missed Caryl Street, and of course their mother. Lily did her best to enjoyed herself under the circumstances, except there was rather too much church for her liking, but she was glad the children seemed to have had a good time. Sister David had organised a tree which they decorated with battered baubles moulded out of papier mâché that they made from torn-up pieces of the *Echo*. She and Aggie and Janet went out and picked armfuls of holly with berries on it and draped ivy over the mantelpiece, and Sister Bernadette melted the bottom of candles so they stood in saucers. They made cut-outs from the *Liverpool Echo* of angels holding hands, so the place seemed cheerful enough. They even soaked dried fruit in brandy for the Christmas pudding with a sixpence in it but there was an almighty fight over that amongst the kids.

But now it was new year and she really was beginning to show. Remembering what Aggie and Janet had said about what the nuns would do if they were to get wind of her 'condition', Lily made her way down the corridor to the children's dormitory. It was early, but she found poor exhausted Bridget in the corridor, bags under her eyes, pushing a mop around in tired circles, half-heartedly cleaning the wooden parquet floor. Lily met her gaze but Bridget's eyes shifted away quickly and back down to the floor.

'You all right, Bridge?' asked Lily.

Bridget bent down, squeezed the end of the mop into a bucket with her chafed and red bare hands. It made Lily shudder. Would she end up like this if she were to stay here? She was glad she had decided she was leaving this place, even though she felt had little choice.

Bridget nodded, continued mopping, and then she paused, called after Lily. 'He won't marry you,' she said. The words echoed off the tiled walls and stone floor. Lily stood rooted to the spot, felt her cheeks burning. Had Bridget been listening at the door? Or had Aggie or Janet told her? 'Once you've had sex with them they never marry you. Liars, they all are. It's the one thing I know about, trust me.'

But Lily didn't want to hear.

Lord Street was quiet. It was beginning to snow. Soon it was difficult to see where the the pavements ended and the roads started. She made her way past the department stores and elegant arcades, knowing that it would be in the back streets in the small shops and cafes where she might be lucky. She headed down an alley that cut through to the promenade. The thought pushed her on – what she needed now was a job and somewhere to stay that would buy her some time. But there was nothing that was remotely close to a job advertisement in any of the shop windows. Someone's missing cat, a mangle for sale, a gardener for hire. Defeated, she was about to go back to the convent when she heard a blast of music, trumpets it sounded like, coming from an upstairs window. It felt familiar and made her nostalgic. She lifted her eyes tiredly. Sullivan's Dance Hall, it said on a board on hinges that creaked in the wind. She stopped, knocked, then tentatively pushed open the door. Inside there was a woman pushing a tea trolley across the polished floor of a small foyer. The daylight coming in from a high window was unkind. It showed up the shabbiness of the room. The wallpaper was peeling off the wall at the cornices, the stacked velvet chairs were balding and the curtains across a set of double doors that fell in folds had holes in them and gold braid fringes coming away at the hems, but it was a room that made Lily feel wistful and homesick.

'Yes, love?' said the woman leaning on the trolley handle with one hand and wiping her brow.

'I'm looking for a job,' said Lily.

*

The children were half awake in the dormitory bunk beds. Bobby clutched a pine cone and Lily unpeeled Deirdre's fingers to find a tiny heart-shaped shell in the palm of her tiny hand. She looked at the children's deep brown, soulful eyes as they stirred, kissed them on their pink cheeks, stroked their hair, and said she was going away, but hopefully not for too long.

'I'm leaving. I've got the chance of a job and a room with it,' she said, meeting Janet and Aggie on the stairs. 'I've already told the nuns. They seem relieved. Especially Sister Assumpta. I've been here longer than I planned.'

Janet raised her head. 'You're leaving. So quickly? What's the job?'

She told them about the woman she had met who had asked her to come back the following day to her house where she would talk to her more about the position that was vacant – she needed someone to work in the ticket office at the dance hall.

'And what about the baby?' asked Janet.

'I'm waiting until Vincent comes home on leave before I do anything. He said he might be going away to North Africa,' she replied sadly. 'But that was months ago so I'm hoping it's soon. In the meantime, I'll write to him and tell him to find me at my new lodgings. Until then, I'm not making any big decisions. Apart from getting out of here.'

'You hoping he's going to take the blame?'

Lily looked shocked. 'No. I didn't force him. And he didn't force me. I'm as much responsible for this baby as he is.'

'Oh, Lily! You're so flipping innocent. You haven't a bad bone in you, have you? I just hope you don't have to find out about fellas the hard way.'

'Please God we won't see you back here,' said Aggie, with a snort. 'But just a warning. You have to be strong, Lily. It's not nice going to a hospital an unmarried mother. Trust me.'

'Why?' asked Lily.

'Because people can be vile. Honestly,' replied Janet. 'Vile. In fact, I wouldn't be surprised if you do end up here again. I don't know which of the two places is the worst.'

'I'd stick to the hospital. If you come back here and have it the nuns will make you have a christening. You have to choose a name. What name will you choose?' said Aggie.

'Name?' she answered, frowning.

'Baby's christening name. You decide for the ceremony. Though, most likely, the new ma and da will change it. Some girls even bring their fellas to the baptism. The nuns don't mind that. They encourage it, even. I think it's cos they think it adds to the drama. All the crying and greeting and sobbing.'

A memory flashed into Lily's head of the time she had walked in on a service in the chapel. The sad spectacle of girls spending their last moments with their baby at a christening font before giving the infant away to complete strangers.

'I'm never coming back here. I don't care how shameful it would be to have my baby in a hospital. I couldn't stand it here,' said Lily. She frowned. A thought occurred to her. 'If the new parents change your baby's name anyway, what's the point?'

Janet shrugged. Is this what had happened to her baby, Lily wondered?

'You say you won't come back now. But if you do ...' Janet's eyes widened with excitement. 'Hey, we could meet in Lord Street and go shopping together. For the baby's christening outfit. I love a good shopping trip, me.'

'What?' Lily said, shocked.

'Just another one of the nun's rules. Like they make you dress the wee one up yourself. If you can't afford to buy an outfit, they make you knit little matinee jackets. I chose a little pale pink dress to set off my Sissy's red hair, and a matching blanket with a pink ribbon stitched around the edges. Cost a few bob but it was beautiful,' said Janet. 'And the clothes go with your baby in a shoebox for your new family to keep and show your little 'un when they're all grown up.'

Sissy? It sounded unbearable. A baptism. Choosing clothes. Christening shawls and blankets! But she could see they were just trying to put her in the picture, trying to make her understand the seriousness of the situation.

'Never. Those nuns won't come anywhere near my baby,' she said.

Aggie nodded. 'Atta girl. But if you do change your mind, I'll keep your spirits up. Janet's leaving next week but I'll be here for a while yet.'

'What about your mam?' asked Janet.

'I'm hoping Vince will get my letter first. Then, when he finds me, we can tell her together. That's why I have to leave here. I don't want the nuns sending me back before I've got word to Vince or I've heard back from him. It's best that I disappear, just for a short time. I'm going now. I've told the kiddies I've gone back home.'

'Toodle-oo,' Janet said. 'And remember, if you do come back here, to the House of Hell, they'll snatch it off you, soon as blink. Sorry. *Her. Him.* But well, you know. Sometimes it doesn't do to think of it as a real live human baby. That was my mistake. Then you start thinking about names and whether it has brown or blonde hair, and whether it will have your nose or his eyes, then you're done for, so to speak.'

'The nuns have an instinct about these things,' said Aggie.

'They might already know. So scram. I would,' said Janet.

'You're not thinking about … well about?' added Aggie, as Lily stuffed a pair of shoes she had left under the bunk bed into a bag.

'What?' asked Lily.

'Going somewhere to sort it out. I'd say you're too late for that, sweetheart,' said Janet.

Lily looked shocked. Did that mean what she imagined she did?

'It doesn't work. Hot baths and gin. Knitting needles. Chucking yourself down the stairs. I know because I tried it and look at me . . .' Aggie gestured to her stomach.

'Word of warning, Lil,' said Aggie. 'Finding someone who can "sort things out for you" doesn't always work either. I know a lass who knew a lass who knew a sweet little woman – but it cost a bloody fortune and she nearly ended up dead herself. Fully tomatoed, she were, by the time the "sweet little woman" had made a right mess of her insides.'

Fully tomatoed. The words sounded blunt and nasty. It felt as though she was being hit about the head with them. And the thought 'of sorting things out' hadn't even occurred to Lily, but now the idea had entered her consciousness, it stuck there like a bad penny. Even more reason to pray for word from Vincent.

Chapter 19

It was a Saturday, a wintry but sunny January day, and Lily knew where she was heading. She felt the cold air sting her cheeks. Walking along the row of shops in Lord Street, she stopped for a moment to look in the window of a jewellery shop, her fingertips resting on the glass for a second or two. Her warm breath blotted the glass. It was full of trinkets, tarnished silver spoons, gold watches, yellowing pearl necklaces. But she had never seen anything as beautiful as the carriage clock in the centre of the display. She read the words on a small tag, the string of it tied around one of the gold bars. Charles Cinq, it said, with its tiny hinged door open to reveal the delicate mechanism on display, a perfect intricate balancing of cogs and wheels. Inside the shop she saw two people moving about – a soldier in uniform with his sweetheart on his arm, bending over the ring display case. This town was full of military, so there must be a camp nearby, maybe where the musicians she had met at the Copper Kettle were stationed.

She turned to walk towards the Victorian war memorial. The fountains spewed showers of glittering droplets of water that oscillated in the sun in front of the bandstand that stood empty but proud. A stack of deckchairs was covered in a tarpaulin that had come loose and flapped in the breeze, revealing the candy-coloured striped canvas. You would hardly know there was a war here, she thought. They had had word that back in Liverpool, after the three days and nights of pounding from the air just before Christmas, huge parts of the city had now been demolished.

She had half an hour to spare and found herself around the corner to the Copper Kettle. Remembering it had been welcoming and friendly, she decided to go inside to stay warm. She pushed open the door and straight away recognised the waitress, with her starched white pinafore and lace cap, as being the same one who'd been serving when she had come here with Aggie and Janet. She was standing behind the counter, slightly bored, sucking the end of a pencil. There was the sound of piano music floating over from the corner of the room – and there he was again, Clarence!, sitting at the battered piano, working out a tune that wasn't familiar to Lily.

She made her way to the counter and ordered a tea when she heard a voice saying, 'We've met before, haven't we?'

It was Clarence smiling at her and the first thing she noticed, once again, was the flash of gold in his teeth. He hesitated. 'I do know you, don't I? Do you dance at the Kingsway?'

'No. But I came here once with my friends Janet and Aggie.'

'Ah. Aggie often used to pop by here. We got to know each other. Not so much lately. Sorry, you'll have to remind me of your name. I remember you're the girl who knows about syncopation, but not your name, I'm afraid.'

Her eyes widened and she blushed, impressed that he had remembered her at all.

'If you ever do make it to the Kingsway, you'll have a dance with me?'

She shrugged, feeling her cheeks stinging again.

'Maybe see you there, then. It's in Eastbank Street. I'll write it down so you remember.'

'Want to borrow my pencil?' asked the waitress, taking it from behind her ear and handing it to him.

He bent down, scribbled the address on a scrap of paper that he took out of his pocket, then slid it under Lily's saucer.

Half an hour later, she drained her tea, stood up to leave, and headed to the door.

'Miss, have you forgotten this?' She turned around. It was Clarence, who had got up from the piano, and had followed her out, holding up the piece of paper with the address of the Kingsway on it. 'You'd love the Kingsway.'

'Would I? But you don't know anything about me,' she shot back.

He grinned. 'I know you like music – I saw your foot tapping when I played "Sleepy Lagoon". I know you can dance, dear, just by the way I saw you walk across the room. I know drinking tea here with old ladies in feathered hats is not your style and you'd be more at home at the Kingsway. Am I right?'

He had said it so politely and with such charm, such ease and grace, and despite the turmoil going on in her life, all the worry and fear of what was going to become of her, she couldn't help but smile.

When she arrived at the address on the advert, the woman who answered the door, large with broad hips and a mass of tangled hair, was friendly and introduced herself as Joyce. It took her no time over a cup of tea to tell Lily the story of her husband who had left for France three months earlier after he had been called up. Lily would be doing a man's job because there were no men left here who wanted to do the work. She had put the notice in the cafe because she knew it would attract the folk who liked to dance at Sullivan's.

'Barmaid job is long taken, but I need someone on the booth. You're a girl, but you'll do. I need you to take the tickets at the door and make sure there's no trouble. Maybe folk will be more polite if a pretty girl like you is laying down the law. So, now you've heard my side of the story, what's yours? What is it that makes you think you'd be suitable for this job?'

Lily took a deep breath. 'I've been staying at St Jude's. My brother and sister are evacuees there, taken in by the nuns. My mum and dad ran a dance school in Liverpool – Laffertys' Dance School. That's shut up now, and they wanted us to get out of Liverpool to be safe.'

'I see. You've a sweet face, Lily, but you've also got a strong jaw and sharp eyes. You can have the job. There's a camp nearby. That's why they bus in the girls from around to the dance hall. Passion vans, they call them. Do you think you'll be all right with that?'

'Passion vans?'

'Women. Girls. For the fellas.'

Lily shrugged.

'We've had some trouble – a few hoodlums picking fights with a couple of the West Indian soldiers stationed at the Mere Lane camp. You can guess why, but these West Indians are good men. They only want to fight for the King and Empire. Most of them are sons of dockers in Liverpool who jumped off the boats from Trinidad and suchlike and settled here so this is their country, the only one they've known. Others are young men who have signed up in their home countries when the war commission went looking for more fellas after Dunkirk.

They love the British Empire, consider the war as much as their fight as any man who comes to drink here, or spin a girl around the floor on a Saturday night. Tea?'

Lily nodded. Joyce poured her a cup and pushed a plate of carrot and ginger buns over the checked tablecloth. Covering her bump with one arm, desperate that Joyce wouldn't notice, Lily reached out and took one. She gobbled it up almost in one go.

'Have another,' said Joyce, smiling.

Lily blushed. Being pregnant had given her strange urges. The week before she had lifted a piece of coal from the coal bucket up to her lips and licked it. She would have bitten off a chunk of it if Sister Assumpta hadn't come in and seen her.

She started her new job that evening after unpacking her small bag and hanging up her few dresses in the maple wood wardrobe, but before she left the house, wrote a letter to Vincent telling him her new address. Please God, she would hear from him soon. In the meantime, she was going to make the best of it, welcome him with a bit of money and the hope that he would be understanding about their baby. Then they would tell their mothers, get married quietly and quickly, and life would go on just as it had before, but with a baby on her hip. At least, that's what she hoped.

There was already a queue forming outside the dance hall. There were some men in uniform – the uniform that gave them a confidence they didn't possess in their humdrum lives. No doubt these fellows were quite ordinary – butchers, clerks, truck drivers – but she could tell that the army made them feel special, different to their civilian friends.

Meanwhile, the women hanging onto their arms more than outmatched them in the glamour stakes. Their hair was done up in elaborate styles with cascades of curls held by marcasite hairpins, diamanté earrings and other jewellery glinting in the soft, shell-like light. Their lips were painted deep red, their faces powdered and creamy. One or two wore A-line skirts belted at the waist; others wore swing dresses and teetered in high heels.

'Eh, Gladys. You going with him or seeing him?' shouted one of the soldiers.

A woman in the queue giggled.

'Leave off, she's mine! I'm on a promise tonight! Don't you be thinking you can waltz her out from under me feet tonight!' cried the fellow with his arm snaked around so-called Gladys' waist.

There was a ripple of laughter.

'Oi, is that Slack-Mouthed Sally you're on about? She was my dance last week!' someone cried.

'And she was mine the week before!'

The woman didn't seem to mind. 'You're a bloody case, you are,' she said to the one who had started it off. She took a cigarette out of a pearlised case, put it to her lips and laughed so hard that she began choking, so that one of the fellows had to thump her on the back so she could catch her breath.

When they got to the booth, Lily spoke to them through the round hole cut out of the glass. Some commented that she was new. Some tried it on just as Joyce had warned her they would.

'You're a corker. Right little belter. Fancy a drink later, love?'

Lily raised her eyes, shook her head, said not likely, and smiled. It was mostly harmless banter.

She had been told to ask their ages, that she should demand to see proof if there was any question they weren't old enough. But she knew what it felt like to be desperate to get inside, to be part of the dancing and the music and the heady smell of cigarettes and cheap cologne, so more than once she turned a blind eye. Each time the door opened to let someone in, there was the tantalising sound of notes piling on notes.

A man handed over a ticket with long, graceful fingers. When she looked up, her brown eyes widened in surprise. It was Clarence, looking even more handsome than the last time she'd seen him, with his Brylcreemed tight brown curls, smiling eyes, and smart army uniform.

'Lily!' he said.

The door to the ballroom swung open and a head stuck out. 'Hey, Clarence, glass of liquid sunshine?

You're on in a minute,' the person – another soldier in uniform – said.

'Liquid sunshine. He means rum,' Clarence said to Lily, grinning. 'Perhaps you'll have a glass with me?'

'A shilling to get in,' she replied. 'And I'm working.'

'You have a break sometime this evening, right?'

'Oh, I don't think so.'

'Well, if you can't slip out before, how about if you'll have the last dance with me?'

'No,' she said, with a toss of her wavy hair and a flash of her serious brown eyes. That would put an end to that. Or so she thought.

Two hours later, when she had counted up the money, put it in the tin box Joyce had told her to and locked it away in the back room in a safe, she slipped into the hall. Just a quick look, just a quick peek around the velvet curtains, she promised herself, because the music sounded so joyous. Through the fog of cigarette smoke, which made her feel a little nauseous, and through the gap in the velvet curtain, she could see a sliver of the musicians on the stage. When she opened the musty-smelling curtain further, she saw one of the group sitting on an upturned box, slapping the side of it. He was smiling as he did so, cigarette drooping from his lips. And there was Clarence, playing the double bass, swaying with the instrument as if he was dancing with a woman, complete looseness in his hips, in perfect time to the music. It excited her to see him playing. She stood, her back against the wall. They seemed to be playing a Caribbean song and she vaguely recognised the lilting melodies, or perhaps it was just a memory of the music they played at the Rialto and the Grafton.

There was a couple dancing in the middle of the floor and people were making way for them. They were better than everyone else, might even be professional, Lily thought. Watching the woman's dress unfurling in ripples, the man in his uniform, she wished it was her and Vincent. Would people have made way for them? The thought nagged at her. Was it unusual that she hadn't heard from him for months now? Please God, he would be back soon to find her. Oh, she hoped that he had read her letter, that he was safe and alive and happy about his baby. Any day now. Any day …

Now the music was another song she couldn't quite remember, the lilting melody vaguely familiar. There was a round of applause when it came to an end.

She returned to the booth, but half an hour later when she came out from her little cubbyhole, there was Clarence waiting. He was smiling and had an expression on his face that said he was pleased to see her. Swallowing down great gulps of air, she readjusted her collar, smoothed down her skirt.

'Next time you're not working, will you let me take you dancing?' he asked.

'Oh,' she replied. 'Not sure I can . . .'

She saw his face fall.

'You know where I am. But I understand if . . .' His words tailed off into silence.

'If what?'

He shrugged. 'I'm not so stupid as to not realise what a sight we would make.'

Lily suddenly realised what he meant. 'Oh. I don't care about *that*. I was brought up not to give a damn what the world thinks about such stuff. And well, why wouldn't I want to be seen out on your arm? You're a lovely-looking fella and charming with it, Clarence. No, it's not that. It's just that—'

She had been about to tell him about Vincent, her sweetheart, about how it wouldn't be right to accept Clarence's offer because she was taken, but in a whirl of coats and instruments, laughter and shouts across the room, the musicians came hurtling into the foyer, slapping Clarence on the back, winking at him and grinning. And the moment slipped between her fingers like grains of sand and passed.

'If you change your mind, I play at the Copper Kettle on a Friday, and then I go for a drink at the Bull, then some dancing after. Every Friday, yes? So you know where to find me,' he called, as he was bundled out into the cold by his friends, his arm waving his cap above the throng, Lily smiling as she watched them go.

Chapter 20

10 January
SS Empire Minerva

My dear love, Lily,

I really wish I could shake it off, this feeling of worry. I'm back in a week. Would you like me to go and check on the house? I'm sure you don't mind me saying Caryl Street has always looked pretty down at heel, but I've heard there has been the most fearsome bombing around your way and now I'm just hoping your house is still standing and still has the Lafferty name on it above the front door! I am planning to come to St Jude's as soon as I can. Mam has told me where you are. I am hoping to whisk you away for a night so I can take you dancing in Liverpool. I still think of your eyes as soulful and deep as the ocean, and how I'm lost at sea without you.

With all love my dearest,
Vincent

The letter sat on the floor in the corner, pushed up against the skirting board of Sister Assumpta's office. She hadn't bothered to pick it up. It had remained there for weeks, gathering dust, and unopened.

Chapter 21

Three weeks had passed since she had arrived in Southport. It began raining that evening, suddenly and unexpectedly. Lily could hear the rain battering the roof, from the window she could see hailstones bouncing off the pavement. She got up from the kitchen table, placed a tin bucket underneath the leak in the ceiling to catch the drops, and another by the window on the instructions of Joyce. When one was full, she had to run outside quickly to empty it in the gutters, but by the time she had come back there was another brimming over on the floor. Joyce's patience was beginning to fray; bad-tempered and tired, she began shouting at Lily, asking her why she was slopping water all over the place, or why she hadn't moved the bucket quickly enough before it had overflowed on the rug.

'This bloody place, more damp creeping up the walls. This is a catastrophe!' Joyce said darkly.

Lily said nothing but bridled. Finding herself pregnant, Rosie dying, not hearing a word from Vince, was a catastrophe – not a bit of rainfall. She took some rags and began to mop up the water. Then, when she had done, she kicked off her sturdy lace-up shoes, and put on her heels with the delicate strap that fastened over the arch of her foot.

To hell with it. She wasn't staying in the house tonight! There was still no letter from Vince and she was bored and fed up. What harm could it do, meeting Clarence? He was kind, and funny and seeing him might make her forget not only about a leaky ceiling, but also what was happening to her, at least for a couple of hours.

When she walked into the cafe, Clarence looked surprised and happy to see her.

'Lily! You came to see me!' he said. He was wearing civilian clothes: a pair of smart flannel trousers and a Fair Isle sweater over a crisp white collarless shirt.

'Why wouldn't I?' she responded. 'I'm glad you're still here. Didn't want to walk into the Bull on me own, looking for you.'

After the initial burst of conversation – Lily talking to him about her job, and Clarence telling her about the trouble at the barracks, with some of the new arrivals less than impressed with the state of the place, the awful wartime food – stuffed marrow and cheese and tomato potato loaf – the uncomfortable bunk beds, the endless drills, they both sat, shy and nervous, each of them waiting for the other to speak first.

'I honestly didn't think you'd want to come back here,' Clarence said, after a pause.

'Why ever not?'

'I don't know. Maybe I was worried you wouldn't want to be seen with me, whatever you said.' He smiled. 'Anyway, I'm glad you're here.'

He suggested it might be a better idea that they went somewhere else to dance, not Sullivan's.

She agreed. 'Doesn't do to mix work and pleasure if I'm to be at the booth the next night.'

And then, without warning, he reached across the table and went to take her hand. She drew it away quickly, as if she had put it into a fire. Then thought better of it and gently placed her fingers on his.

'I have to tell you, Clarence. I have someone in my life. A fiancé.'

His face clouded over. 'Oh. I see.'

'I'm so sorry,' she stammered. 'I should have said straightaway.'

'Well, we didn't really have much chance to talk about things like that.' He shifted awkwardly in his seat. 'Stupid. Stupid of me to think that you would ...' The sentence tailed off again. He seemed to make a habit of that.

'No. No, it doesn't mean I don't want to go dancing. Besides, I've not heard from him for so long. And they tell you nothing. It's just that I do love him and ... and ...'

Tears welled in her eyes.

'Hey, darlin'. I understand. I'm just lucky to have met you,' he said, with a smile.

There was a pause. The sound of the low murmur of voices in the cafe filled the silence, and there was the tinkling of spoons against saucers, the gush of water when someone switched a tap on.

'Doesn't mean I don't want to be here,' she said, tossing back her hair.

And he smiled, a smile that lit up his brown eyes, a smile that was the very start of something. A friendship? Or ... something else? But she didn't know what.

She opened her mouth to speak, Was now the time to tell him about the baby? Would he notice her belly under her ruched dress? She had hidden it well, but close up against him, *dancing,* surely he would realise?

'I must say, you look beautiful,' he said. 'Can I say that? It's not too forward? Given that you're well, you know, someone's sweetheart.'

Listening to him speak, his soft voice, kind words, she suddenly decided she was prepared to risk it and tell him about the baby. She looked at his brown soulful eyes. But then again ... Why destroy this moment?

'Truth is, Clarence, I think dancing would be the perfect tonic. Makes me forget, you know. The worry of my chap being in the merchant navy.'

Clarence smiled. 'I can do that for you,' he said. 'I can do that. I'll take you somewhere and I promise it will be magnificent. As long as you're sure?'

'Oh, Clarence. Of course I am.'

He faltered. 'Only, Lily, there are some who don't like seeing fellas like me with girls like you. Do you have the stomach for it?'

She grinned, leaned in to him. 'Fellas like you? Good-looking, talented, and kind? I'm grand with it.'

On the walk over to Percy Street, Clarence told Lily a little more about himself and Lily told him a little more bit about herself, how she had worked for the WVS in Liverpool before she was evacuated with her brother and sister. 'Aggie calls it stitch and bitch,' she said with a smile, 'but it's not like that. We help make medical supplies like bandages.'

He told her how he came to be in Southport, that the news of Dunkirk had made everyone feeling very gloomy in his home town, Port of Spain in Trinidad. But how soon after, allied troops started arriving and, in an agreement with the British government, set up desks in the town halls and market squares and started recruiting for the British army.

'There was an appeal by Winston Churchill to Commonwealth and colonial countries, for them that didn't need training because they already had the skills, like me. You should see me with a wireless and a soldering iron, Lily. I'm a wizard!' She smiled. 'Within a week I was called to the GPO engineering department for a test. I passed with flying colours. After a slap-up party and farewell to family and friends, I was issued with an army paybook. Signalman Aimé, Royal Signals. My family was *so* proud. And here I am. I'm waiting to see where they'll send me next. Catterick, I think. Yorkshire.'

She laughed at the way he said Yorkshire, pronouncing the end of it 'shire', the way Americans often did.

'Very glad you are here,' she said.

And for a short while, enjoying the sound of his voice, she decided she was going to forget her dreadful secret.

When they reached the Floral Hall they went through the large glass doors, passing a roped-off area and down the stairs. People were gathered around the tables, whilst some couples lounged against the walls. Clarence and Lily were an arresting sight, she in her best ruched organza frock, one of Stella's cast-offs that she had darned, stitched and hemmed, he in his smart tweed jacket, broad and high-shouldered.

But when they walked onto the beautifully sprung maple dance floor, full of excitement as they took their place amongst the swirling bodies and a feeling of happiness she wanted to be part of, something tugged at her. A doubt, a niggling worry. Something she hadn't expected.

'What's the matter?' asked Clarence. It was as though he knew what was coming.

And Lily had a feeling. She couldn't quite put her finger on it. But it was a feeling that the voices around her had lowered in pitch. That some had stopped talking, were looking over their shoulders. She could have sworn a couple nudged one another and sniggered, spoke behind their hands, glasses raised to their lips to disguise what they were saying.

Maybe she was imagining it.

She clutched his hand, feeling it warm in hers, prepared to shake the feeling off.

And they began to dance. It was different to dancing with Vincent – not better, no worse. Just different. And who was to find fault in that? She felt waves of pleasure shudder through her body. From the tips of the toes all the way up to the top of the head, the way he spun her around the floor made the hairs on her neck stand stiffly on end. Dancing is like dreaming with your feet, a conversation between body and soul, Stella had always said. And she was right, thought Lily. That's what this felt like.

They moved together, oblivious to people's stares. Oblivious to people wondering what was going on under the ruched silk and pleats of her dress. Oblivious to the woman saying, 'She's *pregnant,* I swear on my mother's life. Look at her when he spins her around, *the line of the dress! Look at her bump!*'

'Do you think that fella is the father? If she is, she's in trouble all right. She's not wearing a wedding ring.'

'And neither is he,' said a second.

A third woman leaned in and sneered. 'I'm sure she's one of the Lafferty lot. She works at that dance hall just off the prom. What's she going to do when he disappears back to Jamaica or Barbados or wherever it is he's from? Her father would drag her out of here by her hair if he could see what a holy show she's making of herself.'

And then there was another conversation about how the girl was lucky Cliff wasn't here to witness such a terrible thing, very fortunate indeed for Lily Lafferty that he's in some godforsaken distant corner of the world – didn't you hear? He's bashing the ivories in Egypt?

'Young people, these days. They just don't care, they have no shame.'

Meanwhile, Lily and Clarence continued to dance. People moved around them but it just felt like shapes rearranging themselves in the room. And pushing aside all these snippets of conversation around her, the stares and the gossip, he led her around the floor as if she was on air, made her feel dizzy with his touch, awaking feelings of joy that she had almost forgotten. Holding each other tight, looking into his eyes that she thought were warm and sweet, it was as if they melted into each other, and their movements were in turn gentle, and then spirited. She didn't care about anything, because she danced and danced and danced some more, and with him in her arms, she felt better than she had done in months and there was nothing that anyone could say that would ruin that.

The bottle, with its jagged, spiked edges – the consequences of an ugly brute of a man smashing the end of it against a table – was thrust towards Clarence, directed straight between those beautiful eyes. If he hadn't lunged to the side it might have done more than just snagged the skin of his temple. Lily could do little but stare as she watched the hulk slam his fist into the side of Clarence's face, and then the brute look stupid and mildly surprised at the Roman candle of blood spurting out in an arc and splattering all over a faded framed picture of Lord Kitchener on the wall. The music wasn't playing any more and it felt strangely quiet for a brief time. And then someone shouted, 'Call the police!'

She had expected them all to run away. But the monster, defiantly unapologetic, the group snorting and stamping behind him, stood with his feet planted firmly apart, hands on hips, waiting to see what was going to happen next.

There was a whack of boots on the floor, men's voices, at first low and indistinct, then rising to the pitch of cackling hyenas. Lily's heart began to pound. Finally, Clarence, focusing, swung back his arm and struck his clenched fist at the man. Then someone rushed into the dance hall, clutched Lily's arm, and told her that she had to leave.

The big question everyone was asking was: what had Clarence done to cause this? And in the meantime, the hulk still stood there, hands on hips, lazy, challenging.

'What did they expect me to do? Not defend myself?' muttered Clarence, nursing his head. He stared ahead, accepting of his fate, frustrating Lily and making her feel sad at the same time.

'Come outside,' she said, pulling him by the sleeve. 'Please, Clarence! Come outside!'

He followed her, his hand pressed against the side of his head, gulping in the fresh air and reeling. Only to find, rounding the corner, that there were four youths leaning on a Rover, the engine idling, watching them, waiting for their next move.

'Here, let me help you,' one of them said, reaching out a hand.

'Thank you,' said Clarence, staggering towards him, but at the last minute, the miserable idiot snatched it away and Clarence fell, stumbling face first onto the pavement. He could hear laughter, slow hand-clapping, someone shouting, 'It's an ambulance he needs, let's get out of the bloody place!', then the sound of doors slamming shut as they prepared to roared off in the car.

Lily could feel herself shaking, but it was as if she was overtaken by some new courage, as if a ferocity ran through her veins as she stood in front of the car, hands on the bonnet, legs apart, and jabbed a finger at them. She knew what she was about to say didn't make sense, but she was going to say it anyway.

'Leave him alone!' she said determinedly. 'You bullies! What the hell has he done to deserve this?'

The driver, got out, grinning. 'Ooh, fiery little lass, aren't we?'

And there were no words. She was suddenly lashing out and kicking at his shins. The man yelped, clutched his leg and hopped in circles. The other three in the car laughed.

Lily raised her head and raked her hands back through her tangled hair.

Clarence placed a calming hand on her shoulder. 'That's enough now, Lily. That's enough.'

'Come on, fellas!' she yelled. 'If you have any argument, you can start it with me. Say it to my bloody face, why don't you?'

They laughed harder, then, as the sounds of police-car bells grew closer, one of them shoved his fingers into his mouth and whistled. The man got into the car and it roared off.

'Come with me. Let's get you away before the police get here and get you cleaned up,' she said to Clarence as the car disappeared around the corner.

'No,' he said. 'I'll be fine. I don't want to get you into any more trouble. This was a mistake. I should never have asked you out.'

'It was nothing of the sort,' she said. 'Those people will always see badness where there is none, so what's the point in worrying what they think?'

Oblivious to disapproving looks from the few passers-by, they headed down the promenade, he limping slightly, she propping him up with his arm draped over her shoulder. She was distracted by the worry of him becoming weaker and weaker. Blood trailed on the paving slabs, a dribble of it was on her skirt she noticed. All this over dancing. He hadn't been causing trouble, just dancing with a girl.

Lily took him up the narrow, creaking stairs to her flat. Once inside, she told him to sit on the small put-you-up bed in the corner of her room. She took the frayed towel hanging over the rail under the sink and her touch was soft and gentle as she pressed it against his skin and sopped up the blood. And she only realised then quite how bad the bruising was, and he winced as her fingers glanced across his cheek.

'OK. Don't think about anything else. You're here now. And you can stay tonight if you want.'

'Here? In your room?' he said, shocked.

'I don't care. The world is a cruel place. But inside this room, it's different. Is that better?' she asked, rinsing the towel out in the sink.

Later, they sat together on the floor, backs against the wall.

Above his lip, she noticed there was a small scar, like a silvery eel under his skin. He saw her looking at it.

'Walked into a door when I was twelve,' he laughed. 'No heroics involved, I'm afraid.'

'You were brave tonight. To stand up to those men.'

'I don't know about that. If you hadn't sent them packing, it could have been a lot worse. That brute was right. You're a fiery lass!'

She smiled. 'You're a grand dancer,' she said. 'Where d'you learn to dance like that?'

'Can't hardly remember. Danced before I could walk, I learned holding onto the table leg and the back of a chair.' But then the smile slid from his face.

'What's the matter?'

'The time,' he said. 'Ten o'clock, I reckon. I go back like this, and I'm for it. I go back this late, I'm also for it. They won't let me go to Manchester, that's for sure and I'm supposed to be going for a month to help with the electrics on a new communications bunker they're building over there.'

Lily frowned. 'You're not in a fit state to go anywhere.'

'I'll mend. And it's the rules. And, you know, punishments. They live by them in the army. This won't go down well at all.'

'We'll see about that,' said Lily.

There was a knock on the door. Lily started, opened it an inch, and placed her foot in it to stop it. It was the landlady, cold cream on her face, her hair sticking out in tufts.

'I heard what happened.'

Lily's heart beat fast. 'I'm s-sorry,' she stuttered.

'Nothing to be sorry for. I'm not the type to judge and I couldn't give a fig. You wouldn't be the first couple to be expecting a baby. I take as I find. And I don't see anything wrong with two people in love,' said Joyce.

Lily nodded, took the fresh jug of warm water Joyce was holding, gratefully.

'Baby?' said Clarence, in shock.

Chapter 22

When Joyce left, Clarence and Lily talked. It was the release that she needed and, in a great outpouring of sadness and anguish, but also huge relief at being to say the words out loud, she found she was able to say, yes, I'm pregnant and I'm terrified, and to her surprise, he didn't seem to think it was the end of the world. In fact, he seemed just as hopeful as she was that Vince would marry her when he returned home. 'Why wouldn't he want to be with such a lovely girl as you? To hell with everyone, it's only a baby,' Clarence said. And she felt as if the cloud of worry about her head was beginning to lift.

Clarence left to return to the barracks, cuts dabbed clean, bruises soothed – and took with him the knowledge that there were people in this town who were kind, who would help a stranger because it was the right thing to do.

*

What had she been thinking of? Lily asked herself the next day. Every time she looked in the mirror, the growing bump looked back at her. Even though she was still able to disguise it sitting behind the booth taking tickets, large coat draped over her lap and her shoulders, she should have known dancing would have been impossible and that her stomach would show through the dress she was wearing, too flimsy for this time of year – a cold January morning. She should never have gone dancing with Clarence in the first place. But she was here to put that right. The officer at the barracks looked across his desk at Lily and smiled.

It wasn't often that he had such a pretty girl sitting in his office. If he could, he would have just leaned over the desk, reached out and touched her glossy curls, stroked her smooth white cheeks. He wondered what it would be like to kiss those lips …

'So I wanted to say thank you,' said Lily, bringing him back to the present, 'to Sergeant Aimé for his bravery. Stepping in to save me from the hoodlums who were trying to steal my purse. Will you reward him in some way?'

The officer faltered.

'He's so looking forward to Manchester,' she added. 'He's so proud to serve.'

Her words certainly helped. But it was her smile that did it.

*

Two days later, Lily turned her head to look at the light slicing between the curtains. It was early. Swinging her legs over the side of the bed, she sat with her fingers pressed against her temples. The knots of worry in her stomach grew tighter. Padding barefoot across the room she flung open the curtains. The sky was cloudless and unending and she made her way into the bathroom. She felt herself panic about how much her body had changed in these past months. Her instinct was to push down the fearfulness, try to move on past it and start her day. She made her way downstairs, got dressed, and set off to meet Clarence. She was going to say goodbye to him.

The gardens were quiet at this time of the year. There was a woman with a child feeding the ducks at the boating lake and someone had tied a forlorn-looking dog by a thin leash to the railings. She took a deep breath and followed the path through the manicured lawns sloping towards the sea front. The pale January sun shone through the bordering trees, dappling the ground with bright spots of light. Her muscles relaxed and she could feel her face soften. Could it be that the fresh air might smooth out the frown lines that had appeared between her brows over the past few months? There was a stream running from a fountain that was an arrangement of misshapen rocks, winding its way here and there, trickling over mossy stones, then through clumps of weeds. A robin hopped across the path then fluttered up into the branches of a tree. She unbuttoned her collar. It felt good. Nothing had changed, nothing at all beyond this garden, her father was still away, her mother was still crazy, she was still pregnant, but this moment of tranquillity was a brief respite.

She heard a sound behind her – a twig snapping. She turned and saw Clarence bobbing through the trees, ducking to avoid a low-hanging branch.

'See, told you I would be here,' she said to him, smiling, revealing the slight gap in her front teeth.

'I would have been heartbroken if you hadn't turned up,' he said, and they walked, arms linked, enjoying the feel of the sunlight on their faces.

'I did, though. One thing this war is teaching me is to try and march on to happiness, not look back all the time.'

'What's everyone saying? That you should be ashamed of helping me?'

'Don't be stupid. Anyway, we're a right pair, aren't we? Here's you, in trouble just because you danced with me, and me because … well, because of this baby. But I don't give tuppence. I told your officer as much. He said he would see to it, that he would take care of things for you.'

'Oh, Lily,' he said, with a sigh. 'I can't thank you enough. I nearly fainted dead away when the captain told me. But mostly I can't thank you enough, for standing by me against all those people. Not many would do that. You could have run away. But you took me to your lodgings. That really meant something.'

When they reached the Italian Gardens, they linked arms with one another as they walked along, falling into a steady rhythm. There were a few people in the gardens, a man raking the gravel paths, a woman pushing a pram, glancing away when she noticed them. Lily really didn't care. This was important. She was going to show the world she didn't give a fig. Behind the trees she could see the Palm House ahead with its delicate lead windows, glinting panes of graceful sloping and curved glass, reflecting the sunlight. As they got closer, you could see the throng of bright green tropical plants inside, otherworldly and vibrant, with their rubber leaves, thick and prickly.

They walked along the side of the boating lake and he put his arm around her shoulders. Then they stopped and stood in front of the floral clock.

'So what's for you now?' he asked. 'You've got to face this, Lily.'

'I know. But my mam. It'll kill her. Thank God my dad is away.'

'She might surprise you.'

'Trust me,' said Lily, 'I know exactly what she'll say.'

They rounded the corner and she found herself in front of a large flower clock. She was reminded of *when she and Matt were little, spending what felt like* hours, waiting for the hands to move of the clock in St George's Hall Gardens, with yellow posies on the large one, violets on the small one. The thought of it made her feel homesick suddenly. She remembered how she never seemed to catch the hands jerking even an inch when you watched them, and yet the time moved on, imperceptibly and inevitably. That's what she felt like now, her hand on her belly. How time had time moved, imperceptibly, and tragically inevitably.

She didn't see Vincent coming through the gates, shading his eyes and scanning the park, then walking with purpose towards them. She didn't see him stop in his tracks, his heart thudding against his chest, feeling as though he had been hit by a truck, reaching out to steady himself against a lamp post.

So it was true! He hadn't believed what they were saying, because Lily was his girl. But there she was, cavorting around with the fellow everyone was talking about. And my God! The rumours weren't just gossip! How *sickening*. They were right, there was no mistaking it. She *was* pregnant. He could see the swell of her stomach, the rise of her breasts. He felt the blood rush to his head, was ready to stride over and hit the fellow square in the face. There they were together, bold as brass, leaning against the railings of the bloody bandstand, thigh against thigh, heads bent, deep in conversation.

Lily! She's just like the others, he thought, smarting. All those wives sending letters saying they want a divorce, or girlfriends breaking off romances because they had got sick of waiting for their men to come home. And now it was the same for him. His sweetheart, in the arms of another man. He clenched his fist, wondered what it would feel like if he were to run over and leap across the railings, and smash the low-life's face in.

His mind was in turmoil. With the sun bleeding through the blurred edges of their silhouettes, he decided revenge might be sweet, but the humiliation would be worse. Better to pretend he didn't care. But how could he walk away? Much as he knew this was sensible, he felt such rage, such fury bursting through his veins, that he found himself running towards the bandstand, leaping up the stairs, one, two, three at a time, scrambling over the stunted flowerbeds, then drawing back his hand and pounding his fist into Clarence's face.

Lily screamed. 'What the hell are you doing!' she cried.

'Here's another for luck,' he yelled, swinging wildly.

But Clarence was strong, caught his forearm and twisted it behind his back in a painful arm lock.

'You another that's been hanging around the barracks looking for trouble? What is it that you can't stand so much about me and this girl? Bloody animals, *all of you!*'

'He's not an animal,' cried Lily. 'That's Vince! My fella.'

Clarence dropped the arm in shock. Vincent nursed his shoulder, twisted it in its socket, and winced.

'Your fella! I'm not anyone's fella, least of all yours. Sod you, Lily. You can keep your sloppy seconds. You're welcome. Just eff off!'

She moved forward, reached out an arm. 'It's not what it seems!'

'Not what it seems? State of you! Knocked-up the minute my back's turned! Don't bloody touch me!' he cried, shrugging her off roughly, then strode away and Lily could do no more than watch as she slumped to the ground, crying and sobbing, a cold fear gripping every atom of her body. What was to become of her now?

Chapter 23

The following day, with dark clouds threatening rain, Stella stood looking wanly at the fishmonger's slab. The glass window with its arc of gold letters reading 'Sandy's' was dripping with condensation, water wriggling down the inside of it and pooling on the sill. The man behind the counter, his pristine apron tied around his huge stomach and a doughnut of fat wobbling around his neck, smiled at her apologetically. The single piece of dried plaice that she was staring at looked forlorn and unloved, curling up around the edges. Fresh food, particularly meat and fish, was becoming more and more difficult to come by as the war dragged on; even so, Stella decided, rationing wasn't such a bad thing as at least it had brought an end to greedy folk up at the crack of dawn, cleaning out the stores before others had time to get there. For months now, the Laffertys had got by on turnip and curried carrots, and parsnip and onion stew, and Stella's mouth watered at the thought of something different: fish, meat, anything at all.

Stella leaned in to him, spoke in a low voice, and crinkled up her face into a sweet smile. 'Haven't you got some cod under the counter?'

'No, love,' he replied, flatly.

'Nothing for the Laffertys?' said Stella, plaintively. 'Just half a cod? Just to put a bit of fish on our plates?'.

'I've got diddly-squat, love. Sorry.'

She had half a mind to ask him how he'd managed to stay as fat as a house with food so hard come to by these last three months.

'Look, queen, if I had a bit of cod under the counter I'd give it you. But I haven't.'

'Oh, come on, love,' said Stella, as she leaned forward, tossed her coppery hair and smiled sweetly and seductively.

'Stella, I've no cod! Watch my lips. No C.O.F.D.'

Stella pursed her mouth.

'There's no "F" in cod,' she said, frowning.

'That's just what I've been trying to tell you. There's no effin' cod!'

She humphed and went to leave.

'Stel,' he said, stopping her as she walked out off the door. 'Heard your Lily's got another fella? Heard about that fight at the Floral Hall with the coloured fella.'

The words hit her like a fist punching her stomach. What are you talking about? She wanted to say. But she was too worried where that would take her. Surely this was just back-fence talk? What on earth did he know about Lily? How could the gossip have travelled all this way from St Jude's? But then when she arrived home, a letter sat on the doormat to confirm it.

24 January
14 Scarisbrick Road
Southport

Dear Mrs Lafferty,

I hope your children are thriving at St Jude's. I've heard the evacuation programme has been a huge success in Freshdale. It's amazing how the sisters can turn things around for youngsters. When this war is over they will send them back to the back streets of Liverpool quoting Shakespeare and reciting Latin. However, onto graver matters. I feel it is only proper to tell you that the gossip is that Lily is pregnant. There was an ugly fight at the Floral Hall, which I had the misfortune to witness, so you might want to reach out to your daughter. The father is a soldier at the barracks in Mere Lane. He was stationed at Burtonwood for a time. I believe he is from the West Indies. Jamaica. Or Trinidad. Nellie's daughter, Bridget Mulcahy, a girl I know who is at St Jude's, confirmed it to me in a letter. She said he is some kind of a pianist. I didn't want to be too hasty. Rest assured, I have urged Bridget to keep the talk from the nuns. But I expect it will only be a matter of time before they find out so I will leave it to you to perform the worrisome task of informing them.

Yours sincerely,

Mrs Callaghan

Stella, feeling waves of panic rising through her body, screwed up the letter, flung open the door of the range, and shaking, threw it inside, where it curled at the edges and reduced to ash and floated away. She wasn't going to read another word. This awful woman, a friend of Annie's, had always been a terrible gossip. She didn't believe a single word of it. And yet . . . And yet . . .

Stella went upstairs, got dressed out of her overall and, without thinking what she was doing, changed into a ridiculous velvet frock with flounces around the bottom of the skirts that looked as if she was about to set off to a dance, and an ill-matching pair of white Mary Jane shoes. She came back downstairs, slipped off the shrug she was wearing, took the iron from the range, set up the board, and prepared to go through the motions of smoothing out the creases in order to distract her from the tide of worry in her head. When she turned around, Lily was stood there, hat in one hand, umbrella with a handle shaped like a bird's head in the other.

'I'm sorry I missed Rosie's funeral,' she said, forlornly.

'Oh, love. I wasn't expecting you to come. Besides, it was too too sad.'

And whether by accident or intention, Lily sighed and unbuttoned the worn trench coat she was wearing, allowing it to gape open to show her mother the awful truth.

Stella dropped the iron onto the board; it hissed steam, burnt her wrist, and she gasped.

'Jesus, Mary and Joseph!' cried Stella. 'You *are* pregnant! That Callaghan woman wasn't lying! Oh, love!'

She staggered backwards, fell into a chair and dropped her head into her hands as though she could barely look at her. 'Oh Lily, just when I was getting back on my feet! And now this! Do the nuns know?'

'The nuns?'

'At St Jude's. Sister Assumpta. I received a letter from Iris Callaghan. She said there had been gossip, talk. I didn't want to believe her. She's always been a muckraker, that one. I didn't have enough room in my head to cope with the dreadful things she was saying.'

'Talk? Who from?'

'I don't know. Doesn't really matter. Whoever started it, gossip is like quick-fire, love. But how are you going to hide that bump? You're not even trying! Have you no shame?'

Lily shrugged.

'What are you going to do?'

'Do?' Lily looked at her vaguely. 'I don't know. That's why I've come home.'

'How far gone are you?'

Shrugging again, Lily turned and faced the other way. It was too painful to meet her mother's eyes.

'I didn't know I was pregnant. No one told me. You never told me a thing,' she said, sadly.

'Don't be so ridiculous. Are you blaming me? I asked you if you were pregnant! You said no and I believed you, fool that I am!'

'I had no idea.'

'Did you not have morning sickness? And what about the curse?'

'I thought it was the nun's porridge making me ill. Or the sour milk. I thought I had my Auntie Mary. Turned out, I probably hadn't. Just something that happens sometimes, Aggie said.'

'Who's Aggie?'

'Just a girl I know.'

'How could you have been so stupid?' Stella cried.

'It's not my fault.'

'Whose is it then?'

Lily shrugged again. 'Dunno.'

'Is that all you've got to say for yourself? Dunno?' Stella marched over, took her daughter's chin, and twisted her head to face her. '*Dunno*?' she repeated.

Lily winced, looked at her mother sadly, and felt even more stupid and ashamed.

'Perhaps we should speak to the nuns. They'll know what to do,' said Stella.

'No!' said Lily.

Stella sighed.

'Please, Mam. I'm tired. We'll decide later.'

'Decide what?'

'What to do about this baby.'

'Oh Lily,' said Stella again. 'My heart is breaking for Vincent. Does he know? They say if you love two people at the same time, always choose the second because if you really loved the first you wouldn't have fallen in love with the second. But I don't know, I don't know. Perhaps, well, if Vincent is away perhaps you could pass this child off as his? You're dark enough with that olive skin and those brown eyes ...'

Lily looked at her bewildered. 'What?'

'This fellow from Jamaica, or wherever he's from – does he love you? Or was it just, you know, a quick fumble? That you got carried away?'

'What are you talking about?' Lily said, bewildered.

'This fellow of yours—'

'What?'

'The Callaghan woman told me you've been hanging about with a – well—'

'Pianist?' interjected, Lily, sarcastically. 'Say it.' She jutted out her chin. 'Mam, now who's the stupid one? It's not Clarence's baby. It's Vincent's!'

Stella frowned, confused, trying to make sense of what Lily was saying

'Wait. What do you mean, "*it's Vincent's*"? That Callaghan woman has been running around telling everyone that it's a blessed piano player from Jamaica!'

'Oh, good God!' cried Lily. 'Why on earth would she say that?'

'She said you were at a dance hall with him. And that someone there said you were having his baby. Bridget-someone confirmed it?'

'Bridget's lost the plot. Bridget doesn't know the time of day, Ma. Why anyone would listen to what Bridget had to say I don't know.'

Stella reeled with shock or relief – she couldn't decide which was the stronger of the two emotions.

'And what does Vincent say?' asked Stella.

'Vincent? Vincent doesn't think it's his.'

'Well, at least that's one thing we can put right,' said Stella, grabbing her coat and heading out of the door, pulling Lily behind her.

Chapter 24

The Whartons' clock had a tick that was the loudest Lily had ever heard. Though perhaps it was just the disconcerting silence that made it appear so.

'Scotch pancake?' asked Mrs Wharton, pushing a saucer of the limp, stale cakes over to Stella and Lily who sat facing her on the other side of the parlour table.

'Scotch pancake*?* Is that all you've got to say?' said Stella.

'The baby's not his,' said Mrs Wharton, flatly.

Lily felt her legs wobble. It was as if the fringes on the red lampshade of the wooden standard lamp had begun to sway back and forth, or was it just her eyes losing focus? How could a person change from being so friendly, so charming, to such a cold-hearted witch?

'But Mrs Wharton, look at me,' Lily stuttered, fixing her with a desperate stare as she gestured towards her stomach, appealing her to listen, to make her believe that she was telling the truth. 'I know about the gossip.

And how it would suit some folk to spread this version of the story around. More colourful, I suppose. In every way. But I'm not that sort of a girl. I've only ever been with Vincent. And apart from that, it doesn't even make sense. I've only really known Clarence these last four weeks! So how can I be this far gone? It has to be Vincent's!'

Mrs Wharton, stared at her coldly, without a shred of compassion.

'I'm only saying what I know to be true.' She tossed back her head, stuck her chin out, and gave her a withering look. 'Anyway, you're lying. What kind of girl gets herself pregnant? A liar, and a selfish one at that.'

Lily looked outside, blinking back tears, took the gloomy weather and the bombed houses opposite that she could see through the window as a perfect accompaniment to how she was feeling.

'I know what you're up to, Beryl Wharton,' said Stella. 'You're trying to pin the blame on Clarence because you don't want your Vincent left with a child to feed and raise. Very convenient, these rumours. Was it you who put the poison into Vincent's head? You know it's not this Clarence fellow's. And so do I. God, I actually feel sorry for Vincent.'

Lily was praying for Vincent to come in from the other room.

'There's nowt you can do about that. Vincent went off to sea again this morning. And we've no idea when he's back. Except that it won't be for another six months at least.'

'I don't believe you,' said Lily.

Vincent's mother shrugged and turned away from them. 'I must say, I never would have thought it of you, Lily. So disappointing. Will he marry you, this Clarence character?'

'It's not his!' she cried. 'I've told you. It's Vincent's! Why do you keep going on about Clarence?'

Beryl Wharton looked at her, the corners of her mouth turning down into a sneer. 'Rot,' she said.

Lily felt herself trembling. All the life drained out of her in an instant.

'You really think it's Clarence's baby? I'm nearly six months pregnant.'

'You don't look six months pregnant,' she snapped. 'Anyway, everyone is saying it's this chap's baby.'

'Everyone?' said Stella. 'And who have you told this lie to?'

'Please, Mrs Wharton. You have to help me,' said Lily.

'What can I do? I'm only the monkey. Tell that to the organ grinder.'

'What are you on about?' yelled Lily, losing her temper, her cheeks flushing.

Mrs Wharton stood. She began clearing away the plate of untouched cakes and the jug of water. 'Look, leave now. How can I believe a word you say? Liar, liar, pants on fire,' she snapped, bitterly. 'I'll not having you trap our Vincent into thinking the child's his.'

'No! It *is* our baby. Mine and Vincent's. I love him! We love each other!'

'It doesn't look like it. When did you last hear from him? He told me he wrote a letter to you, breaking it off. Didn't he? Have you not received it, then?'

She fixed her with a cruel appraising gaze, glacial and unfeeling.

'I-I . . .' Lily stuttered, feeling defeated and alone.

Stella gathered up her shawl, pulling it tight across her body, and drawing herself up with an expression on her face that showed the strength of her feelings, announced that this was a waste of flaming time and she had never heard such nonsense in her life.

They left the house. Mrs Wharton heard the door slam shut and watched Stella and Lily from behind the blackout curtain, two hunched desperate figures, making their way down the ravaged street.

Ten minutes later, the door slammed open.

'You had callers, Mam?' said Vincent, shaking out his mackintosh.

'No,' she replied.

'Then what's with the pancakes?' he said, stuffing one into his mouth.

'Nowt. Don't bother yourself, son. Just a bit of summat over nothing.'

*

When they arrived home, Lily curled into herself, the pale blue coverlet bunched up around her, hugging her knees to her chest. When she rolled onto her back, Stella saw the whole truth of what had been happening over the past six months. Lily placed her hand on her bump, not shrouded in a coat, or covered with a blanket, but exposed, smooth, and white, with her belly button protruding. Her face looked sad and frightened.

'It's not fair, Mam.'

Stella took her hand, stroked the back of it. 'Life's not fair. This bloody war has shown us that.'

'What d'you mean?' asked Lily.

Stella pressed her lips together. It was still too painful to speak about. 'I mean Vincent.'

Lily pulled the covers back over her, and played with the tassel on her mother's shawl as she had as a child.

'So what now?' said Stella, tenderly.

What Stella had dearly wanted to say was, if you decide to keep the baby, I'm sure we could sort something out. Why should we care about what anyone thinks? What with this war on, everyone coming and going, I could even pass the child off as mine. But she knew this was a fantasy. The shame would be too much for any of them to bear. She pushed a tendril of Lily's hair behind her ear.

Lily winced. She looked at Stella, bewildered. 'Without Vincent, what's the point of keeping the baby? How would we manage? What would everyone say? They'd call me a slut or a fallen woman. I couldn't bear it, Mam.'

Stella paused. Was now the time to bring up St Jude's?

But suddenly, Lily cried, 'So, don't you see, that's why he *has* to come back and find me!' She banged her fist on the bed as if to underscore her feelings. 'I can't believe he won't change his mind. Can I please stay here until I have the baby in case he does?'

'Of course,' said Stella, despondently. It was agonising to see her daughter still so hopeful, so in love with Vincent.

Then Lily felt something suddenly, lifted up her blouse. There was no mistaking or hiding this baby now. And to her amazement, she could actually see it, a wave, a ripple, a stubby shape moving under her skin, a bump, but there it was, the heel maybe, a fist. Good grief. It was a baby. An actual baby.

'Mam, the baby. You can actually see it moving!'

Stella gasped. She came back over to the side of the bed, placed her hand on her daughter's stomach. And there it was.

'She's turning. Oh Lily ... Lily ...'

'What?'

Was now the moment to tell her? thought Stella. If she was a good mother, wouldn't now be the time to share her awful secret? But how would that help things? This really was a hopeless situation.

'Try and get some sleep, love. Everything will feel better when you're not so tired.'

Lily sat up, wrapped herself up in the bed covers. No, it won't, she thought. And then suddenly she felt a kick. A little angry kick. And a reminder that time was running out.

Chapter 25

This time Stella wasn't going to put the letter from the Corporation away in a drawer, under the mattress, or into the range. It had been bloody mindedness that had made her shove all the others to the back of the roll-top desk with the rest of the unopened letters, gathering dust and causing problems. But now she thought of Lily, and of Cliff, and what he would be saying if he was here instead of sweltering in another continent: Don't just stand there, love, get a shovel! She had to change things if she was going to be in any fit state to help her daughter. And so this was what she was doing.

She moved from room to room, picking up laundry, throwing away old newspapers from behind the sofa. If there was something good to come out of these last couple of months, it was the fact that it had jolted her out of her depression, brought on so unexpectedly with missing Cliff, and into the present. She had decided she was going to became the mother that Lily remembered, though she was still Stella, still crazy, but a survivor.

Lily on the other hand, had just slumped over the past two months. It was painful to watch. For weeks they had had conversations about adoption and the nuns, but she just looked at her vaguely and refused to talk about what was going to happen after the baby came. She barely even noticed the bombs that were being dropped, and even started to refuse to go to the shelter. She was so quiet these days, though the crying had stopped, at least on the outside, and Stella knew that was dangerous. Any day now her daughter would either explode or fall to pieces so someone was going to have to hold things together. But pulling herself up by her bootstraps was just so hard, Stella thought, as she opened the Corpy's letter, and laid it next to all the others. There was one from the bank, telling her that they had exactly two pounds and four shillings in savings. There was one from the co-op – the divvies she had collected left her with one shilling in that account. Then there was the pawnshop – five shillings she owed there. And the tick man, Carroty Des. He had lent her two pounds for the kids' presents last Christmas, the lead soldiers with the arms that pivoted, the jewellery box with a ballerina that rotated when you opened it, and she still hadn't *paid it.*

The weight of these responsibilities came crashing down on her. She had no idea what she was going to do, so she wandered from room to room, picking up clothes that Lily had left lying where she took them off, a discarded shrug, a crumpled ribbon. She was relying entirely on Matt and Annie now for money. Of course, apart from the church that lurked, omnipresent, their divine protector, sending her news of how the children were doing, '*Bobby is improving his arithmetic skills and Deirdre is enjoying baking, both are enthusiastic members of St Jude's Digging for Victory programme in the nuns' garden*', the last letter from the nuns had said, but she didn't trust St Jude's one bit. Why would she? She knew all too well that you didn't get something for nothing. And what about if they decided to swoop in on the little ones and she never saw them again?

The biggest fear for her as a child had been the nightwatchman who knocked on the door while they were sleeping, checking for illegal overcrowding and whether the adults in the house were in a fit state to look after the kids, followed by a prompt visit from the health visitors. The bogeyman, they called him. No one was going to tell her she wasn't well enough to look after the kids. St Jude's had been a brief respite. That was all it was ever going to be, she told herself. She would bring them home when she had sorted out the problem of Lily.

But she had decided she was no longer going to abandon herself to self-pity and so the first place she went was the labour exchange. She left Lily sewing a patch on the knee of Matt's trousers, told her she would be back in an hour.

Weak after the two mile walk in shoes that were giving her a blister, she knew she had to find some strength. When she walked into the building, and her heels clicked over the tiled floor, a small, hunched man looked up from the desk that he was sitting at.

'Can I help you?' he said.

She nodded. 'I need a job.'

She tried to present a version of herself that was bright and optimistic.

'Good, where d'you live?'

'Caryl Street. At the other end of the road to the tenements. It's spelt C.A.R.Y.L. but everyone says Carly.'

'Yes, I know. I used to play footie down at the brickie. Now, what hours can you work?'

'I have young children. They're not with me now, but they will be soon,' she said.

'What does your husband do?'

Her voice shook. She thought she was going to cry. 'He worked at the docks. Reservist. But now he's in Egypt. My son's the only man in the house.'

Thank God for Matt, she thought. Each time, when he came home from his war work, he seamlessly took over where Cliff had left off, but she wasn't going to tell this man this. He squinted up at her. Come on. Let's see how deserving you are, his expression seemed to say. True, thought Stella, the deserving poor were hard to separate from the grasping malingerers that this war seemed to breed. But surely he could see she wasn't one of them?

'And you have your husband's wages?'

'No. Not yet.'

'I see.'

'We've got so much on tick. We had a little bit of savings from my mother, which we've been managing on. But now we have nothing.'

'And what did he do before the war?'

She traced a finger over the contours of her face. 'What's that to do with anything?'

He began to soften when he saw the frown on her brow. 'Just the form, love. You can't just expect to come in here without filling in a form.'

'Please, I don't want a lecture. I've had that all my life. I just want a job.' she said, bitterly.

'I know, love. Sorry.'

He was kinder than she had first thought, this man, and she regretted snapping at him.

'I worked at the parachute factory but that was only a fill-in. I want something more permanent now. Before that me and my husband ran a dancing school.'

'Name?'

'Laffertys.'

'Ah, I know it.' He put down his pen, laid it on the desk. 'My daughter used to do the Saturday morning swing class. Had a smashing time.' He hummed the famous opening bars of 'Puttin' on the Ritz', tapping his pen on the desk. 'She loved that. I'll sort you out, Mrs Lafferty. Maybe the Bryant and May factory?'

She smiled a tremulous smile. She was thinking, well, at least some good would come out of this; it would pay the housekeeping and they might have Scouse for tea with real meat, and cherry pie. There would be money for the electric, and maybe even some ollies for Bobby to give him when she next saw him. He was always the only one without a bag of marbles in their street, and it pained her to watch the other lads run off without him, or to see Bobby hanging back, able to do no more than look.

'That's about it.' He pushed the form over the table, slipped it over to fill in. 'Here y'are, missus. Good luck. And I wish you all the best.'

'Well, I'm glad you've got some good news. But I'm afraid I haven't,' said Lily when Stella returned home. She could feel her hand shaking, the letter fluttering as delicately as a hummingbird as she read it. 'Read this. It's taken months to get here. Must have sent it from his ship. Anyway, that's why he hasn't tried to find me. Nothing more to be done. His awful mother has got to him. But now it's final. I've been kidding myself he might come back. If I can't have Vincent, I don't want his baby,' she said, suddenly crumpling the letter up and throwing it down. Shocked by Lily's outburst, Stella picked it up from the kitchen floor and scanned the page.

Dear Lily,

I'm afraid this will be the last you hear of me. I'm sorry about what happened in the park, but I daresay if I met the chap another time, I'd do the same again. I only wish you had had the courage to tell me yourself. I thought you and I were stronger than this, but it seems our love affair was as much of a sham as all the others that have withered on the branch of this bloody war. I don't blame you. Merchant navy means a fellow is away for so long, but I do find it painful. How long have you been seeing this chap? You must have met him as soon as I left. That hurts, but there it is. I am sailing with the Harrison Line. They run transatlantic voyages so I won't be home for a good while, which is fortunate given the circumstances. The sea has a way of keeping one distracted.

Please don't contact me again. Despite everything I wish you well.

Vincent

'I want to kill myself, Mam,' she wailed.

'Love, that's the hormones talking.'

'But, Mam. You said yourself he doesn't want me. So that means it's just me and this baby. You've been saying it for weeks now. How can we afford to keep a child? And what would it do to this family, me being unmarried? I was so hoping it might not come to this. Thought something might change as I got closer to having the baby. But I've got to face it.'

The words hung in the air, unanswered, guilt-laced, and shameful.

'I'll go and get the coal in,' said Stella. 'Your father and I . . . well, your father . . . I only wish he was here. He would know what to do.'

Lily looked around at her, at the bare lamp bulb, the blackened Valor gas stove, the sagging curtains, and all the other distinct signs of wear and tear about the place like the yellowing damp patches and loose, drooping wallpaper that Stella had tried to stick up with pieces of blackout tape. And then rage took over her, and without reason, she took off her shoe, and flung it at the wall.

'Whatever did you do that for? Chucking shoes around isn't going to help things,' Stella said flatly as she left.

And then suddenly Lily had another desperate thought that overtook everything she had just said. *The shoes. Vincent's shoes. The ones he danced in,* with the battered heels, the frayed laces and the worn crevices she knew and loved so well. She had noticed them sticking out from under the sofa when she had been at the Whartons'. It had been a niggling concern that had stayed with her over the last couple of months. What were they doing there, downstairs in the parlour? Had Vincent actually been at *home* when they had visited, not at sea like his mother had said? Was there a clue in those shoes? And if the shoes hinted at a lie, what about the letter? It didn't look like an airgraph or one that had been sent from a ship. There was no stamp or signs that it had been censored. More like someone had just pushed it through the door. What if he had *been* away and was now back on leave? Was it worth one last try to find him and speak to him?

And so, whilst Stella was sleeping, she slipped outside into the alley beside their house. It was a stupid thing to do. The black sky was lit up here and there with fires burning. The colours were beautiful, a green hue above the Mersey, and she wondered if some kind of factory was burning. It was in Birkenhead or Wallasey, New Brighton perhaps.

'What d'you think you're doing? It's not safe out here!' cried an ARP man in his hat, battering on the doors of Caryl Street to tell them to turn off all the lights and take cover in the shelters. 'Bloody reckless girl! Get to the shelter! You're going to die if you don't.'

She didn't care; she moved off, walked down the hill towards the river. The streets were deserted apart from the occasional army vehicle or ambulance hurtling by. You could smell the sulphur in the air. It prickled her nostrils.

She reached the Whartons' house. The step was grimy, the front of the house, unclean.

Her heart rose to her throat. She stared up to the window of Vincent's room. Picking up a handful of gravel, she threw it at the pane of glass. But who was to hear that pathetic sound against the moan of the sirens? No doubt, if it was Vincent in there, he would just think it was shrapnel, or someone's window being blown out from an incendiary bomb. She picked up a larger stone, cradled it in her hand, and then threw it with all her might.

It bounced off the window as if it was a rubber ball.

'Vincent!' she cried, cupping her hands around her mouth. 'Are you in there?'

The blackout curtains told her nothing and gave her no clue what was behind.

The whole idea was stupid and pointless. The numbing sensation in her brain was causing her actual physical pain. She scrabbled in her pocket for a handkerchief to put over her mouth and she wondered what she was doing, shouting at a window, cramps in her belly, and a searing pain in her head.

She was about to turn and walk away when the window was flung open, and a head stuck out.

'Vincent!' she cried, her heart leaping to her throat.

'*Go away*!' he yelled. And he slammed the window shut as quickly as it had been opened.

And in that moment, her heart broke into a thousand tiny pieces.

Tears coursed down her face as she outstretched her arms.

'Please! Vincent! Please ... You promised! You promised that when you came home you would take me dancing. Please ...' she whimpered. 'Just one more time. And then I can explain everything! All I'm asking is that we have one last dance together ... Vince? Vince are you there?'

But there was no reply. So she looked up to the heavens, and cried, 'Come on, do your worst, then!'

Then her body went limp and she felt her knees buckle as the drone of the German bombers announced their arrival; and here they were, at least twenty of them, flying in formation, and she did nothing except stand there, watching the planes open their doors and drop their black bombs which exploded as they hit the ground. Fires were breaking out all over the city and it was as if the devil was chucking down skittles from the sky, the whizzing sound so terrifying, as if the shells were actually moving past her ears. In the air, there were particles of fire and burning flecks of debris and a cold chill gripped her bones. Up here, on the brow of the hill, she could see the flames licking the wounds of the city as she squinted into the distance and watched the bombing unfold. She stood there, a hole in her shoe making itself felt, furious and desperate and sad.

Next day she found herself dragging out of bed, vaguely surprised and sorely disappointed that she was still alive, as Liverpool woke to another day of mourning.

Chapter 26

Stella came into the room and sat on the bed.

'Bad night last night,' she said. 'Garston was hit. And they got the power station at Lister Drive. I was going out of my mind. Why didn't you come to the shelter?'

'I hate the shelter, Mam. Everyone looking at me. I can't go there. I'm better under the table here.'

The raid had dropped bombs on Menlove Drive and Edge Lane. Lily had heard the roar of engines all the way through until the morning, pressed her hands over her ears in an effort to drown out the terrible sounds. Apparently, her mother told her, Betty from the Rialto had not uttered a single word for weeks since she had lost her husband and two brothers in a bombing in Wykeham Street – the dreadful event had rendered her speechless. Lily blinked away tears; she was so lonely, so desperate, she felt the same might happen to her. She couldn't even bear to tell Stella she had seen

Vincent and he had sent her away. The humiliation was just too much.

She dropped her head and pulled the blanket up to her neck. She felt ashamed. The idea of giving her baby away was so painful. But if Vincent didn't want this child, it meant he didn't want her, and that was unbearable as well. The child would be a reminder of that, every day of her life.

Stella flinched. 'Do you want me to make you a nice cup of tea, love?'

Lily shook her head.

She thought back to Aggie saying that if you couldn't change anything at least you could try your best to give your baby a better start than you'd ever had. Janet and Aggie seemed resilient, you had been happy on the boating lake and in the cafe, and even at St Jude's. Life had gone on: the sky hadn't fallen in on them; the world hadn't collapsed. Besides, she didn't know if she could stand the pointing, the name calling. It was bad enough just seeing the way Matt looked at her. Really, there was no choice. And now was the time to face it.

'Mam, tell the nuns they can have the baby. I've made my decision. I can't keep this baby. What am I to do with a child? What will everyone say about me? It's bad enough those who know about it now, but for the rest of my life? Gossiping behind my back, pointing, and calling my child a bastard and me a slut? I couldn't stand it.'

'But maybe you should—'

'I couldn't stand it! Please. I don't need any more speeches. I don't want this baby. If Vincent doesn't want me, I don't want his child. Write to the nuns. Please. And do it quickly. Please, Mam. I just can't bear it.'

And then suddenly she felt a kick. Another little angry kick. And a reminder that time was running out.

Three weeks passed. Stella was getting ready to leave for work for her job at the Owen Owen department store. The wireless was playing. Another one of the government-manipulated programmes: *Music While You Work*, cheerful, up-tempo popular music for factory workers.

'Help me with this, Lily,' said Stella.

She walked over, switched off the wireless and moved the sideboard so it stood away from the wall. Tying the blackout curtains in a large knot to lift them from the floor, she began sweeping along the skirting boards. The muck was everywhere and the clean was long overdue.

There was a knock at the door.

Over the last month, Lily had got even bigger. She felt like a whale, and she had begged Stella not to to let anyone, whoever it was, Peg Leg, anyone, to come into the house.

'Then make yourself scarce, love,' said Stella.

Lily went upstairs quickly.

Stella opened the door an inch or two, putting her foot in it to stop it swinging open wider. It was the bread man, Mr Weakforth, delivering a loaf.

'Heard your Lily is home,' he said cheerfully. Was that all he had heard? She wondered. She hadn't seen him a while, but surely he knew Lily was pregnant? Nevertheless, she wasn't going to get into a conversation with the flaming bread man.

Lily meanwhile, stood at the bedroom door, opened it a crack and listened to the exchange.

'How's she keeping? Bert's is closed down. She signed up for the WAF?'

'Land girls,' replied Stella. 'She's away on a farm ...'

'Oh, really? That's grand? Which farm?'

Stella cast her eyes around. 'Banana farm,' she stuttered, noticing the empty banana crate that Cliff had once brought back from the docks that now housed the firewood for the range.

'Banana farm? That's unusual,' he said, laughing.

Stella muttered something vague, something about needing to get back to a task she was in the middle of – baking an apple pie. Stella never baked, she'd always bought cakes from Satterthwaites Bakery in St Anne Street before it was bombed and before rationing, and he knew it.

'Don't worry, Stella, I'll not have a word said against any Lafferty, whatever trouble they're in,' he said, with a wink and a tap on the side of his nose.

'Goodbye, Wally,' said Stella crossly, pushing him out of the door. She was in no mood for gossiping about this dreadful situation.

Meanwhile, Lily shuddered. She hated this, having to hide herself away, waiting week after week for the baby to come. She wanted to fling open the window and shout into the street after the bread man that she wasn't the first girl to get herself into this mess. And was it really that awful? Having a baby? She paused. Maybe giving her baby away to a woman who lived in a germ-free kitchen was the really awful part of this mess.

She heard the sound of her mother's footstep on the stairs, avoiding the bottom one, the one that sagged and your foot would go right through it if you were to step on it. When Stella came into the room with a letter, she asked Lily if she wanted her to read it.

'It's not very nice. But you need to hear it, sweetheart,' she said, with a long sigh.

Lily nodded, waved a hand at her to read.

Stella began to read it out loud, haltingly, at first.

26 April
St Jude's
Freshdale

Dear Mrs Lafferty,

Thank you for your letter regarding your daughter's situation. The fact is, one of our girls was due to hand over her baby to a couple from Scarisbrick who are upstanding members of the community. However, there was a tragedy with the child and, as you say, Lily needs a home for her baby. Well, they are a loving couple who have unfortunately found themselves in the unenviable position of looking to adopt an infant to complete their long-wished-for family. I must say I am surprised that Lily succumbed to the way of the flesh like some of these other girls who come through our doors. But I suppose it goes to show …

Stella fought hot, angry tears and the words clutched at her heart. Her voice shook as she continued to read.

I suppose it goes to show you never can assume a girl's nature. We will pray for you and—

'Stop, Mam,' said Lily 'Let me read it myself. Go away.'

'Succumbed to the way of the flesh'. What would Assumpta bloody know about that? Lily thought bitterly. She shivered and sat on the top stair. She thought of the couple, desperate to take the child. Had the room been decorated? Was there a Babar book on a shelf? A stuffed Winnie-the-Pooh propped up in the corner? A drum for a boy? A doll's house for a girl? A pretty paper mobile, no doubt. A pink or blue (or yellow to be safe) blanket that she had lovingly crocheted. An eiderdown. A crib. With a Lloyd Loom chair for her to sit in and rock the baby to sleep. All the things she had dreamed of giving her own children one day but knew that if she kept this baby, it would have to make do with hand-me-downs from the Sally Army and home-made toys that fell apart in days.

Lily continued to read.

We will pray for you and hope God will guide Lily back to the path of righteousness. Be reassured that Lily's misfortune will in some way give hope once more to the lady and gentleman in Scarisbrick after the disappointment of the stillborn.

She felt herself shaking and the paper quivered in her hand, making the words shimmy across the page as she read it and reread it. Was it Bridget's baby they were talking about? Or Aggie's? No, it couldn't be. Aggie would have already had her baby by now. So had Bridget's baby died? Was it now one of the babies buried in the nuns' garden after a sad little funeral, a few Hail Mary's and a Novena rushed through by Father Donnelly? Or had she left without giving her up? She hoped she had.

If Lily needs our help, she can have her baby here in our labour ward. Her child would be going to a much-needed loving family. It would be an act of God, a gift, a sacrifice to Jesus, if you will, which would make her decision so much more the better. If you bring her back, we will put her in the annex, and then when the child comes, she will give birth, supervised by Sister David who is a qualified nurse and will most likely see her through the birth. If there are complications there are health professionals at hand. The necessary forms will be sent for you to sign. The adoption papers will be signed after the child is born. Giving the baby away won't mean that one day she might not be reunited with her child. A christening ceremony will be arranged after the birth, if Lily wants to be there. We encourage the mother's attendance, though she should understand that the adoptive parents will probably change the name of the child. The baptism is a deeply moving religious experience and sometimes the fathers attend and often it has the happy consequence of atonement for both parents.

May God be always with you in Jesus Christ and the Heavenly Father.

Sister Assumpta

Lily shuddered. She thought of the couple, desperate to take her child from her. Images blurred from one into the other: the faceless woman cradling her baby, Sister Assumpta waving a pen at her, squinting at her through those wire-rimmed spectacles, Vincent dancing alone in a ballroom with shards of light from a mirrorball moving across his face, all mixed up with her sadness, all there to complete the circle of shame and self-hatred.

And then suddenly she felt a twinge. A sudden movement in her belly, her baby, another anxious rest-less kick.

Chapter 27

Matt came into the house carrying a bucket of sand. He had been on fire watch. That morning he had announced that, as he was seventeen now, he was old enough to leave home and, as he had been offered a volunteer job guarding RAF Morecambe aerodrome, that's what he was going to do. But they all knew the real reason he wanted to get away from Caryl Street, and besides, sleeping on Aunt Mary's sofa was hardly leaving home. Since Lily had come back home from St Jude's, he had found it difficult to look her in the eye, and they had barely exchanged a word. Just the sight of her, her protruding belly, pillowy breasts and glowing skin, was painful and shocking for him to see.

Stella stood at the stove with her back to them, frying an egg, waiting for an argument to ensue. She scooped a forkful of lard, slid it off the prongs with her finger, and watched it bubble up in the pan. When a tiny globule hissed and spat and shot out, landing on the back of her hand, she winced. Pain adding to more pain.

'Matt,' Lily asked, 'what's up with you?'

He sat across the table from Lily, turning a coin in his hand. 'What's up with *you* more like?'

'Don't start, you two,' said Stella. She could sense what was happening, had an instinct for it after all these years.

'Don't tell me you're ashamed of me an' all?'

'Just glad Da's not here to see it. Might be better if he gets blown to pieces by the Jerrys rather than have to look at that,' he said, nodding at her stomach.

'Matt! That's a terrible thing to say!' cried Stella, clattering the spatula into the pan.

'It's true,' he replied. 'What did he used to say? Children are pieces of the heart. And you would break his in two . . .'

Lily started to cry. 'Even Matt hates me,' she wailed, when he had left.

'No he doesn't. He's your brother, that's all. You have to understand it's hard for him. For all of us.'

Lily stared into the bottom of the cup of milk she was drinking. Maybe it was the thought of it, but there it was again, the pain. Only this time it was different. It increased in intensity, became so bad, that she let out a whimper, and then a moan.

'Are you all right?' asked Stella.

'Fine,' she lied, pressing her fingers to her temples.

She got up, left the room and went upstairs. Outside, the familiar clatter of the milk crates and the clip-clop of the milk cart coming down the street grew more distinct as it approached the house. At the same time, the knot of pain tightened in her stomach. This is the worst it's ever been, she thought.

She walked over to the window, hoping she could shake it off, saw the milk cart disappear around the corner, and moved back to the bed, but had to steady herself against the wall now that the stabbing feeling was coming over her in waves. She looked at herself in the mirror that was hanging crooked. Like every wonky picture in the house, it was a reminder of the bombing, like the cracks in the wall in every room, the dust on every surface. Rubbing her tongue over her lips, she barely recognised the face staring back at her.

Once again the pain came over her in waves and she felt like vomiting, and swayed backwards and forwards. She went into the bathroom, held her hair back from her face as she leaned over the sink and was sick. Her forehead rested on the edge of the basin and it felt cool on her skin. She ran the tap, swooshed water into her face.

But then there it was again, the throbbing pain, coming in waves again. It was when she reached the other side of the room, as she made her way over to the bed, that it morphed from a griping, cramping, stabbing feeling, to something bigger, something awful, a pain such as she had never felt before, terrifying and unfamiliar.

'Mam!' she cried. 'Mammy! Help!!'

The doctor, Stella already knew, kind Dr Blinkhorn, was away in Algiers.

'Joined the services. Temperature doesn't agree with him, poor man,' the woman who answered the door of the surgery told Stella. But Stella didn't give a fig that he was suffering with the blessed heat in Africa – she just wanted someone to come and see if her daughter was all right. Probably half the doctors had joined the Forces.

'Go to the hospital. You'll find a midwife on duty there,' the woman said.

When Stella got to the infirmary, the front doors were shut. She pulled the bell pull and the matron appeared. Stella recognised her as someone who had once come dancing at Caryl Street but she didn't have time for that conversation, just told her in a panicked voice that it was an emergency.

'Emergency? This city is full of emergencies. I've twenty mothers on my labour ward here. All in dire straits, all in hopeless situations.'

'Please,' said Stella, desperately. Finally, the Matron took pity on Stella and she agreed to send one of the midwives to Caryl Street.

'Though it will cost you five shillings. And as a favour, you understand, Mrs Lafferty.' Stella gave her a disgruntled nod and mentally raised her eyebrows; was that all the thanks she got for teaching her to foxtrot?

'What are you doing in here? Let's go into the kitchen where it's warm,' said Stella, when she got back home to find Lily had come downstairs and was sitting in the 'ballroom' on the tatty chaise longue. The room hadn't been used for months and there was debris and bits of plaster on the floor that had been swept into piles that no one had bothered to clear up. Lily looked at her vaguely, round-eyed with sadness, looking as desolate as the room did.

'What's that?' asked Lily as Stella handed her something wrapped in tissue paper. Lily opened it carefully. 'A ring?' she asked, frowning.

'Don't want tittle-tattle. Bought it you from Owen Owen. Only cost a few bob with my discount.'

'Oh,' said Lily sadly, as Stella took her gently by the arm and led her into the kitchen.

The midwife arrived at the house a few minutes later. Lily was still feeling the sharp pain in her stomach, but the midwife's presence, as she bustled into the room with a large bag and a stethoscope around her neck, and her no-nonsense shoes and practical hairdo, seemed to calm her.

'So, Lily, if the pain is getting worse, take some Epsom salts. You're not in labour yet. Your waters haven't broken. I'll come back and check on you tomorrow. You have Epsom salts, do you? A leave baby, is it?' asked the midwife, bustling about with bottles and powdered milk.

Lily winced, twisting the cheap ring. It was tight and her skin bulged around the edges of it. But with some people there were barriers that could never be crossed, and she had an instinct that the woman was one of them.

'And when is your husband back?'

She saw the look flashing between Stella and Lily and Lily bridled. 'My husband's dead. I'm having her adopted.'

'Oh,' said the midwife. 'Shame. And has that been arranged? Have you signed the forms?' she said, placing a bottle of cod liver oil, and a carton of orange juice on the mantelpiece. Though what she was supposed to do with that, Stella had no idea.

'The nuns at St Jude's are helping us with that.'

'St Jude's?' She glanced at Stella. 'They're very good. Very kind,' said the midwife. 'Your baby will be in safe hands. And Lily, you will be able to live your life. As long as that's what you want. You do want that, don't you?'

Lily nodded sadly.

Outside, there was the sound of a siren. Of course she didn't want to give her beautiful precious child to the nuns! But she had no choice. They were too poor. How could she bring a child into this world, with no father, with the bombing and death all around, in a city of dust and dirt, now built on rubble and heartache?

'Now, you'll need this. Give it to the nuns when you hand baby over . . .'

From a bag, the woman produced the strangest-looking contraption Lily had ever seen. It was black rubber and looked like a pod with plastic windows. A strange tube came out of it.

'It's baby's gas mask. You put her in it like this . . .'

She pumped the valve and gave a brisk smile.

'See, easy.'

Lily watched, horrified; surely a child would look like it was something out of a Frankenstein film in this.

'Use the Epsom salts and here's bandages for your breasts. They will help stop the flow. I can't promise they will be one hundred per cent successful because we can't work miracles, but try your best. That's about it,' she said. 'I must say, with this dreadful bombing nearly every blessed night, who would want to bring a baby into the world?'

Not me, thought Lily. Certainly not if Vincent doesn't want me.

'But at least you can have the baby adopted and pretend this never happened. Now, your mother has said you don't want to go to the hospital, so I should leave for St Jude's as soon as you can. I think this baby is ready to come sooner than we think. Eight months or so, your mother said? You should thank your lucky stars for the sisters. And your mother, of course.'

Tears streamed down Lily's face.

'Now what on earth are you crying for? Your secret is safe with me, dear,' she said, with a reassuring pat on the knee, which only made Lily feel a thousand times worse than she already did for misjudging the woman so badly.

Barely an hour later the gush of water from between her legs was frightening and shocking. Wet against her thighs, her sodden underclothes stuck to her flesh. Why had no one told her about this?

'Mam!' she shrieked. 'What's happening to me?'

She reached for the mantelpiece to steady herself.

'Mam! I think the baby's coming!'

Stella, downstairs cleaning the hall tiles, dropped the mop. It clattered down onto the floor and the bucket spilled as she tripped over it in her panic. She raced up the stairs, three at a time. When she got to the top, Lily had stumbled to the door, clutching the bottom of her stomach, and moaning.

'Go back and lie on the bed!' cried Stella.

Lily clambered on top of it, grabbing on to Stella's arm to help her. When she released her mother's arm, her fingers had gripped her so tightly she had left slender imprints on the flesh. Stella shoved her from behind, each hand placed firmly on her bottom, and Lily rolled over and lay on her back, moaning. Stella wiping her shiny forehead, holding a clump of her hair away from her face,

Lily let out great breaths of air through puffed-out cheeks. The pain was coming in great, rolling waves and she could feel moisture pooling under her arms and dripping down her face as beads of sweat broke out all over her body. Stella pulled her daughter's underclothes off in one quick tug and told her to push.

'Oh Jesus! That was quick! I can see a head! A little head!' cried Stella, gasping in shock, when she moved around to the foot of the bed. 'Push, love! Hold my hand, squeeze it and push as hard as you can!'

Lily felt as if she was being torn in two. She was bathed in more sweat now.

'Make it stop, Mam!' she cried. '*Make it stop*!'

The walls seemed to bend and curve in on themselves and more beads of perspiration broke out on her forehead, glistening, a kind of fear-dew that couldn't be stayed, no matter how many times Stella wiped her forehead with the coverlet. The pain was unbearable. And then suddenly, with one final push and yell, she raised her head, and she felt something slither out of her, soft and wriggling between her knees. There it was. A baby. In Stella's hands.

'Is it dead?' asked Lily, panicked.

And as if to answer the question, the little girl, for so it was, took a breath, opened her mouth, and started crying for all her worth, announcing to the world that she had entered it.

'Of course, she's not dead!' replied Stella, smiling. She wiped the child with a piece of greyed towel and placed her on Lily's swollen breast. She knew Lily would always have flashes of memories of the baby all tangled up in her shift dress, which was unbuttoned to the neck, her mouth searching out Lily's nipple, her big round eyes blinking up at her.

She went over to the chest of drawers, found the sewing basket, and knew what she had to do. Groping around in it, she found what she was looking for: a pair of small silver scissors.

'This won't hurt,' she said, and snipped the cord.

For a moment, a great blanket of calm was wrapped around Lily and her daughter, round Stella and this shabby room.

The child had a mop of black hair and her skin had a dark hue to it, but that was just the colour of a newborn baby, Stella said, as she adjusted the pillows for Lily. The colour of a plum. Lily touched the baby's hand and the tiny fingers grasped her thumb. The nails were like flakes of butter, the downy hair on her shoulders like fur.

'Prudence,' she said, forlornly. 'I've always loved the name Prudence. Can I call her Prudence, Mam?'

'Of course. She's your baby,' she replied. And Stella's heart broke.

Lily breathed in the smell of her daughter – the smell was like nothing she had ever smelled before.

In the distance there was a rumbling, the ground shaking, more bombs, but not even that was going to spoil this moment.

But that was all it was. A moment of sheer unadulterated happiness as she locked eyes on her child and felt an intense love for her. And then nothing. That was all Lily could allow it to be.

Tears welled in her eyes. Suddenly she held the baby away from her. 'Mam, I can't. I can't. I can't start to love her. If that happens … if that happens, I'm done for. Please take her. What's the point of even giving her a name?'

Numbly, Stella took the child and cradled her in her arms.

Lily rolled onto her side and stared at the blank wall. She traced a finger around the familiar cracks and indentations. She was telling herself that without Vincent's love this child's life would have no meaning for her, that the baby would forever be a reminder of that sadness. Would she always feel so dead, so incomplete as she felt now?

Meanwhile, Stella wanted to reach out, place her hand on her daughter's pale, colourless cheek and tell her everything was going to be all right. But that would be a lie. She couldn't. She just couldn't. Because she knew it wasn't true.

Lily dozed whilst Stella swaddled the baby in an old crocheted blanket, cushioned the bottom drawer with some worn-out children's clothes, and laid the baby in it. And left them both asleep.

Chapter 28

Lily woke after three restless nights in a row, dreading the thought of what the day might bring. It had felt more like a doze than a proper sleep, waking up before dawn in a sudden terror, desperately afraid that something had happened to her baby, falling asleep, waking again after what felt like only minutes.

The baby was still sleeping. Lily got out of bed, leaned over the drawer and lifted her out. Every movement seemed to require a huge effort. Her limbs ached, her head ached – but there it was again, that great gush of love that had overwhelmed her the minute she looked into her daughter's eyes. For a moment she allowed herself to luxuriate in her baby's warmth, her folds of soft skin, her eyes that shut and blinked opened, fingers that curled around her thumb. And she couldn't believe it. Surely, if Vincent saw this miracle, surely he would want her, want them both?

The infant's tiny chest rose and fell. She leaned in closer, kissed her on the soft dimple on the top of her head, felt each exhalation of breath on her cheek.

It was twelve o'clock when the doorbell rang.

She heard the voices, low and indistinct, but just loud enough to make out what they were saying.

'Mrs Lafferty, this ends now. My son has asked me to return Lily's letters. The fact is, Vincent has a new girl. What did you expect? That daughter of yours, having a baby, out of wedlock and trying to trap my son! I'm sorry. She's made her bed, and she must lie in it.'

Lily's heart began to hammer.

'I'll do nothing of the sort. I'll not tell her that,' replied Stella. 'Now go away, we're busy!'

'I'm sure you are,' she sneered. 'The fact is, if he wanted to have any part of this, he would be here, wouldn't he? Well at this very moment he's with Mary Connors, making eyes at her and enjoying a pleasant conversation in our best room. Tonight he's taking her to the Rialto, which speaks for itself, I'd say.'

'Doesn't it just,' said Stella, trying to shut the door in her face. 'I thought he was supposed to be away!' she cried.

'We owe you Laffertys nothing. Least of all an explanation!' Beryl Wharton muttered, as she made her way down the hill, her face pinched, her back ramrod straight and defiant.

*

She could stand it no more. As Lily washed and bathed the baby in an enamel bowl the way Stella had shown her to, scooping up the warm water with her hand and dribbling it over her little squirming body, then as she changed her, using a large nappy pin to hold together the clean terry towel before dressing her in flannels, an old pink matinee coat and knitted boots that had belonged to Deirdre, she went over and over in her head what she had overheard. She was too tired and too weak to fight the despair that was taking hold of her. Was it true? She couldn't imagine being able to look forward to anything without Vincent, and as she washed herself in the basin and pulled a comb through her matted hair, tears coursed down her face. When her baby slept, she buried her face in her pillow to stifle the sound of her crying. Finally, exhausted from lack of sleep and worry, she said to Stella, 'Mam, take Prue. Take her now to St Jude's. At least I know she'll be safe away from this city. I can't be taking her down to the shelters every night. So you may as well. Before even more people start gossiping. Please. Then it will be as if I never had a baby.'

'Lily!' said Stella, in shock. 'You don't mean today?'

'Yes. Today. I can't bear it!' she replied. She felt the strange, stuporous sensation in her brain. 'Vincent doesn't want me or her!'

Stella tried to say something comforting, but turned her head aside and went through the motions of picking up the bucket and a pile of terry cloths as her eyes filled with tears because she could think of nothing.

'You're certain this is the right thing to do?'

'I've never been surer in my life,' Lily lied.

'Shall I leave you alone with her for a moment?' Stella asked.

Lily shook her head, but Stella made an excuse about going to get the gas mask to pack and moved out of the room.

The baby was in the drawer; she made a small, sweet sound and Lily looked over, couldn't help but lift her daughter out, hold her close, smell her, kiss and stroke her forehead, marvel at her eyelashes like soft brushes, her searching gaze, her tiny fingers curled around the top of the blanket. She faltered. For a second, she nearly changed her mind. But to put her feelings before this child's future, in the vain hope that Vincent would want her back, was wrong. At least, that's what the world was telling her. That the infant would go to a better home, have a better future, with two loving parents. And hearing her begin to cry and not having a single idea how to stop it, not even feeding her seemed to do any good, it summed up everything about why keeping her was a mistake. And finally, she had no tears left. All she could say was, 'Sorry, I'm so very sorry, little one. Perhaps you'll find me one day, Prudence ...'

She started when she saw Stella standing at the door.

'Come on,' she said. 'This isn't getting the baby bathed,' she said briskly – and immediately regretted her choice of words.

'Goodbye, angel,' whispered Lily, bending down and speaking close into her face, so that the child wrinkled her nose as if she was luxuriating in her mother's breath. 'Goodbye, Prue.' She straightened up, stood, took a step back. Then taking a deep breath, shaking, she reached in to the drawer, picked her up and handed her over to Stella, who took her and wrapped her up in a blanket she had brought in with her, and moved quickly away to the door. Lily lay back down on the bed and rolled over to face the wall, her eyes squeezed tight shut to stem the flow of tears.

Stella paused. 'Cry, love. You have a good cry. There's nothing wrong with crying,' she said, closing the door with a soft click.

And when she had gone, Lily felt a sharp pain in the pit of her stomach and was overtaken by a terrible sadness, worse than even she had thought possible. Burying her head in the pillow, she stuffed a corner into her mouth so that her mother wouldn't hear her cry and knew then that this was a decision she would regret for the rest of her life. And that guilt, like a shadow, would follow her everywhere, consume her heart and mind, forever. What on earth had she done?

Chapter 29

Stella primped herself in front of the hall mirror, pursed her lips, and checked for lipstick stains on her teeth, then set off to get on the train with the child. There were a few stares, but she sloughed them off, certain that Lily's decision was the right one. This would break Cliff's heart. Thank goodness for Egypt so he wasn't here to see it. Besides, whether it was right or wrong, they had no choice. They had no money. The child had no father. She didn't want her daughter to be called a slut, a harlot, a fallen woman, by every new person she met, for the rest of her life. Who could forget what had happened to Nellie's girl? Driven mad by it, wasn't that what they said? But when she reached the gates of St Jude's, she hesitated. Sister Bernadette was waiting for her at the top of the stone steps leading to the front door.

'Where's Lily?' the nun asked.

'At home,' replied Stella.

'Do you have the letter?' the sister asked.

Stella nodded. The brief note with Lily's sloping handwriting, her signature scrawled at the bottom, was pressed between her handkerchief and her skirt pocket.

'The couple will be ready to meet you soon,' Sister Bernadette said. 'Come inside. She looks a little poppet,' she added, cooing, peering in at the bundle of blankets.

There was a fancy car outside on the gravel drive. A shiny bottle-green Rover. Was that theirs? The adoptive parents'? Stella wondered.

Sister Bernadette took her into Assumpta's office and sat behind the desk. She asked for the letter from Lily, which had been witnessed by Matt, and the form that Father O'Casey had delivered and Lily had also signed.

'That all looks in order,' said Sister Bernadette. 'Come with me. How is Lily?' she asked, gently.

'As well as can be expected,' replied Stella.

When she went into the room, Stella saw the man first, silhouetted against the window, nervously puffing on a cigarette. Surely this wasn't the couple who would be adopting her granddaughter? They seemed far too old. The woman looked ancient, with her papery skin and grey hair escaping from a mustard velveteen hat; she was far, far, too old to have a baby. She was heavily made-up, with a scarlet gash for lipstick and trowelled-on face powder. When the woman took off her gloves and put them into her handbag, Stella noticed the skin on the back of her hands also looked old. Stella frowned. The clothes she wore had the same kind of outdated look that her own mother wore!

Sister Assumpta entered the room and walked briskly over to Stella, opened the blanket an inch more and peered in at the child, as if to check it was alive. Thank God Lily wasn't here to see this, thought Stella, feeling sick.

The woman, Mrs Potter, as she was introduced, with her lace-up sturdy shoes, and an A-line tomato red skirt and tree-trunk legs wreathed in wrinkled stockings, nodded a brief hello. Her arms hung stiffly to her sides, and then, just as awkwardly, she held out her hands. The man placed one of his hands on the hollow of her back and walked her over to Stella. The woman faltered as she took the bundle; it was like she didn't know what to do with the baby. Stella might have handed her a neatly folded pile of clothes or a leg of mutton.

'This won't take long,' said Assumpta. 'Follow me back to my office.'

'Sister, it's crying,' Mrs Potter said, panicked.

Sister Assumpta looked at her, surprised. 'Babies cry. Isn't that right, Stella?'

Stella nodded.

The woman turned her head. Her mouth was formed in a taut O shape. She was still holding the child away from her, awkwardly, as if it was an expensive piece of china she was worried about dropping, her arms stiff.

'Come now, Stella, show her.'

'Oh no, Sister. I couldn't . . .'

'Show her,' repeated the nun.

Stella took the child, rocked her gently in her arms, moving from foot to foot, a dance that steadied the baby, soothed her; she cooed 'there, there', and finally she stopped mewling. She bent her head, spoke quietly to the bundle, turned her back as though this was a private moment, some unspoken exchange between her and the child. My God! The child's expression as it looked into her eyes was Vincent's and Lily's all rolled into one, and it shook Stella to the core.

'L-like that,' she said to the woman, speaking over her shoulder.

Assumpta took the bundle of swaddling from Stella and gave her a perfunctory nod. 'Now you can take baby home. Give her some formula as soon as you get in. She's probably starving. What are you going to call her?' she said, brightly as they walked along the corridor to the door and down the steps to the car.

'We're going to call her Gertrude,' said the man.

'Good Grief. Gertrude?' Stella knew a Gertrude. Dirty Gertie, the boys all called her at school. Why would anyone call their child Gertrude? 'My daughter,

Lily. She liked the name Prudence. That's what we've been calling her. That's her name.'

'No. We prefer Gertrude. Family name,' he replied, with an unflinching stare.

The woman grimaced. 'And Prudence? There's an irony. Perhaps if your daughter had placed a three-penny bit between her legs . . .'

Mr Potter looked shocked. 'Gwen!' he exclaimed. 'Come on,' he said quickly, opening the passenger door. 'Thank you, Mrs Lafferty,' he added, glancing back over his shoulder.

Stella breathed deeply. It was all she could do to stop herself running after the car when it started and throwing herself on the bonnet, demanding they handed the child back. Mr Potter wound down the window and called goodbye, accompanied by an insensitive, cheery wave.

The woman turned, looked through the back window. Stella lifted a hand to return the wave, but it seemed inappropriate, and she lost heart halfway through the gesture. Instead, she slipped her hand into her pocket and watched the car move down the sweeping drive and swing through the gates. 'That wasn't too bad was it, Stella?' said Assumpta, coming to stand quietly next to her. 'Thank the Good Lord for the Potters. Now, if you want my advice, you'll go home and tell that little harlot daughter of yours to stop spreading her legs for strange men in dingy dance halls. And confession. She has confessed, Stella? Do we need to get her to a priest?'

The witch! thought Stella, her cheeks smarting. She could feel the tears in her eyes, pricking like silent stabs. It was as if hot needles were poking through her eyeballs, but she blinked the pain away. Sister Assumpta was not going to see her cry. She might have known she wouldn't have been able to resist the urge to sound so smug. She used those words and that tone of voice deliberately, it was no accident and she hadn't needed to. Why was she so unkind? She couldn't shake the pain of it off, even when she returned home, even after she had put Lily to bed with a hot cup of milk and a few pathetic words telling her she had done the right thing. Assumpta really hadn't needed to be so cruel.

Chapter 30

The newspapers might talk of the morale, but there wasn't much of it in Caryl Street, thought Stella, after another night of monstrous bombing. Things were grim on every front, the air raids heavier than ever, and, unsurprisingly, nobody had visited lately – when you might get killed just walking down the street, who would leave their home or shelter for a cup of tea and a natter at the Laffertys'?

'Oh Mam. I can't stand it,' Lily said, twisting a tea towel in her lap when Stella came in with a jug of milk and placed it in front of her. 'I've just got to get out of here for a bit!'

Earlier, Lily had struggled with the drawer upstairs in the bedroom, now sad and empty apart from the rumpled pink crocheted baby blanket in the bottom of it, as she tried to slot it back into the casing. Finally, with a shove she'd bashed it into place and removed the clothes from the top drawer back to this one, hiding the baby blanket so she wouldn't be reminded of Prudence every time she opened the drawer. At least, that's what she hoped. She sat back on her heels and looked around. The smell of her baby lingered, which was perhaps the worst thing of all. How quickly this room had gone from being so full of the clutter of her little girl – bottles, the gas mask contraption, blankets and nappies, and pins, and buckets – and now it was to back to its sterile, bare, shabby look of poverty.

Her head hurting, and her womb aching, she had sat down to finish one last, important thing.

Dear Vincent,

I know you don't want to see me again. And I know I have to stop writing these letters to you. But I still think you don't believe me that my child is yours. Vincent, I can only tell you that it's true. I have had the baby. A girl. She came quickly. Earlier than expected. Your child. Our *child. I still don't believe you wouldn't at least want to hear my side of the story. Not until you hear it from myself. In the meantime, I am sending this to your home. I am not sure your mother won't destroy it but am doing it anyway. Our little girl is beautiful. She has thick black hair and brown eyes. I have called her Prudence. Everyone is agreed that the nuns know what is best.*

Lily.

PS I hear you have another sweetheart. My heart is breaking but I can't for the life of me think about how I can change that.

Now all she had to do was go to his house and post it through the letterbox. Without getting killed in the process.

Lily hurried past the recreation ground. She had her gas mask around her neck in the cardboard box and the park railings had been taken down, to be used for armaments. From the top of the hill, she could see the Big Bertha gun firing. She could now tell the difference in sound of that and a bomb exploding, and the ground was already shaking. She should have known better to be out in the streets again, but the bombings were a tragedy, so a fitting backdrop to her own tragedy. The sirens had been sounding for half an hour and beyond; down by the docks, the explosions looked like a red sunset on the horizon. You could see the glow for miles, fire leaping up around them.

All around the roads were cordoned off. Delay-action bombs, probably. A couple of ARP men were waiting nervously at the top of the hill for someone to arrive. There was the curious sight of six cats following each other, padding off in the opposite direction to the docks. Did they know something that humans didn't? The steady drone, the heavy thrumming sound, was ominous. She knew the sound of the Luftwaffe heading back home – a good deal lighter after emptying their bombs on the city – to get more munitions, but this was not it. Suddenly, a man came running down the street, shouted at her to take cover, and shoved her inside the doorway of a grocer's shop.

The ground shook harder. It felt like an earthquake and shrapnel was falling around her. The anti-aircraft guns were louder now, the sound of the guns firing into the air, popping in her ears. There was a tall structure, blotting the way ahead, with a tangle of metal scaffolding and corrugated iron holding up the front of a house.

She darted out of the doorway – and that's when she saw the Whartons' house. It was the only one in the street that was damaged – tiles from the roof blown off, windows shattered, glass on the pavement.

Breaking out into a run, she sprinted towards it. The front door was barely hanging on to its hinges and she pushed it open wider, put a handkerchief over her mouth, and went into the hall. The living-room door had fallen off completely, becoming a bridge into the parlour. Wiping the smoke out of her eyes and coughing, she walked gingerly over it, noting that two pictures, one of the Mersey, another of a field and a hay cart, were hanging off the wall. The doors to the bookcase were open and the books were lying open all over the floor like dead birds. Very little was intact.

She heard a voice in the parlour.

'Help!' it cried.

It was Vincent's voice! *She was sure of it.* But the thunderous sound of more bombing made it impossible to make out what he was saying.

'Vince! Is that you!?' she cried.

She saw the blurred figure form into a shape through the clouds of thickening smoke and dust.

'Lily! Lily, help me,' he shouted, choking, groping helplessly as he moved across the room back to the door. Panic-stricken, he cried, 'Lil! Thank God you're here! Help me pull open the door! Please! Please help! Ma and Pa are in the cellar and a pipe has burst and is flooding it!'

He went back into the living room, began pulling at the handle of the door to the cellar that was wedged shut. She knew exactly where the door led. She had been in the cellar – his father had proudly shown her the chintz armchair he'd put down there, the small table with his pipe and matches, the three camp beds, the shelf he had built, even a rug and a wireless.

'Help me, Lil ...' Vincent's knees and hands were covered in grease, his trousers and shirt were torn, and blood was seeping out from his shirt cuff where he had cut his forearm.

Lily stood in shock for a moment and then she picked her way through the rubble that was all around the room – pieces of brick, lumps of concrete and plaster. Curling her fingers into the grooves of the door's inlay, she pulled with him, but it was no good. Vincent looked at her with frantic eyes as they fell against the wall, panting and gasping for breath. Lily felt her legs buckle underneath her. 'I have to open the door! We haven't got much time, Lily. There's water. It's filling up like a bloody fish tank! They'll drown if we don't get this door open.'

Suddenly Lily heard muffled voices from behind.

'Vincent! Push! Oh God! Help us!' It was Mrs Wharton wailing.

Together, she and Vincent put their shoulders to the door, trying to push it inwards, now. But it was impossible.

'There's an axe in the backyard. If we can split the door open . . .' Vincent panted.

'It's up to my chest! Please help, Vincent!' cried Mr Wharton. His voice sounded indistinct, but what was clear was that this was a tragedy that was about to reach its inevitable conclusion.

She could hear whimpering. And then more wailing. More clouds of dust billowed through the front door.

'Vincent, do something!' came a cry from beyond the door.

Lily raced outside, found the axe propped up against the privy door, raced back and thrust it into his hands.

'We're trying, Mam!' Vincent called desperately.

There was more smoke now and Vincent's features had dissolved into a blur. Lifting the axe over his shoulder, he whacked it hard against the door. Splinters flew off but that was all. 'This axe is useless. The head's flamin' loose!'

'Who's with you?' shouted his father, in a muffled voice.

Vincent took a moment to look at Lily. She looked so young and frail.

'Find someone, Lil! Go outside. Just find someone!' he said.

Heart bursting, thumping at her chest to clear her lungs, she ran out into the street. The bombing seemed to have stopped and there were two soldiers in a van coming up the street. It screeched to a halt as she dashed in front of it, and she banged frantically on the windscreen. Just then a man in an ARP hat appeared, head down.

'We need help!' she said. 'Number forty-two! It's been hit. And the cellar, it's flooding and—'

'Number forty-two Fisher Street?'

With a rope under his shoulder, the ARP man ran. Lily followed, as did the soldiers who leaped out of the van. When they got to the house, Vincent was hacking at the door with a chair leg.

'It's up to their necks! Time's running out' he yelled.

'Stand back!' said the man.

He took something from the rucksack he was carrying, an explosive of some sort. 'Stand back.'

Vincent dragged Lily to the end of the room and, pulling her down, he put his arms around her. There was a loud explosion, and then, through the dust, the sight of the door blown right off, hanging like a wobbling tooth on its hinges. The silhouettes of Mr and Mrs Wharton were just visible as the ARP man shone a torch through the gaping hole. There was the ominous sound of creaking.

With the help of the soldiers they were hauled out of the murky liquid terror, dripping wet, hair stuck to their faces, clothes in tatters, and distraught. Beyond, in the gloom, Lily saw an armchair, an upturned table and a kettle, floating on the surface of the black water.

And as the clouds of smoke dispersed, they saw the water had reached right up to the bottom of the door. Mr and Mrs Wharton seemed in shock, but mostly from discovering that they were still alive.

'Lily? Is that you? What are you doing here?' asked a confused Mrs Wharton.

Vincent just looked at her.

'Saving your life, Mam.'

Chapter 31

The rescue men put blankets over their shoulders and took them to the nearby church hall where they were told to wait until they had further instructions. As they walked through the streets, numb and dazed, the whole place looked like it was collapsing in on itself. A wall had come crashing down, then a tree had fallen and smashed on top of a car that had crumpled in on itself as if it was made out of plasticine. At the church, tea was brewed, and the first thing Vincent did was make it clear to his mother and father that he wasn't going to hear a word spoken against Lily. Mrs Wharton sniffed pitifully and apologised and said that now was not the time to talk about the matter of the child.

'This war makes monsters out of people and I'm ashamed to say it did out of me,' Mr Wharton muttered over a cup of tea rattling in a saucer.

'Oh God, Lily. Will you ever forgive me?' said Vincent clutching her hands. 'It's as though I was overtaken by a kind of madness. When I punched that chap, it wasn't so much that I was angry with you – or him for that matter. It was because I was so hurt. Oh, I love you, Lil. I do. I really do.'

Seeing the sadness in her large brown eyes swollen with tears and her plump, trembling lip, he felt incredulous that he had listened to his mother for even a single second. He loved Lily, and that was an end to it, baby or no baby, whoever's child it was.

'Vince, it can't be Clarence's baby. You can see that, can't you? Because I've never been with anyone but you ...'

And in the cold light of day, it became clear to him that what she was saying made sense. Of course it was his child – why on earth had he listened to his mother?

She looked at him through eyes brimming with tears. His hair doing that thing where it flopped in a front lick over his forehead. 'I wish I could say something to put things right,' he faltered.

'You're here,' she said. 'Alive. Let's be thankful for that. There's not been one night that I haven't worried about that.'

'Right, we're all going to Lewis's basement,' said a man with a clipboard. 'Safer there than here.'

Vince clutched Lily's hand. His parents followed along with the other tired and frightened dozen or so people. Smoke billowed through the city. The pavements crunched with the sound of broken glass when they walked over it and a man using a stirrup pump to put out a blaze from an incendiary bomb started shouting at them to hurry. They knew what was coming. Everyone could distinguish the friendly Spitfires from the sound of the ominous Heinkels.

They reached Lewis's department store and went inside. A man with a torch led them between the shop counters, his flashlight giving them tantalising glimpses of scarves and gloves hanging on steel hooks, ties laid out in neat rows under glass counters, perfume bottles and jewellery on shelves. Lily stopped for a minute, gazing at all the goods on sale. It was a wonder people didn't reach out and take handfuls of the stuff. But it was when she walked past the counters with bassinets and baby mobiles, knitted and crocheted blankets for newborns, and teddy bears, that her heart lurched.

'Come on, love,' whispered, Vince.

They walked on, under chandeliers dripping with glass pendants, and trod as softly as they could over marble floors, their footsteps echoing and mirrors throwing back rippling reflections. They were taken down a flight of stairs to the basement. It was a huge storage room with sofas and chairs wrapped in plastic, but also the place where the music department was.

'You can all find a spot here,' said the man.

Vince took Lily by the hand and led her to one of the sofas. They sat together, he with his arm around her, she with her head on his shoulder. She had missed him so much, missed the smell of Brylcreem in his hair, the pink crescents of his fingernails. She had missed the sound of his voice, the constant jigging of his knee and his fingers tapping out a rhythm on tabletops or countertops. She had missed the dancing, of course, and the milkshakes at the Regal in town, and his easy charm – but most of all she had missed this feeling, that together, despite whatever was happening around them, everything was going to be all right. Including the matter of their child.

'Are you OK?' he asked. 'I mean, you've just, well, just had a baby – *our* baby. Doesn't that . . .?'

She felt a shiver through her body. Blinking away tears, she felt his breath on her face as he leaned his forehead on her brow and spoke softly to her, clasping her hands with his.

'I'm right as rain,' she answered, but then her bottom lip quivered again and tears spilled down her cheeks. 'What about your new girl?' she asked.

He had made her cry. It wasn't the first time he had made someone cry in his life. But this felt so much worse than any time that he could remember.

'There is no new girl. Just you,' he replied. 'Just you now. But what about the baby?' he asked.

She felt his arms around her and it was an overwhelming feeling, as if she had come home. She sniffed, touched his cheek. When his face moved towards her, she grasped him by his shirt and kissed him.

'Vincent. She was your child. I swear she was …'

Was? he thought.

'I know that, Lily, of course I do. But when can I see her? Where is she now?' he asked. 'With your mam?'

And then panic ripped through her and her eyes filled with tears.

'Oh God, Vince! Didn't your ma put you in the picture? My mam wrote to her.'

There was only one thing for it, and that was to tell him every last detail. To be truthful. And so, hopeful that he would understand, that he wouldn't hate her for it, she spilled out the whole story in one outpouring of grief and apology and regret.

'Slow down, slow down,' he said. He reached out and stilled her with his hand, squeezing hers firmly, twisted to her, put her head under his chin and spoke into her hair. 'We'll just get her back. Surely we can do that?' he added with a shrug. For him, it was simple. If the nuns had taken her, well, she was still their child, they would just get her back, wherever she was.

Lily looked at him. 'D'you think so? I've signed the papers, Vince.'

'You might have signed the papers, but I haven't. And I'm the father. I could kick up a right stink about that. Couldn't the couple just have another baby? It's not been that long. There must be others.'

The way he said it, so certain, so sure, so young and optimistic, sent waves of relief passing through her and her eyes shone as her spirits rose.

'Maybe we *can* get her back. Janet told me you have six weeks to change your mind. They make you stay for at least six weeks at St Jude's after you have your baby, just in case. And surely the nuns would want any child to be with their parents? Surely that's what God would want? So why wouldn't they? Oh, Vince! I feel better already.' She smiled hopefully at him and in response, he squeezed her hand and kissed the top of her head.

A man in an ill-fitting suit sat down at the piano stool.

'Give us a tune?' someone said. 'Something to get this wretched sound of bombing out of me head.'

The pianist's fingers began to wander over the keys, picking out single notes, then chords, then harmonies and gentle tunes.

'Sing something to get the kiddies asleep,' said a woman.

People began to settle onto the camp beds that were arranged in rows between the supporting pillars.

'A lullaby?' someone asked. 'Something to drown out this blessed droning of them flipping planes ...'

He began to sing 'The Sandgate Dandling Song' as he played. 'Fa la la la ... Hold your way, my bonny bairn.' It was lyrical and easy to pick up and a few joined in, though he changed the words to suit the circumstances. 'Hold your way up on my arm, Dad he's long in coming from the war. Though his mucky face'll be like hell, I like a kiss from Daddy …'

And then came the horrific crescendo of sound as even more planes roared over in waves. The ground shook again and a stack of china rattled, a vase smashed as it fell onto the floor. Someone jigged a crying baby up and down and played peek-a-boo with the child as a lump of plaster fell off the wall behind them. 'I see!' the mother chimed, and put her hands over her eyes, removed them, and delighted in the baby's giggles. Vincent caught Lily watching the mother and child, and whilst the Moaning Minnies, as the sirens had become known, wailed and the ack-acks fired, he reached out his hand and gently squeezed hers.

And still the man played. It was certainly comforting. And then someone, a man in his silk pyjamas and a dressing gown, amidst all this worry and fear, had the idea to dance.

'If we get through this alive, there'll always be the coal-hole, but there's not always a fella sitting at a piano and a polished marble floor like this one,' he said to his wife as he took her by the hand and they began to move gracefully across the floor. As the fellow played 'Dancing Down Lime Street', other dancers began to join them.

'Come on, Vincent,' said Lily. 'Let's dance as well – I've missed that so much . . .'

She stood, took his hand, moved in to him, slowly rhythmically, his arm around her waist, her head on his shoulder. And as they danced, they took comfort in each other's bodies and the music – and the hope that, as soon as they were out of here, something would change for the better. 'You can find yourself and lose yourself at the same time on the dance floor,' Lily remembered her father saying, and it was never truer than now.

Finally, the hellish noise of the bombing that had accompanied the roaring of the aeroplanes receded as dawn began to break and in the silence that fell a cuckoo sang. Then the sirens began to wail again for the all-clear.

Lily felt so hopeful with Vince by her side as they came out blinking into the sunlight. She saw a woman was pushing a pram. Might that be her soon? More often than not, after an air raid like that night's, the sole conversation revolved around who had died, who had survived. But now it was the city of Liverpool itself that gave her courage, battered and bruised as it was, as they walked hand in hand towards home with the Liver Bird's still wings outstretched above them, proud and regal and steadfast.

*

Stella opened the door to them at Caryl Street.

'Good God!' she said. 'Look at the state of you! I've been worried sick!'

Lily's eyes shone with excitement.

'Mam! We're going to get our baby back!' she cried. 'Vincent's coming with me. Everything is going to be all right.'

Stella paled.

'What?' she said, inwardly terrified, her heart leaping to her mouth. How much she loved this daughter who thought life was so simple, so straightforward, and whose greatest fault was that she believed everyone was as good and as kind as her.

'Vincent knows the truth now. Me and him, we're grand, Mam. So, our baby. We're going to get her back.'

Chapter 32

Stella could hear her mother moving about upstairs, washing out her mug of tea, putting on her shoes, clearing her throat. She began to stoke the fire on the range. She noticed damp creeping up the walls. This house really was getting into an alarming state. And it wasn't the war that was to blame for that – it had started to crumble long before. She went to fill the coal bucket.

There was nothing Stella had been able to say to Lily. She'd felt herself spiralling into a mess of incoherent ramblings and, in the end, she decided Lily had to find out for herself, hoping against hope that it would not end the way she feared it would.

She'd sat with her, holding her hand, but then, she'd told her, 'Hope for the best, but prepare for the worst,' and stood to go out to work, planting a tender kiss on her daughter's waxy forehead.

'My friend told me you have six weeks to change your mind – that's why you have to stay for six weeks at St Jude's after you have your baby.'

'Oh love, that's not why,' Stella had said. 'You stay there so you can feed the baby and make sure it's healthy, then wean it before you give it away so the new parents don't have to do the hard work. And Prudence? Well, they took her early.'

Lily had frowned, then light filled her face – for Lily was an eternal optimist. 'They'll understand, I'm sure they will. If Vince tells the nuns we're going to be married, if the couple, the Potters, you said? If they know we want her back, well, maybe they could have my friend Aggie's baby? She was due about the same time as me, I think. I could ask her?'

Stella winced. Through all the horrors, the awfulness of war, the terrible things people were doing to each other, Lily would always see the virtue in the human race, so for her it was simple, but it was painful to hear.

'Why shouldn't we have her back?'

'If only life was that straightforward,' Stella said with a sigh.

But Lily batted the comment aside with a toss of her shivering hair and reassured her mother that nobody, not even Sister Assumpta, would be that unkind.

Lily had practised it under her breath as they took the train, and said it over again, walking hand in hand with

Vincent, down Virgin's Lane. *I've made a mistake, this is my fiancé, Prue's father, we're getting married, and so we've come to take our baby back from the Potters.* They went past the large houses, past the hut painted yellow, past the orphanage with a roller in the front garden. *I've made a mistake, this is my fiancé, Prue's father, we're getting married, and so we've come to take our baby back from the Potters.*

She noticed the front step of the grocer's had been repainted and the baker's had shut up shop for Wednesday half-day closing. *I've made a mistake, this is my fiancé, Prue's father. We're getting married, and so we've come to take our baby back from the Potters* . . .

With each step she felt excited and optimistic. Finally, they reached the fork in the road and a little way ahead rose the turrets of the mother and baby home. St Jude's gates were shut and there was a chain padlocked across them.

'This is it,' said Lily to Vincent.

She went up the path, and clung to the gates, her fingers curling around the bars, and peered at the house. Beyond the gates, walking towards them down the drive, a girl pushing a Silver Cross pram veered towards them.

'Aggie!' Lily cried. 'You're still here!' She turned to Vincent. 'This is Aggie. And this is her baby! You've had the baby!? Oh God, Ag, can I see?'

Aggie faltered.

'Wait,' she said as she unlocked the gates and swung them open. The baby in the pram, its face just visible under the cream hood, began to cry and pull at its ear.

'Your baby, Aggie? You've had your baby?' Lily repeated.

'Oh, this bairn's not mine,' said Aggie. 'This little fella is nearly eighteen months. So it wouldn't make sense, would it? I had my baby six weeks ago. But let's not talk about that. I've a job as a nanny for one of the rich bitches in the village. Well …' She tailed off. 'Anyway, it's a job. The nuns got it for me.'

Lily's face fell. 'Just to be cruel? They got you … a job as a *nanny*? Does that not …' She tailed off.

'Upset me?'

'Yes.'

Aggie looked at her sadly, for once letting her feelings show. 'Of course. But what can I do? Like I said, don't bite the hand that feeds you. And they're not bad, the couple I work for.'

'And Bridget?' she asked tentatively, fearing the answer.

'Ah, poor Bridget. Still here. Never recovered after her little one ended up one of the Breadbox Babies?'

'What's that?' asked Vincent, curious but alarmed at the same time.

'The Breadboxes?' she said to Vincent. 'Hasn't Lily told you? That's what they make the little wooden crosses out of to mark the babies' graves. They say it's just practical. With the war. Some say it was Bridget's fault, that she did it deliberately. The baby was blue when they found her. Anyway, they had a funeral and she's buried in the grounds, just behind the Brussel sprouts. You'll see her baby's name on the Breadbox cross.'

'Oh God, Ag,' said Lily.

For a moment they all just stood there as Aggie gripped the pram handle and jiggled it up and down on its creaking chrome springs to quieten the child who was beginning to whimper. Not daring to say anything out loud, it was all just too painful, too awful to speak about.

'Don't feel too sorry for me,' said Aggie. 'My son went to a good mother. The friend of the couple who I'm working for. So that was nice. They've promised me they'll write to me.' She opened the clasp on her leather handbag, took out a small white lace handkerchief, and blew her nose. 'This blasted hay fever,' she said, tucking it under the cuff of her sleeve. 'Anyway, I've a job waiting for me in Liverpool when all this bombing is over. At the Meccano factory'

'That's good. Why are you still here, though? Why haven't you gone back?'

'Nowhere to go back to. Nothing left of our house, completely flattened like so many other poor buggers in Bootle. Me ma and da are living in Ormskirk with my aunt but I'm not welcome there. You can guess why. In the meantime, remember Clarence? It's him that keeps me sane. He went off to Manchester for a while, but now he's back at the Mere Lane camp. We meet every other Friday if he can get away. And your baby, Lil?' she asked.

'We've come to get her back.'

'Good luck with *that*, love,' said Aggie, her eyes widening in surprise.

Lily clutched Vincent's hand and, for once, standing here under a cherry tree, he looked more scared than she was.

They walked purposefully up the drive towards the front steps. Lily pressed the bell with the heel of her hand, and prayed it wouldn't be Sister Assumpta who answered the door. Thankfully it was David, who smiled.

'Lily,' she said. 'Lovely to see you.' She didn't mention the baby, and Lily wondered for a moment if she knew.

'The children are ready,' she said.

Lily paused. 'What d'you mean?'

'The children. Bobby, and Deirdre. You said in your phone call you were coming to get the children. They're all ready. In the schoolroom.'

Vincent frowned. 'I think there's been a mistake,' he said. 'We've come to get *our* baby.'

Sister David's hand flew to her mouth. 'I'm sorry?'

'*Our* baby,' he repeated. 'You must have misheard my fiancée.'

'Why would we take the kiddies back? The bombing is horrendous in Liverpool right now. Never seen anything like it. No, we want our baby. Where is she?' asked Lily, firmly.

'Oh Lily, dear. She's gone.' She touched her arm in a kind gesture. 'You can't have her back. You signed the forms. Surely your mother told you? It will only make things worse if Sister Assumpta sees you.'

Lily began to put together the pieces of what they were saying. She felt as if she needed air, took great gulps, her hand flying to her cheeks.

'No, you don't understand. We want the address of the couple who have taken her. *Where is she*? *Our baby*?' asked Lily. She felt a surge of panic rise to her throat.

'I can't tell you. I just can't tell you.'

Vincent stood, feet firmly planted apart, crossing his arms over his chest angrily. 'What are you talking about?'

Sister David, trembled. 'There's been an unfortunate misunderstanding,' she said, stammering apologetically.

Vincent asked her again, demanding and insistent, 'I thought we had six weeks to change our minds? Well, we have thought about it and we've changed our minds. And we want our baby, Sister.'

'No, dear. Six weeks, yes, whilst you're here with the child. Not when the child has already been given away. Not when the papers have been signed.'

Lily's heart lurched. How could she have been so stupid? She thought back to the letter her mother had made her write, saying she gave permission to have Prudence adopted. Thought back to her bad spelling and young girl's childish round fat handwriting sloping across the page. Surely anyone could see from that that she was only a child herself, that she hadn't been responsible enough for anyone to take it seriously?

Just then a figure appeared in one corner of the bay window, partly visible from the front step. It moved away quickly and moments later the door opened wider. There, like a huge black crow, standing with hands thrust deep in her pockets, keys glinting on the chain hanging from her waistband, light flashing as a burst of sun hit her glasses, stood Assumpta with an expression on her face that was challenging and obdurate. Lily began to tremble.

'Why don't you come with me?' said Sister Assumpta.

Lily felt Vincent's hand squeeze hers tight. She could see from the hardening expression on his face that he was getting angry.

'Please, Sister David,' said Lily, turning to the younger nun, feeling as though a fist had reached around her stomach and twisted it. She began to shake.

'Leave this to me, Sister David. Follow me into my office, all of you,' said Assumpta.

When they walked into the small cluttered room, yellowing palms fashioned into crosses stuck into the frames of the pictures of the saints and the Virgin Mary, rosary beads hanging off a lamp shade, shelves groaning with Bibles, Sister Assumpta suddenly swung around, directing the full force of her cruel words at Lily. 'You knew when you signed the papers that this was something that we had explained very clearly. Your mother assured me she had spoken to you, had told you every detail about the Potters and your baby, the adoption. This is not the time to change your mind.'

'But we want her back!' said Vincent, angrily.

Assumpta laughed, revealing her gums, pink and fleshy, and the greying enamel of her teeth.

Sister David looked like she was going to cry.

'Sister, go back to chapel. Stop snivelling,' she snapped.

Lily's heart kicked at her ribs and fear flamed up in her body. Vincent's throat clogged with rage. Sister David shifted from foot to foot, not knowing what to do as Lily threw her a look, entreating her not to go. *Please don't leave, please don't leave*, it said. The weight of Assumpta's words crushed Lily. As a girl she had vividly imagined and reimagined the story of St Margaret Clitherow, lying on a sharp stone, a door on top of her frail body being piled with more stones until she was crushed to death. She felt like St Margaret, as if Assumpta was the sharp stone cutting into her back, and the regret of giving her child away was the weight of the rocks pressing down on her. 'There's nothing I can do. You've left it too late. The baby has already been adopted.'

'No!' said Vincent.

'Don't blame me. You're too late, sonny boy. Lily signed the papers.'

Lily gasped and a sob rose up from her throat. Please God, this wasn't true.

'You can't d-do this,' Lily said, her voice quavering. She wanted to scream, but she could barely make a sound. Optimism was overtaken by a hopelessness that made her stomach lurch and her eyes fill with tears.

What was to become of her child now? The thought hit her harder than the bombs dropping on Liverpool. Her whole body began to shake. She could see nothing, it was as if black ink had been injected into her eyeballs. She could feel herself falling, could hear sounds, muffled, indistinct, but she could make no sense of them. She could hear distant voices but had no idea of what they were saying. The pain seized her senses, the dull ache that gripped her was all-encompassing, overwhelming. She felt that there was nothing she could do; she couldn't speak, or walk, or stand, or breathe, or see.

She could feel someone picking her up and it was as if she was made of fluff, that she might float away if you were to breathe on her. She heard more distant voices, muffled, but she knew what they were saying all right, that someone better get word to Stella and the kids.

She managed just enough strength to open her eyes. She had a picture of Bobby, standing with a balloon on a stick. Was she imagining this? Was she imagining the balloon, bobbing, bright yellow flashes of colour? She remembered, snatches of conversation, 'Mam, the Tatters Men are coming. It's "Toys For Rags" day ...'

She imagined the children were standing there before her, looking frightened. More frightened than she had ever seen them.

'Vince? What's going to happen now?'

Was this real? Or was this something that had happened to her years before? 'I can't stand this,' she said suddenly, leaping forward and running out of the door. Where she was going? In what direction was she heading? She had no real idea, but she ran all the way down the corridor, calling her baby's name as she did, the repetition with each gulp of air spurring her on. 'Prudence, Prudence? Why did I let you go?'

But her words were lost on the wind, which now sounded like the wailing of banshees. There was a vicious flash of lightning and a growl of thunder crackled, morphing into what sounded like a volley of gunfire, as she stumbled and fell, face down, on the polished corridor.

A nun, hovering in the corridor, looked on aghast.

'Get up,' she said, lifting her up by the arm.

'Lil!' cried Bobby. 'Lily, Lily!' yelled Deirdre, suddenly rushing through the door. They stood there hopping from foot to foot excitedly, in a blur of smiles and gabardines, a jumble of suitcases and bags beside them. 'Are we coming home?' they cried.

'Yes,' snapped Assumpta. 'Time to go. I have Mass now. Father is waiting.'

Lily stared at her, with frozen hatred. 'Come on, kids. I'm not leaving you here. You can go to Morecambe to be with Gram to be safe. But you're not staying here. It's wrong what you're doing! It's wrong! You can't do this – it's—' she shouted after Sister Assumpta.

Vincent was the first to collect himself. 'Don't worry, Lily,' he said, his voice low and growling with anger. 'We'll find a way. We'll be back,' he said, and with that he left, heart raging, head spinning with the madness and injurious wickedness of the situation, but for the life of him, unable to think what they could do about it.

They walked towards the road. A bewildered Deirdre and Bobby clutched Lily's hands, too scared to ask questions. Aggie, who was waiting, knew straight away something was wrong. Sitting on a low wall that ran alongside the side road next to St Jude's, rocking the pram, she sucked on a cigarette.

'Couldn't leave. What happened?' she asked.

Vincent told her, doing his best to keep the children from hearing what he was saying.

Lily could barely speak for crying.

'Oh God. Lily. You'll find a way. I promise. If you want your wee one back, you'll find a way …'

Lily pushed open the door. Stella was sitting hunched over the kitchen table, an old frayed shawl draped over her knees, her eyes shut. She winced when Lily yanked open the curtains and light flooded into the room. The bright sunshine hurt her eyes.

She looked up, saw the expression on her daughter's face, and her heart broke. It was as she had expected. The idea that Vincent and Lily might soften the nuns' hearts was as likely as Hitler calling off this dreadful bombing of Liverpool and taking pity on his enemies.

'No baby?'

Lily shook her head sorrowfully. 'Just these two tearaways,' she said as Bobby and Deirdre ran into Stella's arms.

She held them close. 'Oh, good grief, you've both grown!' she said. 'Come on, let's put a shilling in the meter. Now, Lily, come and tell me all about it. It's not over yet. We'll think of something, I promise,' she added, knowing it was just something to say, meaningless, as desperate and foolish as Lily.

The sun was shining in Southport and the air seemed sweeter It had turned into a lovely afternoon. Clarence, top button of his shirt undone, tie loosened, and jacket slung over one shoulder, met Aggie on the promenade. Together they made their way into the Copper Kettle, the light reflecting off each pane of glass.

'How are you?' she asked, as they sat at a table. Taking off her headscarf and shaking out her naturally wavy hair, she added, 'this weather is beautiful, isn't it?'

He rolled up his shirt-sleeves as they sat down at a table.

'It was a miserable start to the week. I prefer the sun, for sure,' he replied, as they laid their jackets on the backs of the wooden chairs.

'How are you?' Aggie asked.

'I'm doing fine, my love. I have some news though. I might be going overseas soon. They haven't told me where yet. I should find out in the next few days.' He leaned forward and winked. 'Operation Brevity, they're calling it. Keep that under your hat.'

'Ooh, I say, Mr Aimé,' said Aggie. 'Top secret. I'll miss you. I'll miss our Friday meet ups.'

'You want to come along?' he joked, and his eyes twinkled as he said it.

Aggie grinned. 'No thanks. I've got me job at the factory soon.' She leaned forward in her chair. 'Well, you be careful. Still can't see why you want to put your life on the line for this country when people have been so vile to you.'

He smiled graciously. 'I love England. I'm here for King and country. The Mother Country, as we call it. I think we have more of passion for your King than some of your British fellows do. The people here have been good to me. Most of them. Besides, remember what happened with Lily. You can't take one man and blame a whole country for his miserable actions.' He sighed and absently smoothed out the checked tablecloth. 'I'm looking forward to wherever it is they're sending me. Let's hope it's somewhere warm.'

She nodded. 'What'll you do?'

'Same as here. Main thing is making sure the radios are in working order. Batteries, headphones, making sure the leads are kept clean, record voltage readings of the wireless sets for the troops. '

'Sounds grand,' said Aggie.

She glanced outside, lifted her hair off the back of her damp neck. Then her expression changed. 'Talking of that business with Lily. The fight. Terrible what people can do, isn't it?' she said.

Clarence leaned back in his chair, raised his palms, and shrugged. 'Ah well, yes. I've had it all my life.'

Then she paused a moment.

'I didn't mean the fight at the dance hall. I meant the fight with her chap.' She faltered again, as if deciding how to frame her next question. 'Before you go, can I ask you to help me with something? Well, help Lily, really. Something awful.'

'Of course. Anything for Lily. If I can repay the kindness she showed to me, and after what happened with her fellow, if I could put that right, well, that would be grand.'

Chapter 33

Slipping through the side door where the deliveries were left, Aggie went down the corridor, past the crucifixes and the statues of Mother Theresa and St Francis holding a bunch of plastic daffodils, trying not to let her shoes clack too loudly on the stone floors. To her left were the glass windows of Assumpta's office. A little way past it, Aggie stopped and stepped into the alcove. She wanted to get into the office, and into that drawer inside it! She knew that was where the adoption papers were kept, she had seen Assumpta put away the duplicate documents when her own son had been born. The documents that said who the adoptive parents were, and where they lived. She was about to step forward when out of nowhere Sister Bernadette glided swiftly past, right in front of her. She took a sharp intake of breath and ducked further back out of sight, pressing herself right into the alcove. Fortunately, the nun's veil, swishing forward, left Aggie undiscovered.

The nun turned the corner and Aggie crossed the corridor and eased into the cramped cluttered office.

The drawer was unlocked and she quickly pulled out the papers, recognising them immediately. Most were signed, and all had written their addresses below their names.

And there it was. Gertrude Potter. Née Prudence Lafferty.

'Gertrude. Imagine! Dreadful! They want to call Lily's baby Gertrude!' Aggie murmured. Her heart thumped at her ribs. Taking the sheaf of papers, she stuffed them into her pocket. Now all she had to do was deliver them safely to Clarence …

The next day, Clarence got off the bus, turned slowly to his left and looked up the street towards Sullivan's where he and Lily had danced their troubles away before things had turned so ugly. But now his eyes began to cloud over with worry, because he realised she might never be quite the same optimistic, happy, sunny person again if he didn't manage to make a success of what he was about to do. A couple of children were playing in the street with a steering wheel and banging a hubcap, treasures scavenged from one of the few bomb sites in Southport. He turned on his heels and walked briskly towards the station.

Was this completely ridiculous? He carried on, going over what Aggie had told him in his head. He thought back to when he had kissed Lily's hand on the bandstand, a last smile, how that gesture had been so badly misunderstood by Lily's lover. It was the thought of this, how indirectly it had led to Lily having to give her child away, how it was his fault in a way, that pushed him on, and gave him courage to redress the injury.

He was on the train in less than half an hour, resolute and with a clear head. The compartment was empty, the leather straps swinging back and forth rhythmically, which gave him time to come up with a plan. Sitting in the carriage that stuttered and groaned its way towards Bescar Station in Scarisbrick, he decided that he should be as discreet as possible, which was not an easy task for Clarence. He was used to people staring at him, looking over their shoulders, especially to see him in his uniform, nudging, and muttering, and today was no different.

'Just find me the address of the Potters,' he had said to Aggie, and he couldn't quite believe it when she arrived at the Copper Kettle the following week waving it triumphantly.

'But you can't just steal the baby,' she'd replied, puzzled. 'That won't work. How will you even get across the doorstep to have a conversation? Those kind of people will be terrified of you.'

Clarence smiled to himself now. That was precisely what he was relying on. He was going to use the ugliness of the mistrust and hatred he had lived with his entire life to Lily's advantage.

Saltcotes Road wound up from the station. Clarence only knew it, because once, on his way to RAF Woodvale, he'd stepped off the train a stop too soon, and ended up dragging his blistered feet along its entire length, on a road that seemed to lead nowhere. But here he was on that same road, this time the correct one, the one that led towards some kind of reckoning. It crossed his mind that perhaps he should stop for a moment and make a plan. That would be sensible. But as nothing had occurred to him whilst sitting in the train, what did he expect would happen if he stopped now?

He paused at the kerb at the end of the road and, as he waited there, he knew that his next step could determine not only his future, but the destiny and happiness of others. And he sighed at the responsibility.

Suddenly, a car drew up outside the end house, and though he was still a way off, he could see it had a small front garden, and pink geraniums on the window boxes. Two people climbed out of it, a man and a woman. The Potters. It must be – the wife cradling the tiny bundle Clarence knew by instinct was Lily's baby. It had to be – even from here Clarence could see that they were much too old to have a child of their own.

Mr Potter got back into the car and reversed it into the gravelled drive and the sight of it, a Rover, brought the night of the fight back to him. The smell of the exhaust as the engine idled only inches from his bloodied face, the stoop of the man as he looked down at Clarence with contemptuous disregard and told the others to scarper. There would be other Rovers, other stooping silhouettes in his life, but if he ever heard that voice again . . . And yet, this was why he was here. This hatred and prejudice that he was so used to, he was now going to turn to his favour.

He approached the house, which was partly obscured by ivy twisting and spreading up the walls, along the roof and around the chimney stack, and a large apple tree. There was a bird table in the garden and a trellis covered in a clematis. Down the side of the house there was a dog kennel, but no sign of a dog.

His heart pounded and for a moment he hesitated. But his feet weren't stopping, so how could he? And at this moment they seemed to be functioning much better than his brain. With every step his wretched feet moved him forward. It was like a fast walk to the gallows in its grim inevitability. Now they made a right turn, through the gate, his damned feet, into the driveway, his shoes dancing lightly over the gravel surface, the house coming closer and closer, until there he was, at the front door.

No one could make him knock on the door, of course, except even as he thought of rebellion, he realised he was already too late. His hands had taken over and finished the job of his feet. Birds suddenly rose cackling and cawing from the chimney top as his knocks reverberated through the house and he could hear footsteps on the other side of the door – and those feet of his, which had worked so well to get him here, now refused to budge an inch.

In those final moments, as the door slowly opened, he thought he could pretend he was looking for gardening work and later, over tea, charm the lady into allowing Lily to visit from time to time, or maybe hold her one last time, because ... because ...

And there they were, Mr and Mrs Pokerface, he with a look of contempt that he seemed to wear so well, and she behind his shoulder, the grey hair wound up into a tight bun, fearful seeing him, lest this alien interloper at the door might attack them. And once again, standing in the frame of the doorway that was painted a brutish yellow, Clarence was reminded of the gulf between these people and his own.

'What do you want? Where have you come from?' demanded the man.

'Excuse me, sir, can I hear a baby crying?' said Clarence.

Screeching more like, its tiny voice hoarse with the effort.

'It doesn't matter what you can hear. I said, *what do you want*?'

'She cries all the time. So what?' said the woman flatly, which drew a look of rebuke from her husband.

'She misses her mother, I suppose,' replied Clarence, noticing the deep grooves etched into her skin and how dreadfully tired she looked.

The husband, with his braces and sleeveless knitted jumper, shirtsleeves pushed up his arms and held there with silver armbands, bristled. 'What the hell do you mean by that?'

And Clarence, instinctively doing the opposite, hunched his shoulders and held up his palms in an act of deference.

'I'm sorry, sir, ma'am, but I hate to hear the babies cry. My mamma, she would have me comfort my baby sisters when I was a boy.'

The truth was Clarence had never known his mother, and was the youngest in his family, but the strong West Indian accent he'd used to tell this walloping fib did the job that he had planned it to do.

'I'm closing this door now! Get away from here, or I shall have no hesitation in calling the police. Leave now. Or I'll set the dog on you,' snarled the man.

The couple stepped back inside and, eyeing Clarence with a deep distrust, the man moved to close the door, only to find Clarence had placed a foot between the door and the jamb.

'Please sir, wait! There is something you have to know about the baby, something important, really important, sir.'

He had no real inkling of what that information might be, just that this was his chance to do something big, something brave, something that would make a real difference to someone's life – and he wasn't going to let them shut him out so easily. It did the trick; the door slowly opened again.

The couple stared at him, the stranger at their door, this man, so different, so foreign-looking. How could he know something of their newly acquired infant, something that they should know?

'Well? Spit it out. What could you possibly tell us about our baby that we don't know?'

'I know the baby is adopted, sir, from St Jude's. But there is something else. If I may see the child, sir, to make sure I am not mistaken?

Clarence's heart was thumping; he could hear the baby crying inside the house, as if calling to him, 'Don't give up now, you've come this far!' He looked imploringly at the couple, and saw their resolve wither as their concern grew.

'Wait there,' was all the man said, and the door closed.

Beyond, Clarence could hear their voices.

'For pity's sake, woman! Stop the bloody child bawling. I can't hear myself think!'

'You stop her! I can't. There's nothing I can do. *Nothing*,' came the angry retort.

This might be easier than he had expected, thought Clarence. He wondered if they were bringing the child, or calling the police; whether he should stand and wait, or make a run for it. Unable to stay still, he paced, marking a circular route that brought him back to where he'd started. Was he doing the right thing? This was a beautiful house. He'd seen the wooden panelling in the hall, the carpets that touched each wall, the open fields across the road. It was a wonderful place for a child to grow up in, running free, away from the bombs and the dust and the fear. 'But away from your own dear mother,' he murmured out loud, and he knew what that felt like.

He stood outside the door and heard again the footfalls from inside and watched the door slowly open again. The man stood with his hands at his side and the woman held the crying baby against her crisp white cotton blouse.

'Let me see her face? Please?' begged Clarence.

And slowly the woman turned the baby towards him.

When he saw her dark swirls of curly baby hair and her rosy face, he couldn't resist a smile. By a miraculous coincidence, for that's all it was, Clarence knew, the baby stopped crying as soon as she set eyes on him and even gurgled as if to say, 'Almost there, almost there ...'

'She looks just like my mamma,' he said, a dishonest tear rolling down his cheek.

The silence roared as the couple looked from one to another in panic, then back at Clarence.

'What the hell are you saying? Do you mean to say . . .?'

The woman stared at the child, then abruptly held it away from her.

'She is my daughter, sir,' Clarence said managing to put a choke in his voice. 'I-I'm sorry. I only wanted to see her one last time. Forgive me.'

'This is bloody nonsense! She looks nothing like you. She's not a—'

But the woman interrupted her husband. 'Oh my God, Stanley! *Oh my God*!' she cried, uninhibitedly, unashamedly.

And Clarence, now speaking with the thick Creole accent of his childhood, tears springing from an entirely imagined story, stepped forward and said, definitively and proudly, 'Oh, she is mine, sir. Trust me. Her colour will come later. In a few weeks she will be as brown and beautiful as a berry. Look at her beautiful hair and her tiny face. Such thick, wiry hair. Uncanny. She is *so* like my mother. Thank you. Thank you for letting me see her.'

The couple looked down at the child as if seeing her for the first time.

'May I hold her one last time, sir? My mamma said I should bring her back home to Trinidad, but I know that won't be possible. I can see the love you have for her, ma'am, see it plain as can be.'

'Trinidad ...?' said the man.

'But we met the child's grandmother,' stuttered the woman. 'And – and ... Stanley, we met her grandmother, didn't we? She didn't look ... So her daughter ... she ... she ...?'

'Lily? Her parents are Irish. Yes, this little baby will grow up Creole with a dose of Irish, that's for sure. Her blue eyes will soon turn black as coal, as sure as night turns into day.'

She barely knew she was doing it, but the woman felt her own hair, as if to subliminally root her to some touchstone that separated her from this man.

Clarence paused, frowned. 'Did the nuns not tell you about me? Ah well, I expect the sisters wouldn't see colour as a barrier. They only wanted the best for the child.'

'Yes. But, but ... Hold her. Go on,' she said, shaking with fury.

'Really?' he said.

'Woman!' cried the man.

'Why not?' she said, thrusting the bundle into Clarence's arms. 'In fact, now I come to think of it, clearly there's been a mistake. A dreadful mistake.

This was not the child we wanted. All she does is cry. *All the time*. She might be ill. Or something. Yes, that explains it. The crying. We should tell the sisters right away. A mistake. I'm sure of it. Isn't that right, Stanley?'

The man frowned, stuck his hands deep into his pockets, and shook his head, puzzled and disappointed. Clarence, who was rocking Lily's daughter in his arms, hugged her close, kissed her on top of her head, and went to pass her back. The woman didn't seem to notice him, didn't lift her arms to take the child, but remained motionless, seeing only a future with a child that could not be mistaken for her own, a stranger in their house, a cuckoo in their nest.

And Clarence, seeing a look that one might almost mistake for relief cross her face as her husband took the child, knew that at that moment he had repaid his debt to Lily.

Chapter 34

Nearly two weeks had passed since Lily and Vince had gone to St Jude's. They were inseparable, knowing nothing of what had transpired at the Potters', and were united in grief and worry. And in the first five days of those two weeks, as if to underscore their grief, the city burned. The Overhead railway, Cunards, Lewis's and Blacklers, Mill Road hospital, were all hit and nearly destroyed. Wave after wave of bombers flew over Liverpool. There was a different atmosphere. This really was war. Lily and Vince at first talked of nothing else apart from their baby, but as the days went by, it became too painful, too much to bear, going round and round in circles and coming to the same hopeless conclusion, and so their conversation turned to the plight of all the other poor souls around them that were also suffering. A hundred and fifty died last night, another hundred dead tonight. A ship in the docks had burned for twenty-four hours and when it finally exploded, pieces of it were found in people's front gardens and backyards. Death was no longer something that happened to other people. It happened to your brothers, sisters, parents, neighbours, your children.

That morning, after yet again seeing people stagger out from the shelters ready to face the day and piece together what was left of their shattered lives, Lily, full of admiration for the spirit of this city, decided however hopeless the situation was with Prudence, she would never give up on her. But now, as she and Vince sat nursing mugs of tea in the Regal, the window of the cafe steaming up with condensation that made dribbles of water snake like worms down the glass pane, Vince told her what she had been expecting but dreading.

'Lil, I can't just sit around doing nothing watching this place go up in flames. I have to go back to sea. We can't live on fresh air. It doesn't feel right taking handouts from Ma and Pa, even though they're trying to make amends. I've a voyage. Just a week. The Isle of Man. Taking a food delivery to some camps they have there, and then on to Scotland and back again. Not far. But I should do it. I need to keep earning a crust.'

Lily nodded sadly. Her hair fell in a wave over her doleful face as she dropped her head.

'Of course, you must go,' she said, and the following day she went with him to the part of the docks that was still there, stood on the quayside and was shocked at the devastation. She kissed him goodbye.

'Hey, Lil. No tears. I'll be back soon. You've cried enough. I love you. When I come back I'll take you dancing.'

How could she dance? Her feet felt like clay, just at the thought of it. She doubted she would ever dance again.

They kissed once more and she managed a faltering smile as he went up the gangplank to his waiting ship that would leave that night under cover of darkness.

That evening she finished her WVS work at nine. The bluish light of dusk started to take on a deeper hue. She dreaded the moon shining. It had been the full moon that had allowed Hitler to bomb this city with such stunning and awful precision. You could turn off the street lamps and shut the blackout curtains but it was impossible to cover the moon. The smoke that wafted up the hill from the random fires that had broken out across Liverpool smelled acrid and strong and she had a metallic taste in her mouth. She shut the flap of the mobile van, bolted it, and locked it with a click. As she set off on the walk home, a couple of women sitting on their steps clutched their shawls around them, and nodded in approval and gratitude.

'Keep up the good work!' a woman shouted. 'Let's hope tonight's another quiet one.'

But she just looked at them vaguely. Soon she was passing groups of men in uniform, then she dodged past a strange old woman with a bucket on a piece of waste ground, picking up bits of rubbish, looking as though she had gone half mad – not the only one in this city – scouring for trinkets in the debris. She went along the bombed-out street, devastation all around her, a shell of a girl, walking through this shell of a city, thinking only of Vince and her baby.

She could just about make out the bollards at the bottom of Caryl Street as she approached the house. Suddenly she heard a crackling in the air. Was Hitler at it again? The devil chucking down skittles from the sky? Please God, it was just an arbitrary explosion and the wailing sirens weren't about to start up again. She dreaded the whizzing sound that accompanied them these days, then the shells that felt they were actually moving past her ears. A cold chill gripped her bones and she thought back to the days when for months and months the sirens had felt like an empty threat, and everyone had grown used to ignoring them. How foolish they had all been. Now it seemed this blitz – the explosions, the blasts, the shattered windows, bombed buildings, the countless dead, and the random fires, the flames licking the wounds of the city – would never end.

Lily squinted into the distance and wondered what was going to happen tonight and if Vince might not sail at all. She worried too about the children, and though they had brought life into the house, they had brought added anxiety with the danger of more bombing. Stella had talked deep into the night to them about Cliff to help get them to sleep, smoothing out the frowns in their brows with her fingers, telling stories of him in far-off lands, speaking low and sweetly about the times when he had danced and played the piano, and sung to them and hoped that they wouldn't have forgotten him. They had taken it better than anyone had expected.

When she arrived home, Lily looked around at the dishes in the sink, the clothes tangled in bundles on the floor, newspapers in piles that normally would be torn into neat squares for the privy lying about the place.

'Mam, this place needs clearing up …' she said, worrying that her mother was going back to her old ways. The old shift dress, bagging around the waist and gaping at the collar, said as much. Lily stood at the window. It had been a warm May day, but now the sky was packed tightly with dense black clouds and it began to rain, a leaden beat on the roof.

Something's up, she thought, squinting towards the river and out towards the sea.

Suddenly there was a knock at the door. The boy had a telegram in his hand and he was smiling. Lily frowned.

'Sorry, missus. Late with this.'

She took it from him with a frown. Was this a telegram about their father? You never knew when one might arrive with bad news. All hours of the day and night. But the boy was smiling. Surely he wouldn't be smiling if this was bad news? But what did the boy know? The smiling meant nothing. Stupid. Stupid to think that this was anything to do with her father, she told herself, desperately. But what about Vince? she thought, her heart pounding. No, his boat would still be at the docks, waiting to leave.

She took it from him. Fingering the beige envelope with the round fat letters in hard-to-read handwriting that was scrawled across it, she broke the seal of the envelope, opened it up. And felt her knees buckle. And then she screamed. 'Mam! Mam! The sisters are asking us to go back to St Jude's. They say they have news! Do you think they've changed their mind about Prue?'

Stella took the telegram, read it quickly. 'Be careful, Lily. They're not saying anything much. Just that they want to see us. It could be about anything.'

'Read it out,' said Lily.

'Are you sure you don't want to read it again yourself?' she asked.

Lily shook her head. 'No,' she said, and closed her eyes, winced, her head thrumming with anxious thoughts,

Stella unfolded the telegram, and from the very first minute she started to read it again, she wished she hadn't.

'They're saying … wait …'

She scanned the page. The words swam before her. 'They want you to come, that's for sure.'

Lily felt her whole body shaking. Suddenly she grabbed the telegram off Stella, held it towards the flickering light of the fire on the range – and let out a wail as she slammed a fist on the table. The sound that followed was low and guttural and came from the very depths of her soul.

'But it's the fourteenth today!' she gasped. 'The date of the telegram is the tenth! And we've only just received this! Four days have passed already! What if something has changed?'

Lily was pacing frantically. Stella tried to stay her with a trembling arm.

'Stop, Lil. What can you do?'

'Got to find Vince,' she mumbled. 'Before his ship leaves. Got to find him!'

She felt a rush of anxiety. She remembered the times when they were younger, he calming the dramas when she had argued with Stella, like the row over a ridiculous tulle and chiffon dress with pink bows that Stella had taken three days to make and expected her to wear for the Grafton and she had refused; or when she had run away after her father had forbidden her to go out dressed in new silk stockings, saying only common hussies wore stockings. Vincent was the one who always seemed to bring her back and know how to make things right.

'Let's wait and see what Matt says,' said Stella.

'Matt says? I don't give a damn what *he* says!'

'But maybe it's for the best. You can't do much about it if—'

'*No*,' said Lily. 'He's never wanted me to find my baby, because he's ashamed of me. He's never actually said it. But I know he is. I can tell by the way he looks at me. But this time, I won't be shamed. Vince and I are going to find her and bring her home. And you, Matt, everyone, can like it or lump it.'

And then she gathered herself and rose to her feet in a great flurry of snarls and unintelligible muttering.

'Where are you going?' cried Stella. 'Come back!' she shouted after her, into the street.

But Lily was gone, and Stella, too tired to go after her, too exhausted to care, went back inside to wash the pots.

That morning when she had been at the Pier Head, scurrying along in the shadow of the Liver Buildings with the magnificent Liver Birds perched on top of two bronze plinths, the metal gun boats refracting off The Mersey, shimmering in the winter sunshine, she had thought nothing of finding her way to the docks from Caryl Street, winding through back alleys, and narrow streets and paths. Now that it was dark, it felt a very different, more sinister and dangerous place in the inky blackout. When she got to the quayside, she craned her neck to look at the boats on the horizon. The few anchored at sea were blurred and fuzzy but the small tugboat that was waiting to transport a gaggle of sailors to the larger ship gradually began to take shape as it slipped into the estuary. There was such secrecy about what went on at these docks. The *Mersey Star* had just come back from Scotland, or was it Panama? The *Andorra* was going to the Isle of Man, then to Canada. The *Princess*, supposedly a sturdy tub that could resist a torpedo, had been blessed by a priest and a rabbi, but nevertheless she had been blown to smithereens before she reached the other side of the channel.

Lily had walked away, waving a handkerchief at Vince who stood on deck with a mop and a wan smile, having promised her he would be back soon. But he had said they weren't leaving until the ship had been prepared and cleaned that evening, and they had to leave under the cover of darkness so as not to be detected by the Germans.

Please God, he wouldn't have left. Please God! There was still a slim chance.

The lights that in peacetime would spill a yellow arc onto the wide pavements and the cobbles of the dock road, were out as usual now, but it had stopped raining a little while ago, and the moon shone brightly in the sky. Lily could see the silhouettes of the silver barrage balloons, cranes, and battleships with their tangles of masts and naval guns, as she approached the quayside. The *Liver*, once a cruise ship, was noble and proud, with its funnel at a slight angle, now painted regulation army grey and with guns bolted onto the decks. She frowned, gazing out towards the other boats anchored further down the docks towards the mouth of the River Mersey.

Suddenly she felt someone at her side. Two men in uniform, one in a workmanlike coarse blue jumper and black trousers with hobnailed boots, must be from the merchant navy, she thought; the other, a Royal Navy officer was wearing a slightly longer version of a pea coat, creases neatly ironed into his trousers. The merchant navy fellow introduced himself as the foreman of the docks, then asked, 'What are you doing here, missus? Do you have permission?'

She saw the other man strike a match, his face hollow-eyed and his grinning mouth, stuffed with crooked teeth, lit up in the sudden light. In a rush of words, with panicked gestures and disjointed sentences, she tried to explain that she had to get a message to her fiancé who was due to sail on a ship called the *Liver*, and she wanted to know was it still here in the docks and if so, how could she get to it quickly?

'What's so important?' the foreman asked her.

She said she couldn't tell him; all she wanted to do was to get a message to Vincent before the *Liver* set sail. But as the words left her mouth she knew this fellow wasn't going to help her. He didn't care about some sad desperate girl and the other chap with him wouldn't care either. But she had to try.

'I need to get a message to one of the seamen,' she said. 'Before the boat goes.'

'I shouldn't think you'll have much joy. I'd go home if I were you. This is no place for a woman to be wandering around at night. You know what happened with the explosion on the Malakand ship? This place is still a tinder box,' said the foreman. 'Go home, love. What if the sirens start?'

She realised it was hopeless, they had only confirmed what she had expected, and so she said goodnight, clutched her coat around her, and turned to hurry away. She continued to walk down the quay past a booth that had a chain attached from one end of a post to a second post on the other side. The boat anchored up in front of it didn't look as though it was going anywhere that night and the curling barbed wire on the top deck made her shiver.

She looked at the lidded black water of the Mersey. Suddenly, everywhere was sunk into all-enveloping blackness. This blasted blackout, she thought. Her instinct was to use the chains looped between each post to feel her way along because she could barely see her hand in front of her face now that a cloud had scooted across the moon and it was so dark. She moved off down the cobbles. Using one hand to steady herself, she gripped an iron railing and reached for the chain, but the shock of grasping a moveable structure caused her to stumble and she toppled forward.

The cold water as she hit the surface shocked her into awful terror. She could feel the spiralling, muddy waters of the Mersey deepening to strong currents and under she went, deep under the cold, cold water, the river dragging her down with arms of steel for one, two, three, maybe four seconds. And then she came up, gasping for air, flailing, thrashing, screaming out for help.

The sound of the splashing and her cries alerted the two men who came running and the foreman threw a lifebelt. If she could grasp it … But the energy of the water at this part of the dock, where the tributary met the lagoon, was so strong that the river pushed the ring too far from her for her to have any hope of retrieving it.

'Do something, Paddy!' the foreman yelled. 'It's that woman! Fallen in the water!'

Then she heard more voices and found a new energy, began splashing about furiously, flailing and screaming, her arms hitting at the water.

'Stop thrashing about, woman! Save your energy!' cried the foreman. He ripped off his jacket and shoes and, in one heroic leap, jumped in and swam out to meet her. He reached out to grab hold of her and swam back to the post with his hand under her chin, whilst the other man, yanking her outstretched hand as if she was a wet fish, hauled her out of the water. She flopped onto the stone quay, gasping for breath.

He tried to get her to lie on her back but she resisted, spluttered black water and retched more mouthfuls than she had swallowed.

'Let him help you!' said the second man. 'This bloody blackout,' he said. 'It's made more casualties out of Liverpool than the damn war ...'

Lily gagged, coughed and spluttered more water, sat up and gasped and then hollered until the man had to slap her across the cheek to get her to stop. The end of a bad day had just got so much worse. But she was in no mood to care.

She stood dripping on the quay, propped up by the two men and suddenly the air was heavy with an oppressive quiet. With it, a sickness rose to her throat as her legs wobbled underneath her. She gulped down more great gasps of breath and trembled with shock, the sweet taste of blood swilling inside her mouth because she'd bitten a chunk of flesh from the inside of her cheek.

The Royal Navy man took her over to a shed where a woman dressed in blue culottes and wellington boots sat boiling a kettle on a small stove.

'What in God's name did you think you were playing at? You could have been killed!' she said, immediately regretting her harsh tone.

But Lily couldn't speak. She just burst into more tears.

'All right, love. You're fine. Come on now, let's make you a nice cup of tea ...' said the woman. The smell of kerosene and cigarettes was strangely comforting.

'What's your name, love?'

'Lily Lafferty,' she mumbled, her throat aching when she spoke.

'Sugar? Good for a shock ...' the woman said, tipping heaped spoonfuls into each mug.

Stella managed a wavering smile and clasped the cup of tea between her shaking hands.

'Never mind. You're in one piece. And that's all that matters. I take it you didn't see the sign saying Danger?'

She shook her head.

'Let's get you out of those wet clothes. I've some WAAF overalls in the back.'

Somewhere far off, an engine backfired, which made Lily jump. For a moment she thought it was gunshot, and then suddenly the heavens opened and hailstones as big as sugar lumps begin to beat against the roof of the shed.

'What were you doing here on your own? The bombing could start at any minute. What would you have done?'

'My fiancé. I-I ...' she whimpered, her face crinkling into a desperate expression, *half wishing she* could jump back into the Mersey so the icy current might grip at her ankles once again, and pull her down to its watery depths forever.

Then suddenly she heard a voice she recognised calling her name.

'Lily! Lil!'

Jerking her head around, she cried, 'Vince! Vince!'

He was running towards her, waving, then shouting her name again, cupping his hands around his mouth. Behind him, the gangplank banged down on the landing stage, all clanking chains and buffeting up against the huge rubber tyres, water slopping and slapping against the ship's sides.

'What the devil? What are you doing here? Why is your hair wet?'

'The baby,' she cried. 'I think she's back at St Jude's! Please tell them you can't go – I need you to stay and help me bring her home!'

The captain frowned as he watched this animated discussion. 'Vincent. Are you coming or not?' he called.

Vincent opened his mouth to explain, but in a rush of words, it was Lily who told the man the whole story.

'We had a baby. We weren't married – and I gave her away – but now we need to take her back! Please let Vincent come with me? Please?' she said desperately.

She could see him looking at her. Was he shocked? People didn't say these things out loud. But she didn't care. She no longer cared what the world thought. She only had one chance, one sliver of hope that her and Vince's entire future rested on, and all that mattered now was that her baby was going to be part of it.

Chapter 35

Lily had dressed for the occasion. She was wearing a thin summer coat and underneath, a pale blue frock with gaping stitches at the hem, but neatly held together with a blue sash belt, set off with a wide collar made of lace, and edged in white piping at the seams of the ruched bodice. On her head she wore a red beret, pulled over her unruly hair, and around her neck, as a last-minute thought, she was wearing the locket that Rosie had given her. *For luck*, she remembered Rosie's note, saying. She was going to need it today. Vincent wore his best suit in the hope it would distract from his scuffed shoes and slightly frayed collar. It was decided that he should wait in the cafe.

Stella turned to him to reassure him this was the right thing to do. 'I know how this works. You do as they say. Does no good to rub them up the wrong way. They've asked to see Lily and me, so that's what we should do.'

Vincent agreed reluctantly, after being persuaded by Lily. He followed them outside to say goodbye and good luck, pacing nervously, sucking on a cigarette, under the branches of a large sycamore tree.

'Don't be long,' he said, panting a kiss on Lily's cheek.

'You're here to see Sister Assumpta?' said the nun who greeted Stella and Lily at the door.

Lily nodded, expecting there to be eye-rolling and tutting, or head-shaking. But there was neither. The nun placed a hand on Lily's arm. It was as though she almost felt sorry for her.

'They're ready for you in the office.'

Stella and Lily followed her down the corridor and into the bowels of the convent. The smell of incense was sweet and heady. Candles on spikes dripped onto metal trays underneath, forming waxy stalagmites and stalactites. The smiling face of the Virgin Mary, in her vivid blue robes; the snake at her feet with its red forked tongue and unnaturally realistic eyes that Lily felt were following her. A small statue of St Boniface, in desperate prayerful pose, encapsulated the way Lily was feeling. What was she doing here? It felt as if the whole of her life was hanging in the balance with what was going to happen in the next fifteen minutes. With each step of dreadful anticipation, gloom descended.

'Sister, do you know what Sister Assumpta wants to talk to us about?' asked Stella.

The nun shook her head.

Lily wasn't convinced she was telling the truth. She's probably taken a vow of silence on the flaming matter, she thought, darkly.

They followed her to Ambrose, went through the heavy, creaking door, down another corridor, and then, taking out a set of keys, she unlocked one door and then another. It was the nursery! Lily had never been here before and her heart lurched. It was such a sad place. A mobile swayed forlornly on its string in a draft and a dozen or so empty cots were laid out from one side of the room to the other, each with a uniform crocheted blanket draped over the rails at one end.

'Empty now. The evacuees have brought a bit of life to this place, thanks be to God,' the nun said.

But where's my baby? Lily wanted to ask, as panic suddenly took hold of her.

They slowed to a stop outside a large carved wooden door, and went to go into the room beyond.

'Take your hat off,' Stella whispered to Lily. 'The nuns will have a hissy fit.'

Lily pulled the beret off her head, stuffed it into her pocket. 'I'm grand, Mam,' she said bravely.

Sister Assumpta was sitting at a desk and there was a man sitting rigid in a chair, silhouetted against the light flooding in from the window, two empty chairs beside him.

'Clarence!' yelped Lily in a whisper, when he turned his head to see her come in. What on earth was he doing here? And he winked at her. She was sure he winked at her.

'Ah. The Laffertys,' said Sister Assumpta.

Lily felt her heart was pounding so badly it was going to burst through her chest. It was the way the nun said it, with a sneer, a slight turning down of her mouth, peering over her half-moon spectacles.

'The famous Laffertys. Sit down.'

Lily felt the stuffing that was coming through the seat of the chair prickling the backs of her knees and she shifted uncomfortably in her seat.

The nun gestured to the sister to leave. 'So, I shall come to the point.'

She paused for effect, put her elbows on the table and steepled her hands, propping up her chin with her bony middle fingers. Lily felt tears springing to her eyes.

'This man …'

He has a bloody name! Lily wanted to say.

'This man …' Assumpta gestured vaguely in the direction of Clarence. 'Is it true that he is the father of your child?'

Lily's mouth dropped open. And Clarence looked at her keenly, his eyes widening. It was as if he was trying to say something, to signal something to her. Stella, fiddling with the clasp on her purse nervously, clipping and unclipping the brass fastener, started.

'Sister, I . . .' Lily's voice wobbled. It was as though she was unable to utter a single word. She looked over at Stella who was now toying frantically with the pearl necklace around her neck.

'Well, is he?' asked Sister Assumpta. 'Because that's what Mr Potter has told us.'

The silence in the room felt suffocating. Lily hardly dared to breathe. It felt as if the answer to this question was the key to her future. She could say yes. Or she could say no. Which was it to be?

'Come on, Lily. I haven't got all day. Cat got your tongue? You must know. Heavens above, if you're not sure, we're in a more dire place than we are in even now.'

Stella wiped away beads of sweat forming on her brow. 'Sister, I—'

'I'm not asking you, Mrs Lafferty. For the love of God, Lily, it's a simple question: is Clarence Aimé the father of your child?'

Lily paused. She raised her finger and thumb to her mouth, squeezed her bottom lip, didn't look up directly when Clarence crossed and uncrossed his legs and cleared his throat, but there was no doubt that she had seen out of the corner of her eye that he was trying to communicate with her.

'Sister . . .' she replied.

And with that Clarence leaned forward, across the table.

'We only want to give our baby a home,' he said and placed a hand on Lily's knee.

What the devil was he saying? Lily's cheeks stung. She stared down at the hand, feeling it burn through her skirt, then looked back up at the nun, confused and terrified.

Stella frowned. For the life of her, she didn't know what to make of this.

But in that gesture, Lily suddenly realised what was happening. That Clarence was, at this moment, trying to turn all the hate and unkindness in the world into something good, something noble and humane and compassionate.

'Yes, Sister. He's the father of my child,' answered Lily, firmly.

'Not this Vincent character?'

'No. It's Clarence's.'

The nun leaned back in the creaking chair and folded her arms over her ample bosom. 'And doesn't that feel better now you've told the truth, Lily? Why on earth lie? You might be able to keep these things from the world, but you can never keep them from God. So what now?'

'Sorry,' said Lily. 'Are you asking me?'

'The Potters have returned your child. It seems Mr Aimé visited them. Very unusual. And now Mrs Potter says the child is an unnaturally difficult child – something of an unruly spirit in her – to say nothing of her swarthy complexion!'

'Where is she?' gasped Lily, unable to contain herself.

'Be quiet, Lily. I haven't finished. The Potters say that if you want her back, then they won't stand in her way.'

'And you?'

'It's unusual for us to allow a girl to take her child back – after all, you signed the papers. But with this war it's not easy for us to place babies, people have other pressing matters on their minds. So, as the Potters have returned the child, and as we're full to the gills with the evacuees, if you really think you can give her a home – and if you marry, of course, and repent – well, you have my blessing.'

Stella's eyes flashed black. She knew what was happening all right. And so did Lily.

But then there was someone at the door and Lily turned round.

'Sister David!' she cried, seeing the nun standing there with a bundle of blankets in her arms. And in the bundle, a baby. Sister David, seeing them all, beamed a smile.

'Here. Your baby …' she said, holding the child out. Lily leaped up, dashed over, and leaned into Sister David. Overwhelmed, she felt she couldn't breathe and her body was shaking as she took the bundle and cradled it to her. Clutching her close to her body, feeling the newness of her, marvelling at how much she had changed in the two weeks since she had been born, the milk spots had disappeared and her skin was smooth and perfect and her hair had grown. Those little brown curls poking over the top of the blankets made Lily's eyes swell with tears.

The baby gurgled and, by instinct, Lily rocked her gently, shifting her weight from foot to foot.

'She's beautiful,' said Clarence.

The baby gurgled again.

'She's smiling, Mam! Clarence, she's smiling at us!' Tears rolled down Lily's face. She bent her head. 'Home now, darlin',' she said. 'I've found you. And I'm never going to let go of you again.'

Sister David smiled. She stuffed a bag into Stella's hands; it was filled with tissues and nappies, a bottle and cartons of dried baby milk. Clarence drew himself up to his full height and shook the nun's hand.

They moved towards the door. But when they reached it, Lily stopped suddenly. Turning to face Assumpta, she paused.

'Sister,' she said bravely, 'there's one more thing. I've always tried to see the good in a person, and I'm so grateful you're giving me my baby back. But I know that there's something unpleasant in what you're doing – an unkindness to Clarence. When you thought Vincent was the father, you insisted that we had lost our child forever. Now you think she's Clarence's, you are very happy to give her back to us.

You see, I *saw* whatever you have in your heart, whatever cruelty, prejudice, or nasty thoughts you have, because I saw the same look on the faces of those men who kicked Clarence for no reason other than hateful fear.'

The nun's eyes widened in shock and outrage.

'I beg your pardon!' she gasped.

'I want you to know that *I know* why you have given me back my baby. May God forgive *you*, actually, Sister. You like saying that to us, right enough. But it's you who needs to be praying on your knees and begging for his mercy.'

'What did you expect, you stupid girl!' Assumpta cried, her spittle flying across the table as she spoke. 'How am I going to get rid of a child whose father is – is—'

'Say it, Sister,' drawled Clarence.

She jabbed a finger in his direction. 'Like him!' she said. 'Ridiculous.'

Lily shook her head. 'Clarence is a good man. The very best of men.'

'Oh, isn't he the saint!'

'Sister, all it is, is fear. Fear in your heart. But you have nothing to fear. Not from Clarence. Maybe from God, but not from Clarence.'

Clarence's eyes widened. He was mesmerised; he had never heard anyone speak like this before, but then a grin spread across his face. Lily smiled at him.

'Come on,' she said. 'Come on, Mam. Let's get out of this miserable place. We've got some celebrating to do.'

As instructed by Assumpta, a flustered Sister David led them out of a side door into the walled garden, before they headed towards an anonymous-looking wooden door. Clarence opened it and darted a look into the road.

'Let's go before she changes her mind,' he said. 'I'd take on an army over that Sister Assumpta any day of the week!'

'God will keep you well. And I look forward to hearing about the wedding,' Sister David. 'And Stella, I prayed for you. And I'm happy. That this time it's a happy ending . . .'

Lily exchanged a look with her mother.

She wanted to ask Stella more about the nun's words, but Sister David, was shooing them out, locking the door again, sending them away with more prayers and waves. Was this the horrible warning that she'd once talked of? Lily wondered. She would save that conversation for later.

Vincent was sitting in the cafe at a table in the bay window, drinking a cup of Bovril, his hands cupped around it nervously. Lily knocked on the steamed-up glass and beckoned him to come out and join them.

'Vince!'

He looked up and gasped. He rushed to go out, shoving the chair out from behind him, which fell on the floor, apologising as he flung a shilling onto the saucer, then tearing out of the door.

'You found her!' he said. 'Oh, Lil! Is this my baby? My little girl?'

'Yes,' she said. 'And this is Clarence,' she added, in a softer tone. 'It's him we have to thank – he helped us more than you know.'

Vince thrust out his hand. 'I'm so sorry. Seems I misjudged you, sir,' he said,

'You did, Vince. He's a good man,' said Lily.

'Aye,' replied Vince. 'Can I shake your hand and tell you that? I'm so sorry.'

'No need for that,' said Clarence, batting aside his stuttering apologies. 'No need at all. Your Lily is a grand girl and I'm pleased I can return a favour, that's all.'

And as Lily handled the bundle to her love, and his whole body shook with a happiness he had never imagined was possible, she felt emboldened. For at last she had a sense of good things about to happen in their lives, things that were kind and true and virtuous. Things that Clarence would always have a part in, in a world that suddenly felt a better place because of him.

Chapter 36

Annie, idling around the kitchen, picking up pieces of crockery that had smashed on the floor, talked incessantly, blamed the Corporation for not warning people how bad this wretched war would be, and thanked God the children had survived another night in the cupboard under the stairs. 'Didn't I tell you we should have put that shelter up in the backyard, Matt?' she shouted.

'Stella says those Anderson shelters are useless,' he retorted.

There were more and more shocking stories reaching Caryl Street of so many young children dying. Some blamed the parents for being stupid and not sending their children away. Others blamed the priests and the nuns for thinking that prayer had the power to protect them. And then there were those who blamed God for not intervening to save them.

'Just bad luck,' said Matt. 'Like Lily getting knocked up – everybody's at it. Sooner everyone comes to accept that, the better.'

'All those wasted hours on their knees, hands pressed together in prayer, all those rosaries, begging Jesus and the saints to look after them in their hour of need, and it's come to this,' said Annie, her eyes wandering to look out of the window, to the gaping hole between number 23 and 27, where Rosie had once lived. Her head hurt. Further down the road there was a group of kids more concerned with enjoying the sunshine than anything else. She winced, put her hands over her ears and rubbed her temples as they started smashing a football, trying to kick it through the open window of the derelict house opposite, intent on recreating the lawlessness of the Wild West films that they loved. These streets were becoming scenes of desolation and wanton vandalism.

'Some of them,' she remarked to Matt, 'are having the time of their lives. Should have seen Sarah Flanagan with her kids, standing on the wall watching and cheering on the explosions at the docks like it was a firework display. Winnie's boy came with back with three fingers dangling off the end of his hand. She tried to sew them back but it's not looking good. They reckon he might lose the use of his hand all together. Then there was that wee lassie who fell out of the window and the boy who jumped from the first floor and the window frame jumped with him. These kids are feral. This war is making wild animals out of them.'

'Weren't we all like that?' asked Matt, not really listening.

'Not like this, it's different. They're just copying what they see all around them.

Annie sighed and went to see if Lily and Vincent were coming up the road. She didn't dare think of the outcome of the meeting at St Jude's, but wondered if Lily had gone straight to work, had gone to take the van out again, setting up on the corner of Stanhope Street, delivering teas to the rescue men and the ARP soldiers, serving them with a broken heart.

For the next half an hour she sorted out drawers, cooked a pot of vegetable stew, stirred it, dipped the spoon in and tasted it and burnt her tongue, scoured the newspaper for news – and then there was a knock at the door.

She answered it. 'You look white as a sheet, Lily. What – what the jeepers?' She frowned. There was Vincent. And Stella, looking tired and happy. And a man she didn't recognise. Tall and handsome, strong broad shoulders, tight black curls and dark skin, with wise, serious, eyes. And Lily – Lily was holding something.

'Good God! A baby?'

Lily beamed. Vincent draped his arm over her shoulder.

'What on earth? Stella? Lily's baby?'

*

Clarence sat at the table drinking tea.

'Who is this man? What's he doing here?' Annie hissed to Stella, as they washed pots together, facing the sink.

Stella smiled and said Clarence could speak for himself as she turned and offered him fruit loaf and lukewarm tea from the pot. Vince asked if there wasn't something stronger in the house, but Clarence said that he had to return to the barracks before nightfall. The expressions on Lily and Stella's faces, as they rocked the child and stared glassy-eyed, mesmerised by her beauty, were of sheer, unimaginable, joy.

Lily cried, and held her baby, and Vincent apologised once again for his behaviour, and thanked Clarence, and said he was about the most heroic chap that he had ever met, begged forgiveness for wanting to smash his face in, poured more tea, and said he really did need something stronger.

Lily patted his arm, 'Clarence is a gentleman,' she said, and they all agreed.

Stella cried and laughed and yelped with delight when she held the child, and then fluttered around like a butterfly, refilling cups, replacing food, and the children dashed around the table, and burped the baby, and stroked it, kissed it, and fussed over it.

Clarence, meanwhile, after first telling them about what happened with the Potters, hardly had time to breathe when a succession of questions were fired at him from all sides. 'Were they awful?' 'What was Assumpta's face like when she met you?' 'Did you like sister David, the kind one?' 'Did she make you do the University walk?' 'He tried to answer as best as he could without going into details about how cruel the world could be, only he would know that, how the Potters had explained that this baby was a blight on their lives already, how the sisters had assumed it was Vincent who had arrived at the house demanding his child, until finally he veered the subject back to less troubling matters, and told them a little more of his story.

'I was at Dollis Hill post office, doing research for Teleprinter and Reme, then Mill Hill, that's a nice place, for cypher machines ...'

Deirdre climbed on his knee, mesmerised by his strong, chiselled face, put her hands flat against his cheeks and giggled as she felt his bristles tickling her palms. Bobby pointed out the flashes on his uniform and asked what they were, and he told them they were the colours of his country, Trinidad.

'When I first arrived here I was billeted with a family who were good-hearted enough, they had a piano, so I used to entertain them before I was sent to Mere Lane camp.'

'You should hear Clarence play the piano,' said Lily. 'He's as good as Dad.'

'But we won't tell Dad that,' laughed Stella

'Can he mend the wireless?' asked Bobby.

Auntie Annie was worrying about the sisters finding out Vincent was the father, was this whole thing legal? Or would the nuns insist that Lily give up Prue again? And even if Lily kept her, she said, 'People will gossip terribly and Lily might be shamed into changing her mind. Everyone knows the child is illegitimate. What will they say about us?' she announced, the only chord of dissent in the room.

But Stella didn't care. 'We're the Laffertys and the Laffertys have loose morals!' she announced. 'Who gives a fig!'

And then Vincent explained that he was going to marry Lily right away, so that was the end of that conversation, and everyone was happy.

Deirdre tugged on the sleeve of Vincent's jacket. 'Can I be a bridesmaid?' she said. 'Can I wear a veil and a frilly dress and have a posy?'

'Of course,' he replied with a smile, and Deirdre clapped her hands and yelped.

Stella basked in the warm glow of their chatter and then, because this was the Laffertys, there was impromptu dancing and singing.

'Play something on the piano to celebrate!' said Stella and, after a little persuasion, Clarence took his place on the stool, and they drank anything they could find and Stella sang 'We'll Meet Again' and Deirdre put her tap shoes on and wanted to shuffle off to Buffalo with Stella, who said she couldn't do it in her heels, and they danced instead to 'In The Mood' in their stockinged feet. 'Eyes and teeth!' Stella cried. 'Eyes and blooming teeth!' she repeated, lifting Bobby and Deirdre onto the table, sucking on a cigarette stuffed into a gold-tipped holder, coughing like a miner, waving away the smoke, and clapping her hands together. The children danced and it was all wiggling bottoms and winks and blown kisses as they leaped barefoot off the table, making shapes in the air, Deirdre showing glimpses of pink knickers and white thighs, and when they got to the end with a flourish and a pantomime wave of their arms, there was a burst of applause.

Clarence's mouth gaped open.

'What about that?' said Stella.

'What about that, indeed?' he replied, laughing.

Annie burst out into a vigorous round of applause. 'Bravo!' she cried. And she joined them as they all gathered around the piano and sang 'Rule Britannia' and the children sang another song about a cat. 'I love to sing and I love to dance, miaow, miaow miaow,' they chorused, and everyone miaowed more, and laughed even harder and got even more drunk on cheap sherry and gin and cried about the war and shouted about it. And said, 'Thank God for Clarence bringing home Prue!' and raised a toast to him. And then Stella said, 'Lord God Jesus Christ Our Saviour couldn't have done a better job.' and everyone agreed, and Annie added that Clarence bore a striking resemblance about the eyes to the statue of Jesus in St Columba's, and Stella said, 'Well, I don't know about that. Does Clarence really want to hear that?' And Clarence replied with a smile that he didn't mind at all.

It was only when Peg Leg came across the road with the awful news that there was rumour that a ship had just been hit off the coast of Scotland by a U-boat that the celebrations started to come to an end and Clarence announced it really was time for him to leave.

'Goodbye,' he said, sticking his hand out for Vincent to shake. 'It's been a wonderful night. But there's a war on and I can't stay here and go to work on a sore head.'

Vincent paused. 'Thank you. Thank you. I'm going to sea again soon, for two months, but I hope to see you again. You'll always be welcome here, Clarence.'

Later, Stella took Lily into the parlour and she placed the baby on her breast, and prayed there would be no sirens that evening. Stella sat at the table with Annie. She was dictating a to-do list: make bread-and-butter pudding out of the stale crusts, unravel her pink cardigan and knit a blanket for the baby, invite the Whartons, organise a piano tuner . . .

'Organise a piano tuner?' asked a bewildered Annie, reading over her shoulder.

'For the sing-song after the wedding,' she replied.

Some things would never change for the Laffertys.

Of course, the wailing of the sirens started up the minute they got into bed.

'I can't take a chance with the baby,' said Lily, and they all put on overcoats over their nightclothes, and traipsed out, Matt carrying Deirdre on his hip, Bobby trailing along behind in his jim-jams.

Vincent urged them on. 'Get a move on, slow-coaches!' he cried.

Lily marvelled that despite the worry of more bombing, the children were flush-faced and happy, and so was she. How could that be possible? It didn't feel right. Hundreds – no, *thousands* – dead in Liverpool alone from months of bombing, and now here she was, more content than she had ever been, and finally feeling that, after so much heartache over the past year, luck would be on their side that night.

Chapter 37

Stella wobbled as she rose from the chair that she had slept in and, without thinking, reached out a hand to the range to steady herself, then yelped and sucked the smarting flesh to cool it. Her hair was matted and standing up in tufts and she tried to contain a piece of it with a grip, then gave up. She had woken, exhausted, but she knew what she had to do. Fumbling for the letter she had received the week before and shoved to the back of the dresser, not knowing how to respond, she took it out and read it once again, with fearlessness and conviction now she was ready to write her reply.

16 May 1941
Caryl Street

Dear Sister Assumpta,

I have few words except to say except I am a woman who knows what shame feels like; I found that out when I became pregnant at sixteen. But I will not allow my daughter to feel that shame. Thank God the world seems to be changing. All this nonsense you are talking about? I sent Lily to you because I feared that the same would happen to her as happened to me. When I was sixteen I thought I could take on the world and win. Before I met my husband, I was in love with a young soldier and, like so many young men in the Great War, he was killed in the trenches. When I found myself pregnant, I thought my life was over and when I saw that Lily might be falling in love, I didn't want her to face the same loss, despair and fear, that I had felt after making one stupid mistake. Foolishly, I thought that if she evacuated to St Jude's and I could keep her away from trouble, I would prevent this happening. I was wrong.

This war has thrown unimaginable hardships at us, and a slip of a child is not going to defeat us. As to a wedding, it's none of your business. As to the Church authorities and the signing of the papers, don't you even dare!

Yours in Jesus,
Stella Lafferty.

Ha! she thought. Yours in Jesus. Play Assumpta at her own game. She wouldn't like that one bit.

Chapter 38

'Why didn't you tell me?' Lily asked Stella as she sat looking at her mother across the kitchen table in shock.

Stella stared back at her. 'Lily, do we have to go over it again? I didn't tell you because I was so distraught, so ashamed, I still can't speak of it to this day. I didn't want the same to happen to you.'

'Does Matt know?'

'No one knows. That's the way these things work. Not even your father.'

'Who was *this* father, then?'

Tears welled in Stella's eyes and she blinked them away, trying not to cry.

'His name was Harold White – and there's not a day goes by that I don't think about him. He was wonderful. We knew the family. When he was killed in France, when we got the letter, his death was so horrible, we all just went to pieces.'

'Oh, Mam ...' said Lily.

'The Great War had caused so many deaths, but nevertheless, Harold and I felt invincible. I don't think I had any idea of how dangerous it would be for Harold. What do you know of the horrors of the trenches when you're sixteen and the bands are playing and everyone is beside themselves with excitement and the only talk is victory? He had gone off, just seventeen – lied about his age – to fight with the King's Regiment. And there I was, lovesick, waiting for him to come home. Of course, he never did. Killed in the last month of the war, the second day he arrived in France. And then, when I found out I was pregnant . . . Well, you can imagine. And the Whites didn't want anything to do with me.'

'What did you do?'

'Nothing, at first. Too scared of Gram. Too scared of everyone. The nuns. My teachers. And when I finally told Gram she begged me not to say anything because she knew it would break Grandad's heart. Which of course, when he found out, was exactly what happened. He didn't speak to me for two years. I think that's what drove him into an early grave, my poor father. And so . . .'

The sentence tailed off. She just sat there for a moment, twisting the fabric of her threadbare apron in her lap.

'Go on,' said Lily gently.

'Mam took me to her sister's and I had the baby in Morecambe. Then we came home with her …'

'A girl? Was she pretty?'

Stella stared off into space. 'She was more than pretty. She was beautiful. The plan was we would say she was Mam's. Dad was furious about that, said it was absurd, the neighbours would know straight away we were lying, so I would have to give her away immediately. Thank God for the Walshes.'

'The Walshes?' Lily hesitated, frowned. 'Like Rosie?'

'Yes. Just like Rosie Walshe …' Stella paused, took a deep breath. There was a moment of silence before she let it go. Air whooshed from her lips and she said, 'Rosie is your half-sister. Oh no, there I go again. I can't … still can't believe she's gone! *Was* your half-sister, I mean.'

Lily gasped.

'There I've said it. It's out now.' Stella's rigid posture relaxed slightly and she slumped a little further into the wooden wheelback kitchen chair and said, 'Actually, I feel a little bit better about it.'

Lily took her tense hand, enclosed it within hers.

'It seemed the perfect solution. They were desperate for a baby. And when Gram confided in Mrs Walshe how terrible things were – they had heard the baby's cries through the walls so there was no point hiding Rosie from them – well, when she said how we were all too scared to leave the house because of what people would say, they just knocked on the door next day and asked if they could have Rosie. Simple as that. And it was – well, it was wonderful! I could watch my little girl grow into a beautiful young woman. Watch her through a knot of wood in the fence that I poked through with my finger. I saw her take her first steps with my eye squinting through the hole, heard her speak her first words with my ear pressed against the splintering wood. And then, of course, there were so many other times I got to see what a wonderful job the Walshes were doing. I could never have given Rosie that. She was so solemn and serious on her First Holy communion day and she was such a clever girl – naturally clever, I mean. The three Rs might not have come easily to her, but she knew about the world, could make people smile – and she was a wizard with a needle and a thread. And then, when you two became friends, playing ball against that wall out there, or hopscotch, I got to be part of her life. Imagine. I could never have dreamed of that. Taught her little things, how to waltz, and—'

'How to make fingerless gloves out of an old pair of socks. Oh, Mammy!'

'Now can you see why I didn't want the same to happen to you? When I saw you falling in love with Vincent, when his mother told me he was going to join the merchant navy and I saw so many young men being killed … Then when Bobby and Deirdre were going to Freshdale, I thought St Jude's would be the answer. It would put an end to your romance and protect you from the pain of losing him and possibly worse. Stupid, though, wasn't it? Stupid to think I would somehow manage the situation.'

'What about Dad?' Lily asked, plaintively.

'What about him?'

'Did you … Do you …?'

'Love him like I loved Harold? Of course. When I met your dad I soon realised there were different kinds of love. Lily, I fell head over heels in love with your da the first time I saw him – who wouldn't, with those eyes? And when he sang and played the piano, I was finished, I didn't think that would be possible after Harold, but God, he was handsome, Lil. And then it soon became something else: having children, the hard, hard work, bashing out the piano keys day in and day out, trying to earn a crust when we started the dancing school. I found out about real love the hard way. Now I just want him back home,' she added with a sigh.

'Does he not know?'

'No. Not a clue. I just buried it, because it was too awful – and I was frightened because I never had the courage to tell him when we first met, never told him that the little girl over the fence was mine. And when your da became famous around these parts – well, at least, the Laffertys did, the dancing school – it would only have made it worse. I was too fearful of what it would do to us if we were to go raking over it. To me, if I'm honest.'

She cried, and snuffled, and cried some more.

'Oh Mam,' said Lily. And it was as though part of her insides tore in sorrow for her ma, for Rosie . . .

'Come with me,' said Stella when her tears came to an end.

They went upstairs together and Lily followed her into the bedroom. Stella knelt and reached deep into the back of the wardrobe, took an envelope from an old shoebox. With tremulous fingers, Stella took out the faded photograph. There was handwriting scrawled on the back of it and it was fuzzy and faded, as though it had been bleached by the sun, even though Lily was sure it had remained stuffed in the back of this wardrobe for over twenty years. The photograph was of a young man. There was also a woman in the photograph, her face partially obscured by the branch of a tree she stood under. Stella, she suddenly realised. And in the other photo, a baby. Was this Rosie? Yes, she could see it was Rosie. Something about the eyes. Lily knelt beside her mother. How could anyone ever move past this? she thought.

But there it was, the secret which had lain between a linen handkerchief and tissue paper, hidden away at the bottom of a shoebox for all those years.

Lily stared at the picture, ran a finger around the edges, turned it over in her hand. She looked at her mother, shoulders folded into herself, like a bird with broken wings, and realised that one of her biggest mistakes, unknowing though it was, was not giving her mother credit for what she had been through. Life had been so hard for Stella. That was just the way things were, but understanding, talking about it, helped a little.

'So often I wanted to tell you about Rosie, to warn you. But what could I do? I delayed and worried and delayed again – and then it was too late.' The weight of the memory bore down on her and she pressed the heels of her hands against her eyes. 'That's what happened in those days. We just carried on. The Walshes as well. Oh, Lily, I can't talk about it. The pain ... it's ... Even now ... But do you see? I lost my sweetheart. And then my baby. I *knew* what that felt like. Can you now see why I didn't want the same to happen to you?'

Lily reached out a hand and Stella took it. 'I do, Mam. I'm so, so sorry. But perhaps Prudence will bring some joy into our lives. Perhaps that's why she's here. To make up for all the sadness.'

'I daresay she will. She has already, hasn't she? It's time for us to look forward now, in memory of those we've lost. We owe it to them to be happy. It's the least we can do.'

'One more thing. Did *Rosie* know?'

'I have no idea,' Stella said, tears brimming in her eyes.

'I hope so,' replied Lily. 'And I wonder . . . She once told me that her father wasn't her real father.'

'Did she?' said her mother, surprised.

And then suddenly a thought tugged at Lily. The locket. The locket Rosie had left at the WVS for her.

'Wait – does this mean anything to you?' She scooped the locket from around her neck.

Stella gasped. 'I gave her that! That was the one thing I had to pass on. Harry gave it to me. Oh, Lily.'

'Mam! She knew. I know she did. That was what she was trying to tell me. That's why she wanted me to have it. She said we were closer than the closest sisters. Those were the words she used.'

Stella's eyes widened. 'Do you think so?

'I'm sure of it,' she said. And even if she wasn't, she was content to let Stella think she was.

Stella wiped under her eyes, blew her nose on the handkerchief she tugged out from under the cuff of her sleeve.

'I hope so,' she said. 'Wouldn't that be nice?'

Then, as if the subject was too much to bear, Stella stopped crying, stood up and busied herself with fussy flapping out of skirts, and pointlessly moving a china ornament an inch to the right on the mantelpiece. Her mother was a strong person, thought Lily. The kind of person who was strong enough to sob her heart out and then get straight back up and start fighting again.

'This came this morning. Read it . . .' her mother said.

She handed Lily a letter that she had stuffed into the front pocket of her apron. Lily stared at it for a little while. Then, turning it over in her hand, she read the postmark on the top left-hand corner, traced her finger over the stamp. It was a wonder it had got through with all the trouble in the world.

Dear, darling Stella,

Well, I've recently hooked up with some grand fellows. Can you believe it, they've built a theatre here in the barracks!? The heat is still tremendous. Women performers are thin on the ground, so thank God Percy Naylor, my new mate, has a shapely pair of legs. Ha! He does a mean Betty Grable! He even got a love letter from one of the soldiers at our last show. Don't think he realised he was a chap! Anyway, my fingers are sore from all the playing I'm doing, but I do feel I'm making a difference, keeping everyone's spirits up.

How is everything in Caryl Street? How are Lily and Matt and the little ones? Keeping out of trouble, I hope? I shall find out soon enough, as the big news is, I'm coming home! Three more weeks, and I'm sailing back on HMS Patience. *She's a minesweeper, but they say it's pretty safe.*

Your husband, with all love. Save a shilling for the meter,

Cliff.

'Lily, I never realised how much I'd miss your father's music. But he'll put that right, thumping out a tune on the old Joanna when he's back, please God, safely. I do love him, you know. I actually even feel a little jealous of Percy Naylor!'

And Lily nodded and smiled and, like Stella, she was also grateful for ENSA sending him abroad, and that he hadn't been able to fret or rage, or feel shame, because it had all happened when he'd been away – and when Prue was presented, and the wedding band waved with a flourish, she knew all questions and dates would be forgotten in an instant. The house would soon fill with the smell of his cigarettes, the sound of his piano playing, his whistling – always a sure sign of how happy he was – and his laughing at the wireless and shouting at the letters page in the *Echo*.

'I don't doubt that, Mam. Chin up. I can hear Prue.'

'Another baby to be fed and washed and burped. Reminds you that's why we're fighting this war.'

'That's the spirit,' said Lily.

And she felt that this was another beginning of something, another change in her life: the inexorable transition when mother started to become child, and the child began to become mother . . .

In the week before the wedding, the preparations came and went in a whirl of excitement. On 1 June, the tired, battered city of Liverpool had woken in shock after another night of bombing that had hit the docks badly. The dust in the city was awful. It smelt strange, and a muddy brown hue was coating the linoleum. Must be the cement dust mixing with the moisture, seeping out from the sandbags that the Corpy had lined up along the pavements.

'Wouldn't you think Hitler would give us all a break so we could get a bit of shut eye and enough P and Q to enjoy ourselves on Lily and Vincent's big day?' said Annie, bustling around the kitchen.

They went to bed, pulled the covers over their heads, said a prayer, listened out for the distant growling of aeroplanes, tried to sleep and hoped no one was killed before Lily and Vincent's wedding. The bombing might have eased off since the May blitz, but it still had them running back and forth to the new Anderson shelter at the bottom of the backyard, with barely a moment to catch their breath.

'One of ours!' Lily would cry.

'One of theirs!' Bobby would answer, and they would all dive under the tables or squash themselves into the cupboard like sardines, with Stella trying to chivvy everyone along by remarking they had had years of practice as it had always been one of Cliff's favourite parlour games. And against the background of the endless air-raid drills, the relentless testing of the guns with their constant firing, the barrage balloons and the blackouts placing the city under inky curfew, they were going to try and enjoy themselves and look forward to the wedding. Bobby and Deirdre who had just refused point blank to go to Morecambe, seemed happy to be in the city despite the bombings. 'As happy as children who live in a house full of food *every* day of the week!' exclaimed Stella.

Things were looking up all round. Vincent had bought a model of a battleship for Bobby to paint grey and made beautiful puppets on strings out of a couple of old wooden dolls for Deirdre. Stella had settled into the job at the Owen Owen department store and had managed to get a couple of pairs of cut-price stockings for Lily and a tub of Brylcreem and a shaving brush for Matt. Bobby had come back with apple blossom branches to decorate the house – he had gone out and cut off overhanging ones from the big houses down by Princes Park in the dead of night – and Matt, in his cups, had nicked a set of knives and forks for the wedding party and nobody dared ask where. Horrified, Stella had cuffed him around the head, and told him to take them back and said she would rather eat with her fingers. They all oohed and ahhed when Vincent turned up and gave Lily a glow-in-the-dark brooch that he had bought.

'You wear it on your lapel so people don't bump into you in the blackout,' he said, starting to pin it onto her before Bobby asked if he could borrow it and went into the broom cupboard, and yelled 'it works!' and then stepped into a bucket and came clumping out with his foot stuck in it.

The children hadn't slept all night, and they flopped by seven. The following morning they dressed in their best clothes: Lily in her peep-show heels and a white lace dress that hugged her curves, which Annie had made out of a curtain; Stella in ice-blue crushed velvet and an eccentric plumed hat; the little ones in matching hats and scarves. The wedding took place at St Columba's, with the Laffertys out-performing all the choirs of angels. They didn't care about the tittle-tattle about the baby, but they weren't so stupid not to know there were plenty of those that would, so the ceremony was discreet – apart from Stella's hat, and Lily's beauty. No one could hide those two things. Father Donnelly had agreed to do the service at short notice, the war being an excuse for the haphazard nature of it, and no one asked any questions about when, or how, or who, or the banns, as they all had other things on their minds, like picking out frocks and suits, and carnations for the buttonholes. 'Thank the Lord,' said Stella. The baby appeared miraculously in Caryl Street but with the confusion of the bombings, no one knew whether they were coming or going at the best of times, and with so much death around, one more life seemed little cause for concern.

When Matt, who'd had to work, arrived and scooped up the children in his arms and kissed them, there was even more excitement. He still wasn't old enough to join up, but his job at Morecambe aerodrome meant he was an Olympian God to the little ones, Ares returned from battle, even though he had been doing no more than waving his arms and running around with a bucketful of sand, but in in his uniform with its shiny buttons, he looked the business.

'Our Matt's back, safe and sound!' Stella cried, after each air raid. And so there was more hugging and kissing, and holding onto each other for dear life as if, were they to let them go, they would be gone forever, and when some gossiped about the child born out of wedlock and how shameless those Laffertys were, and how dare they cock a snoop to the world like this, with their *'loose morals and their ways*', Stella riposted that with so many lost, why would they push a tiny baby away? A baby who gave them all hope. It made no sense. No sense at all. And after living under the threat of death as they had done so for the last year, why worry about the future if today they were happy?

And when they stood at the altar, everyone agreed that they had seen far worse things than two people in love who wanted to give a child a decent chance in life. So whilst the whole city pulled the covers over their heads and fretted about another raid, another blackout and more lives lost, at Caryl Street, they partied. And everyone had put their ration books together, and the best damask white tablecloth had been shaken out and spread on top of the table, and there were fairy cakes, butterfly cakes with silver balls studded on swirls of piped cream, jellies and sarnies. And after every last scrap was eaten, they pushed back the furniture and danced. And later still they all got drunk and danced the conga up the stairs.

Epilogue

'So, Sister. Now this war is over, everything will change,' said Father Donnelly.

The clock's loud, tick-tock, tick-tock, reverberated off the walls of Sister Assumpta's office. She had already kept everyone waiting, fetching cups and saucers from the kitchen, even though no one was in the mood for lukewarm tea that tasted like dishwater.

'Nonsense. Churchill will get elected again. This idea of the welfare state is nonsense. Would you like tea? Before it stews,' she said, gesturing at the pot.

'No, thank you. The National Health Service will mean you will be held accountable,' the priest said, trying to move the conversation on.

'It'll never happen. We answer to God,' she said, and snorted in derision.

'You might have to answer to Clement Atlee soon.'

Sister David nodded in agreement.

'You behaved in a way in that was highly irregular,' he went on. 'We sent these children here. You had a duty of care. And you failed them. At least, you failed Lily Lafferty.'

'What?'

The doctor with his glasses balanced on the end of his nose – the one who Assumpta had at first refused to allow to the meeting until Father Donnelly had insisted – pushed the glasses up the bridge of his nose and wrote on a notepad with a marbled fountain pen.

Father Donnelly continued, 'You gave her child away without the proper documents – and when Lily wanted her baby back, you refused. Until you decided that you didn't want the baby after all – a very rum affair. That won't do. Paints a very bad picture of us. Someone has told us the whole story of what went on here during the war. Of a young woman, Agnes Parr, who you wouldn't allow to leave until she paid off her debt by working as a nanny. And Janet Fowler. She's trying to find out where her child is, the name of the couple who adopted him in Canada, and you have refused to help her. And Bridget Mulcahy? Her baby died, I believe, and is buried here. What about Bridget Mulcahy, Sister?'

'What about her? Bridget should have been in the Daft House down the road years ago,' she snapped.

'The Daft House? You can't say things like that any more!'

Sister David fixed her eyes on the threadbare carpet that curled up where it met the scuffed skirting board.

She blushed in shamefaced silence. She couldn't help but think of the facile test Assumpta would insist they did on the girls who were 'slow', as she called them. How many buttons make five? Three plus two and if you didn't know that you'd end up the lunatic asylum.

'We have to be accountable if the welfare state is to start running things. There will be no more sending children off without a thought to the girls who have given the babies to you. And the dead ones? You buried them with just a cross made out of an old *breadbox* to mark their graves? Is that true? Surely they deserve more than that? Surely that's just a horrible, *horrible* rumour?'

'Who told you all this?' asked Sister Assumpta.

Sister David flinched; her skin felt clammy between her tightening, interlocked fingers and she stared straight ahead, a blank look on her face.

Assumpta glared at her. 'That's ridiculous. Isn't it, Sister David? We did our best. At least we gave them a funeral and a decent burial.' There was a pause. 'Sister?'

And then she didn't need to ask again. She knew, she just knew.

'*You* told them?' she said.

It was Saturday morning and Stella threw open the doors of Caryl Street and was amazed and delighted to see the gaggle of children waiting to come in for a dancing lesson. Cliff was back where he belonged, at the piano, cigarette in his mouth, braces looped around his thighs, shirtsleeves rolled up to his elbows, revealing his strong tanned forearms with the recent addition of a rippling tattoo of Stella's name inked inside a blushing heart.

The sun was bursting in through the windows and soon the house would be full to the gills with people and chatter and the sound of feet sashaying and tapping as they waltzed and twirled around the ballroom. It was just like the old days again. Stella refused to let anyone talk about the awful things they had seen and been through – why bring them back to Liverpool? she said, forever tainted with the memory of a young man's tragic death that she still refused to talk about to anyone but Lily. And of course, the dancing helped. Of course, there was always dancing. They danced until their feet felt as if they were going to drop off.

They had other reasons to be happy that morning. Father Donnelly had written to the Laffertys saying that Sister Assumpta was leaving St Jude's. Another good excuse for a knees-up and a bottle of knock-off sherry and a sing-song. The final battle of Lily's war, fought and won. Now the job was to remember those they had lost. But not with sadness. They were done with sadness. And with this in mind they had dug a small hole in the patch of land behind Caryl Street and planted a cherry tree for Rosie, which Lily assured her brothers and sisters and little Prue, would blossom every spring and they would remember her with a magnificent explosion of pink and white flowers. It seemed a fitting conclusion to the war. For who better than Lily and her young family, another baby on the way, to make them all feel hopeful and confident about the future?

'Vince! You look like a film star in that suit!' Lily said.

'Your mam dug it out. You remember it?'

'Aye, used to be me da's, didn't it? The one you wore that was way too big for you when we did that dance at the Grafton, the one you were wearing in the photograph of us as kids,' said Lily when she arrived home from Pat Cherrie's greengrocer's to find Vincent standing on the front door step, dressed up to the nines, holding out a bunch of summer flowers for her. 'What's the occasion?'

'Well, if I remember rightly, I still owe you a night out dancing at the Rialto and a promise is a promise. Let's go a walk down there later. I've heard they've a smashing band. Jive is becoming all the rage now,' said Vincent with a smile.

'I've not got a decent pair of dancing shoes. And I can't go in these dreadful old things,' Lily said, indicating her battered sturdy lace-ups studded with nails that she had hammered into the heels to make them last a little longer.

'Then it's a bit of luck I bought you these,' he said.

He took her into the house and handed her a cardboard box that was sitting on the kitchen table.

'What?' she said.

'Open it.'

She took off the lid and gasped as she opened tissue paper and removed the pair of red patent leather T-bar shoes, with a low heel and a strap over the middle that fastened onto a glass button.

'Gosh, Vincent! Are they for me?'

'I reckon I'd look a little daft in them,' he said. 'Got them from Paddy's market. Going for a song. Can't wait to see you dance in those.'

'Oh Vince, they're beautiful.'

She threw her arms around him. When she withdrew, he smoothed down her hair and put a finger under her chin and tilted her face up to his.

'I love you, Lil. Try them on.'

The beauty of them made her catch her breath as she slipped her feet into the shoes and her brown eyes shone; as he hugged her to him, she felt she was going to die with happiness.

'Don't change, Lil.'

'What d'you mean?'

'Just . . . don't change.'

He need not have said it. Because as everyone in Liverpool would tell you, when you hit a wall, some climbed over it, others dug a hole and crawled under it whilst a few canny ones went around it.

But Lily would always be the girl who was dancing on top of it.